BLACK SCIENCE

IMAGE COMICS, INC.
Robert Kirkman — Chief Operating Officer
Erik Larsen — Chief Financial Officer
Todd McFarlane — President
Marc Silvestri — Chief Executive Officer
Jim Valentino — Vice-President

Eric Stephenson — Publisher
Corey Murphy — Director of Sales
Jeff Boison — Director of Publishing Planning & Book Trade Sales
Jeremy Sullivan — Director of Digital Sales
Kat Salazar — Director of PR & Marketing
Emily Miller — Director of Operations
Branwyn Bigglestone — Senior Accounts Manager
Sarah Mello — Accounts Manager
Drew Gill — Art Director
Jonathan Chan — Production Manager
Meredith Wallace — Print Manager
Briah Skelly — Publicity Assistant
Sasha Head — Sales & Marketing Production Designer
Randy Okamura — Digital Production Designer
David Brothers — Branding Manager
Olivia Ngai — Content Manager
Addison Duke — Production Artist
Vincent Kukua — Production Artist
Tricia Ramos — Production Artist
Jeff Stang — Direct Market Sales Representative
Emilio Bautista — Digital Sales Associate
Chloe Ramos-Peterson — Administrative Assistant
IMAGECOMICS.COM

COLLECTION DESIGN: JEFF POWELL

BLACK SCIENCE VOLUME 4: GODWORLD. First Printing. May 2016. Published by Image Comics, Inc. Office of publication: 2001 Center Street, 6th Floor, Berkeley,
CA 94704. Copyright © 2016 Rick Remender and Matteo Scalera. All rights reserved. Originally published in single magazine form as BLACK SCIENCE #17-21.
BLACK SCIENCE™ (including all prominent characters featured herein), its logo and all character likenesses are trademarks of Rick Remender and Matteo Scalera,
unless otherwise noted. Image Comics® and its logos are registered trademarks of Image Comics, Inc. No part of this publication may be reproduced or
transmitted, in any form or by any means (except for short excerpts for review purposes) without the express written permission of Image Comics, Inc. All names,
characters, events and locales in this publication are entirely fictional. Any resemblance to actual persons (living or dead), events or places, without satiric intent,
is coincidental. PRINTED IN THE U.S.A. For information regarding the CPSIA on this printed material call: 203-595-3636 and provide reference # RICH – 678167.
For international rights inquiries, contact: foreignlicensing@imagecomics.com.
ISBN 978-1-63215-686-0

RICK REMENDER
WRITER

MATTEO SCALERA
ARTIST

MORENO DINISIO
COLORS

RUS WOOTON
LETTERING + LOGO DESIGN

SEBASTIAN GIRNER
EDITOR

BLACK SCIENCE CREATED BY
RICK REMENDER & MATTEO SCALERA

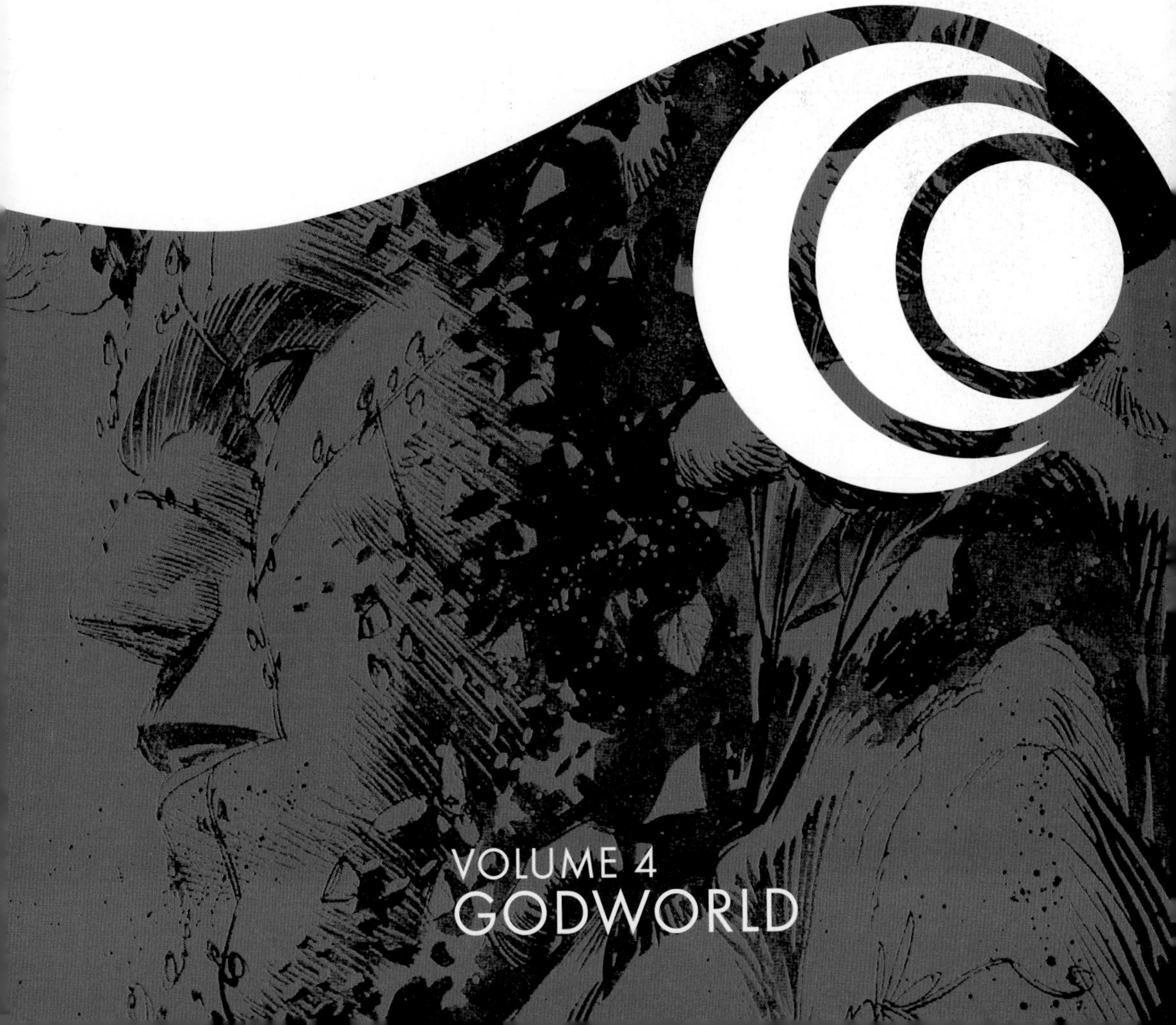

VOLUME 4
GODWORLD

17

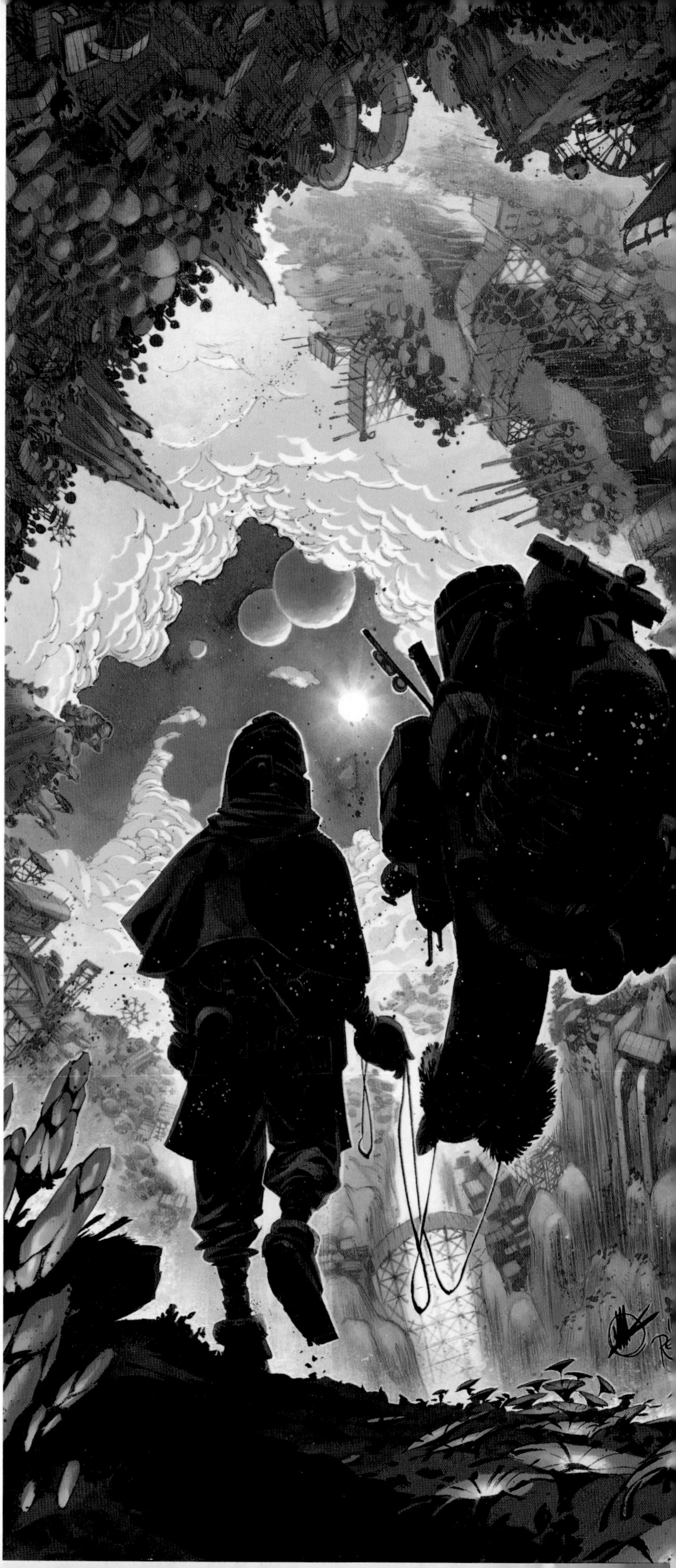

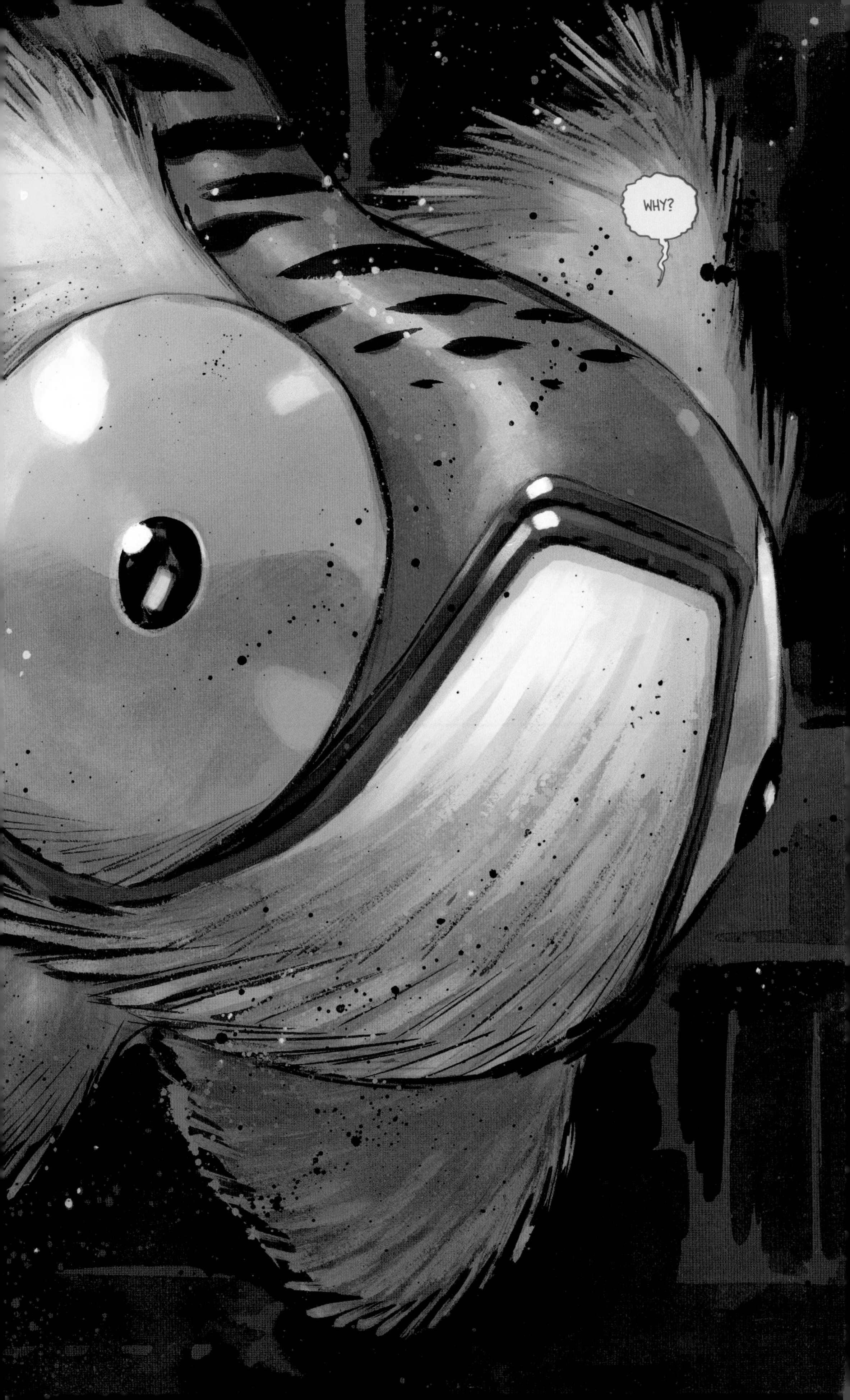
WHY?

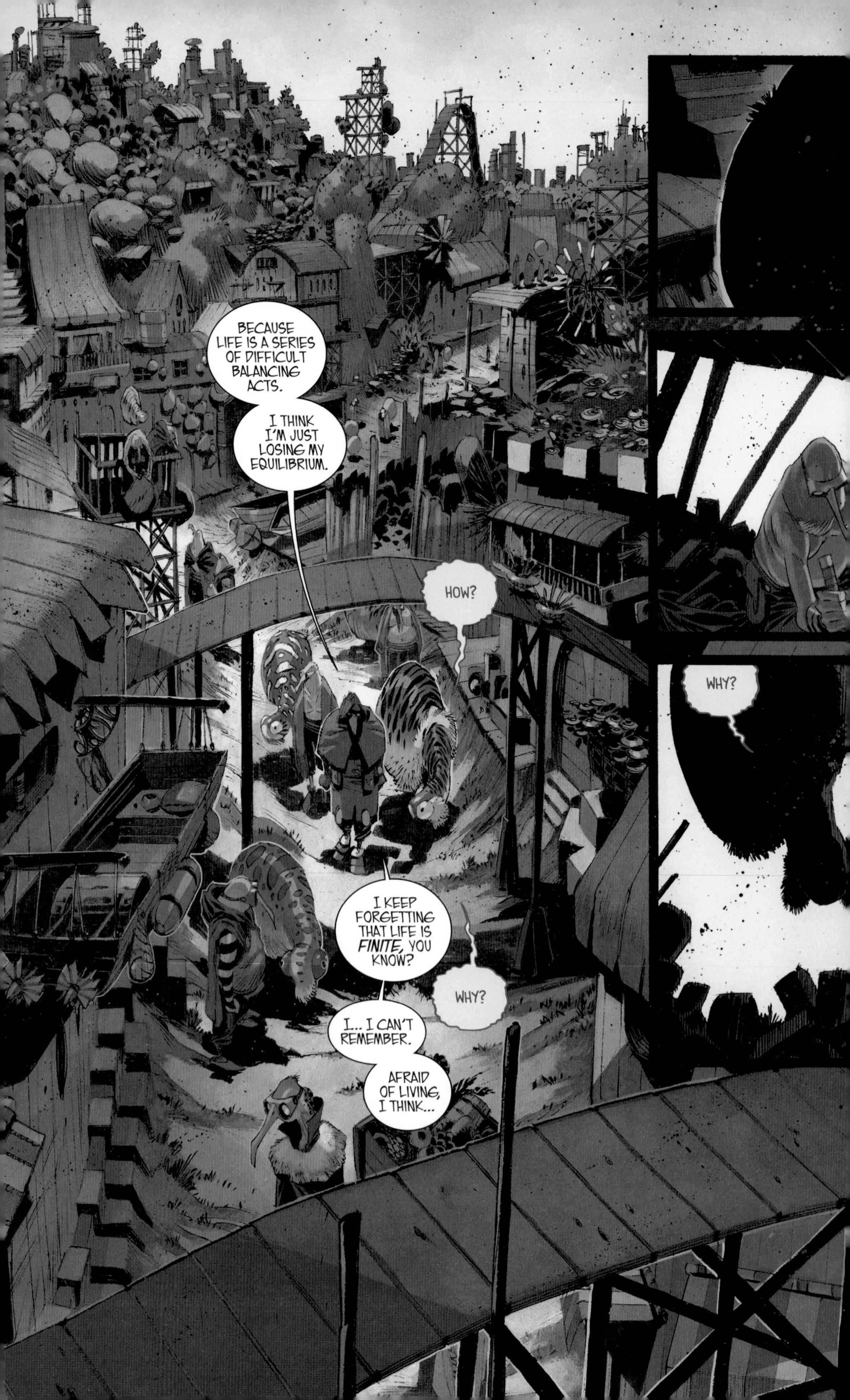
BECAUSE LIFE IS A SERIES OF DIFFICULT BALANCING ACTS.
I THINK I'M JUST LOSING MY EQUILIBRIUM.
HOW?
I KEEP FORGETTING THAT LIFE IS *FINITE,* YOU KNOW?
WHY?
I... I CAN'T REMEMBER.
AFRAID OF LIVING, I THINK...
WHY?

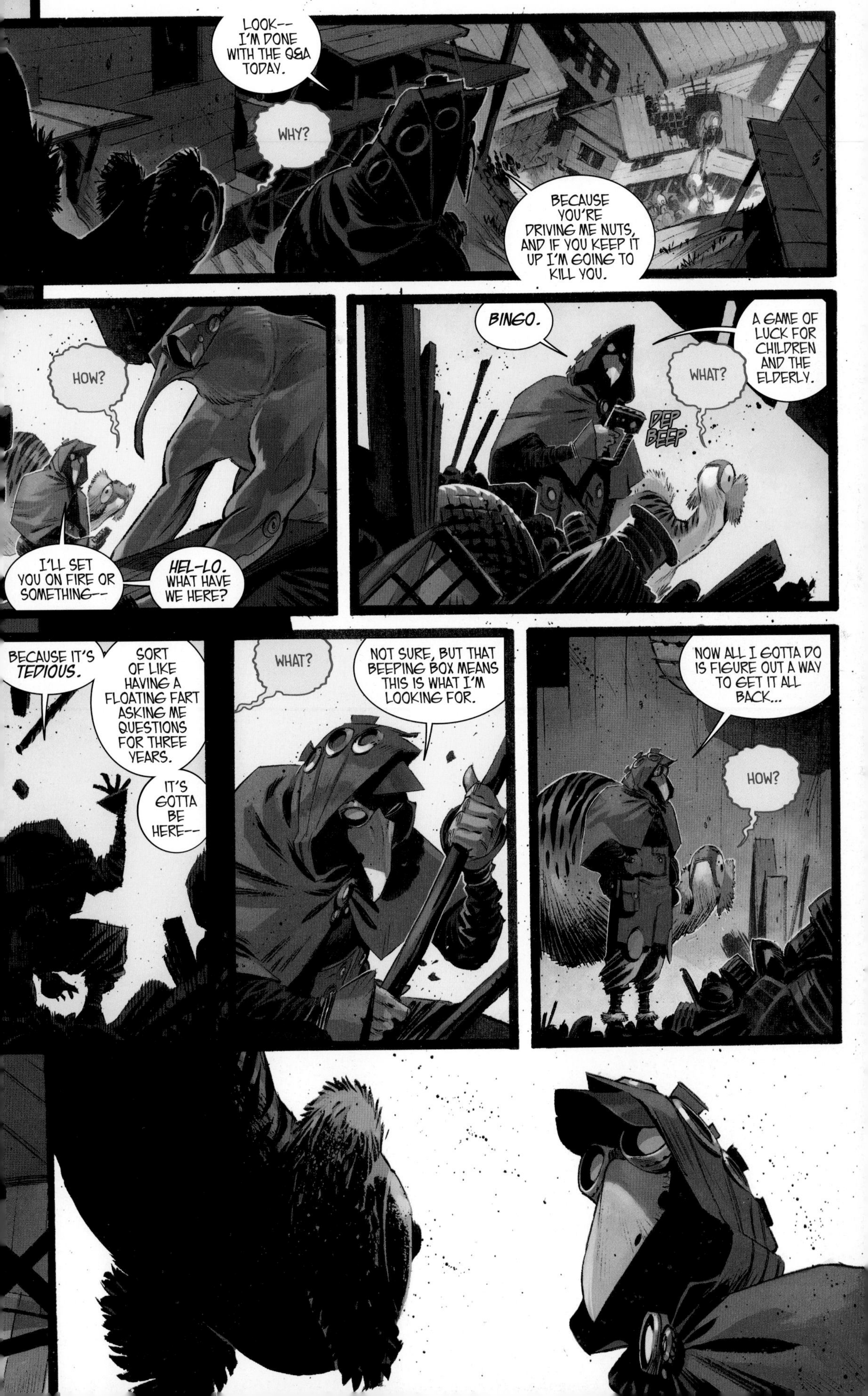
LOOK-- I'M DONE WITH THE Q&A TODAY.
WHY?
BECAUSE YOU'RE DRIVING ME NUTS, AND IF YOU KEEP IT UP I'M GOING TO KILL YOU.
HOW?
I'LL SET YOU ON FIRE OR SOMETHING--
HEL-LO. WHAT HAVE WE HERE?
BINGO.
WHAT?
A GAME OF LUCK FOR CHILDREN AND THE ELDERLY.
DEP BEEP
BECAUSE IT'S TEDIOUS.
SORT OF LIKE HAVING A FLOATING FART ASKING ME QUESTIONS FOR THREE YEARS.
IT'S GOTTA BE HERE--
WHAT?
NOT SURE, BUT THAT BEEPING BOX MEANS THIS IS WHAT I'M LOOKING FOR.
NOW ALL I GOTTA DO IS FIGURE OUT A WAY TO GET IT ALL BACK...
HOW?

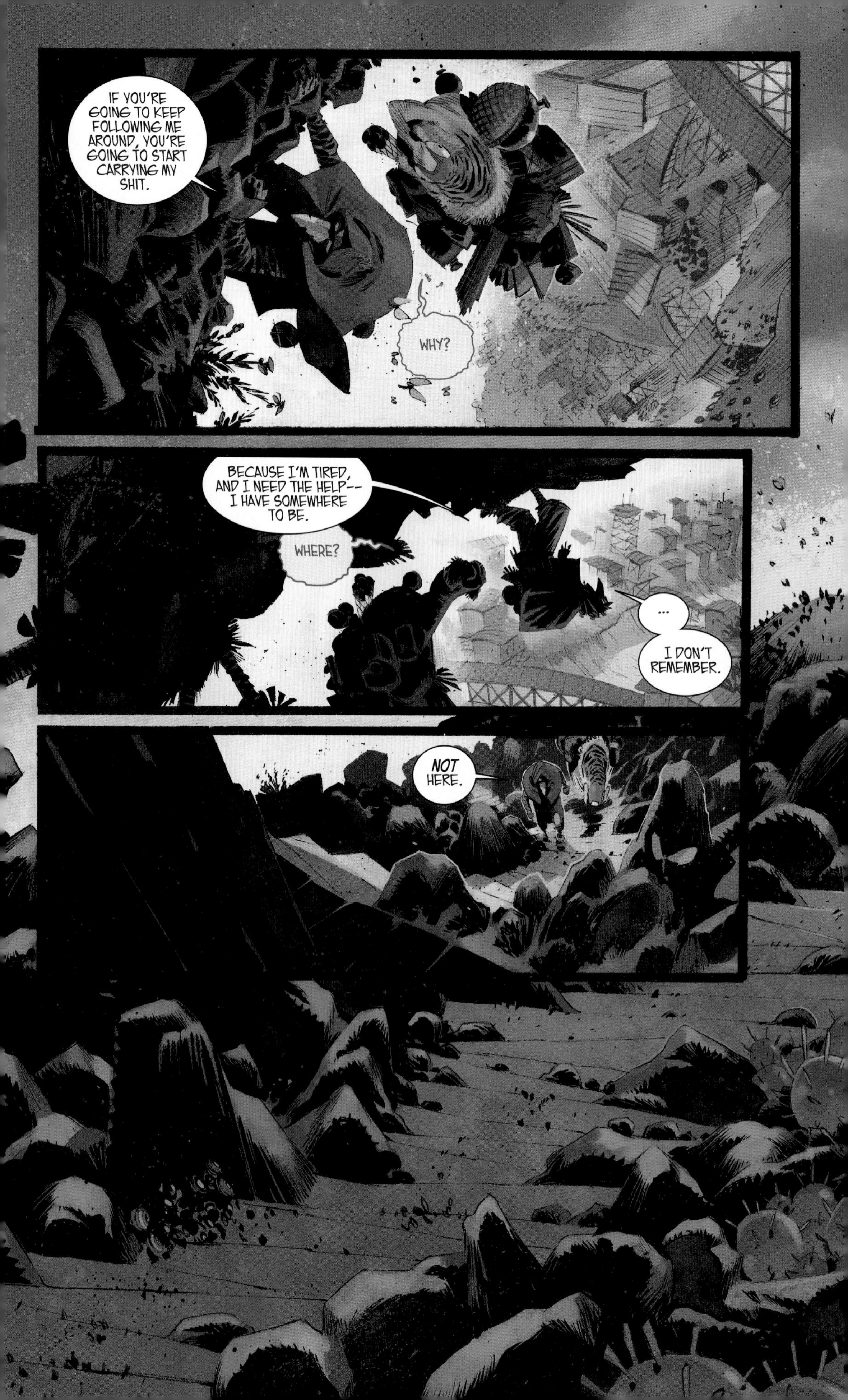
IF YOU'RE GOING TO KEEP FOLLOWING ME AROUND, YOU'RE GOING TO START CARRYING MY SHIT.
WHY?
BECAUSE I'M TIRED, AND I NEED THE HELP-- I HAVE SOMEWHERE TO BE.
WHERE?
...
I DON'T REMEMBER.
NOT HERE.

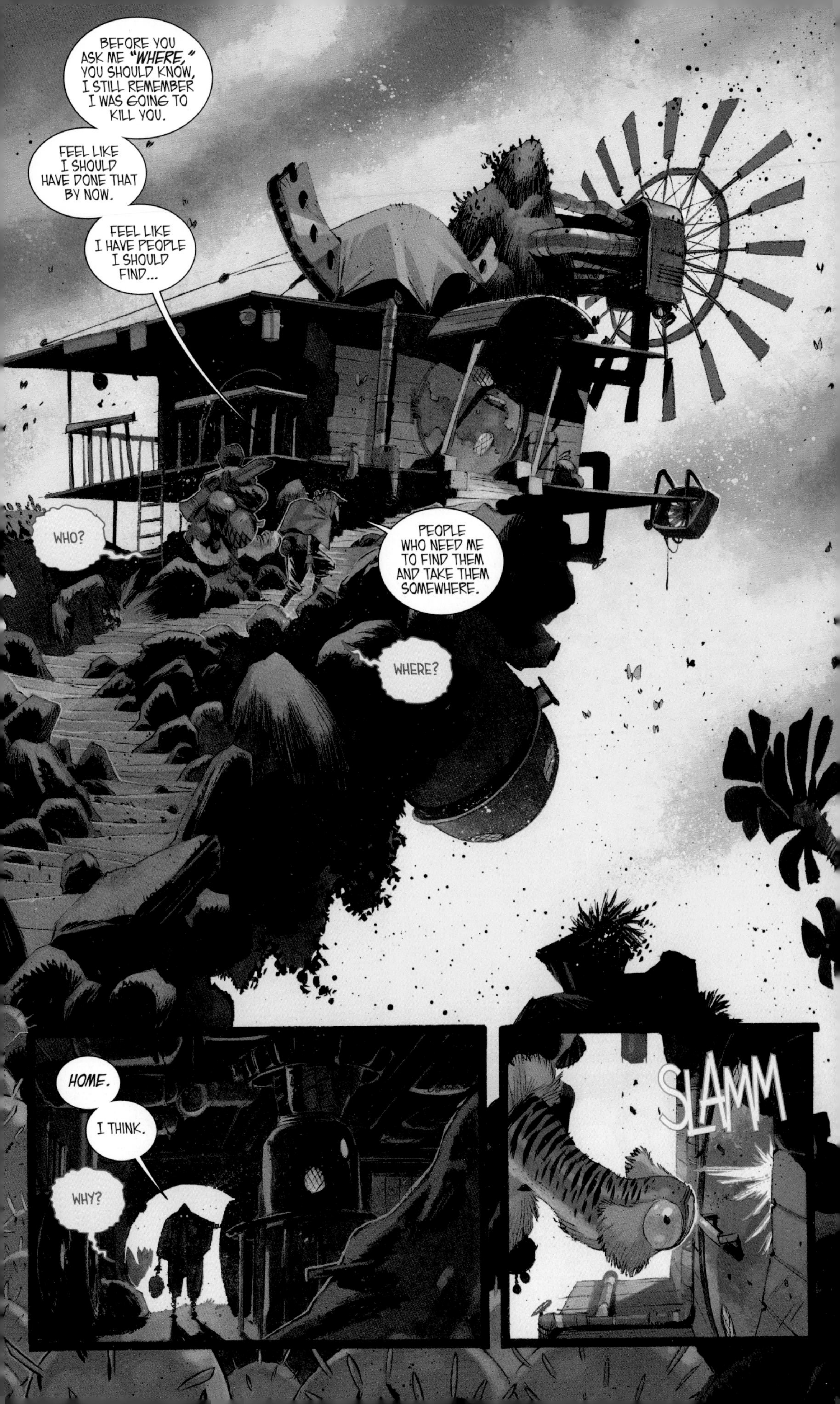
BEFORE YOU ASK ME "WHERE," YOU SHOULD KNOW, I STILL REMEMBER I WAS GOING TO KILL YOU.
FEEL LIKE I SHOULD HAVE DONE THAT BY NOW.
FEEL LIKE I HAVE PEOPLE I SHOULD FIND...
WHO?
PEOPLE WHO NEED ME TO FIND THEM AND TAKE THEM SOMEWHERE.
WHERE?
HOME.
I THINK.
WHY?
SLAMM

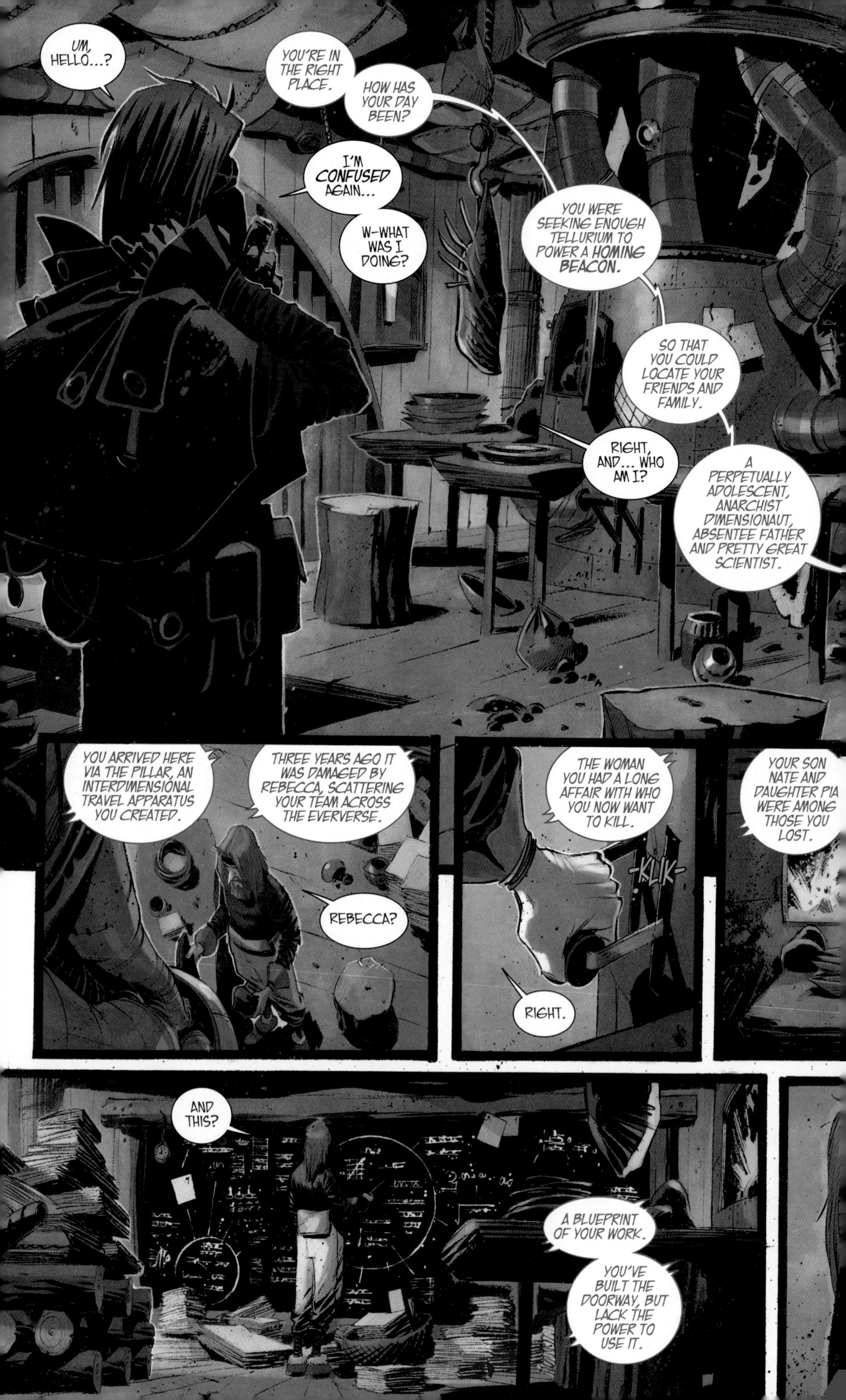
UM, HELLO...?
YOU'RE IN THE RIGHT PLACE.
HOW HAS YOUR DAY BEEN?
I'M CONFUSED AGAIN...
W-WHAT WAS I DOING?
YOU WERE SEEKING ENOUGH TELLURIUM TO POWER A HOMING BEACON.
SO THAT YOU COULD LOCATE YOUR FRIENDS AND FAMILY.
RIGHT, AND... WHO AM I?
A PERPETUALLY ADOLESCENT, ANARCHIST DIMENSIONAUT, ABSENTEE FATHER AND PRETTY GREAT SCIENTIST.
YOU ARRIVED HERE VIA THE PILLAR, AN INTERDIMENSIONAL TRAVEL APPARATUS YOU CREATED.
THREE YEARS AGO IT WAS DAMAGED BY REBECCA, SCATTERING YOUR TEAM ACROSS THE EVERVERSE.
REBECCA?
THE WOMAN YOU HAD A LONG AFFAIR WITH WHO YOU NOW WANT TO KILL.
-KLIK-
RIGHT.
YOUR SON NATE AND DAUGHTER PIA WERE AMONG THOSE YOU LOST.
AND THIS?
A BLUEPRINT OF YOUR WORK.
YOU'VE BUILT THE DOORWAY, BUT LACK THE POWER TO USE IT.

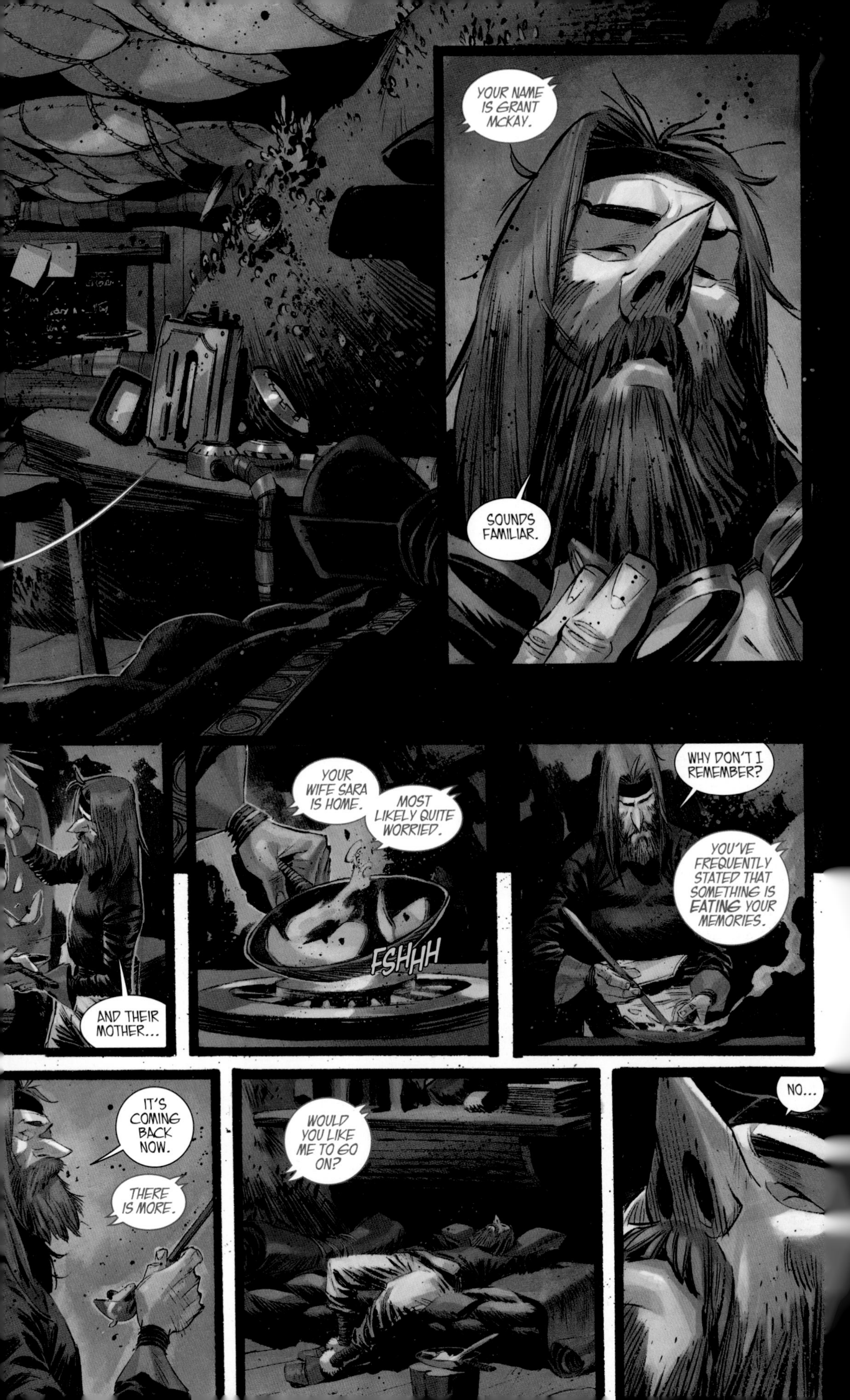
YOUR NAME IS GRANT MCKAY.
SOUNDS FAMILIAR.
AND THEIR MOTHER...
YOUR WIFE SARA IS HOME.
MOST LIKELY QUITE WORRIED.
FSHHH
WHY DON'T I REMEMBER?
YOU'VE FREQUENTLY STATED THAT SOMETHING IS EATING YOUR MEMORIES.
IT'S COMING BACK NOW.
THERE IS MORE.
WOULD YOU LIKE ME TO GO ON?
NO...

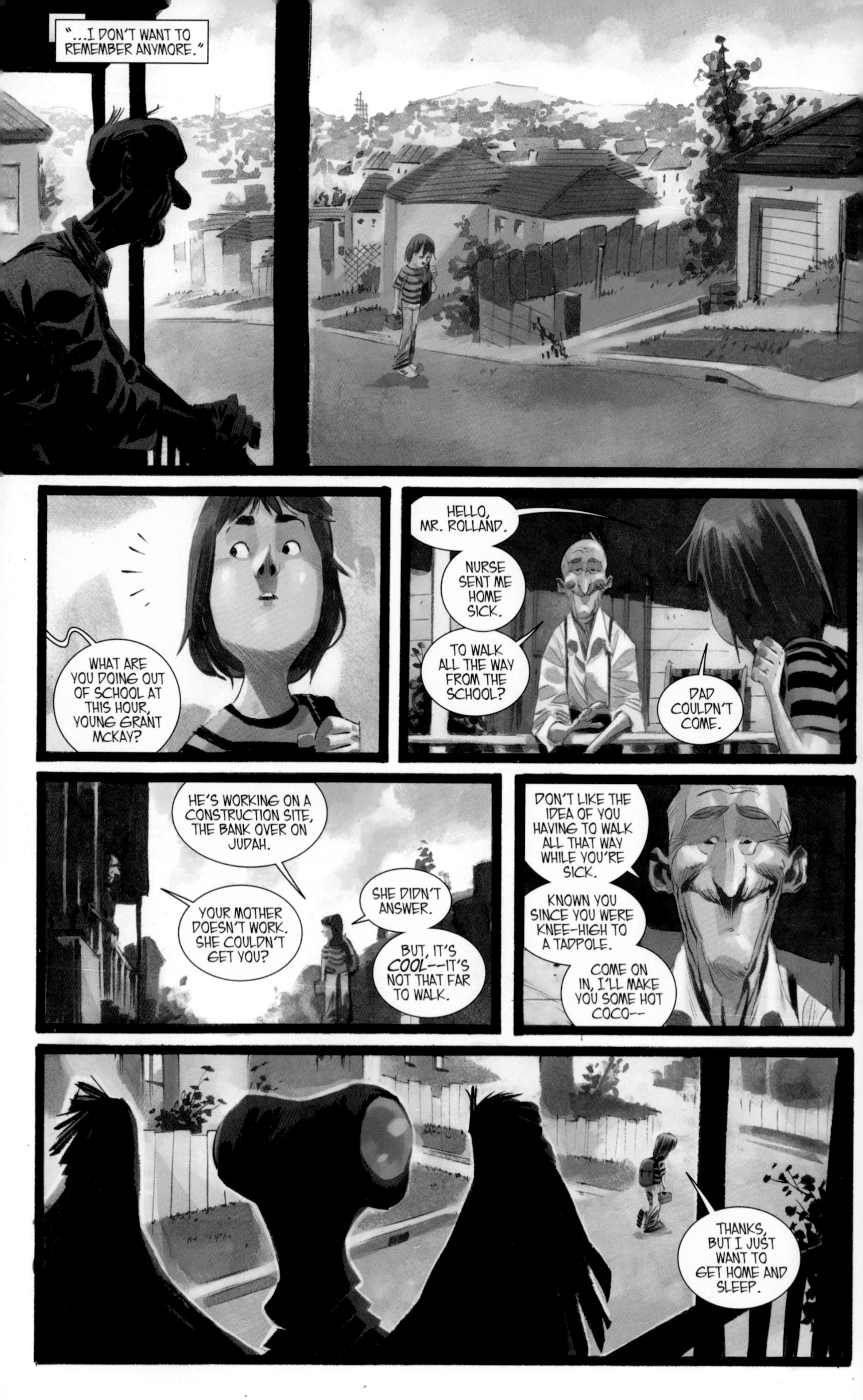
"...I DON'T WANT TO REMEMBER ANYMORE."
WHAT ARE YOU DOING OUT OF SCHOOL AT THIS HOUR, YOUNG GRANT McKAY?
HELLO, MR. ROLLAND.
NURSE SENT ME HOME SICK.
TO WALK ALL THE WAY FROM THE SCHOOL?
DAD COULDN'T COME.
HE'S WORKING ON A CONSTRUCTION SITE, THE BANK OVER ON JUDAH.
YOUR MOTHER DOESN'T WORK. SHE COULDN'T GET YOU?
SHE DIDN'T ANSWER.
BUT, IT'S COOL--IT'S NOT THAT FAR TO WALK.
DON'T LIKE THE IDEA OF YOU HAVING TO WALK ALL THAT WAY WHILE YOU'RE SICK.
KNOWN YOU SINCE YOU WERE KNEE-HIGH TO A TADPOLE.
COME ON IN, I'LL MAKE YOU SOME HOT COCO--
THANKS, BUT I JUST WANT TO GET HOME AND SLEEP.

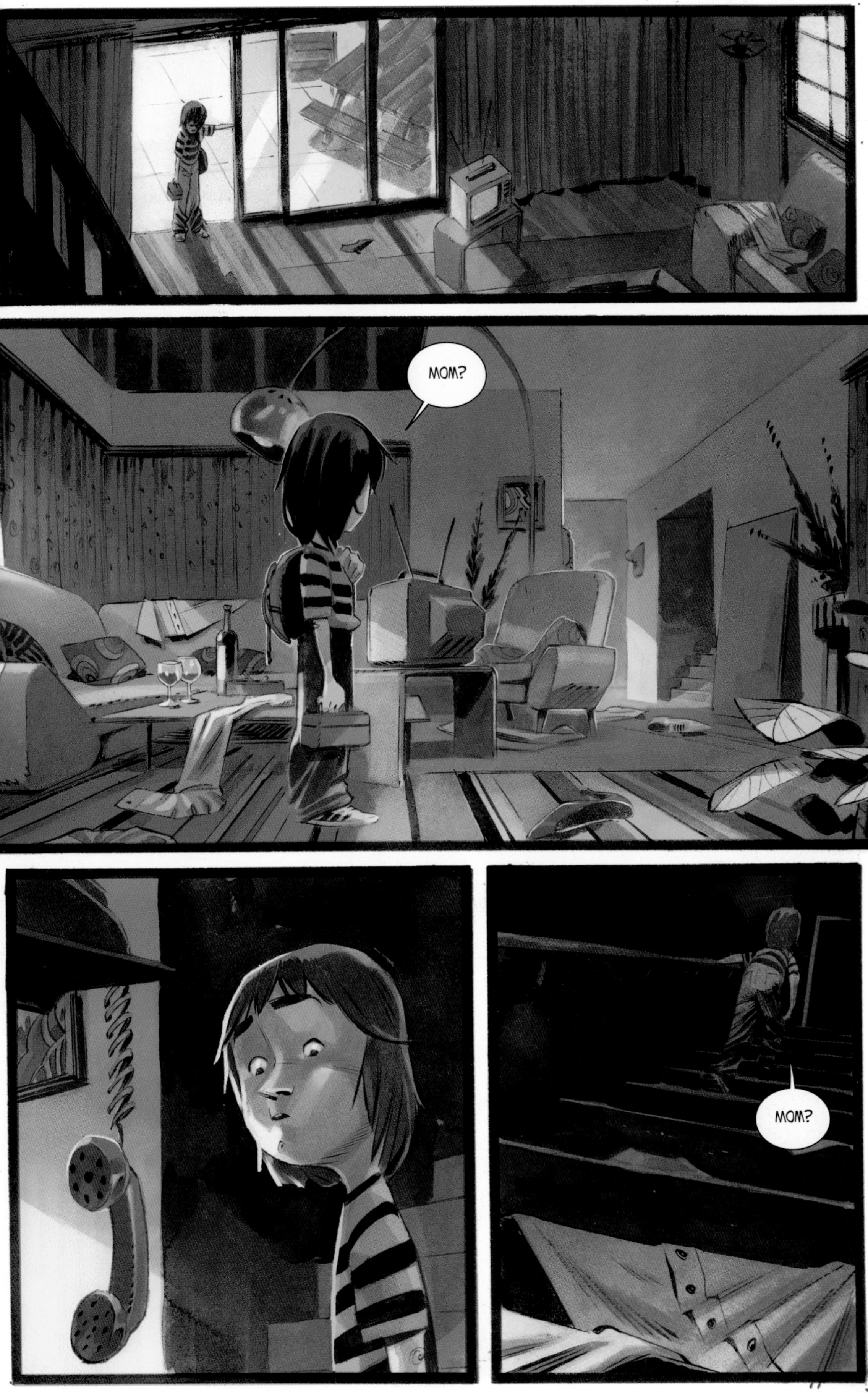
MOM?
MOM?

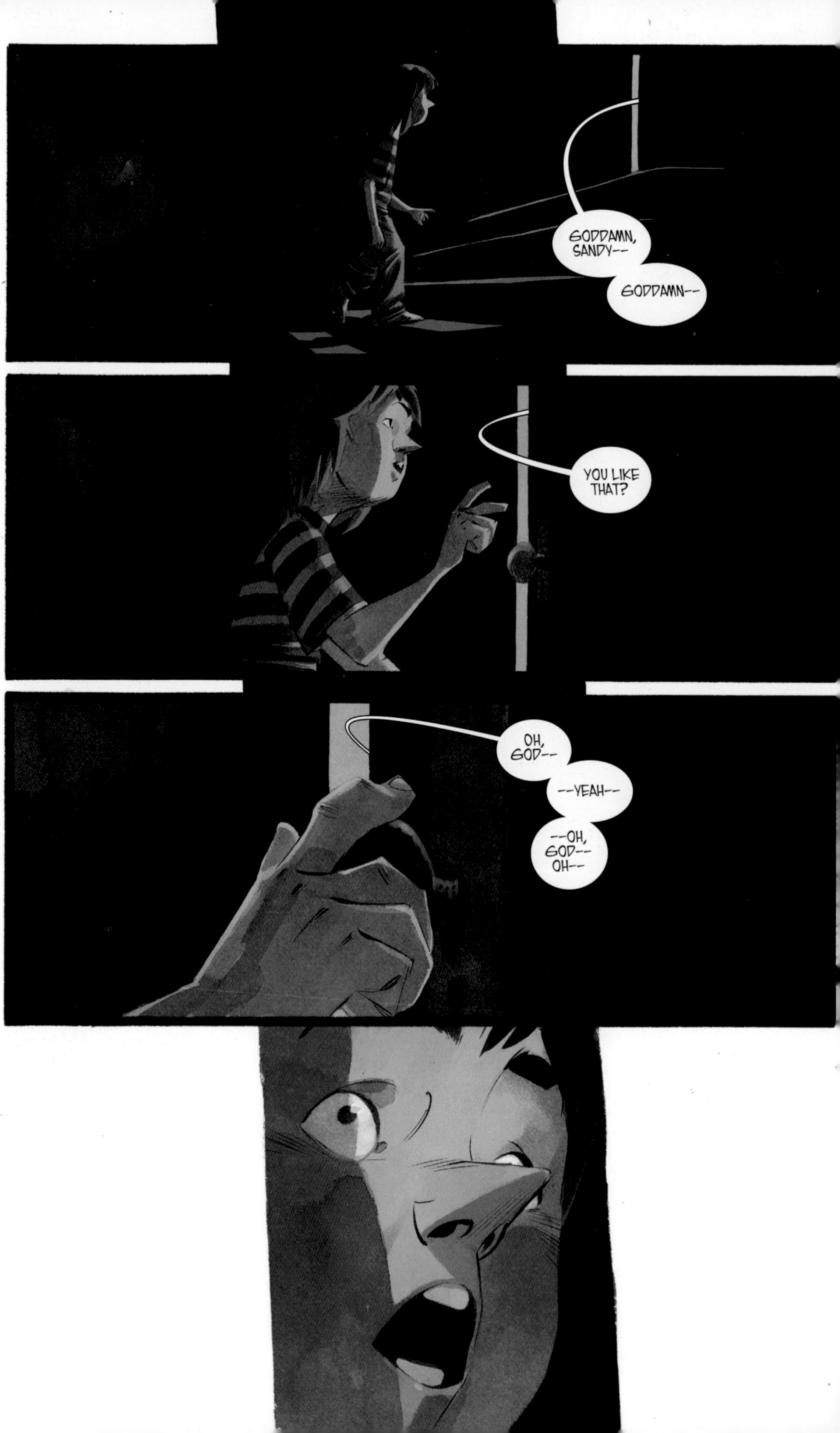
GODDAMN, SANDY--
GODDAMN--
YOU LIKE THAT?
OH, GOD--
--YEAH--
--OH, GOD-- OH--

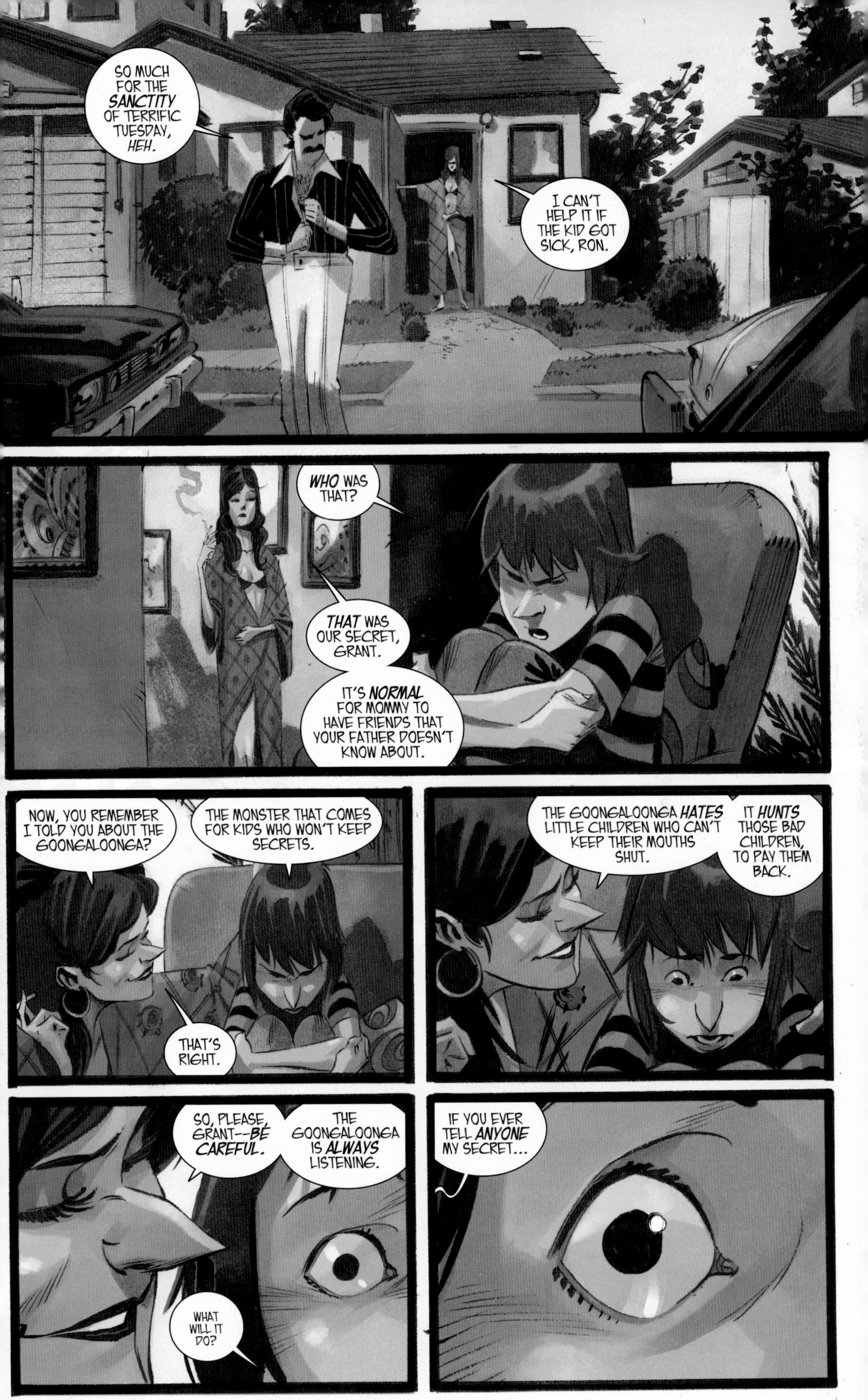
SO MUCH FOR THE SANCTITY OF TERRIFIC TUESDAY, HEH.
I CAN'T HELP IT IF THE KID GOT SICK, RON.
WHO WAS THAT?
THAT WAS OUR SECRET, GRANT.
IT'S NORMAL FOR MOMMY TO HAVE FRIENDS THAT YOUR FATHER DOESN'T KNOW ABOUT.
NOW, YOU REMEMBER I TOLD YOU ABOUT THE GOONGALOONGA?
THE MONSTER THAT COMES FOR KIDS WHO WON'T KEEP SECRETS.
THAT'S RIGHT.
THE GOONGALOONGA HATES LITTLE CHILDREN WHO CAN'T KEEP THEIR MOUTHS SHUT.
IT HUNTS THOSE BAD CHILDREN, TO PAY THEM BACK.
SO, PLEASE, GRANT--BE CAREFUL.
THE GOONGALOONGA IS ALWAYS LISTENING.
WHAT WILL IT DO?
IF YOU EVER TELL ANYONE MY SECRET...

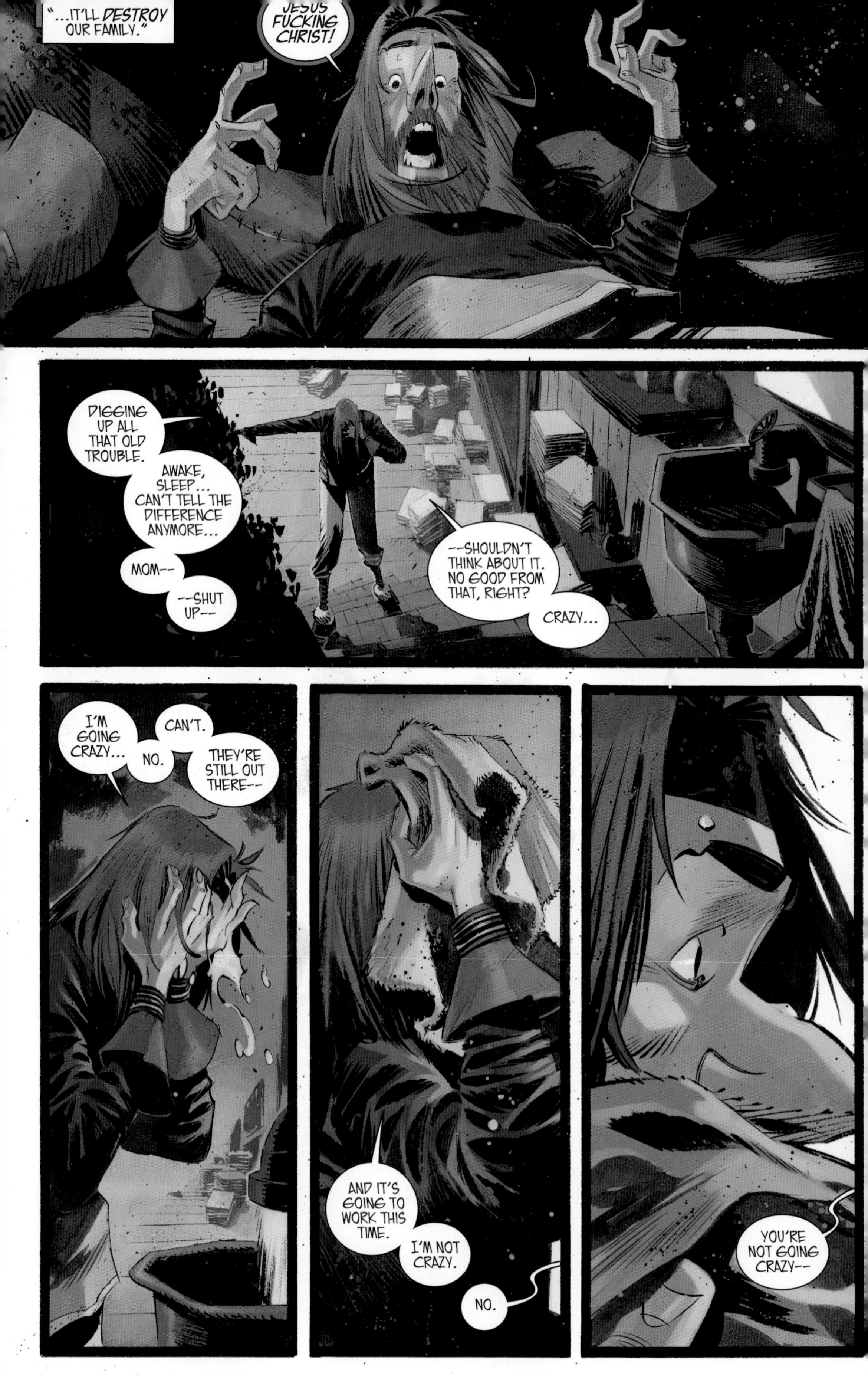
"...IT'LL DESTROY OUR FAMILY."
JESUS FUCKING CHRIST!
DIGGING UP ALL THAT OLD TROUBLE.
AWAKE, SLEEP... CAN'T TELL THE DIFFERENCE ANYMORE...
MOM--
--SHUT UP--
--SHOULDN'T THINK ABOUT IT. NO GOOD FROM THAT, RIGHT?
CRAZY...
I'M GOING CRAZY...
NO.
CAN'T.
THEY'RE STILL OUT THERE--
AND IT'S GOING TO WORK THIS TIME.
I'M NOT CRAZY.
NO.
YOU'RE NOT GOING CRAZY--

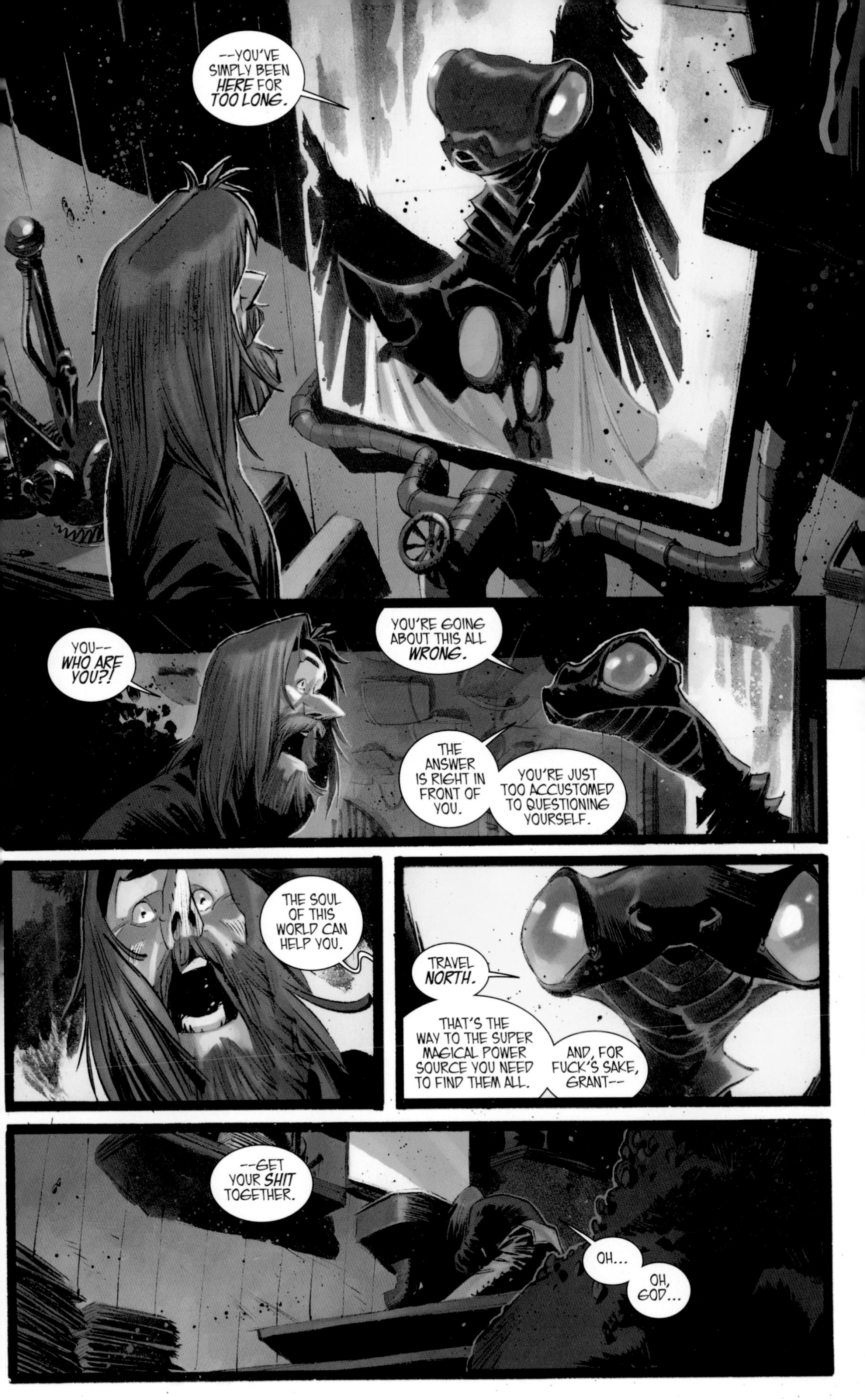
--YOU'VE SIMPLY BEEN HERE FOR TOO LONG.
YOU-- WHO ARE YOU?!
YOU'RE GOING ABOUT THIS ALL WRONG.
THE ANSWER IS RIGHT IN FRONT OF YOU.
YOU'RE JUST TOO ACCUSTOMED TO QUESTIONING YOURSELF.
THE SOUL OF THIS WORLD CAN HELP YOU.
TRAVEL NORTH.
THAT'S THE WAY TO THE SUPER MAGICAL POWER SOURCE YOU NEED TO FIND THEM ALL.
AND, FOR FUCK'S SAKE, GRANT--
--GET YOUR SHIT TOGETHER.
OH...
OH, GOD...

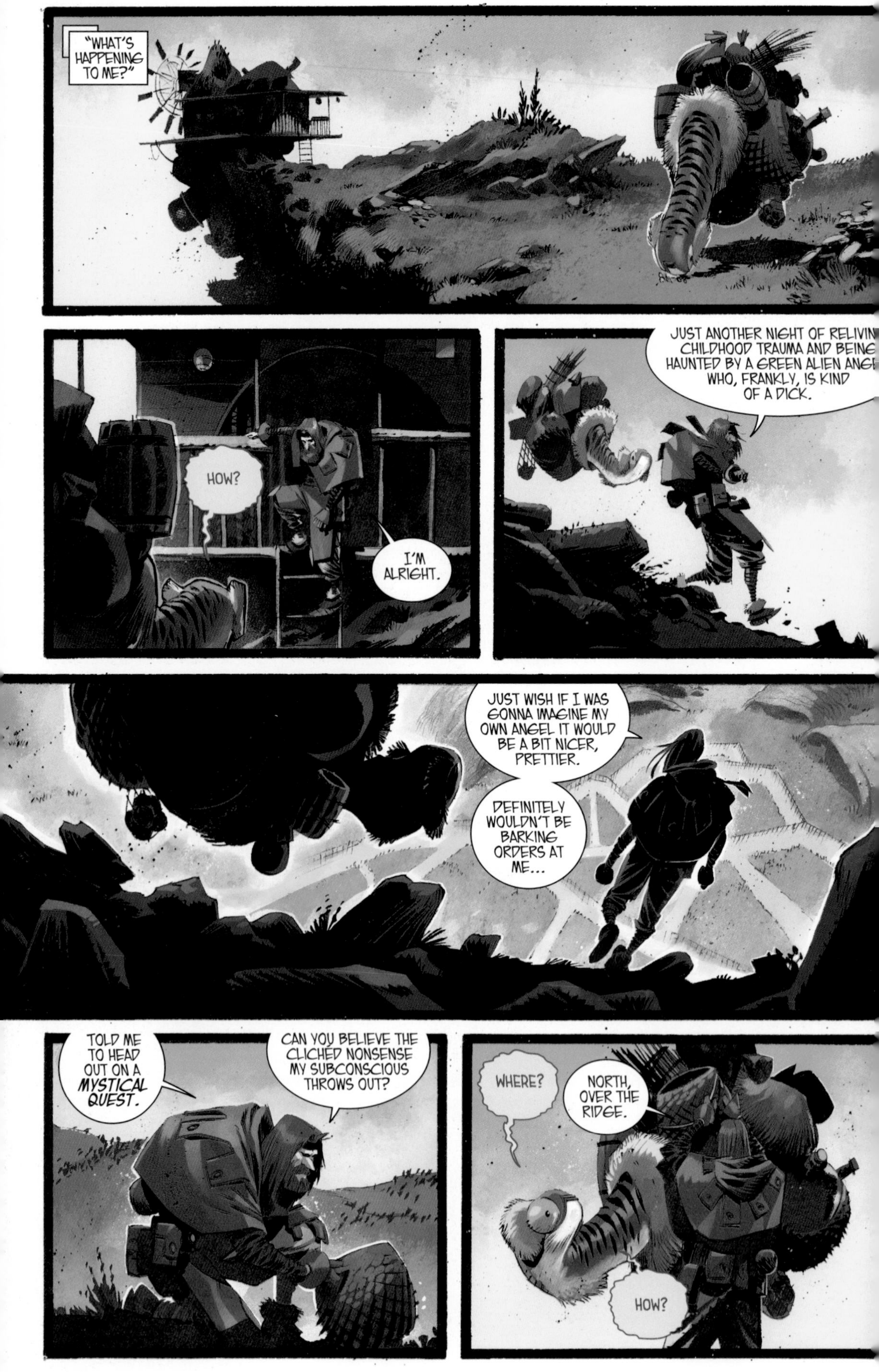
"WHAT'S HAPPENING TO ME?"
HOW?
I'M ALRIGHT.
JUST ANOTHER NIGHT OF RELIVIN
CHILDHOOD TRAUMA AND BEING
HAUNTED BY A GREEN ALIEN ANG
WHO, FRANKLY, IS KIND OF A DICK.
JUST WISH IF I WAS GONNA IMAGINE MY OWN ANGEL IT WOULD BE A BIT NICER, PRETTIER.
DEFINITELY WOULDN'T BE BARKING ORDERS AT ME...
TOLD ME TO HEAD OUT ON A MYSTICAL QUEST.
CAN YOU BELIEVE THE CLICHÉD NONSENSE MY SUBCONSCIOUS THROWS OUT?
WHERE?
NORTH, OVER THE RIDGE.
HOW?

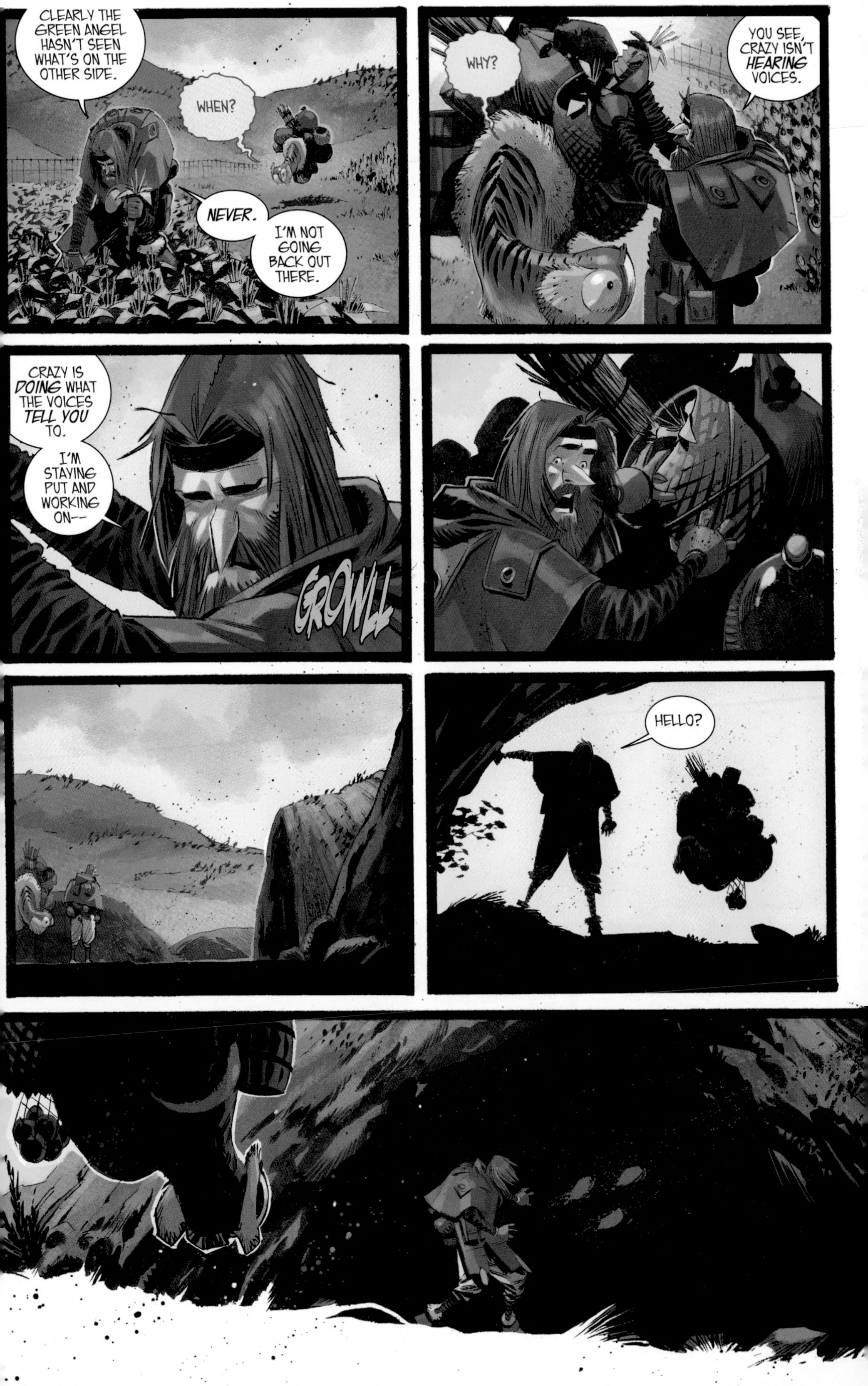
CLEARLY THE GREEN ANGEL HASN'T SEEN WHAT'S ON THE OTHER SIDE.
WHEN?
NEVER.
I'M NOT GOING BACK OUT THERE.
WHY?
YOU SEE, CRAZY ISN'T HEARING VOICES.
CRAZY IS DOING WHAT THE VOICES TELL YOU TO.
I'M STAYING PUT AND WORKING ON--
GROWLL
HELLO?

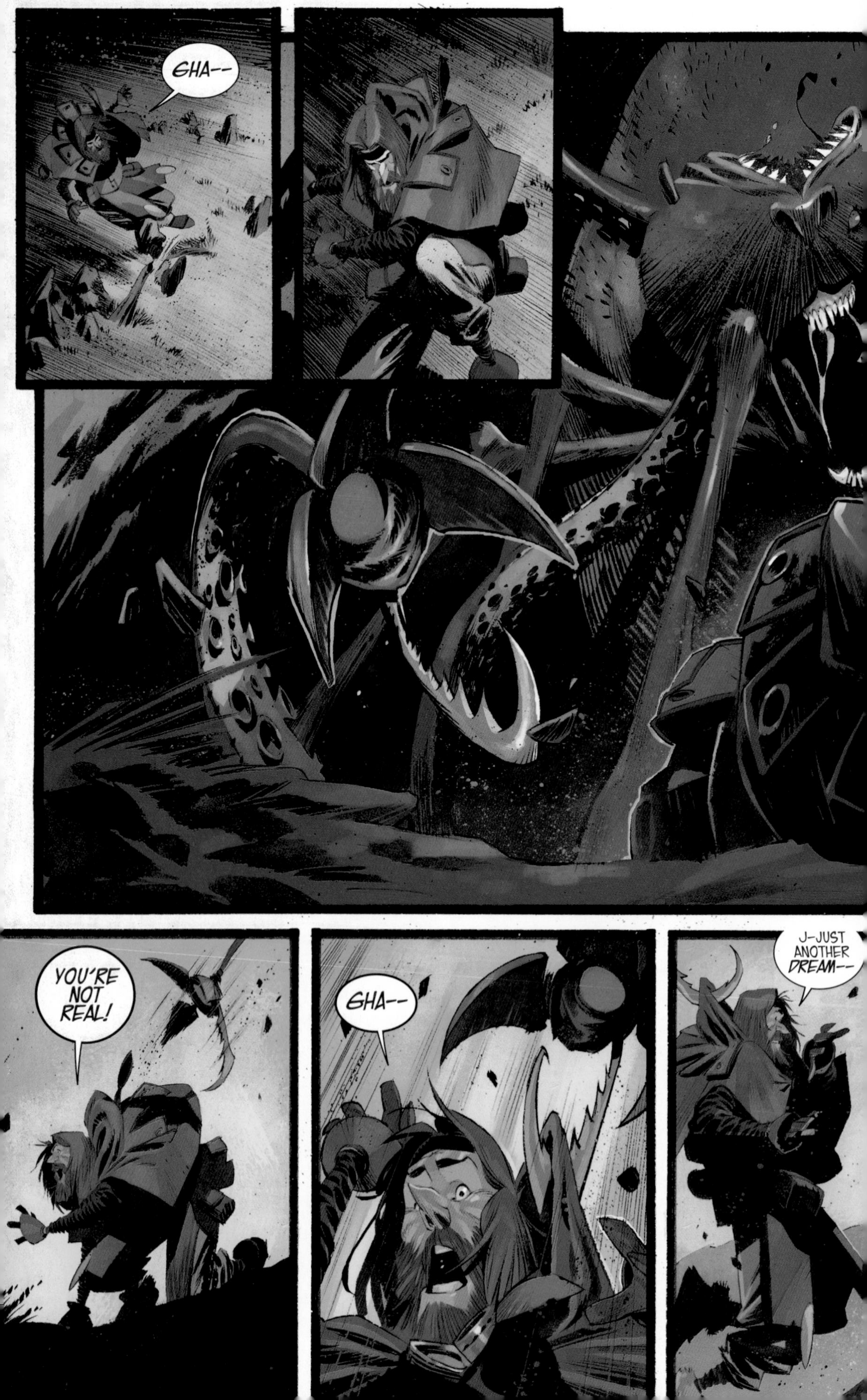
GHA--
YOU'RE NOT REAL!
GHA--
J-JUST ANOTHER DREAM--

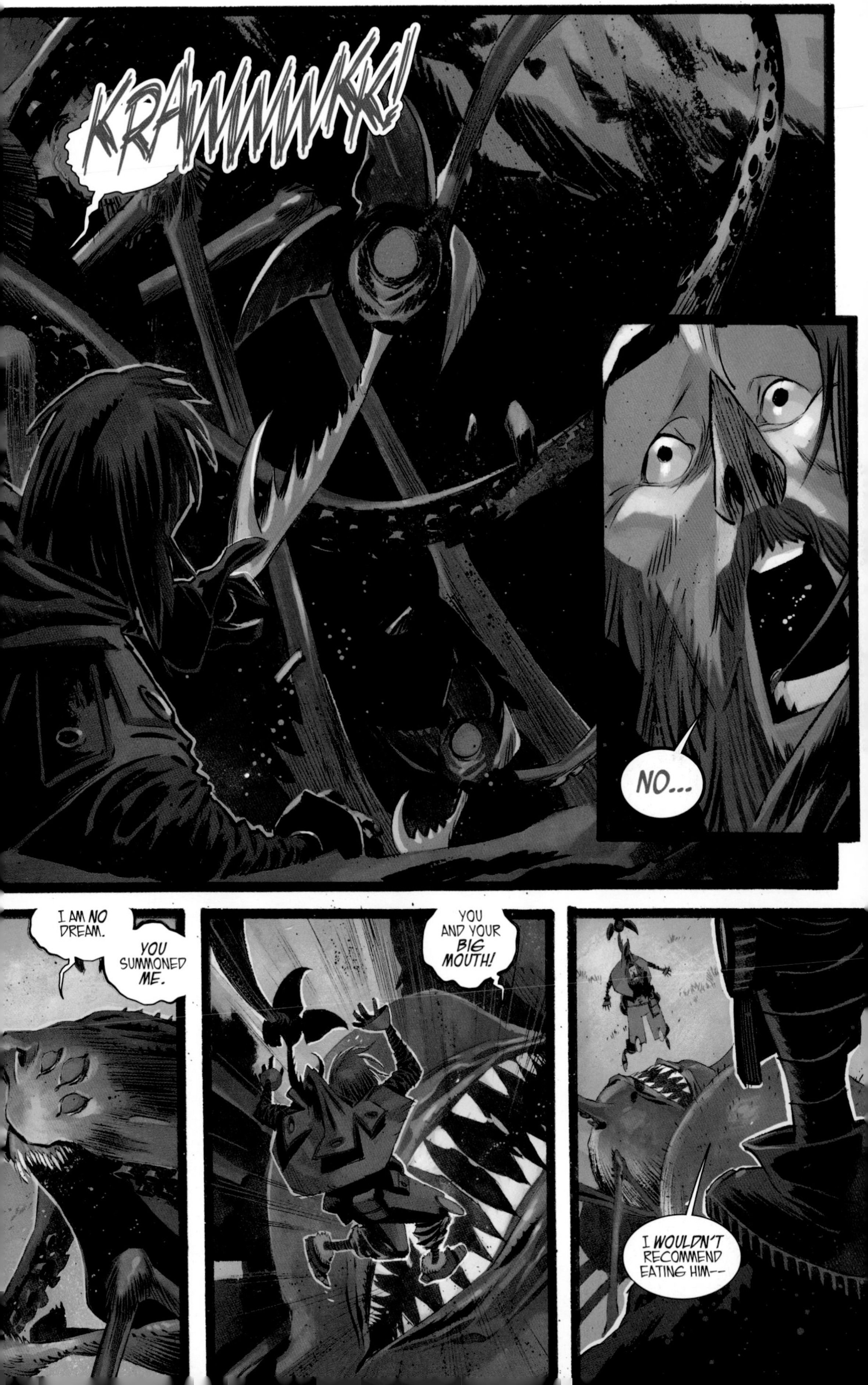
KRAWWWK!
NO...
I AM NO DREAM.
YOU SUMMONED ME.
YOU AND YOUR BIG MOUTH!
I WOULDN'T RECOMMEND EATING HIM--

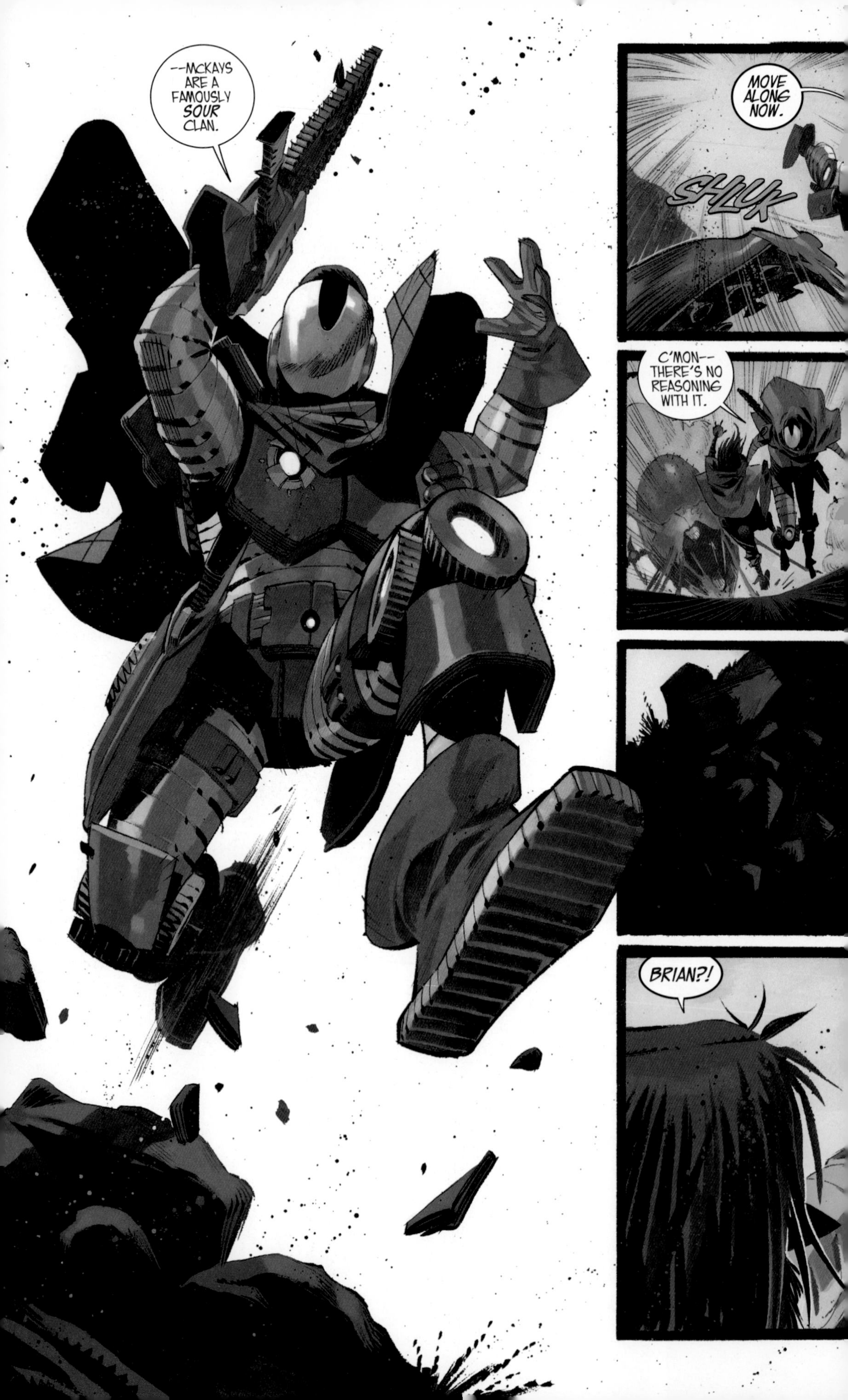
--MCKAYS ARE A FAMOUSLY SOUR CLAN.
MOVE ALONG NOW.
SHLUK
C'MON-- THERE'S NO REASONING WITH IT.
BRIAN?!

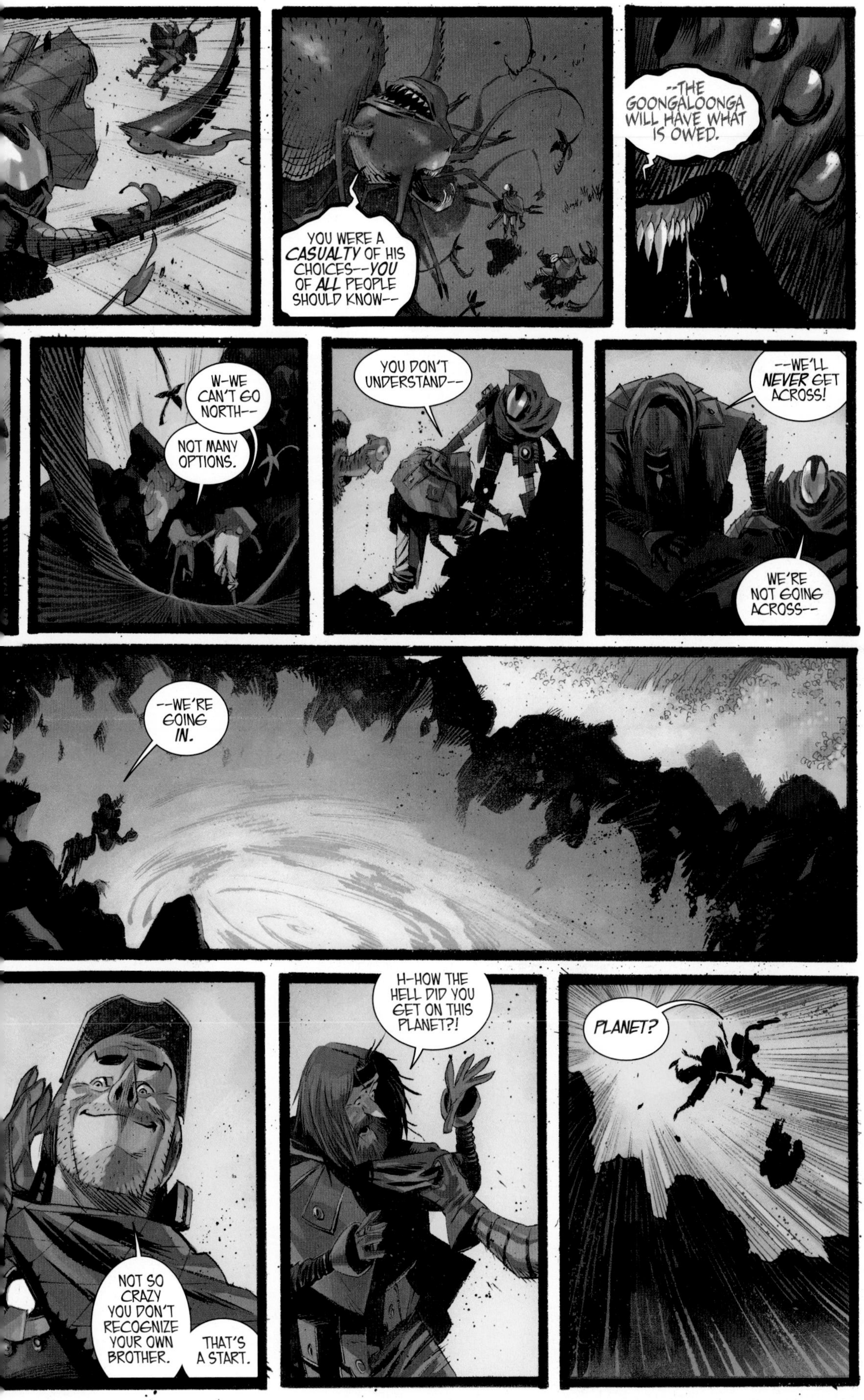
YOU WERE A CASUALTY OF HIS CHOICES--YOU OF ALL PEOPLE SHOULD KNOW--
--THE GOONGALOONGA WILL HAVE WHAT IS OWED.
W-WE CAN'T GO NORTH--
NOT MANY OPTIONS.
YOU DON'T UNDERSTAND--
--WE'LL NEVER GET ACROSS!
WE'RE NOT GOING ACROSS--
--WE'RE GOING IN.
NOT SO CRAZY YOU DON'T RECOGNIZE YOUR OWN BROTHER.
THAT'S A START.
H-HOW THE HELL DID YOU GET ON THIS PLANET?!
PLANET?

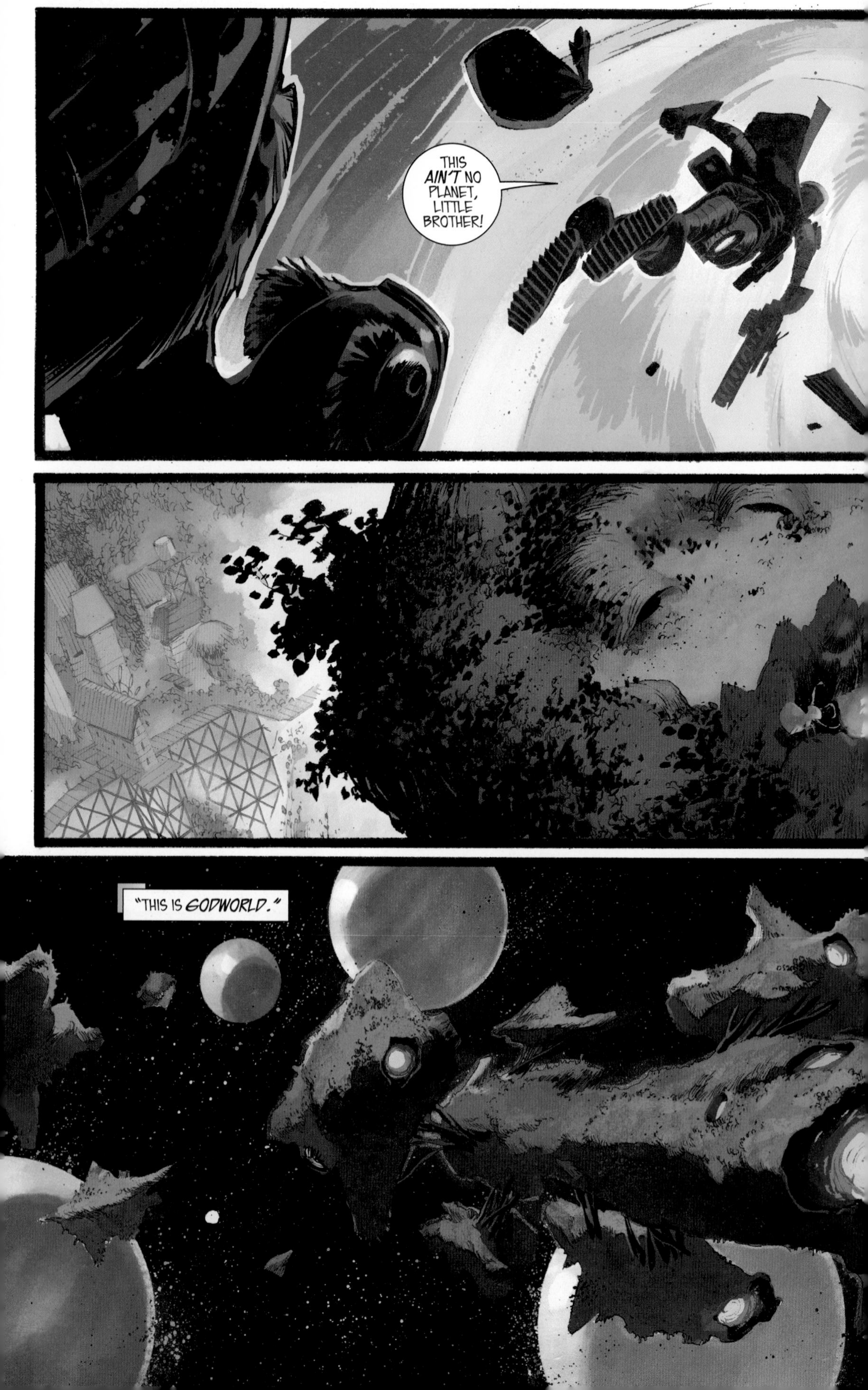

THIS AIN'T NO PLANET, LITTLE BROTHER!
"THIS IS GODWORLD."

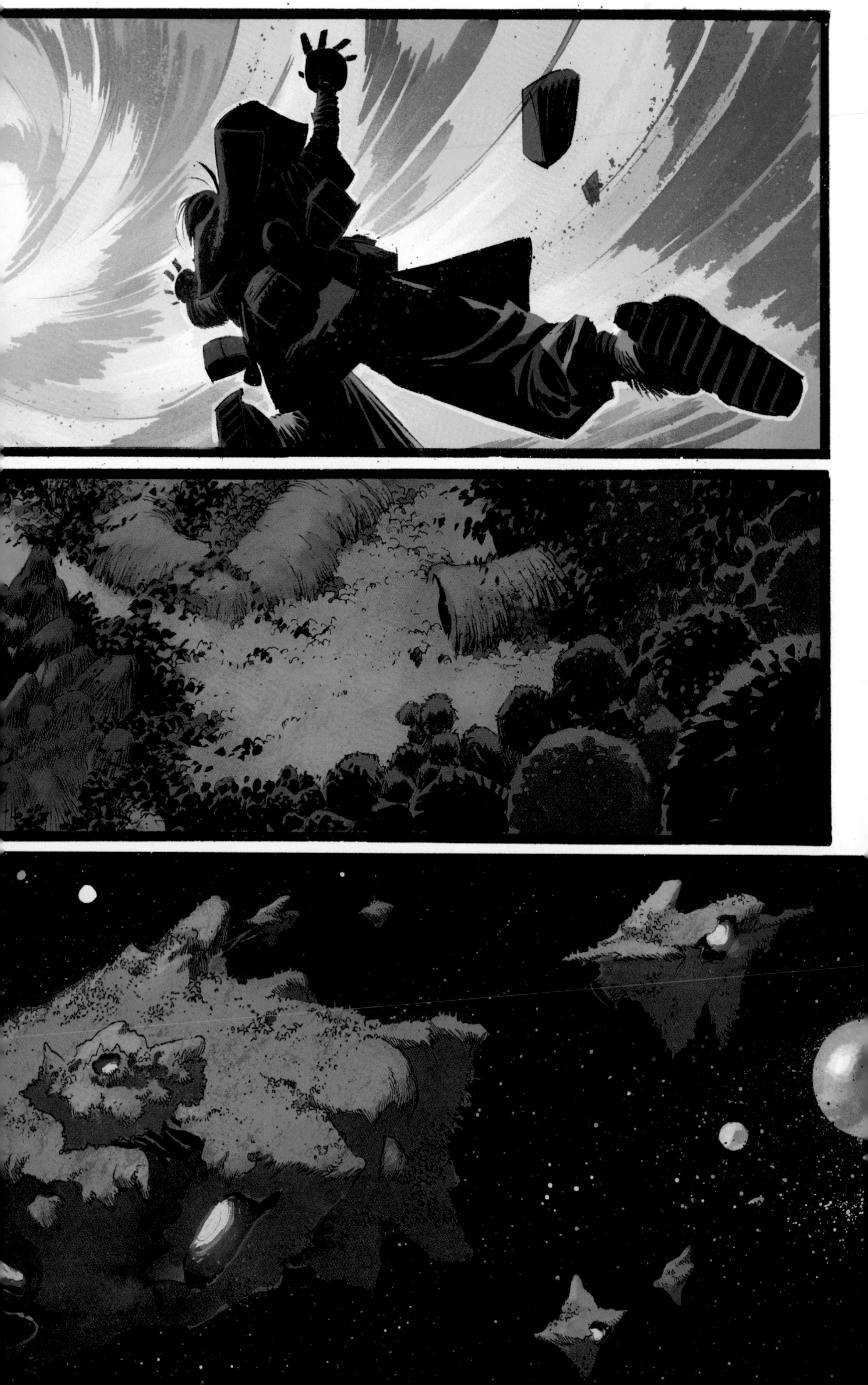

18

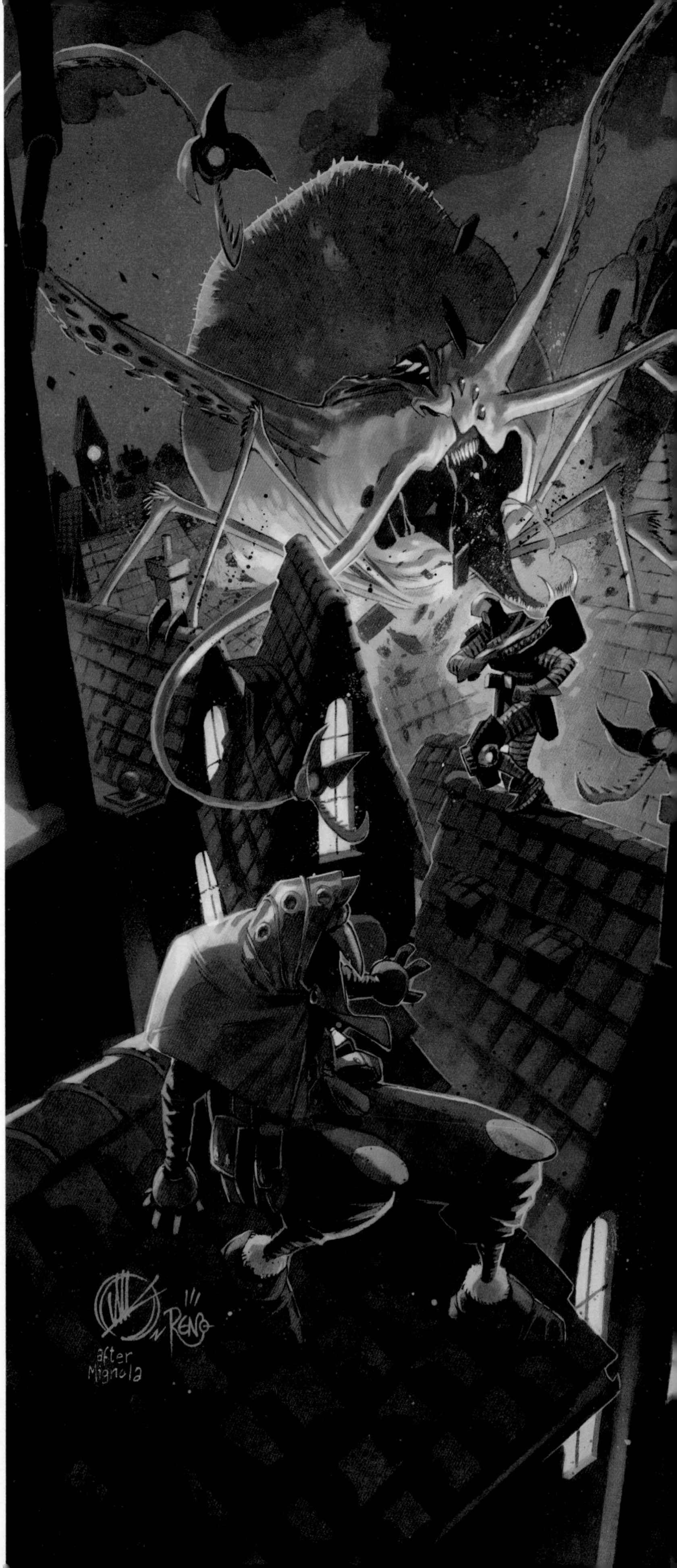
after
Mignola

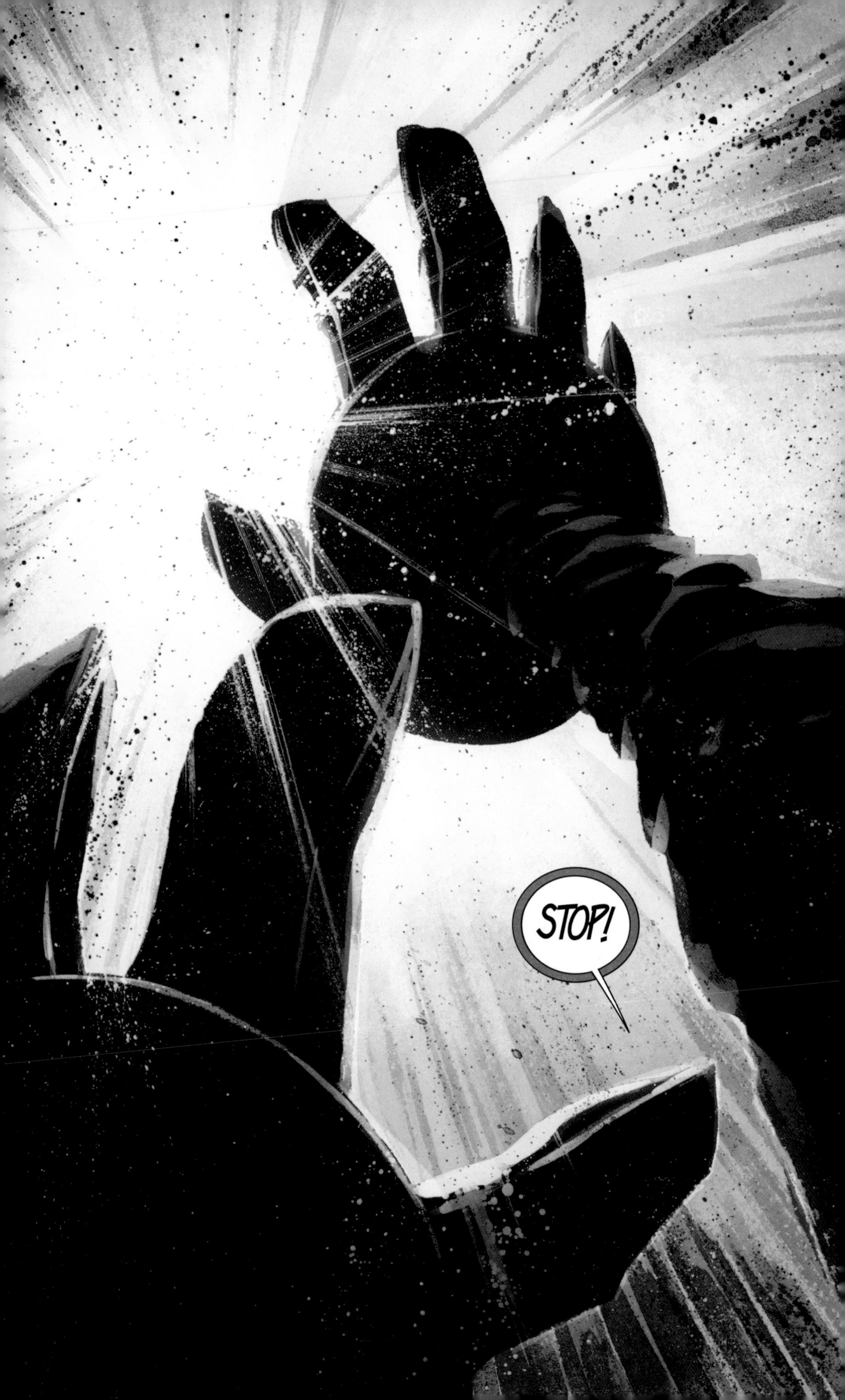
STOP!

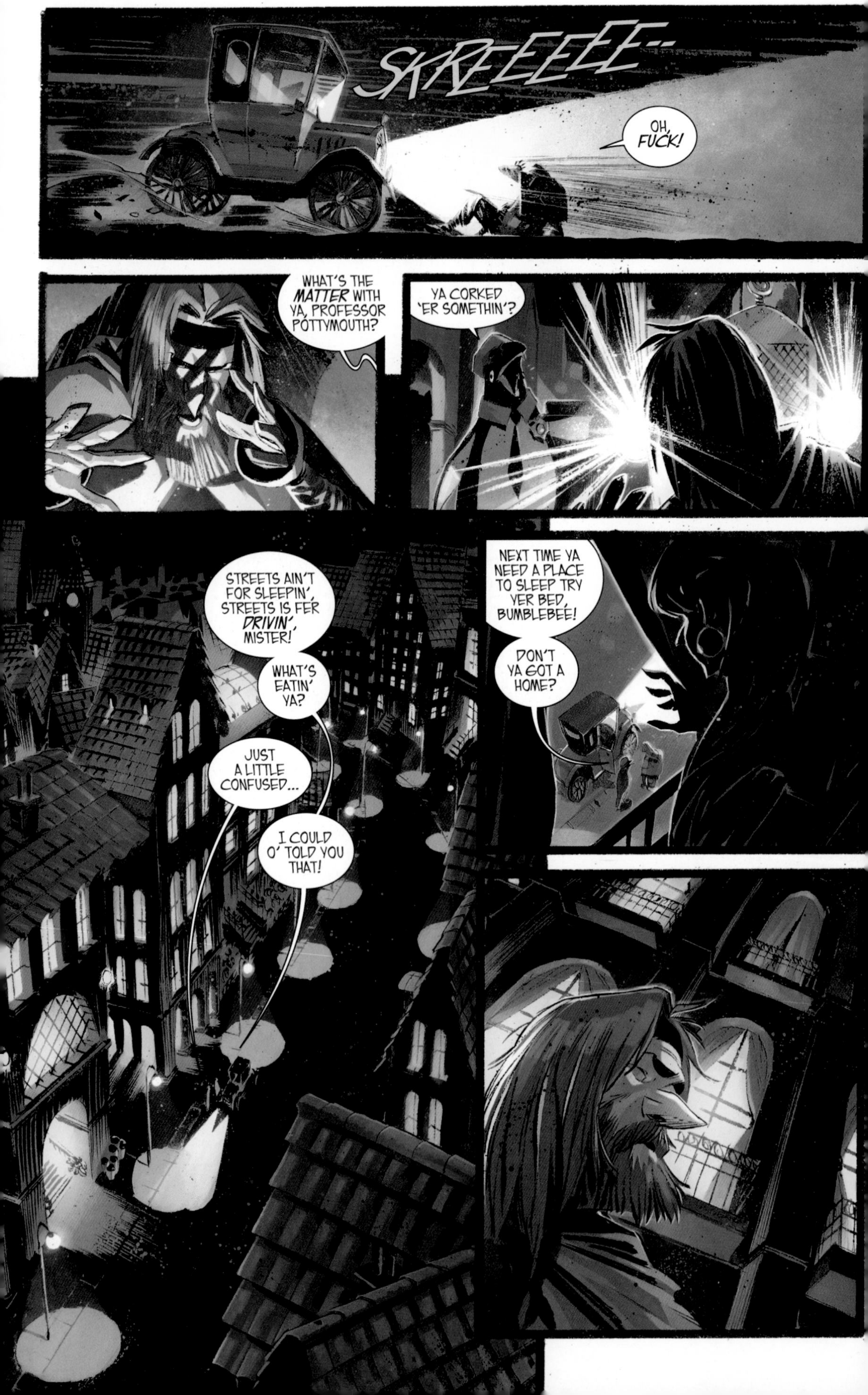
SKREEEEEE--
OH, FUCK!
WHAT'S THE MATTER WITH YA, PROFESSOR POTTYMOUTH?
YA CORKED 'ER SOMETHIN'?
STREETS AIN'T FOR SLEEPIN', STREETS IS FER DRIVIN', MISTER!
WHAT'S EATIN' YA?
JUST A LITTLE CONFUSED...
I COULD O' TOLD YOU THAT!
NEXT TIME YA NEED A PLACE TO SLEEP TRY YER BED, BUMBLEBEE!
DON'T YA GOT A HOME?

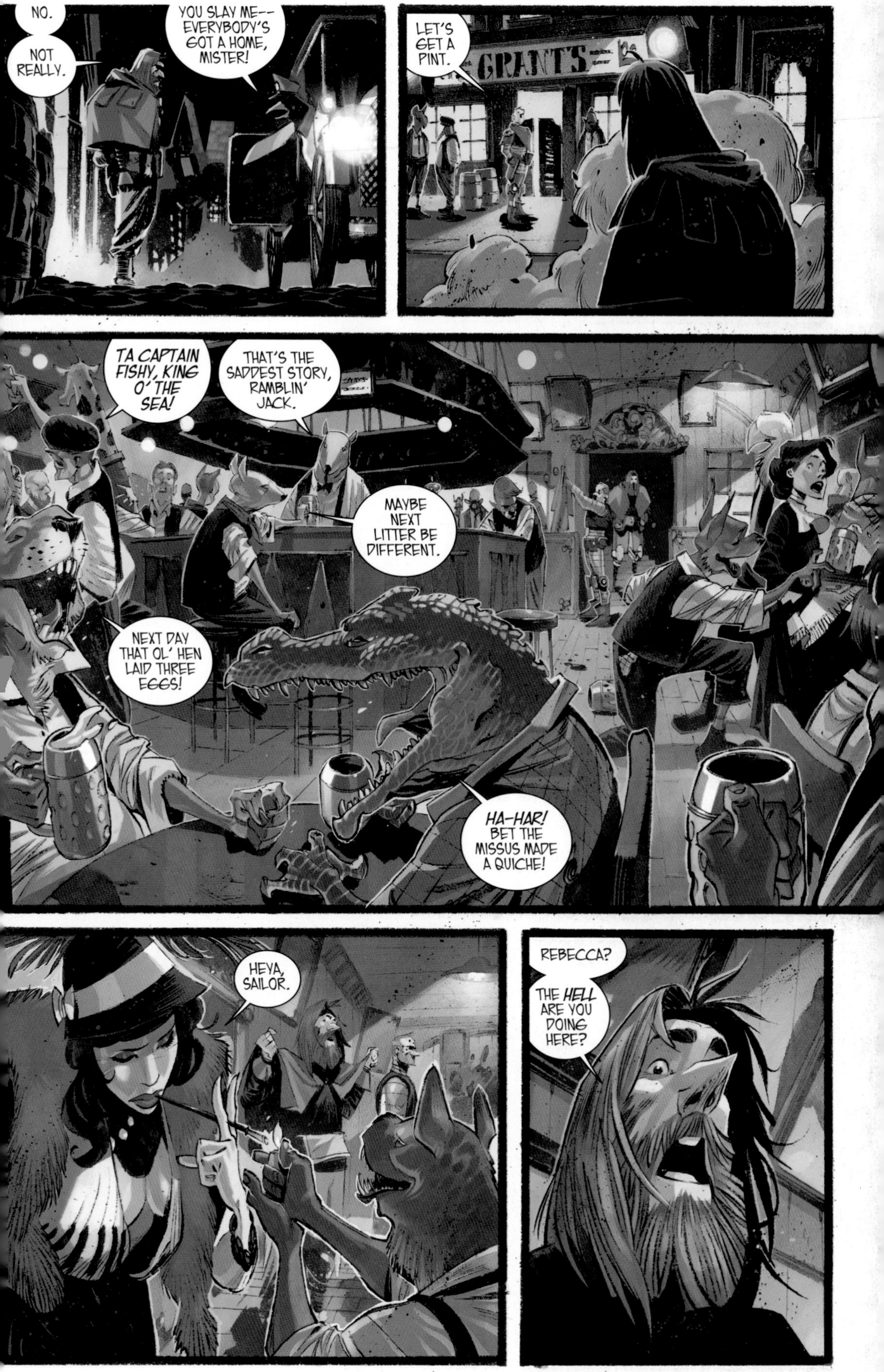
NO.
NOT REALLY.
YOU SLAY ME-- EVERYBODY'S GOT A HOME, MISTER!
LET'S GET A PINT.
GRANT'S
TA CAPTAIN FISHY, KING O' THE SEA!
THAT'S THE SADDEST STORY, RAMBLIN' JACK.
MAYBE NEXT LITTER BE DIFFERENT.
NEXT DAY THAT OL' HEN LAID THREE EGGS!
HA-HAR! BET THE MISSUS MADE A QUICHE!
HEYA, SAILOR.
REBECCA?
THE HELL ARE YOU DOING HERE?

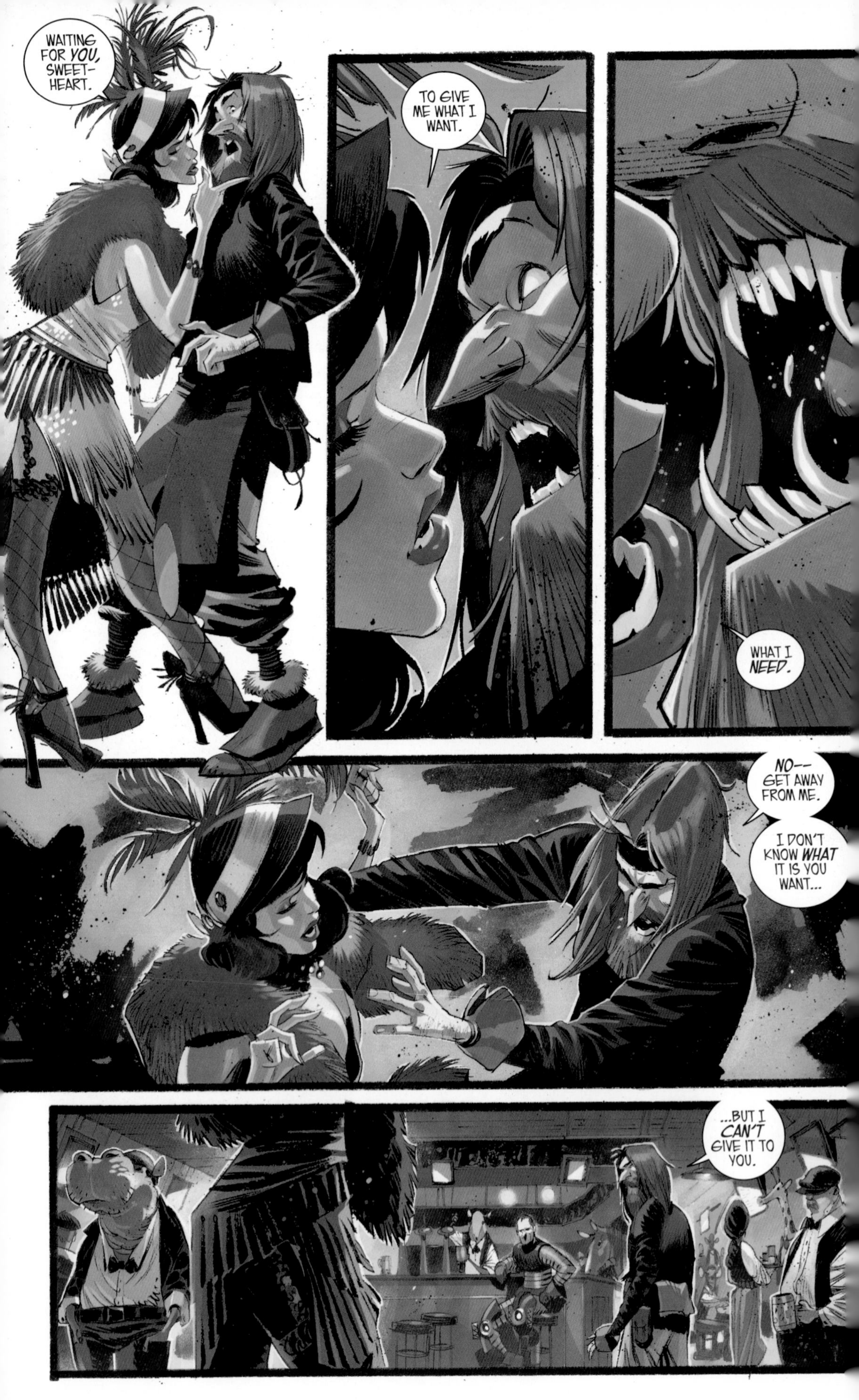
WAITING FOR *YOU*, SWEET-HEART.
TO GIVE ME WHAT I WANT.
WHAT I *NEED*.
NO-- GET AWAY FROM ME.
I DON'T KNOW *WHAT* IT IS YOU WANT...
...BUT I *CAN'T* GIVE IT TO YOU.

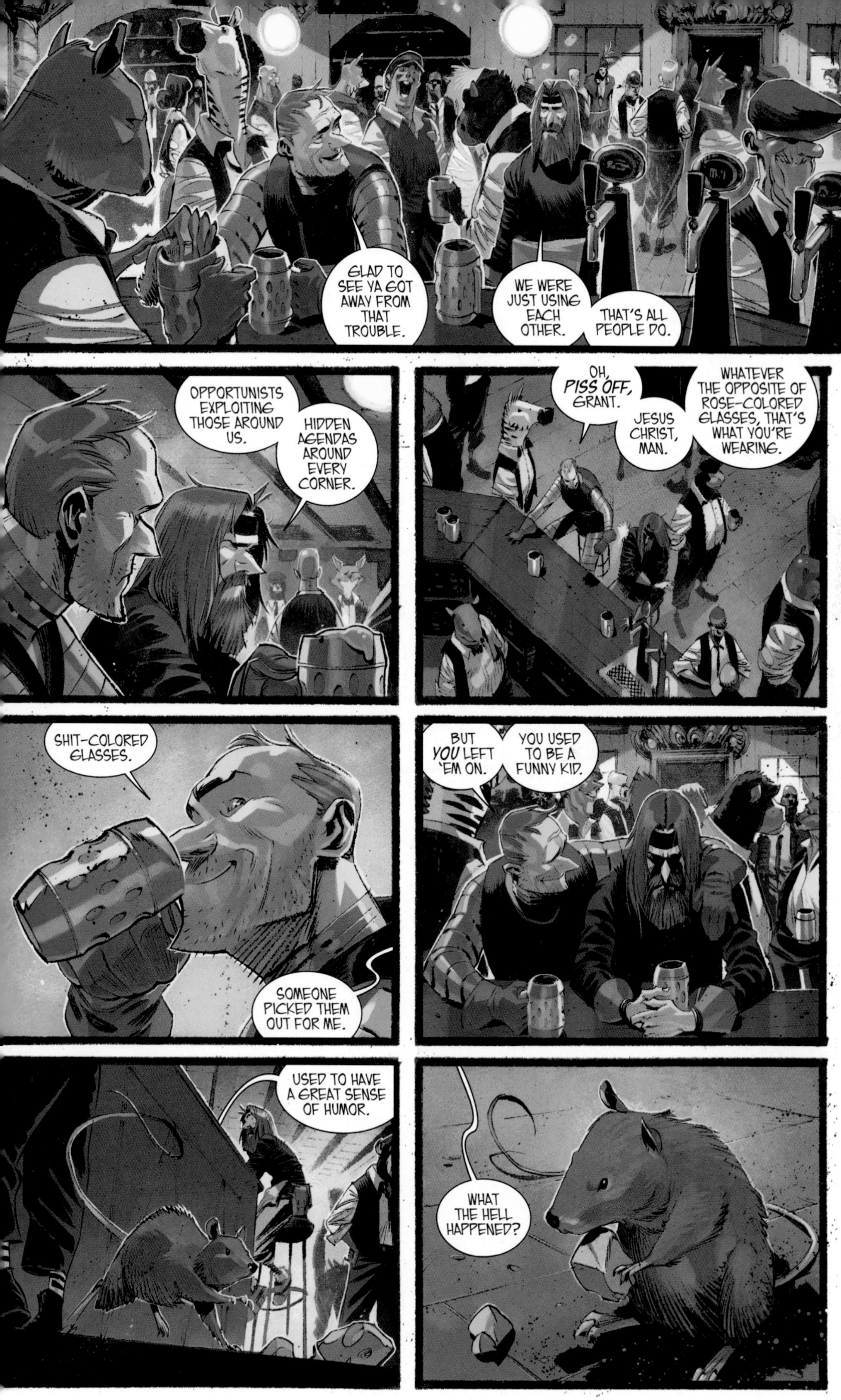
GLAD TO SEE YA GOT AWAY FROM THAT TROUBLE.
WE WERE JUST USING EACH OTHER.
THAT'S ALL PEOPLE DO.
OPPORTUNISTS EXPLOITING THOSE AROUND US.
HIDDEN AGENDAS AROUND EVERY CORNER.
OH, *PISS OFF,* GRANT.
JESUS CHRIST, MAN.
WHATEVER THE OPPOSITE OF ROSE-COLORED GLASSES, THAT'S WHAT YOU'RE WEARING.
SHIT-COLORED GLASSES.
SOMEONE PICKED THEM OUT FOR ME.
BUT *YOU* LEFT 'EM ON.
YOU USED TO BE A FUNNY KID.
USED TO HAVE A GREAT SENSE OF HUMOR.
WHAT THE HELL HAPPENED?

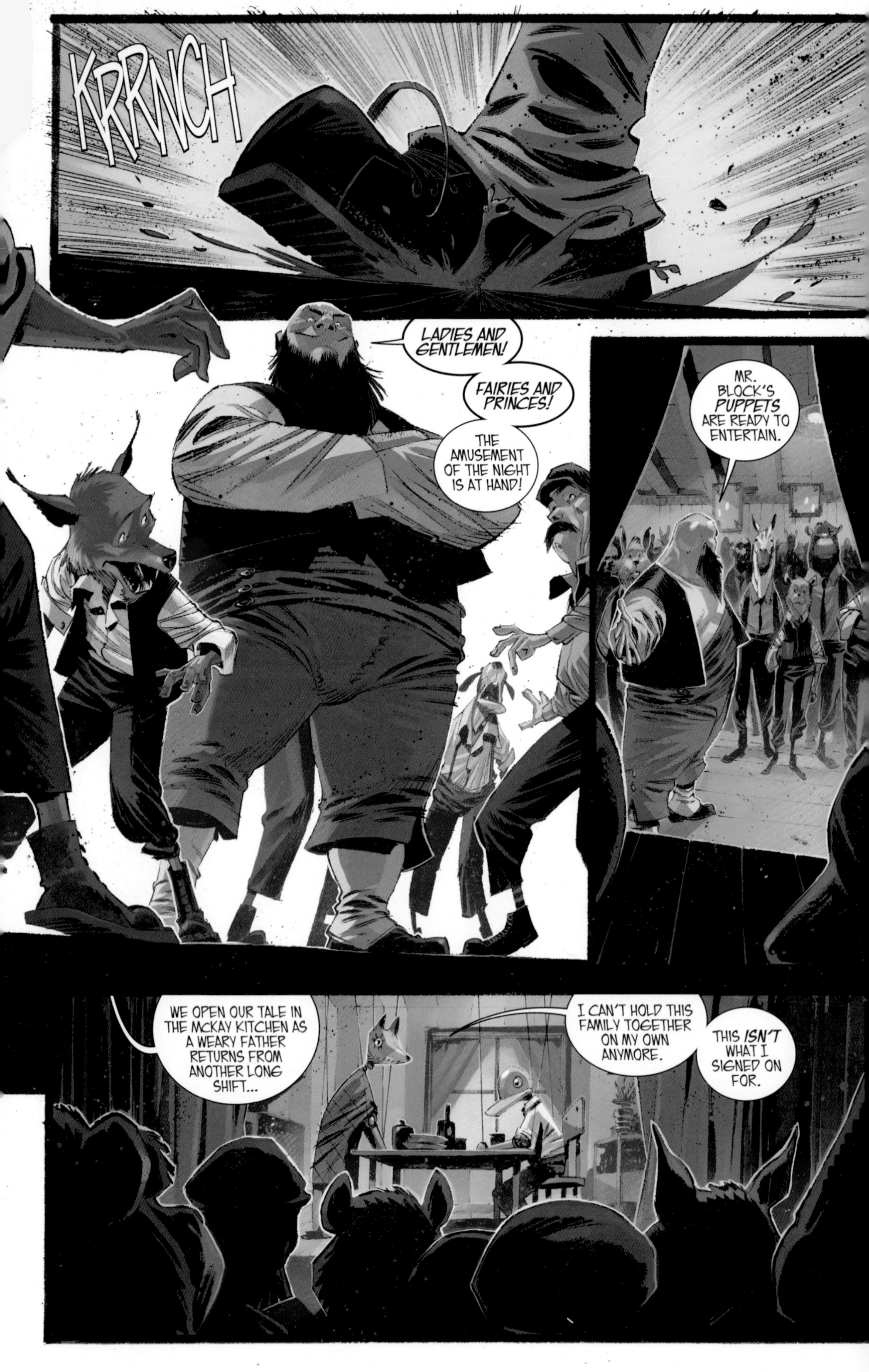
KRRNCH
LADIES AND GENTLEMEN!
FAIRIES AND PRINCES!
THE AMUSEMENT OF THE NIGHT IS AT HAND!
MR. BLOCK'S PUPPETS ARE READY TO ENTERTAIN.
WE OPEN OUR TALE IN THE MCKAY KITCHEN AS A WEARY FATHER RETURNS FROM ANOTHER LONG SHIFT...
I CAN'T HOLD THIS FAMILY TOGETHER ON MY OWN ANYMORE.
THIS ISN'T WHAT I SIGNED ON FOR.

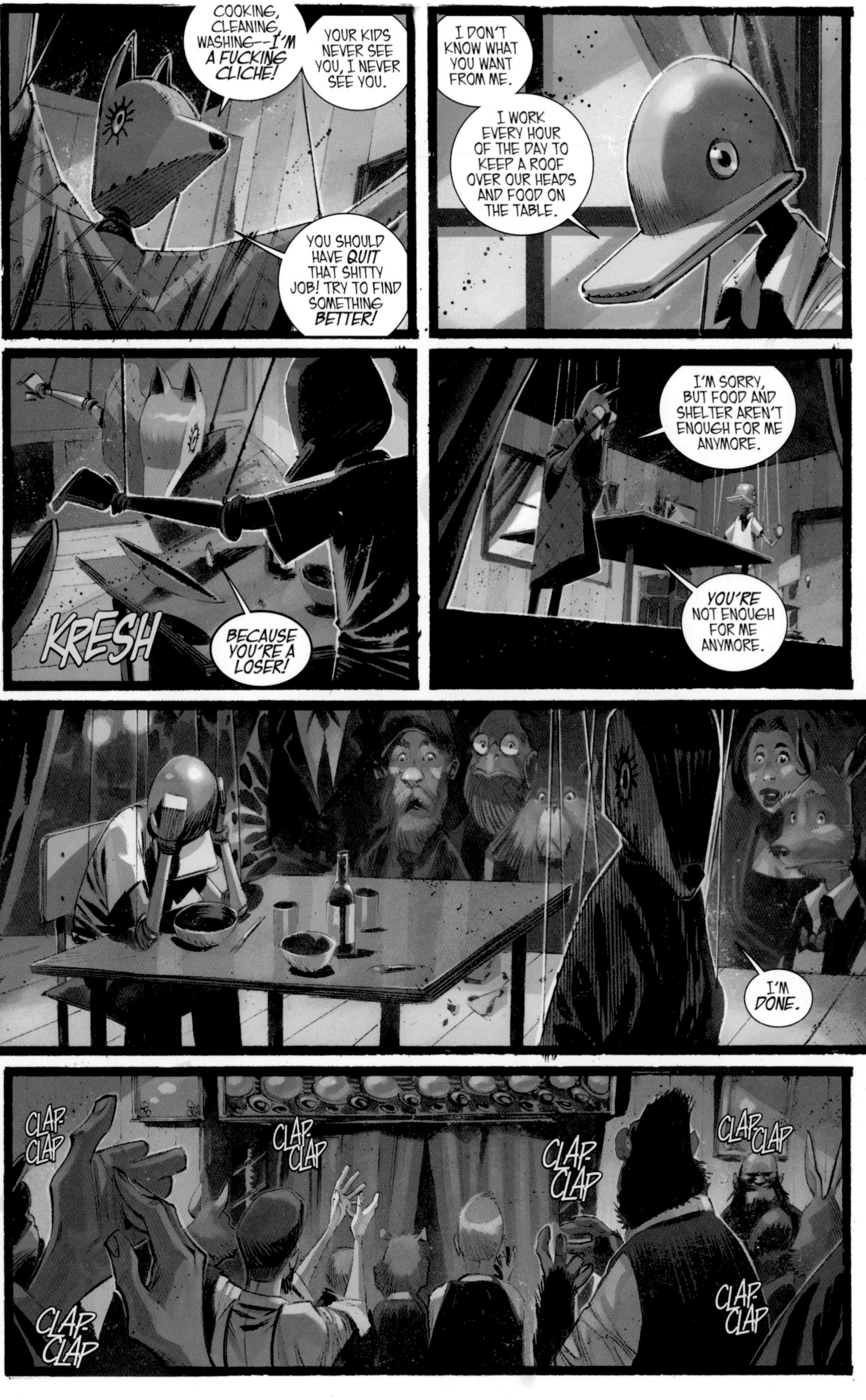
COOKING, CLEANING, WASHING--I'M A FUCKING CLICHE!
YOUR KIDS NEVER SEE YOU, I NEVER SEE YOU.
YOU SHOULD HAVE QUIT THAT SHITTY JOB! TRY TO FIND SOMETHING BETTER!
I DON'T KNOW WHAT YOU WANT FROM ME.
I WORK EVERY HOUR OF THE DAY TO KEEP A ROOF OVER OUR HEADS AND FOOD ON THE TABLE.
KRESH
BECAUSE YOU'RE A LOSER!
I'M SORRY, BUT FOOD AND SHELTER AREN'T ENOUGH FOR ME ANYMORE.
YOU'RE NOT ENOUGH FOR ME ANYMORE.
I'M DONE.
CLAP-CLAP
CLAP-CLAP
CLAP-CLAP
CLAP-CLAP
CLAP-CLAP
CLAP-CLAP

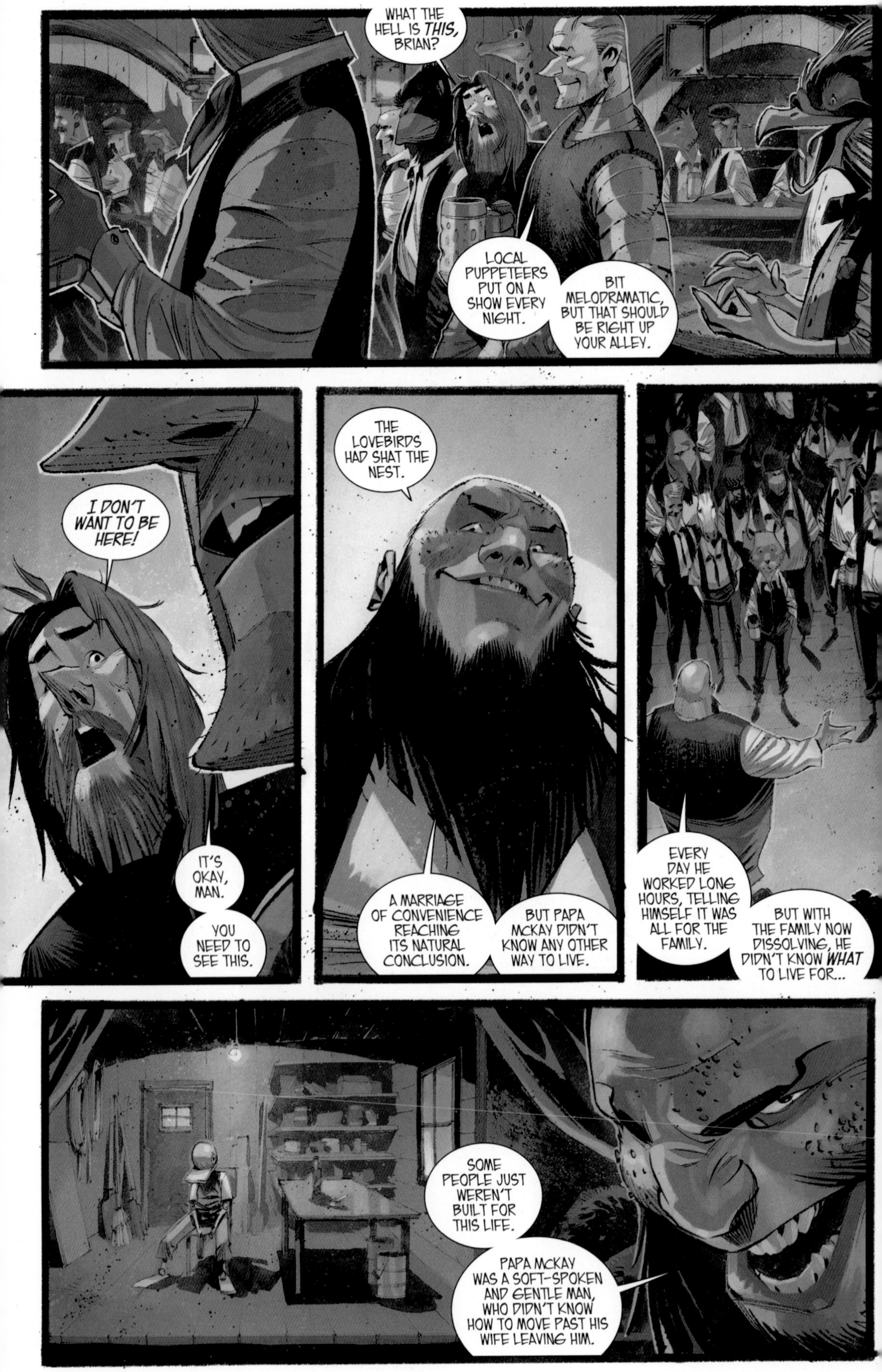
WHAT THE HELL IS *THIS,* BRIAN?
LOCAL PUPPETEERS PUT ON A SHOW EVERY NIGHT.
BIT MELODRAMATIC, BUT THAT SHOULD BE RIGHT UP YOUR ALLEY.
I DON'T WANT TO BE HERE!
IT'S OKAY, MAN.
YOU NEED TO SEE THIS.
THE LOVEBIRDS HAD SHAT THE NEST.
A MARRIAGE OF CONVENIENCE REACHING ITS NATURAL CONCLUSION.
BUT PAPA MCKAY DIDN'T KNOW ANY OTHER WAY TO LIVE.
EVERY DAY HE WORKED LONG HOURS, TELLING HIMSELF IT WAS ALL FOR THE FAMILY.
BUT WITH THE FAMILY NOW DISSOLVING, HE DIDN'T KNOW *WHAT* TO LIVE FOR...
SOME PEOPLE JUST WEREN'T BUILT FOR THIS LIFE.
PAPA MCKAY WAS A SOFT-SPOKEN AND GENTLE MAN, WHO DIDN'T KNOW HOW TO MOVE PAST HIS WIFE LEAVING HIM.

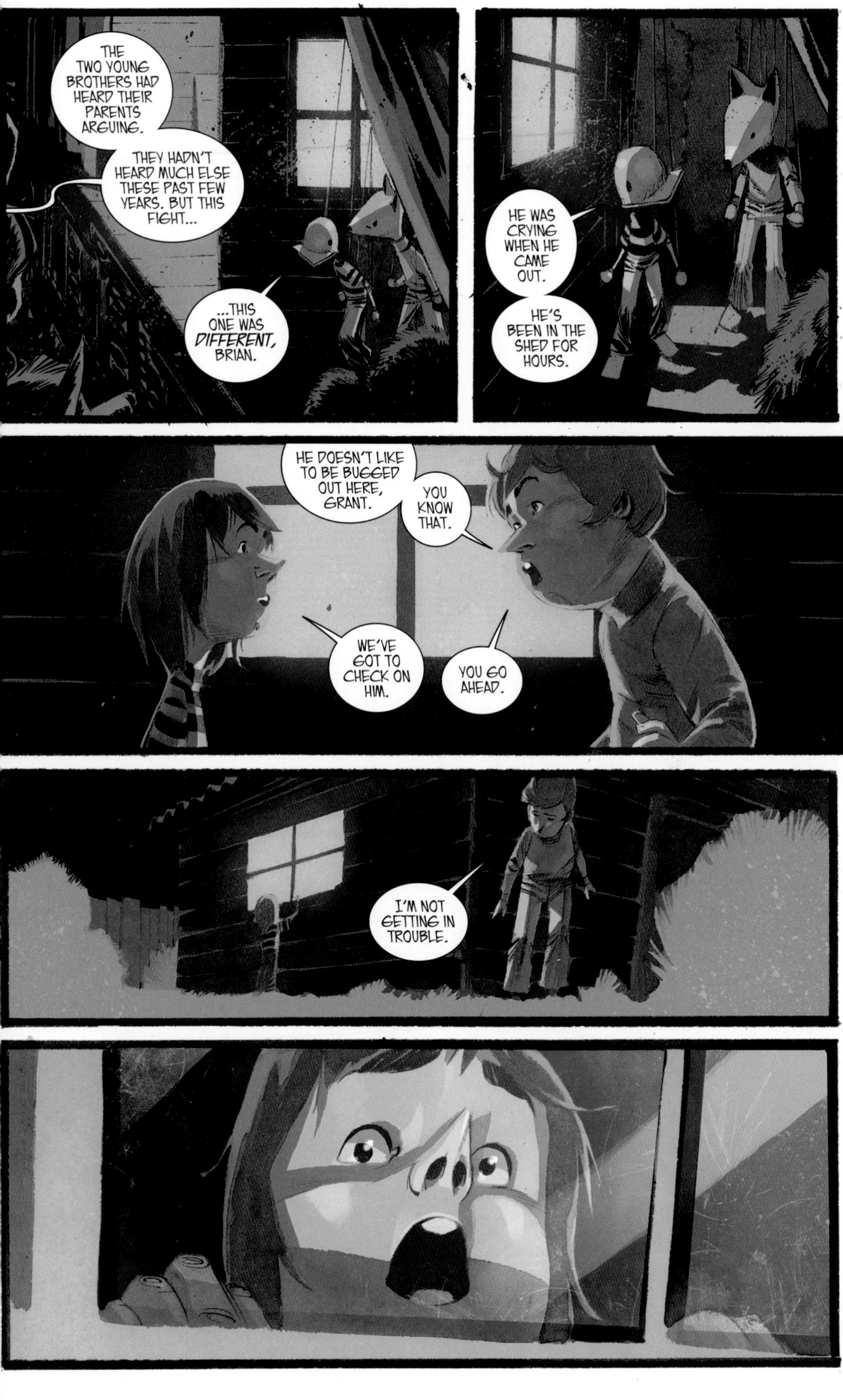
THE TWO YOUNG BROTHERS HAD HEARD THEIR PARENTS ARGUING.
THEY HADN'T HEARD MUCH ELSE THESE PAST FEW YEARS. BUT THIS FIGHT...
...THIS ONE WAS *DIFFERENT,* BRIAN.
HE WAS CRYING WHEN HE CAME OUT.
HE'S BEEN IN THE SHED FOR HOURS.
HE DOESN'T LIKE TO BE BUGGED OUT HERE, GRANT.
YOU KNOW THAT.
WE'VE GOT TO CHECK ON HIM.
YOU GO AHEAD.
I'M NOT GETTING IN TROUBLE.

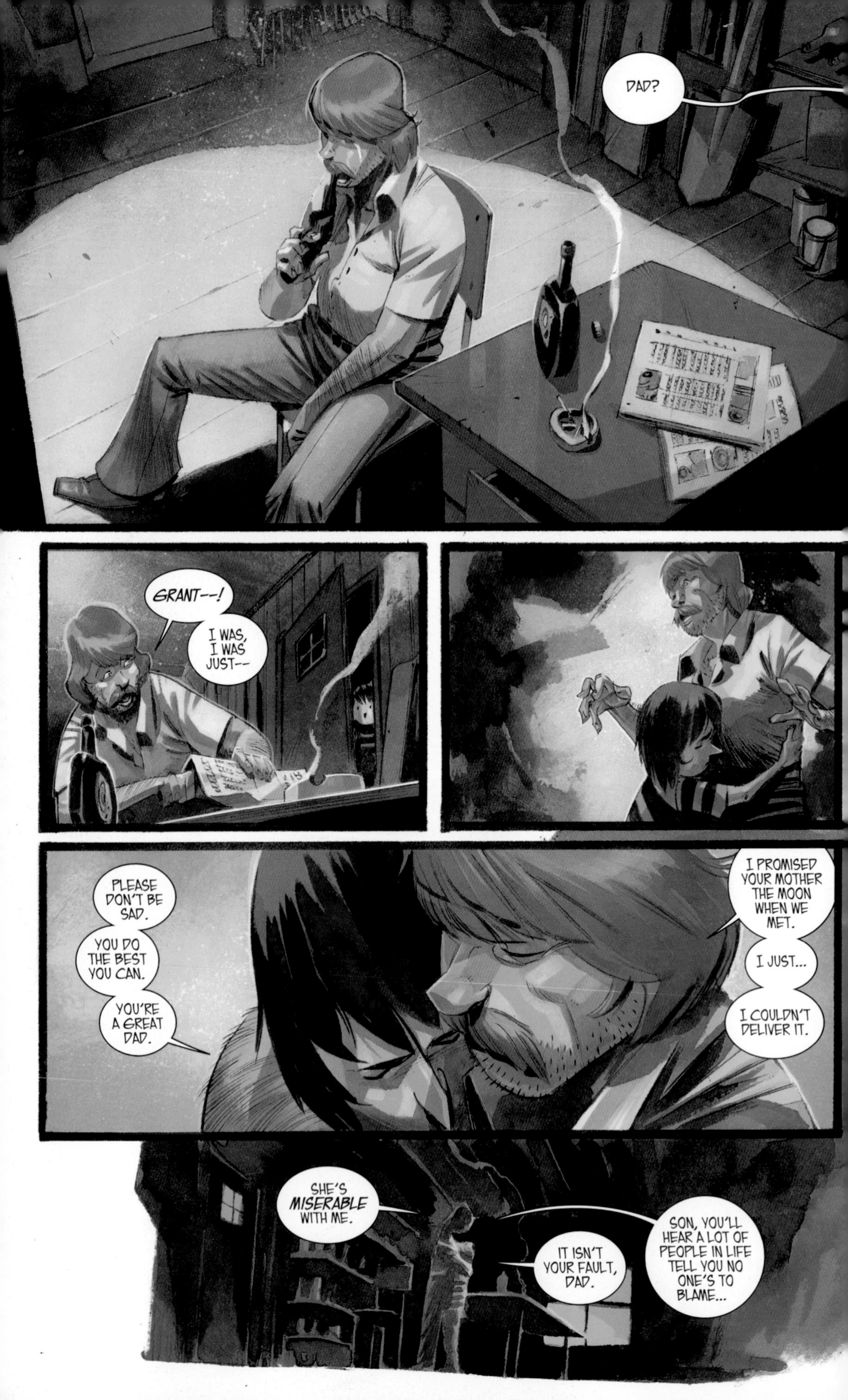
DAD?
GRANT--!
I WAS, I WAS JUST--
PLEASE DON'T BE SAD.
YOU DO THE BEST YOU CAN.
YOU'RE A GREAT DAD.
I PROMISED YOUR MOTHER THE MOON WHEN WE MET.
I JUST...
I COULDN'T DELIVER IT.
SHE'S MISERABLE WITH ME.
IT ISN'T YOUR FAULT, DAD.
SON, YOU'LL HEAR A LOT OF PEOPLE IN LIFE TELL YOU NO ONE'S TO BLAME...

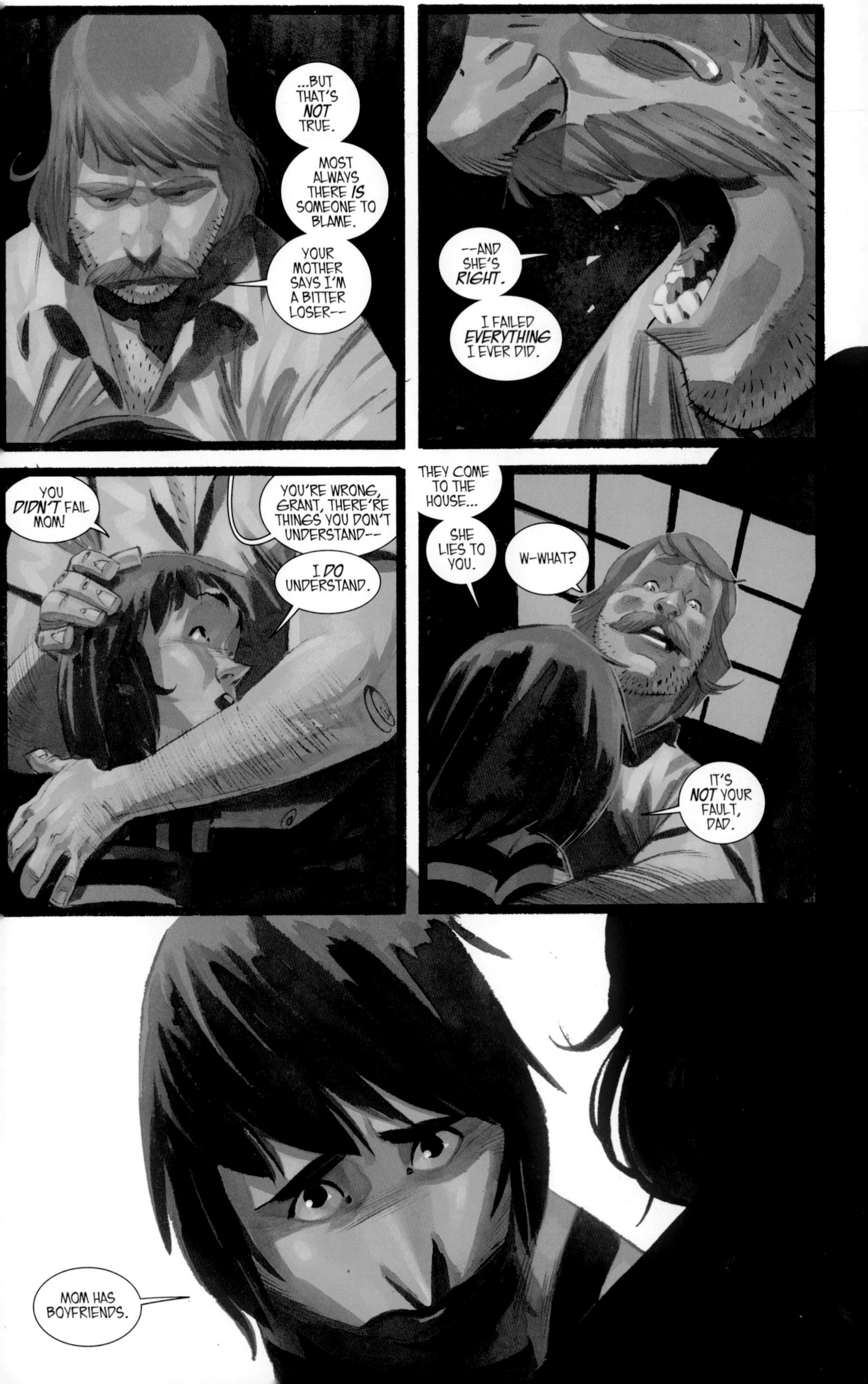
...BUT THAT'S NOT TRUE.
MOST ALWAYS THERE IS SOMEONE TO BLAME.
YOUR MOTHER SAYS I'M A BITTER LOSER--
--AND SHE'S RIGHT.
I FAILED EVERYTHING I EVER DID.
YOU DIDN'T FAIL MOM!
YOU'RE WRONG, GRANT, THERE'RE THINGS YOU DON'T UNDERSTAND--
I DO UNDERSTAND.
THEY COME TO THE HOUSE...
SHE LIES TO YOU.
W-WHAT?
IT'S NOT YOUR FAULT, DAD.
MOM HAS BOYFRIENDS.

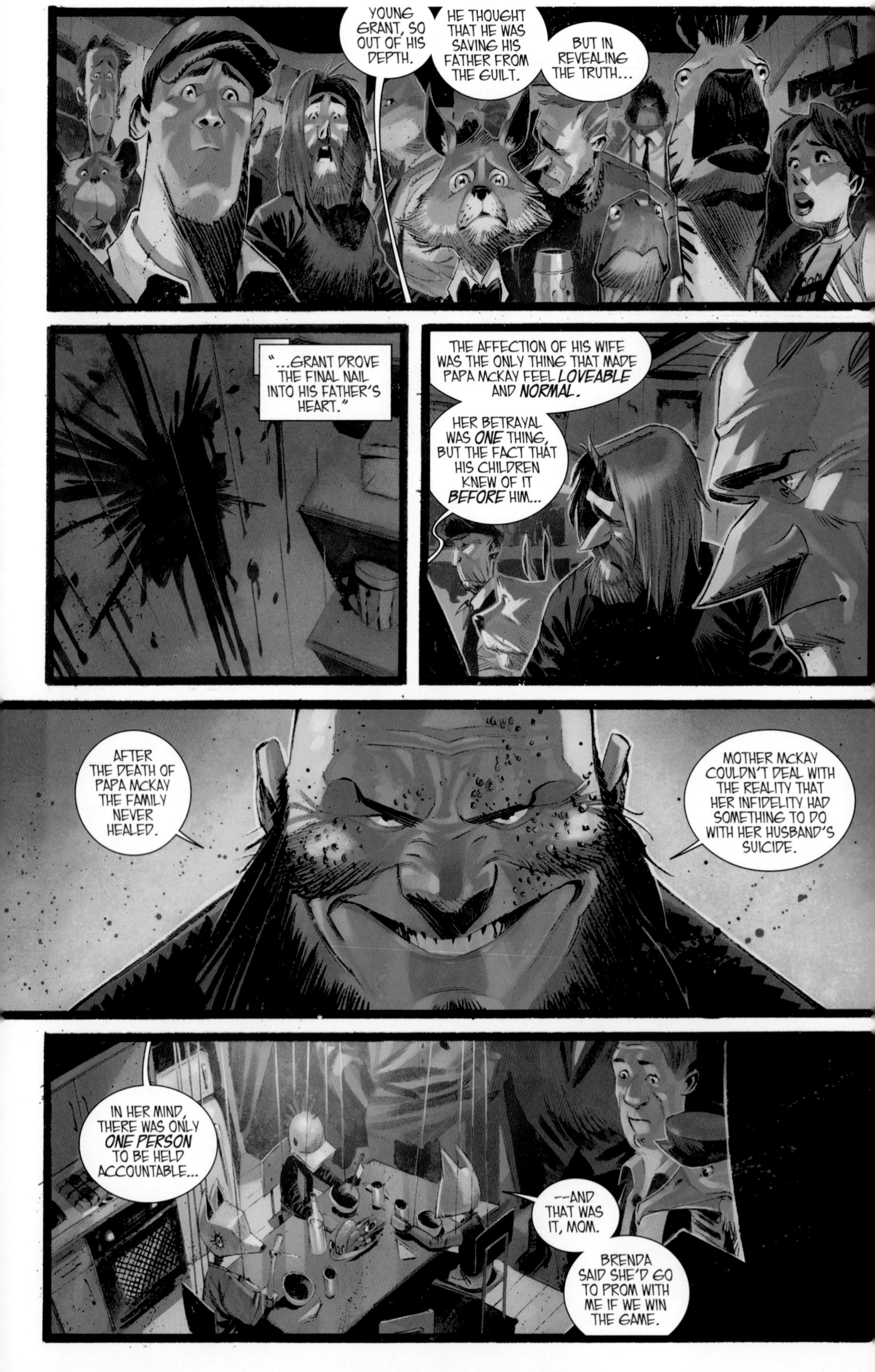
YOUNG GRANT, SO OUT OF HIS DEPTH.
HE THOUGHT THAT HE WAS SAVING HIS FATHER FROM THE GUILT.
BUT IN REVEALING THE TRUTH...
"...GRANT DROVE THE FINAL NAIL INTO HIS FATHER'S HEART."
THE AFFECTION OF HIS WIFE WAS THE ONLY THING THAT MADE PAPA McKAY FEEL LOVEABLE AND NORMAL.
HER BETRAYAL WAS ONE THING, BUT THE FACT THAT HIS CHILDREN KNEW OF IT BEFORE HIM...
AFTER THE DEATH OF PAPA McKAY THE FAMILY NEVER HEALED.
MOTHER McKAY COULDN'T DEAL WITH THE REALITY THAT HER INFIDELITY HAD SOMETHING TO DO WITH HER HUSBAND'S SUICIDE.
IN HER MIND, THERE WAS ONLY ONE PERSON TO BE HELD ACCOUNTABLE...
--AND THAT WAS IT, MOM.
BRENDA SAID SHE'D GO TO PROM WITH ME IF WE WIN THE GAME.

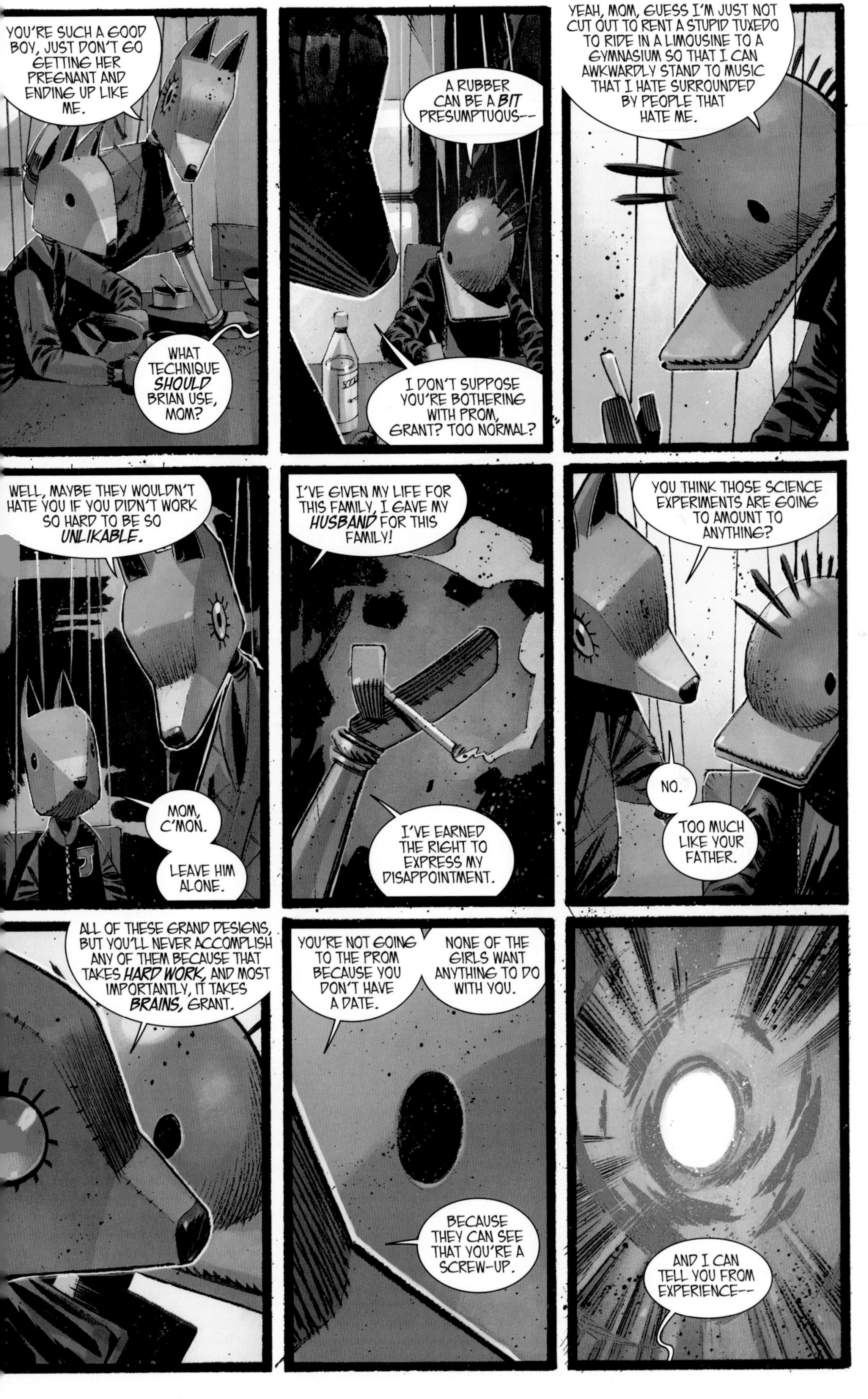
YOU'RE SUCH A GOOD BOY, JUST DON'T GO GETTING HER PREGNANT AND ENDING UP LIKE ME.
WHAT TECHNIQUE SHOULD BRIAN USE, MOM?
A RUBBER CAN BE A BIT PRESUMPTUOUS--
I DON'T SUPPOSE YOU'RE BOTHERING WITH PROM, GRANT? TOO NORMAL?
YEAH, MOM, GUESS I'M JUST NOT CUT OUT TO RENT A STUPID TUXEDO TO RIDE IN A LIMOUSINE TO A GYMNASIUM SO THAT I CAN AWKWARDLY STAND TO MUSIC THAT I HATE SURROUNDED BY PEOPLE THAT HATE ME.
WELL, MAYBE THEY WOULDN'T HATE YOU IF YOU DIDN'T WORK SO HARD TO BE SO UNLIKABLE.
MOM, C'MON.
LEAVE HIM ALONE.
I'VE GIVEN MY LIFE FOR THIS FAMILY, I GAVE MY HUSBAND FOR THIS FAMILY!
I'VE EARNED THE RIGHT TO EXPRESS MY DISAPPOINTMENT.
YOU THINK THOSE SCIENCE EXPERIMENTS ARE GOING TO AMOUNT TO ANYTHING?
NO.
TOO MUCH LIKE YOUR FATHER.
ALL OF THESE GRAND DESIGNS, BUT YOU'LL NEVER ACCOMPLISH ANY OF THEM BECAUSE THAT TAKES HARD WORK, AND MOST IMPORTANTLY, IT TAKES BRAINS, GRANT.
YOU'RE NOT GOING TO THE PROM BECAUSE YOU DON'T HAVE A DATE.
NONE OF THE GIRLS WANT ANYTHING TO DO WITH YOU.
BECAUSE THEY CAN SEE THAT YOU'RE A SCREW-UP.
AND I CAN TELL YOU FROM EXPERIENCE--

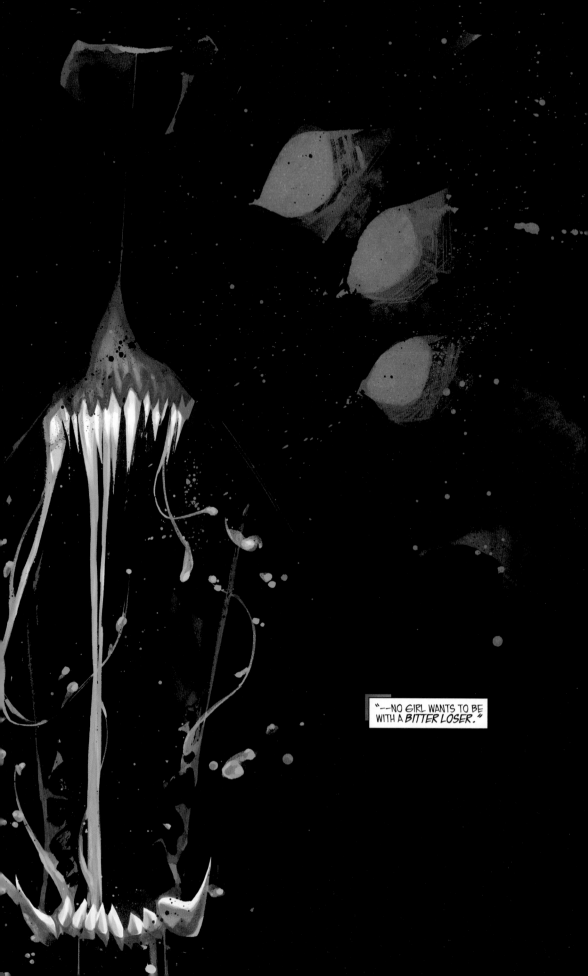

"--NO GIRL WANTS TO BE WITH A *BITTER LOSER.*"

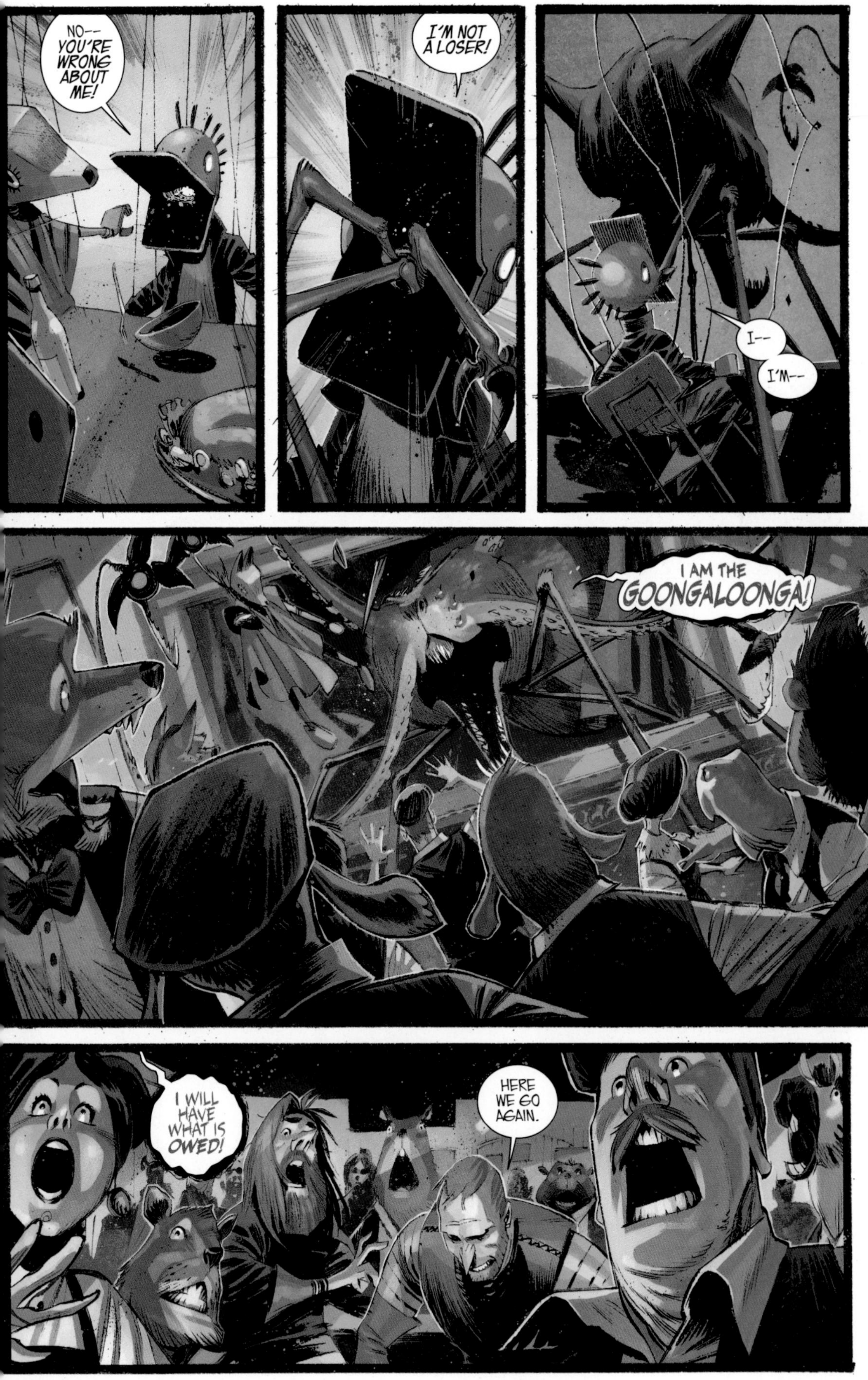
NO-- YOU'RE WRONG ABOUT ME!
I'M NOT A LOSER!
I--
I'M--
I AM THE GOONGALOONGA!
I WILL HAVE WHAT IS OWED!
HERE WE GO AGAIN.

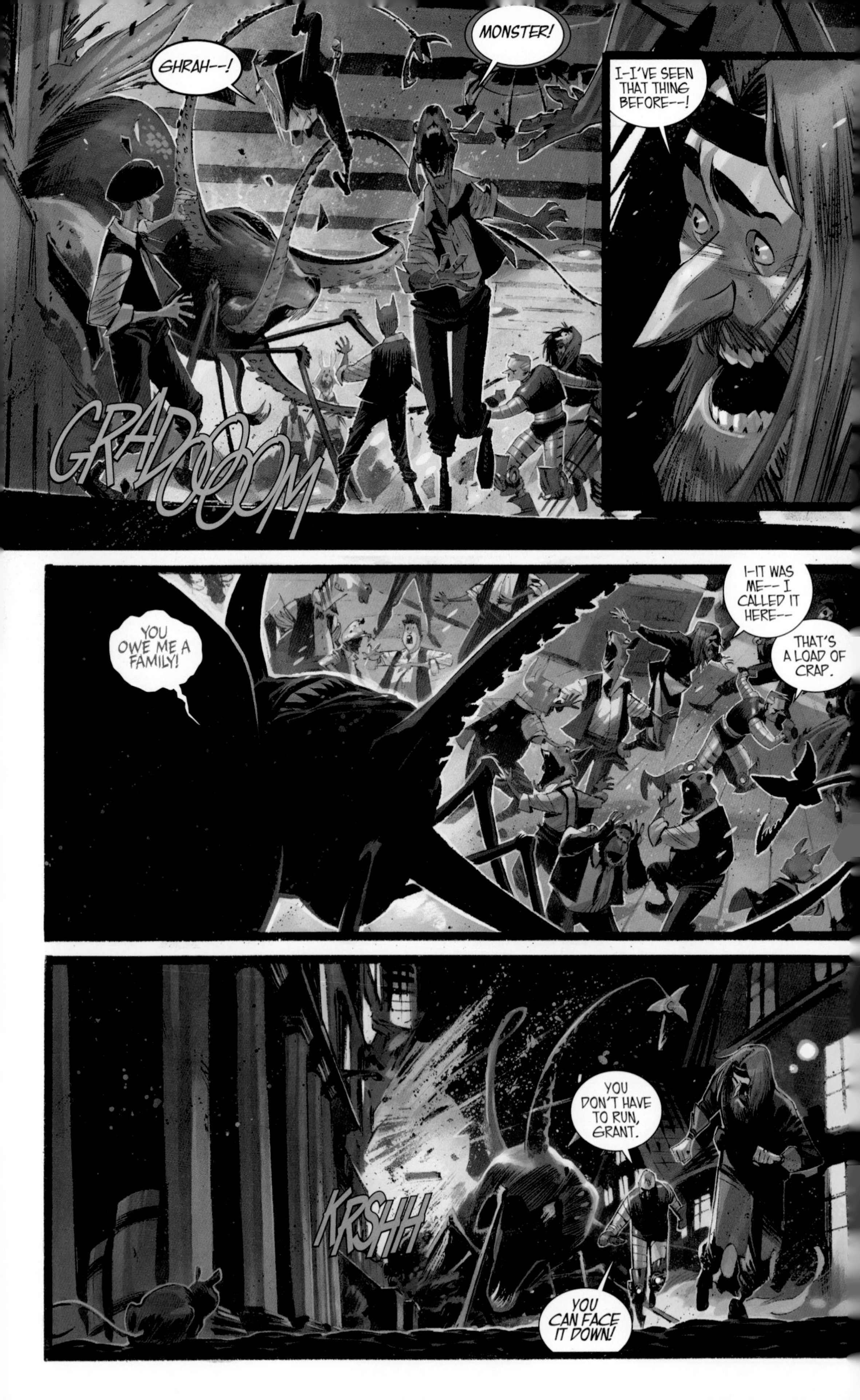
GHRAH--!
MONSTER!
GRADOOOOM
I-I'VE SEEN THAT THING BEFORE--!
YOU OWE ME A FAMILY!
I-IT WAS ME-- I CALLED IT HERE--
THAT'S A LOAD OF CRAP.
YOU DON'T HAVE TO RUN, GRANT.
KRSHH
YOU CAN FACE IT DOWN!

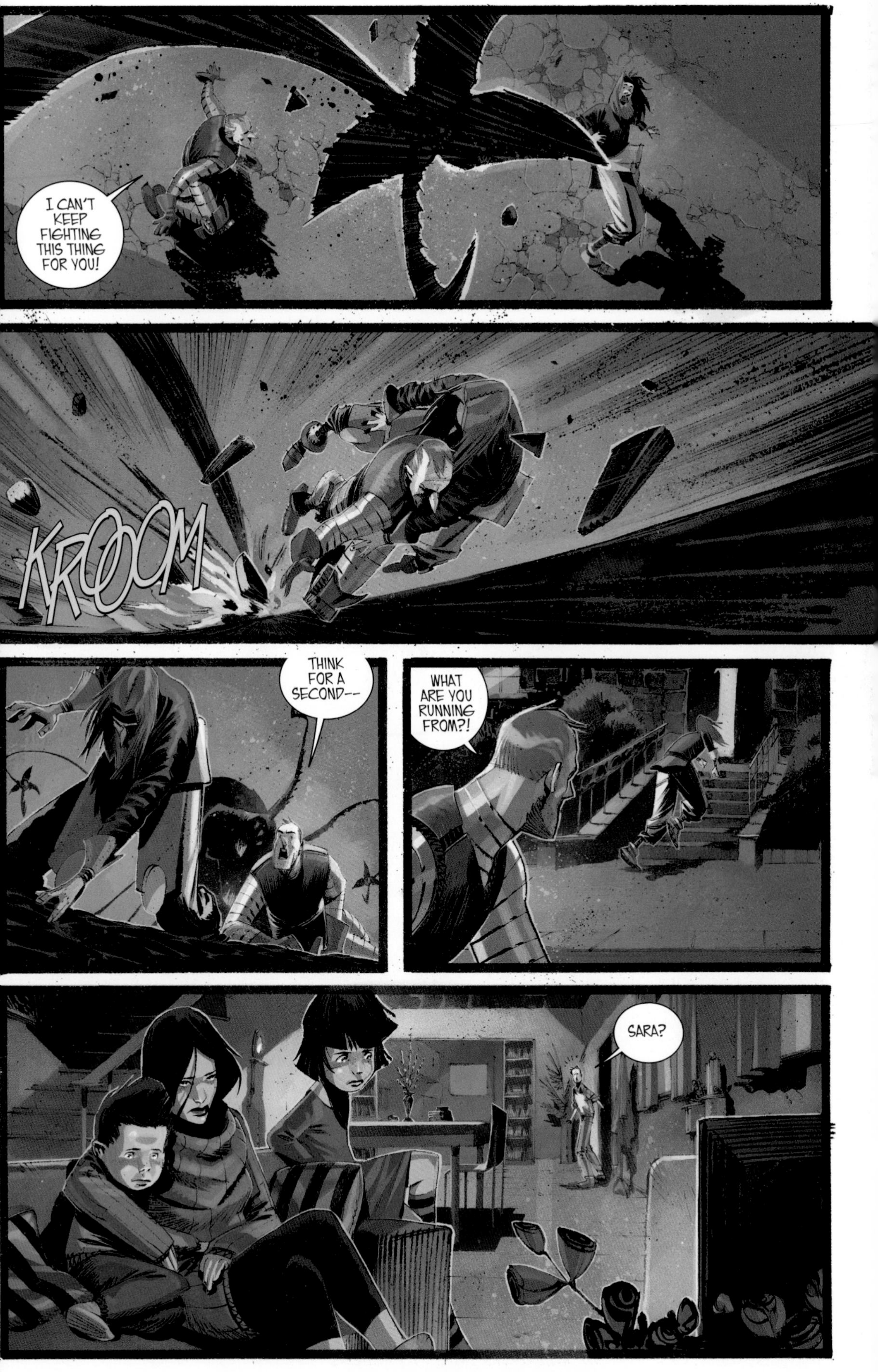
I CAN'T KEEP FIGHTING THIS THING FOR YOU!
KROOOM
THINK FOR A SECOND--
WHAT ARE YOU RUNNING FROM?!
SARA?

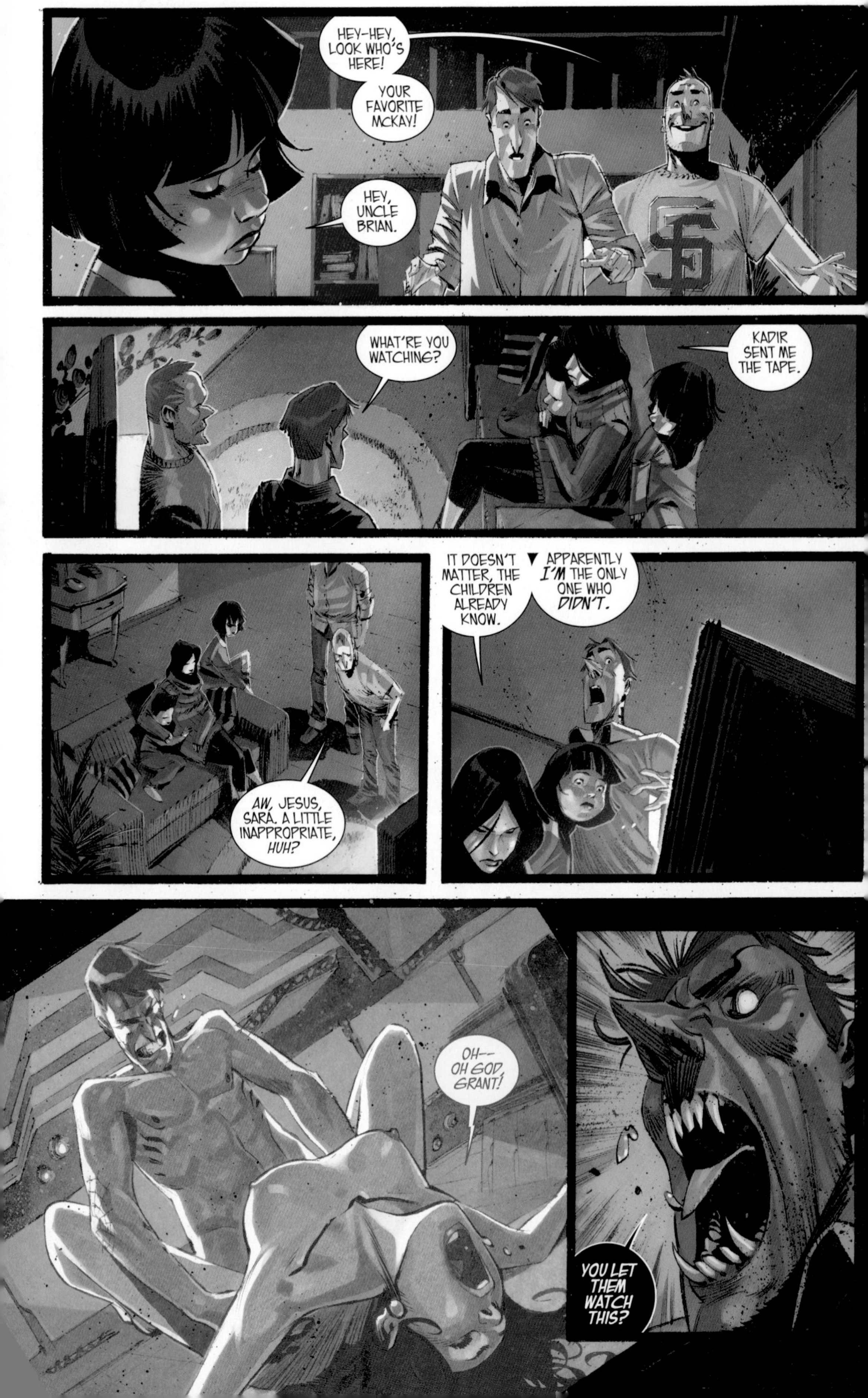

HEY-HEY, LOOK WHO'S HERE!
YOUR FAVORITE MCKAY!
HEY, UNCLE BRIAN.
WHAT'RE YOU WATCHING?
KADIR SENT ME THE TAPE.
AW, JESUS, SARÁ. A LITTLE INAPPROPRIATE, HUH?
IT DOESN'T MATTER, THE CHILDREN ALREADY KNOW.
APPARENTLY *I'M* THE ONLY ONE WHO *DIDN'T*.
OH-- OH GOD, GRANT!
YOU LET THEM WATCH THIS?

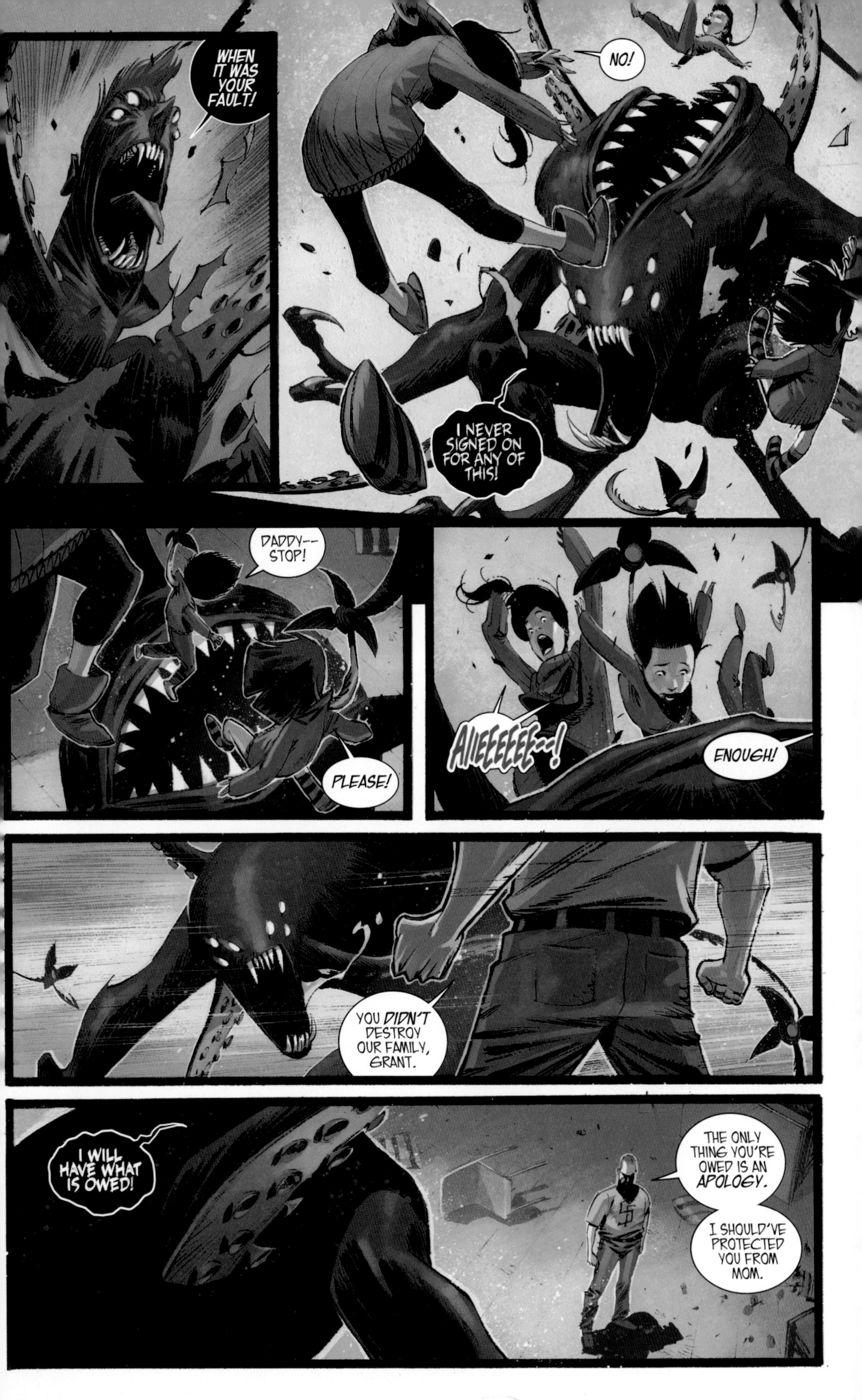
WHEN IT WAS YOUR FAULT!
NO!
I NEVER SIGNED ON FOR ANY OF THIS!
DADDY-- STOP!
PLEASE!
AIIEEEEEE--!
ENOUGH!
YOU DIDN'T DESTROY OUR FAMILY, GRANT.
I WILL HAVE WHAT IS OWED!
THE ONLY THING YOU'RE OWED IS AN APOLOGY.
I SHOULD'VE PROTECTED YOU FROM MOM.

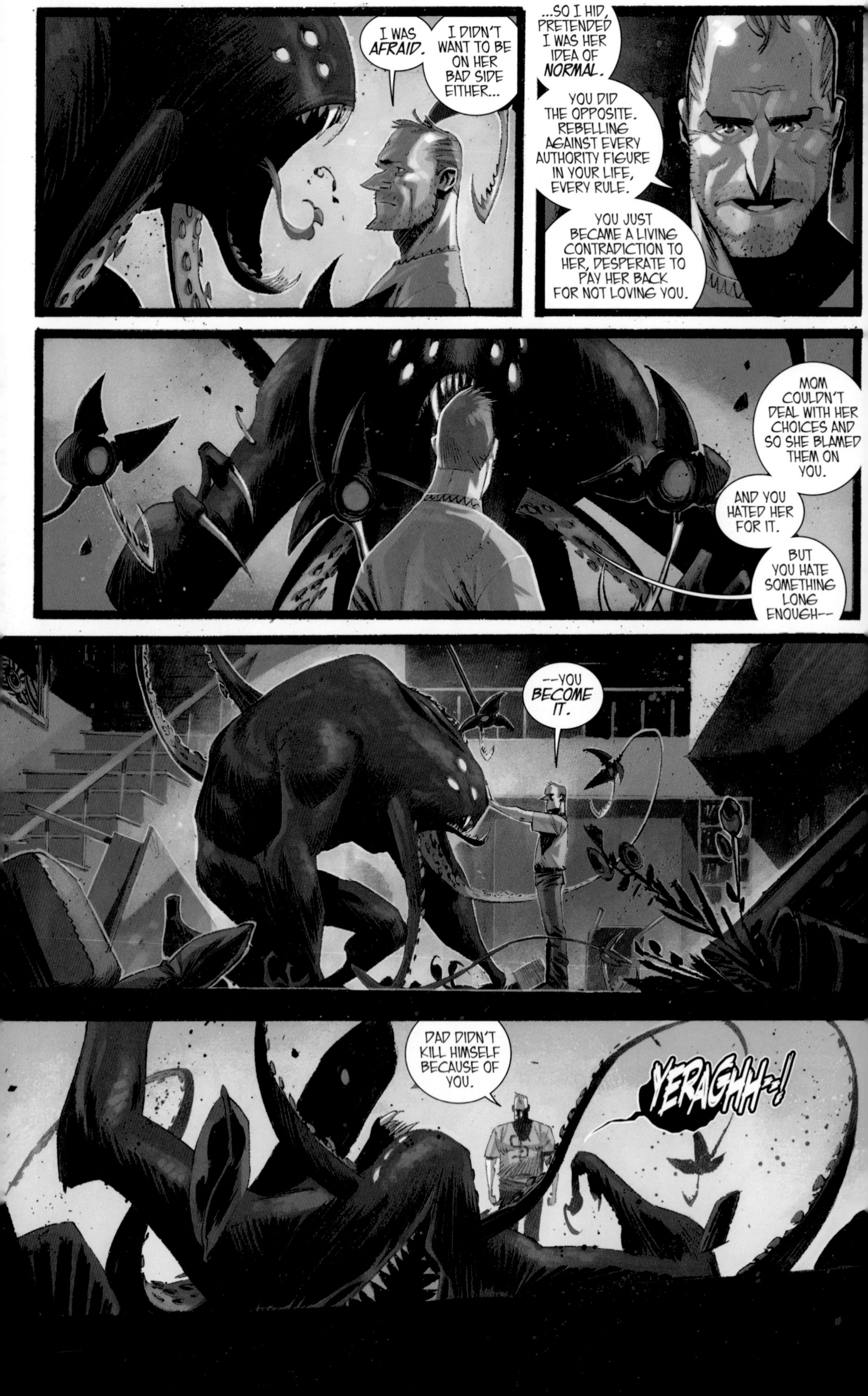
I WAS AFRAID.
I DIDN'T WANT TO BE ON HER BAD SIDE EITHER...
...SO I HID, PRETENDED I WAS HER IDEA OF NORMAL.
YOU DID THE OPPOSITE. REBELLING AGAINST EVERY AUTHORITY FIGURE IN YOUR LIFE, EVERY RULE.
YOU JUST BECAME A LIVING CONTRADICTION TO HER, DESPERATE TO PAY HER BACK FOR NOT LOVING YOU.
MOM COULDN'T DEAL WITH HER CHOICES AND SO SHE BLAMED THEM ON YOU.
AND YOU HATED HER FOR IT.
BUT YOU HATE SOMETHING LONG ENOUGH--
--YOU BECOME IT.
DAD DIDN'T KILL HIMSELF BECAUSE OF YOU.
YERAGHH--!

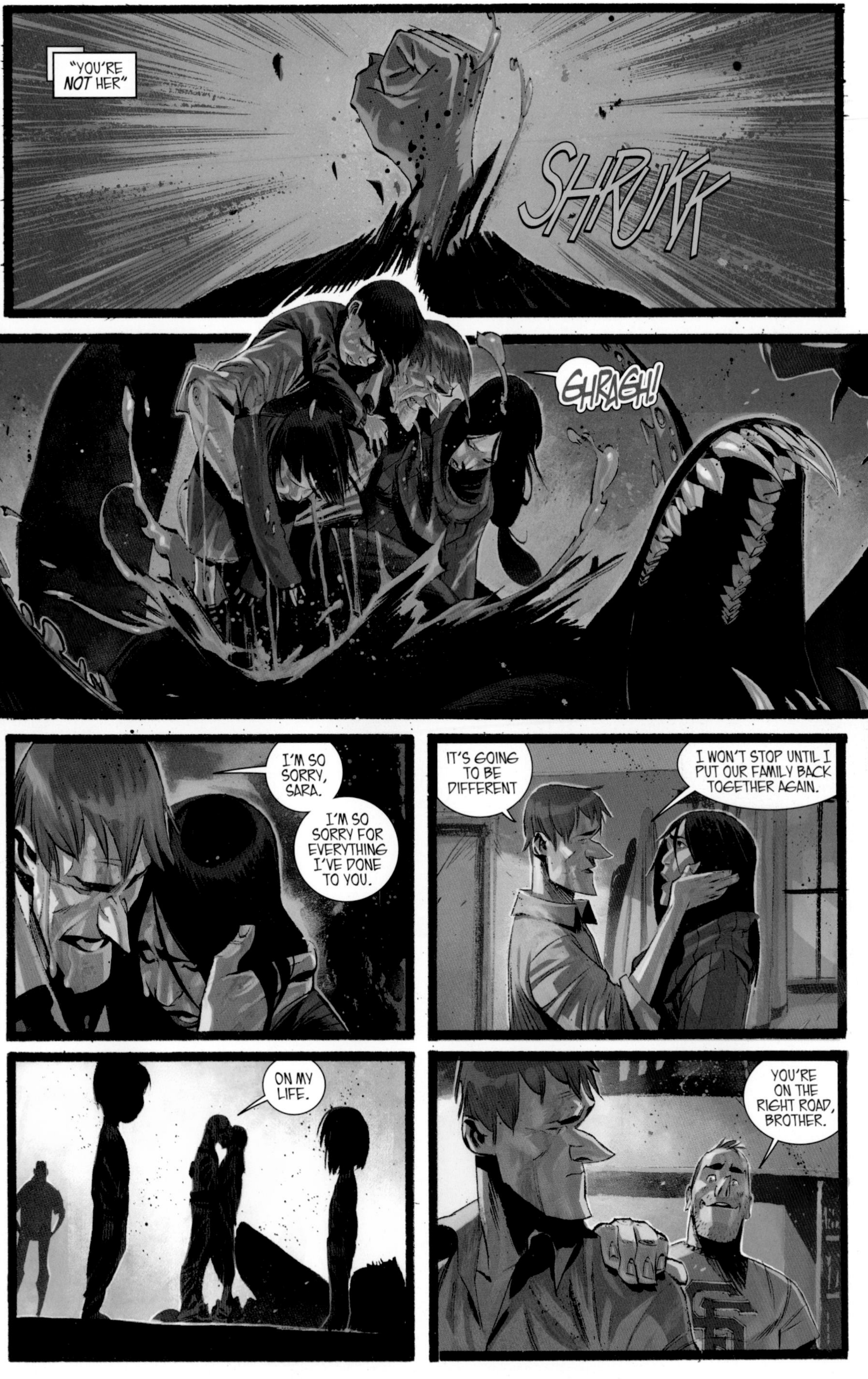
"YOU'RE NOT HER"
SHRUKK
GHRAGH!
I'M SO SORRY, SARA.
I'M SO SORRY FOR EVERYTHING I'VE DONE TO YOU.
IT'S GOING TO BE DIFFERENT
I WON'T STOP UNTIL I PUT OUR FAMILY BACK TOGETHER AGAIN.
ON MY LIFE.
YOU'RE ON THE RIGHT ROAD, BROTHER.

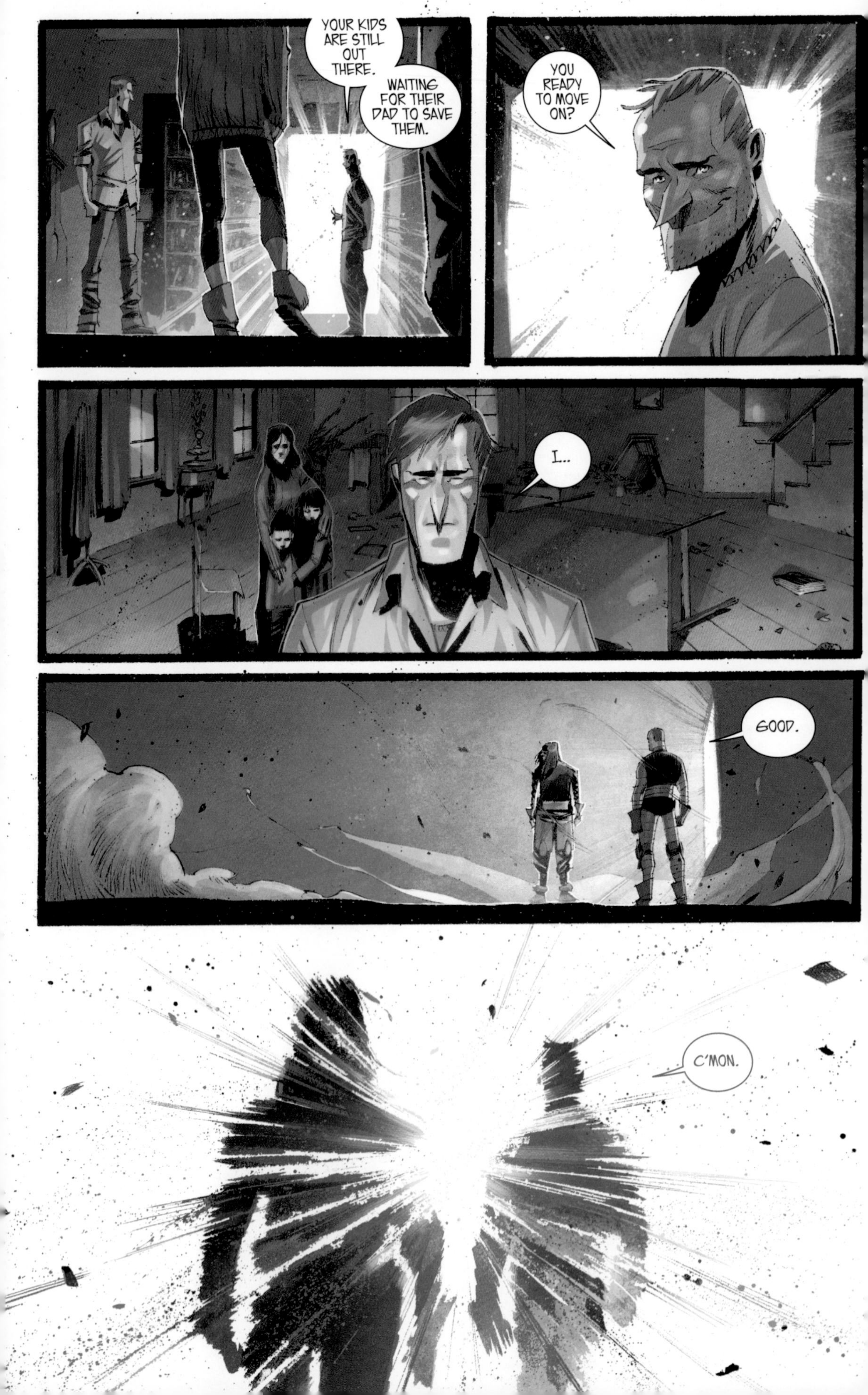
YOUR KIDS ARE STILL OUT THERE.
WAITING FOR THEIR DAD TO SAVE THEM.
YOU READY TO MOVE ON?
I...
GOOD.
C'MON.

THERE'S
SOMEONE
WHO WANTS
TO HELP.

19

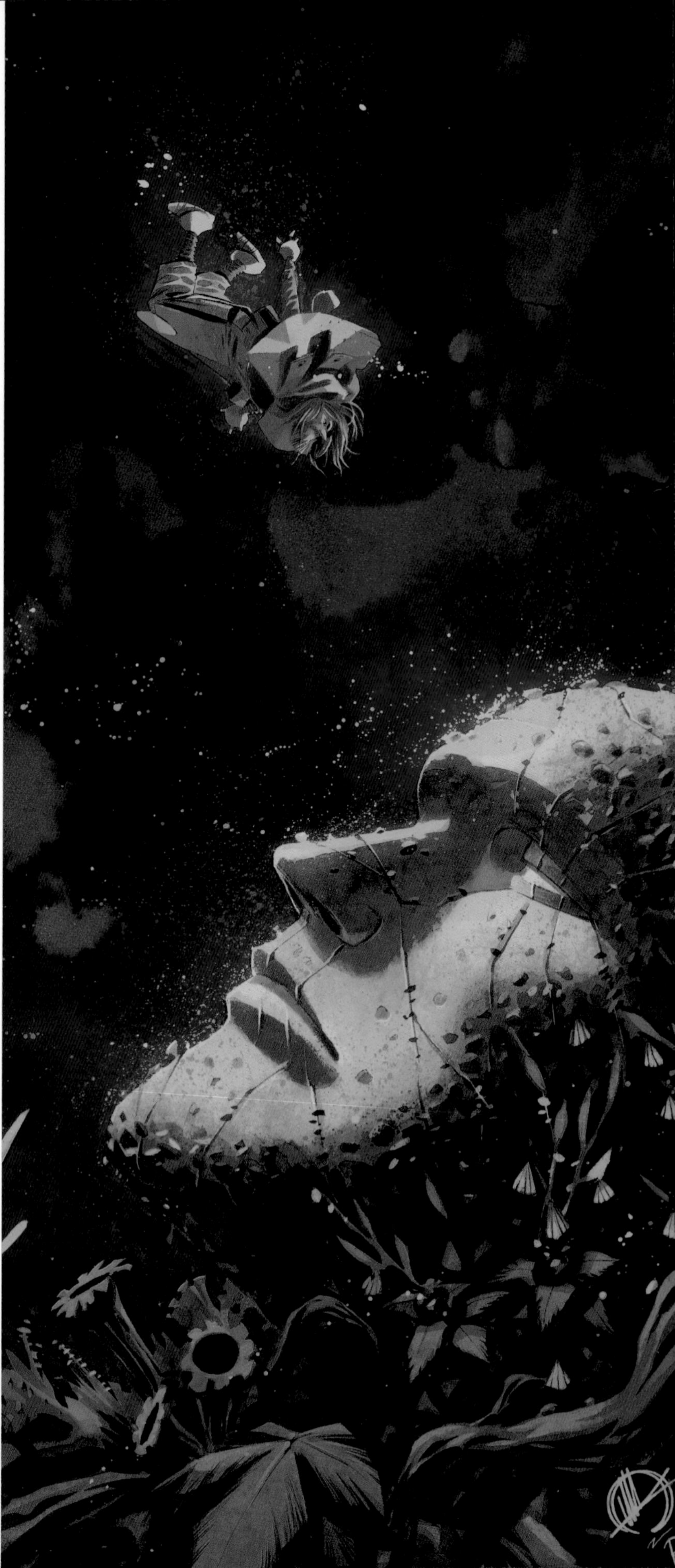

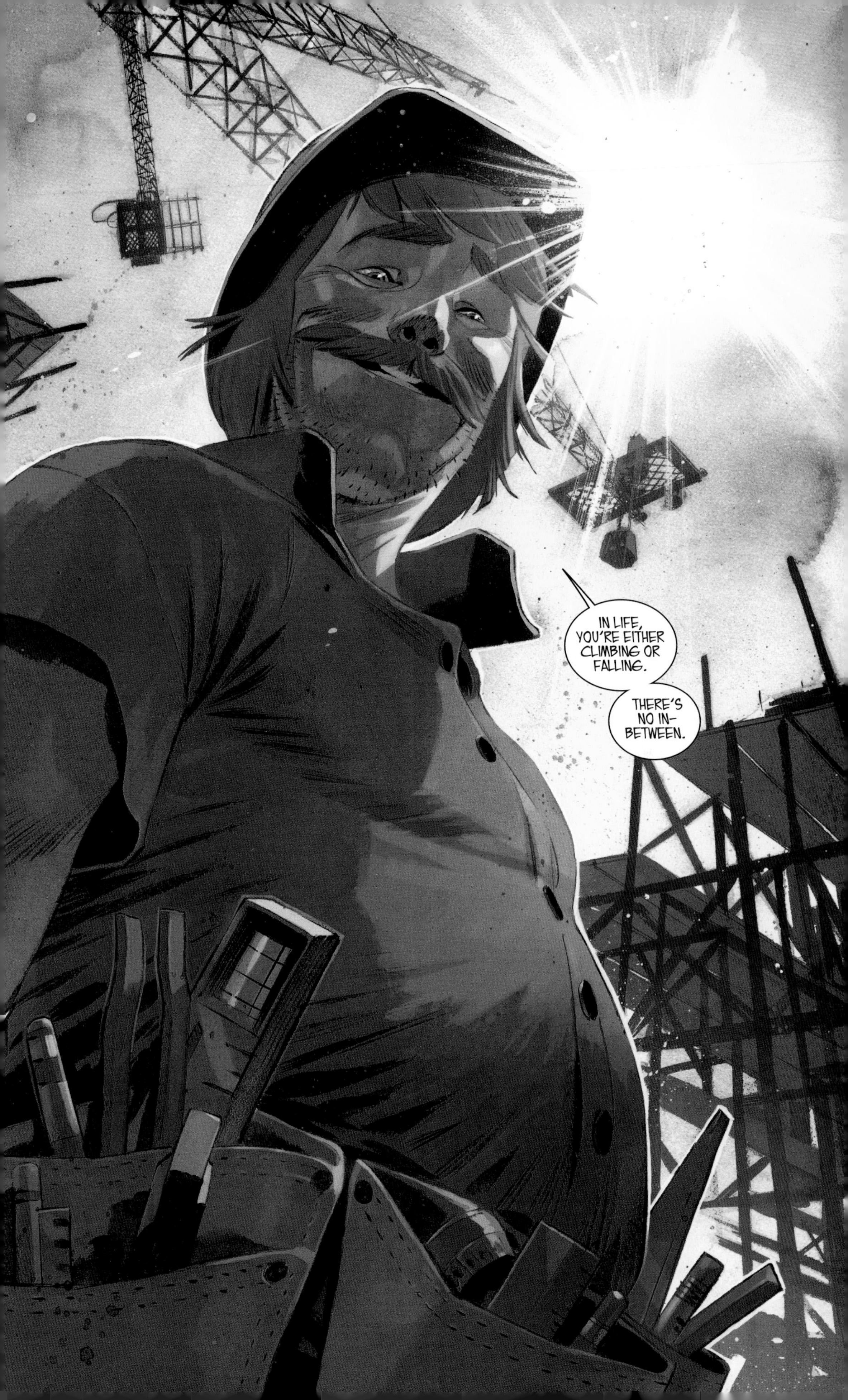
IN LIFE, YOU'RE EITHER CLIMBING OR FALLING.
THERE'S NO IN-BETWEEN.

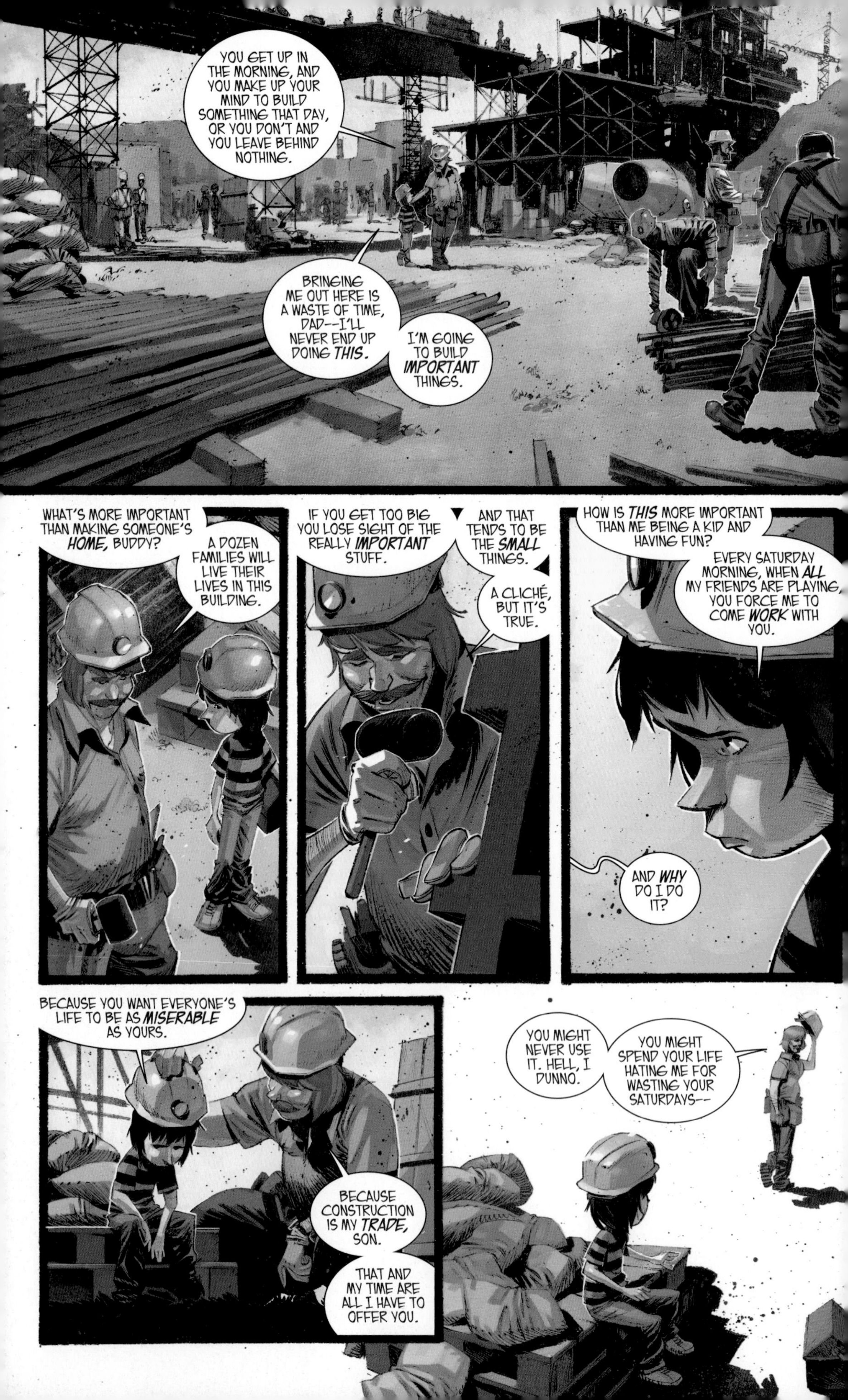
YOU GET UP IN THE MORNING, AND YOU MAKE UP YOUR MIND TO BUILD SOMETHING THAT DAY, OR YOU DON'T AND YOU LEAVE BEHIND NOTHING.
BRINGING ME OUT HERE IS A WASTE OF TIME, DAD--I'LL NEVER END UP DOING THIS.
I'M GOING TO BUILD IMPORTANT THINGS.
WHAT'S MORE IMPORTANT THAN MAKING SOMEONE'S HOME, BUDDY?
A DOZEN FAMILIES WILL LIVE THEIR LIVES IN THIS BUILDING.
IF YOU GET TOO BIG YOU LOSE SIGHT OF THE REALLY IMPORTANT STUFF.
AND THAT TENDS TO BE THE SMALL THINGS.
A CLICHÉ, BUT IT'S TRUE.
HOW IS THIS MORE IMPORTANT THAN ME BEING A KID AND HAVING FUN?
EVERY SATURDAY MORNING, WHEN ALL MY FRIENDS ARE PLAYING, YOU FORCE ME TO COME WORK WITH YOU.
AND WHY DO I DO IT?
BECAUSE YOU WANT EVERYONE'S LIFE TO BE AS MISERABLE AS YOURS.
BECAUSE CONSTRUCTION IS MY TRADE, SON.
THAT AND MY TIME ARE ALL I HAVE TO OFFER YOU.
YOU MIGHT SPEND YOUR LIFE HATING ME FOR WASTING YOUR SATURDAYS--
YOU MIGHT NEVER USE IT. HELL, I DUNNO.

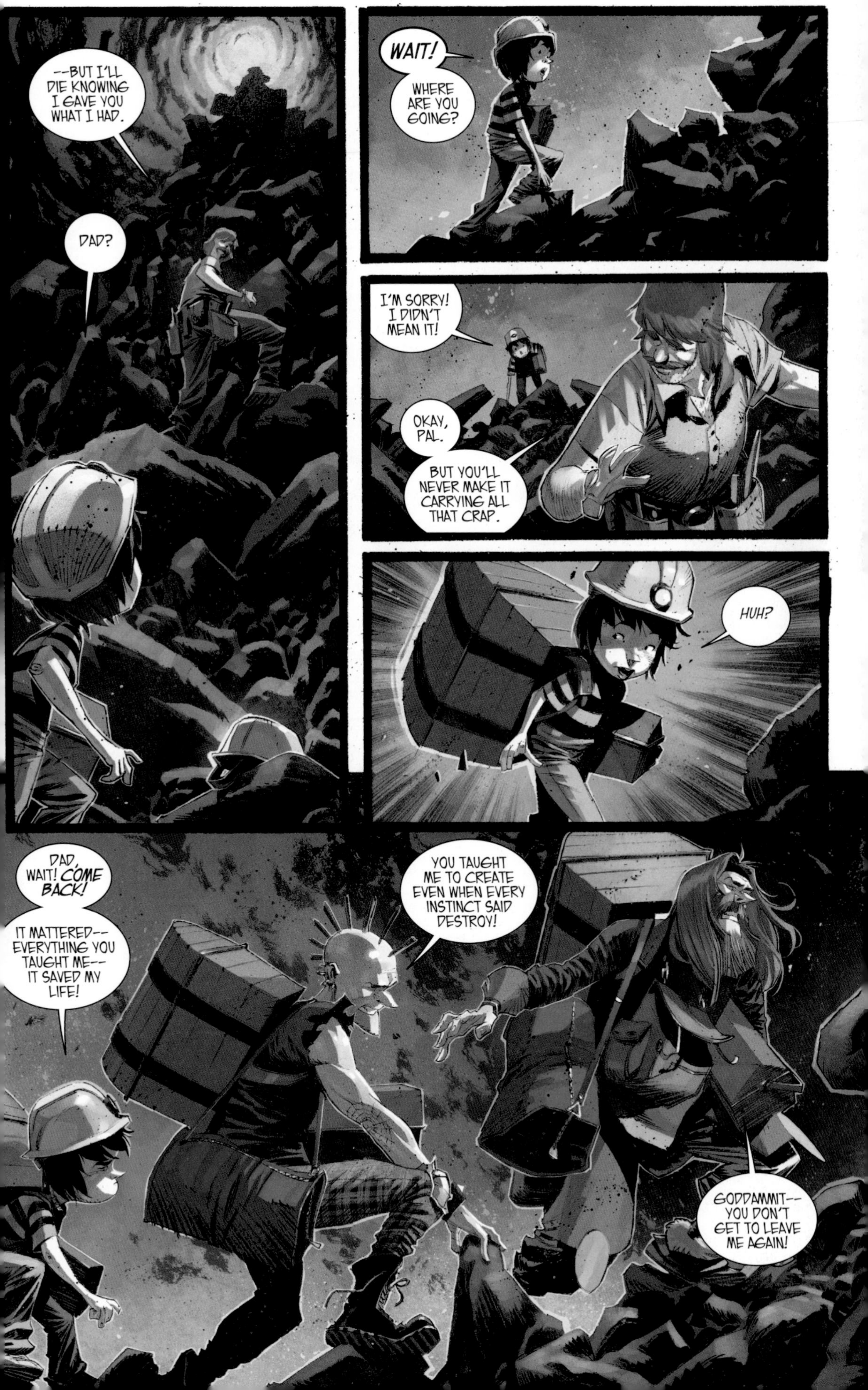
--BUT I'LL DIE KNOWING I GAVE YOU WHAT I HAD.
DAD?
WAIT!
WHERE ARE YOU GOING?
I'M SORRY! I DIDN'T MEAN IT!
OKAY, PAL.
BUT YOU'LL NEVER MAKE IT CARRYING ALL THAT CRAP.
HUH?
DAD, WAIT! COME BACK!
IT MATTERED-- EVERYTHING YOU TAUGHT ME-- IT SAVED MY LIFE!
YOU TAUGHT ME TO CREATE EVEN WHEN EVERY INSTINCT SAID DESTROY!
GODDAMMIT-- YOU DON'T GET TO LEAVE ME AGAIN!

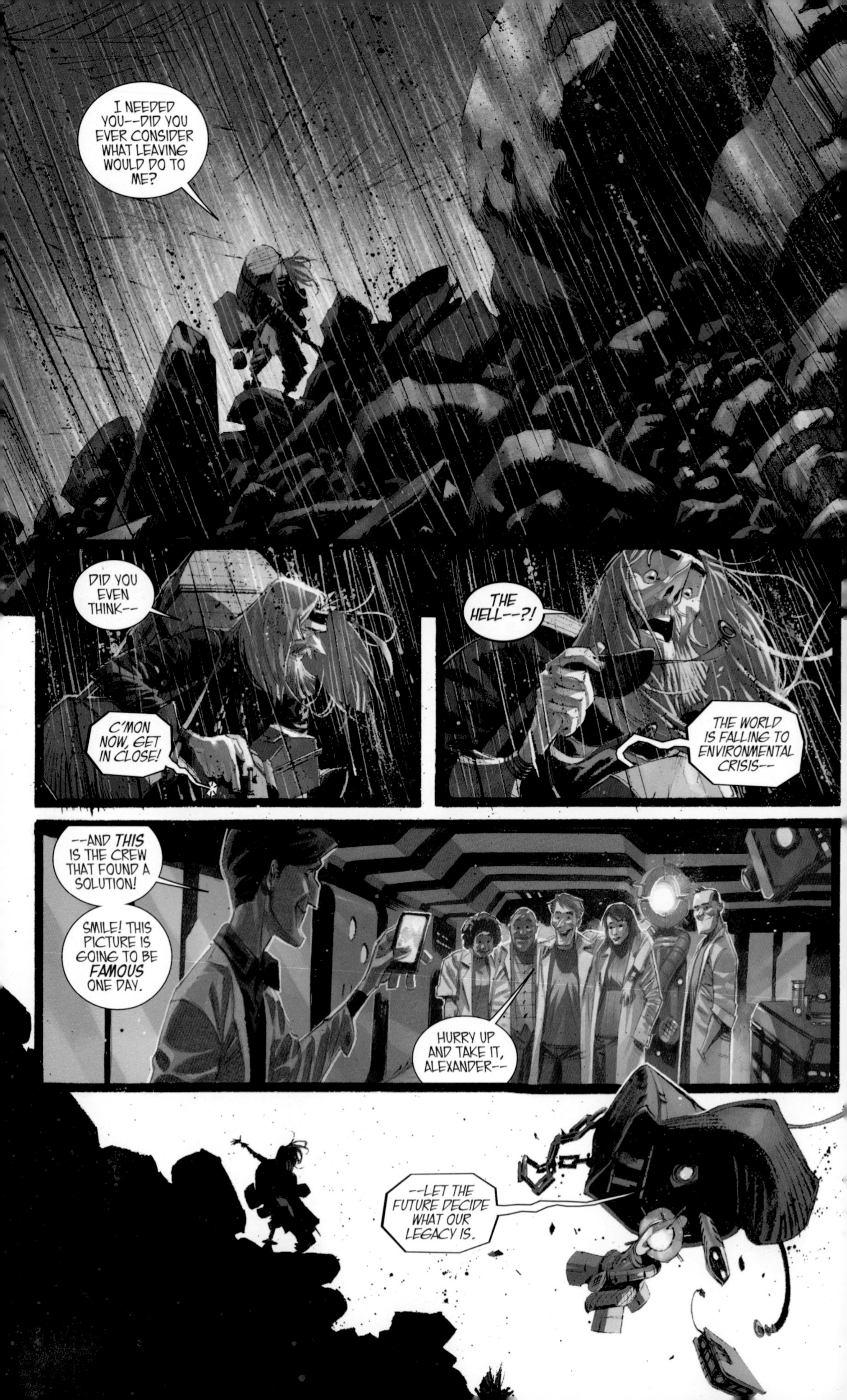
I NEEDED YOU--DID YOU EVER CONSIDER WHAT LEAVING WOULD DO TO ME?
DID YOU EVEN THINK--
C'MON NOW, GET IN CLOSE!
THE HELL--?!
THE WORLD IS FALLING TO ENVIRONMENTAL CRISIS--
--AND THIS IS THE CREW THAT FOUND A SOLUTION!
SMILE! THIS PICTURE IS GOING TO BE FAMOUS ONE DAY.
HURRY UP AND TAKE IT, ALEXANDER--
--LET THE FUTURE DECIDE WHAT OUR LEGACY IS.

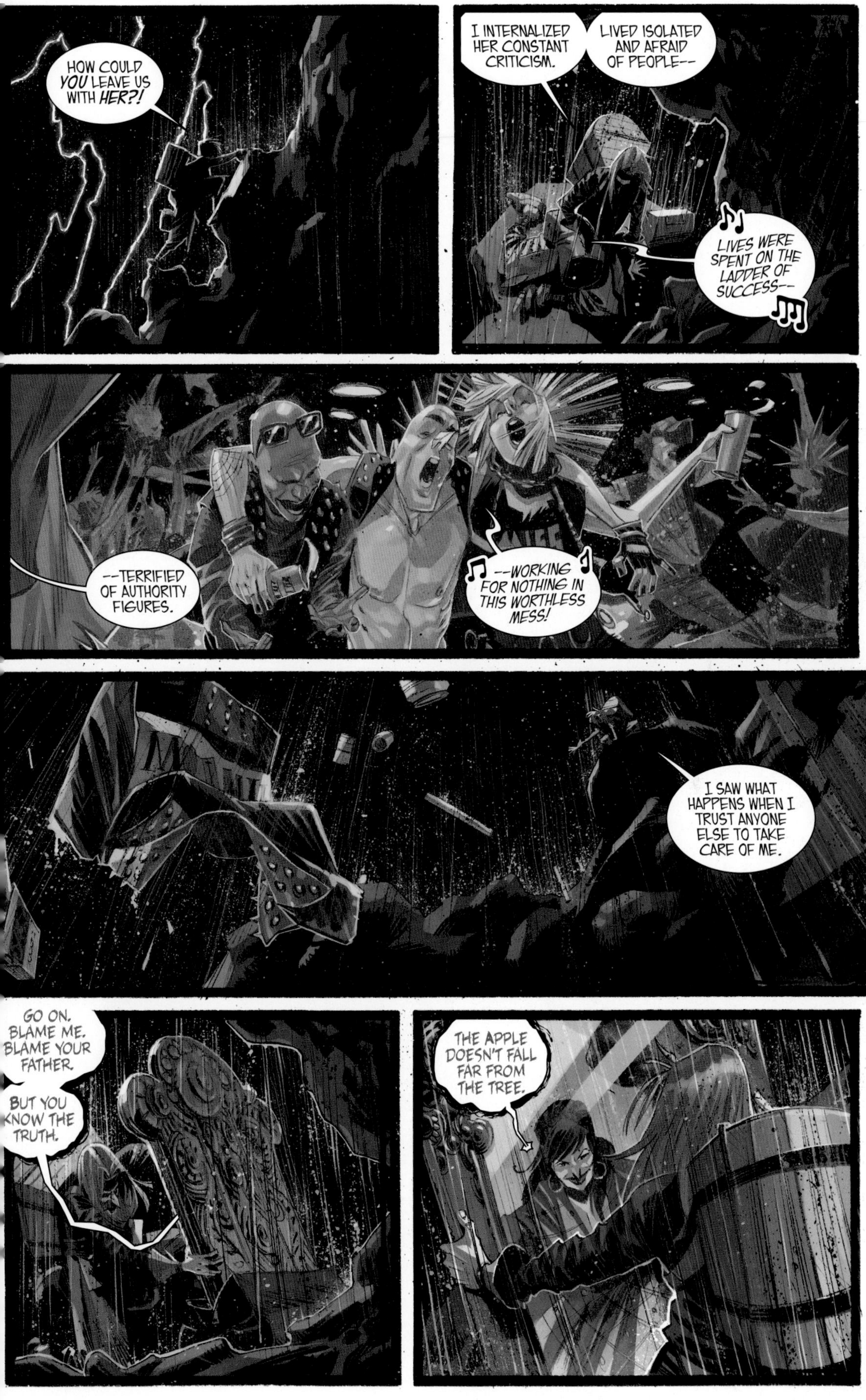
HOW COULD YOU LEAVE US WITH HER?!
I INTERNALIZED HER CONSTANT CRITICISM.
LIVED ISOLATED AND AFRAID OF PEOPLE--
LIVES WERE SPENT ON THE LADDER OF SUCCESS--
--TERRIFIED OF AUTHORITY FIGURES.
--WORKING FOR NOTHING IN THIS WORTHLESS MESS!
I SAW WHAT HAPPENS WHEN I TRUST ANYONE ELSE TO TAKE CARE OF ME.
GO ON. BLAME ME. BLAME YOUR FATHER.
BUT YOU KNOW THE TRUTH.
THE APPLE DOESN'T FALL FAR FROM THE TREE.

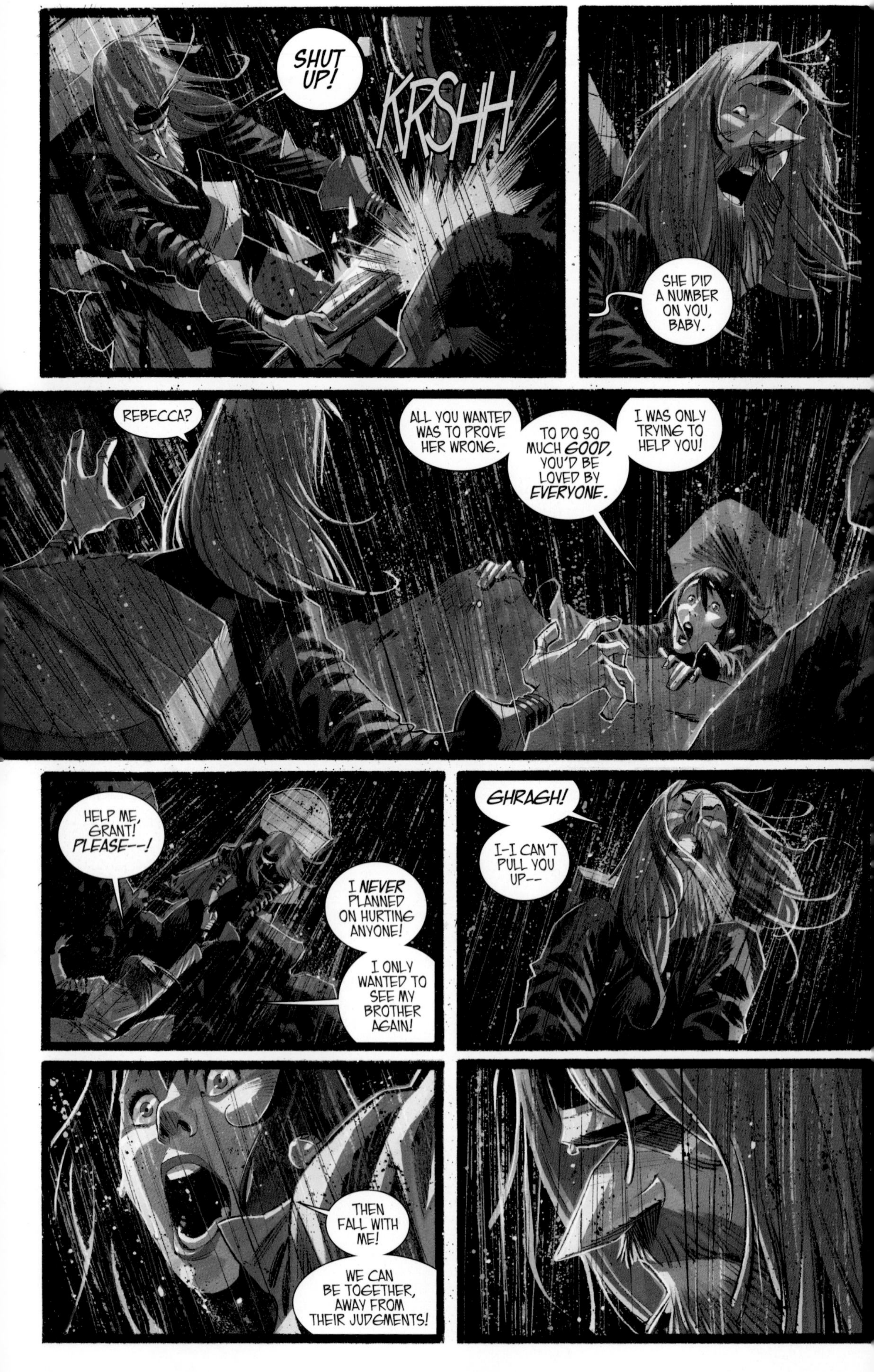
SHUT UP!
KRSHH
SHE DID A NUMBER ON YOU, BABY.
REBECCA?
ALL YOU WANTED WAS TO PROVE HER WRONG.
TO DO SO MUCH GOOD, YOU'D BE LOVED BY EVERYONE.
I WAS ONLY TRYING TO HELP YOU!
HELP ME, GRANT! PLEASE--!
I NEVER PLANNED ON HURTING ANYONE!
I ONLY WANTED TO SEE MY BROTHER AGAIN!
GHRAGH!
I-I CAN'T PULL YOU UP--
THEN FALL WITH ME!
WE CAN BE TOGETHER, AWAY FROM THEIR JUDGMENTS!

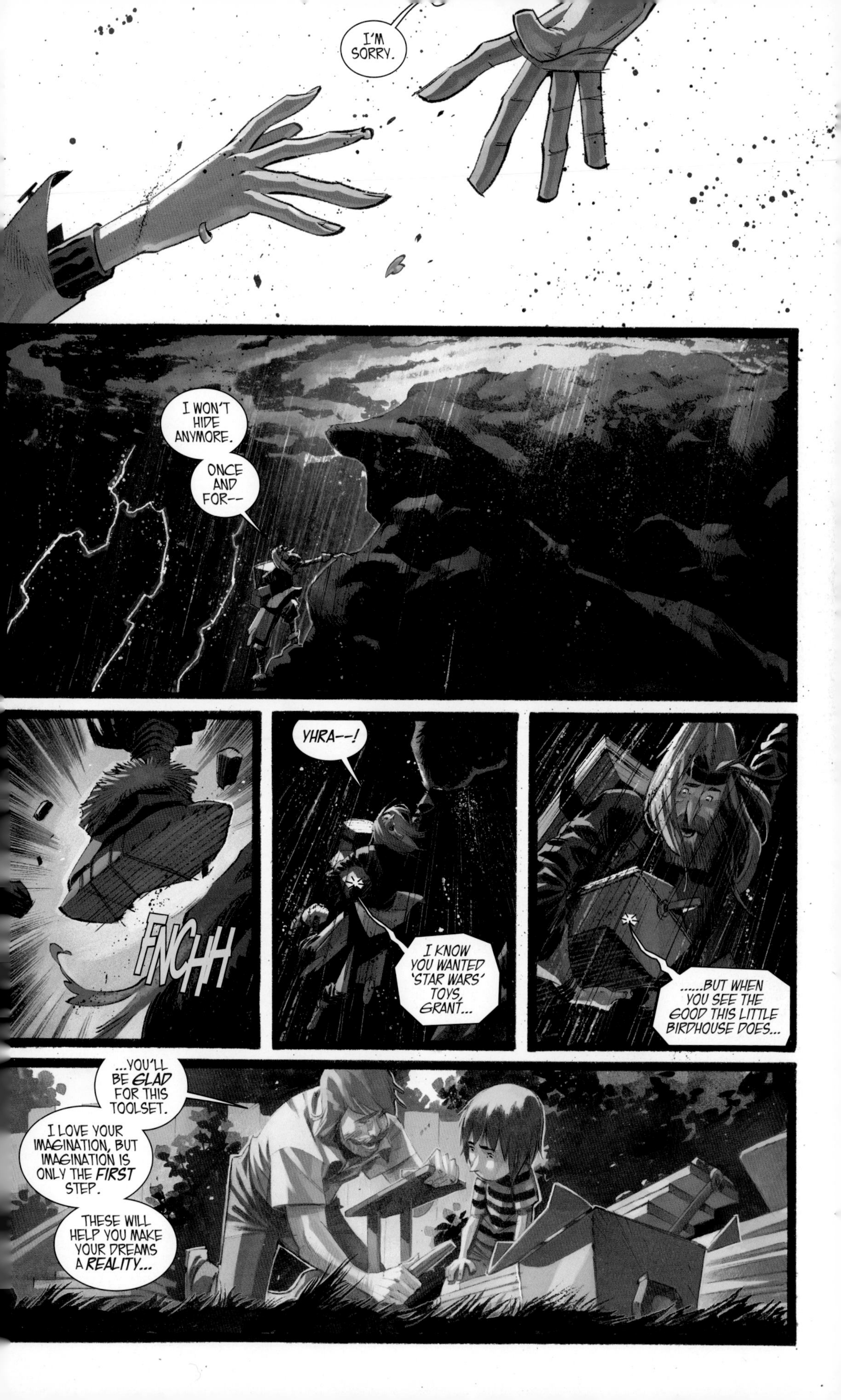
I'M SORRY.
I WON'T HIDE ANYMORE.
ONCE AND FOR--
FNCHH
YHRA--!
I KNOW YOU WANTED 'STAR WARS' TOYS, GRANT...
......BUT WHEN YOU SEE THE GOOD THIS LITTLE BIRDHOUSE DOES...
...YOU'LL BE GLAD FOR THIS TOOLSET.
I LOVE YOUR IMAGINATION, BUT IMAGINATION IS ONLY THE FIRST STEP.
THESE WILL HELP YOU MAKE YOUR DREAMS A REALITY...

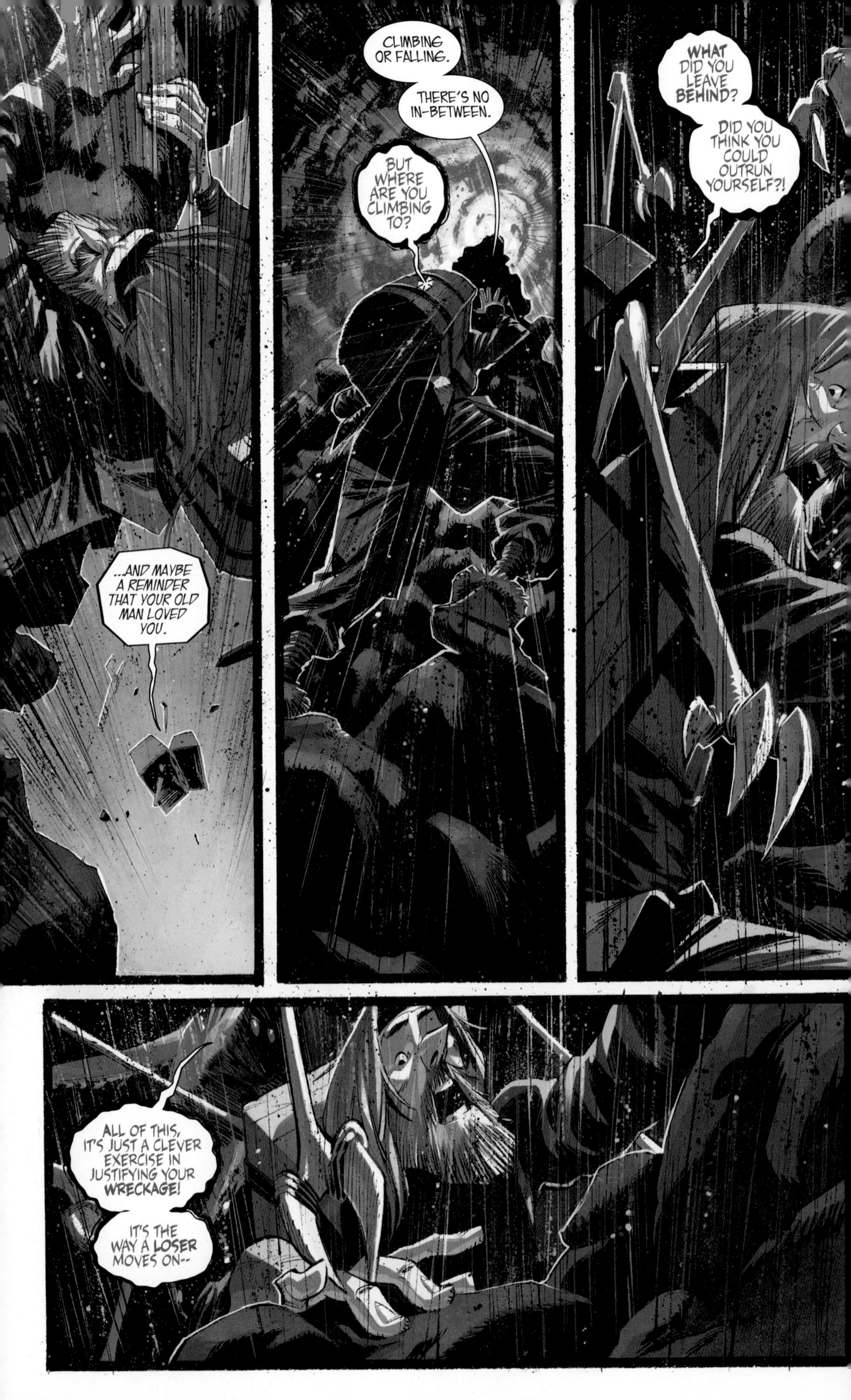

...AND MAYBE A REMINDER THAT YOUR OLD MAN LOVED YOU.
CLIMBING OR FALLING.
THERE'S NO IN-BETWEEN.
BUT WHERE ARE YOU CLIMBING TO?
WHAT DID YOU LEAVE BEHIND?
DID YOU THINK YOU COULD OUTRUN YOURSELF?!
ALL OF THIS, IT'S JUST A CLEVER EXERCISE IN JUSTIFYING YOUR WRECKAGE!
IT'S THE WAY A LOSER MOVES ON--

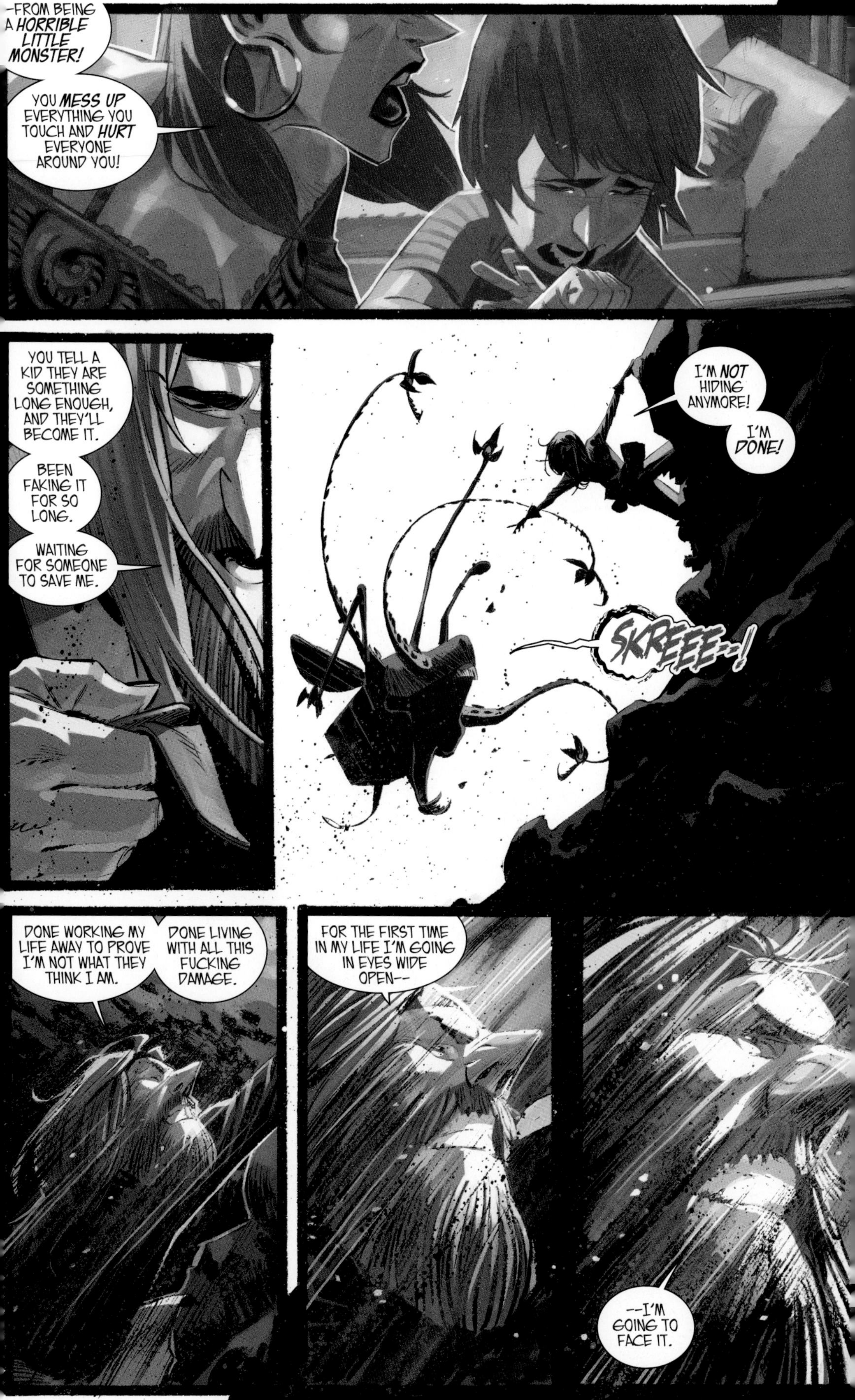

–FROM BEING A HORRIBLE LITTLE MONSTER!
YOU MESS UP EVERYTHING YOU TOUCH AND HURT EVERYONE AROUND YOU!
YOU TELL A KID THEY ARE SOMETHING LONG ENOUGH, AND THEY'LL BECOME IT.
BEEN FAKING IT FOR SO LONG.
WAITING FOR SOMEONE TO SAVE ME.
I'M NOT HIDING ANYMORE!
I'M DONE!
SKREEEE--!
DONE WORKING MY LIFE AWAY TO PROVE I'M NOT WHAT THEY THINK I AM.
DONE LIVING WITH ALL THIS FUCKING DAMAGE.
FOR THE FIRST TIME IN MY LIFE I'M GOING IN EYES WIDE OPEN--
--I'M GOING TO FACE IT.

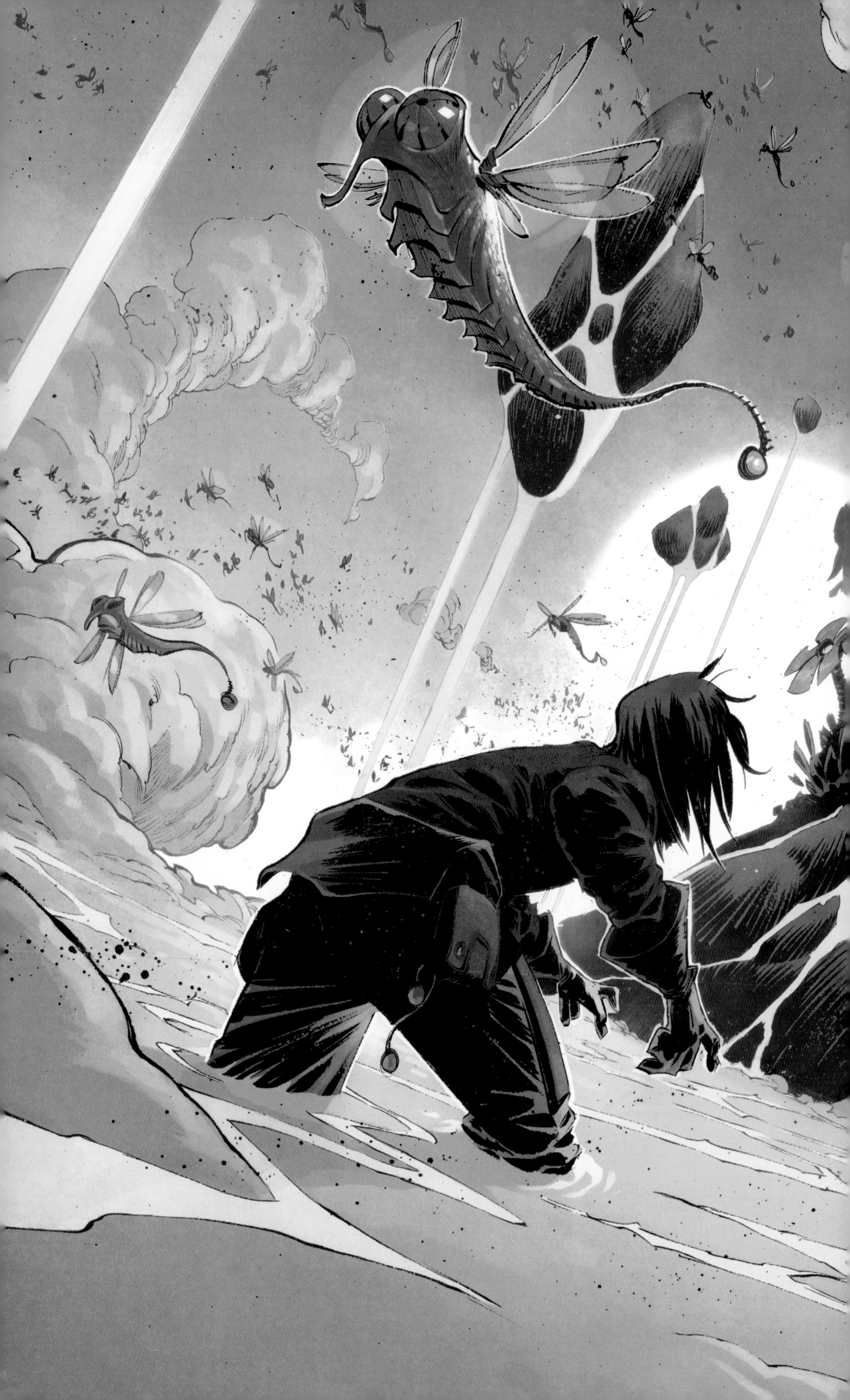

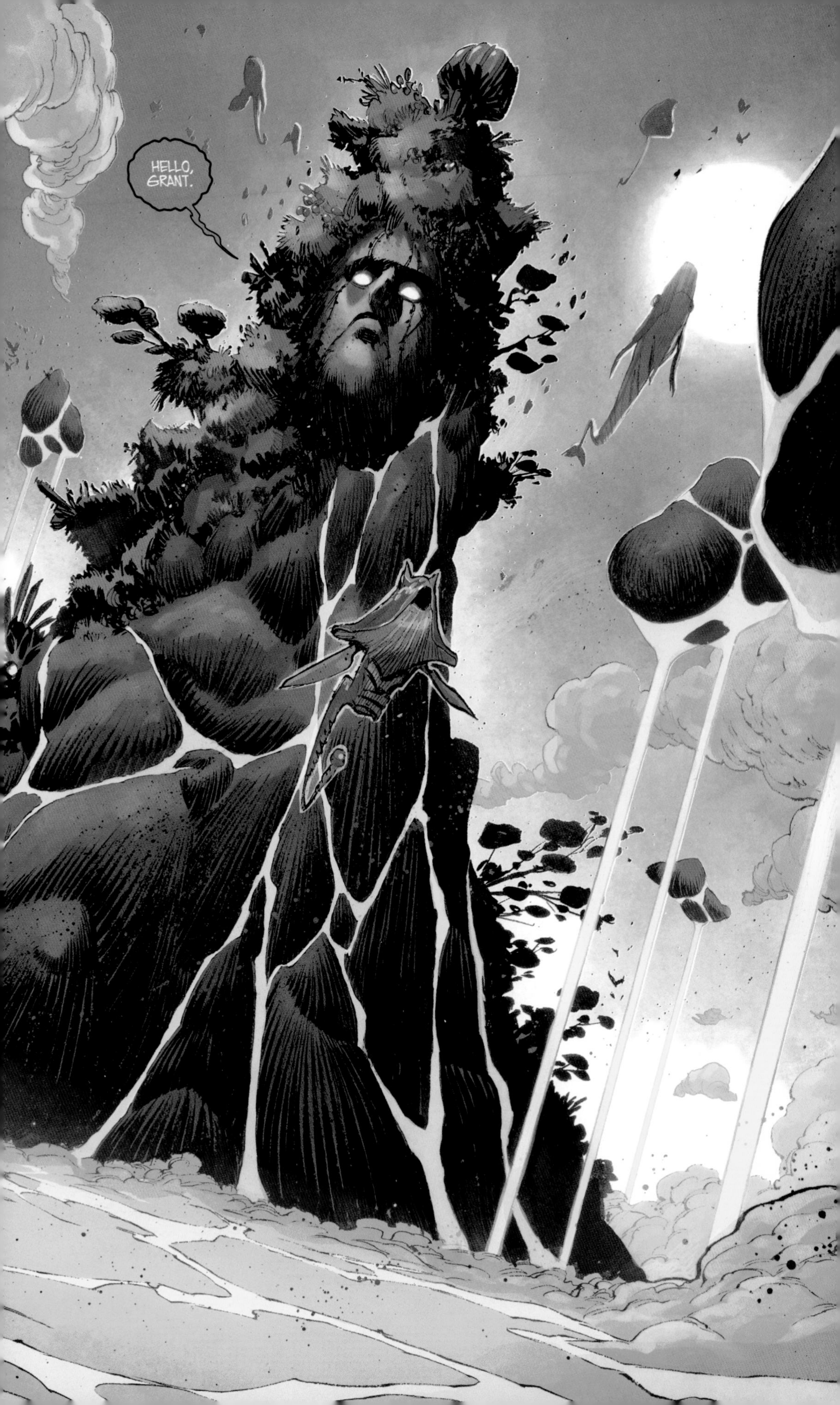
HELLO, GRANT.

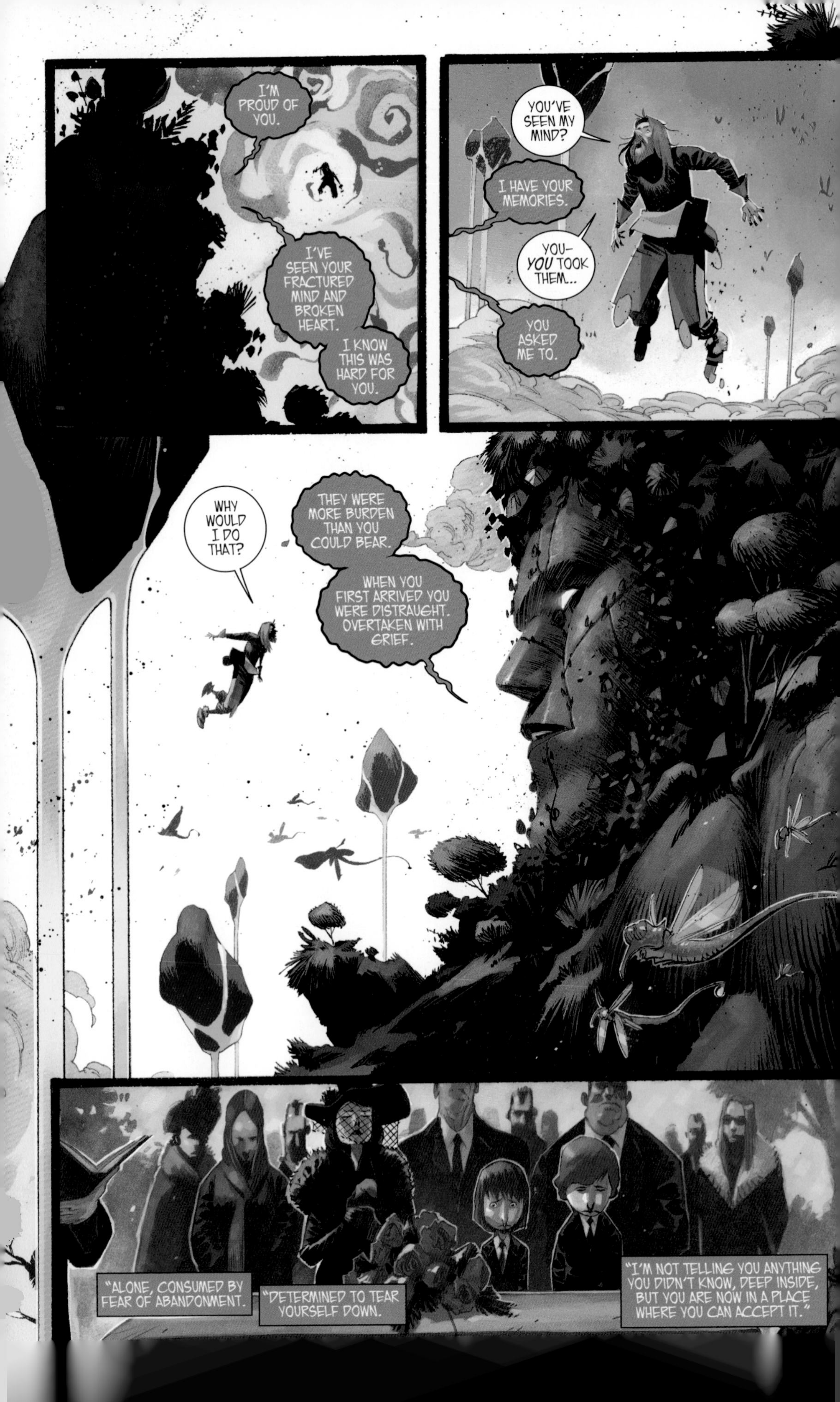
I'M PROUD OF YOU.
I'VE SEEN YOUR FRACTURED MIND AND BROKEN HEART.
I KNOW THIS WAS HARD FOR YOU.
YOU'VE SEEN MY MIND?
I HAVE YOUR MEMORIES.
YOU– YOU TOOK THEM...
YOU ASKED ME TO.
WHY WOULD I DO THAT?
THEY WERE MORE BURDEN THAN YOU COULD BEAR.
WHEN YOU FIRST ARRIVED YOU WERE DISTRAUGHT. OVERTAKEN WITH GRIEF.
"ALONE, CONSUMED BY FEAR OF ABANDONMENT.
"DETERMINED TO TEAR YOURSELF DOWN.
"I'M NOT TELLING YOU ANYTHING YOU DIDN'T KNOW, DEEP INSIDE, BUT YOU ARE NOW IN A PLACE WHERE YOU CAN ACCEPT IT."

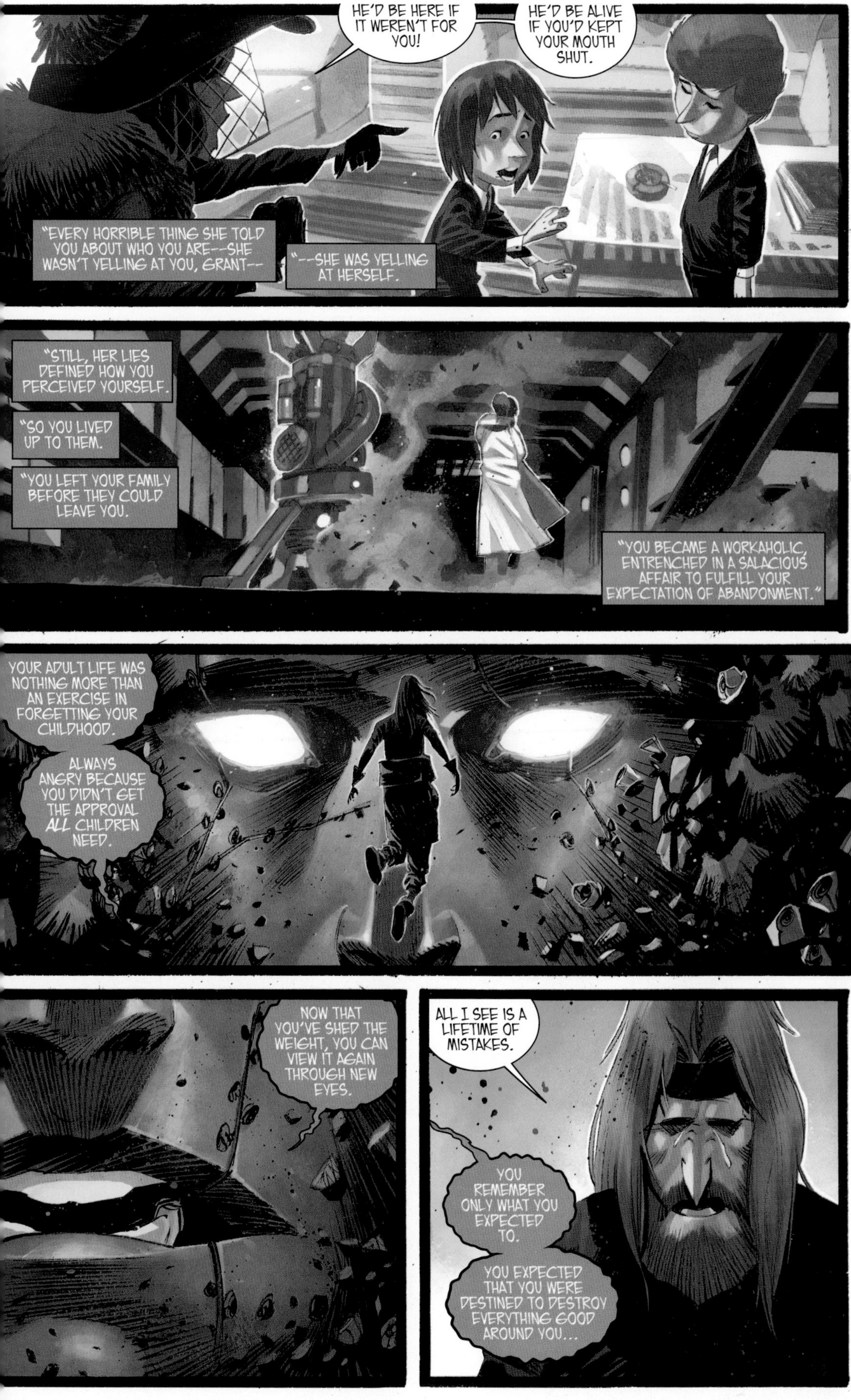
HE'D BE HERE IF IT WEREN'T FOR YOU!
HE'D BE ALIVE IF YOU'D KEPT YOUR MOUTH SHUT.
"EVERY HORRIBLE THING SHE TOLD YOU ABOUT WHO YOU ARE--SHE WASN'T YELLING AT YOU, GRANT--
"--SHE WAS YELLING AT HERSELF.
"STILL, HER LIES DEFINED HOW YOU PERCEIVED YOURSELF.
"SO YOU LIVED UP TO THEM.
"YOU LEFT YOUR FAMILY BEFORE THEY COULD LEAVE YOU.
"YOU BECAME A WORKAHOLIC, ENTRENCHED IN A SALACIOUS AFFAIR TO FULFILL YOUR EXPECTATION OF ABANDONMENT."
YOUR ADULT LIFE WAS NOTHING MORE THAN AN EXERCISE IN FORGETTING YOUR CHILDHOOD.
ALWAYS ANGRY BECAUSE YOU DIDN'T GET THE APPROVAL *ALL* CHILDREN NEED.
NOW THAT YOU'VE SHED THE WEIGHT, YOU CAN VIEW IT AGAIN THROUGH NEW EYES.
ALL I SEE IS A LIFETIME OF MISTAKES.
YOU REMEMBER ONLY WHAT YOU EXPECTED TO.
YOU EXPECTED THAT YOU WERE DESTINED TO DESTROY EVERYTHING GOOD AROUND YOU...

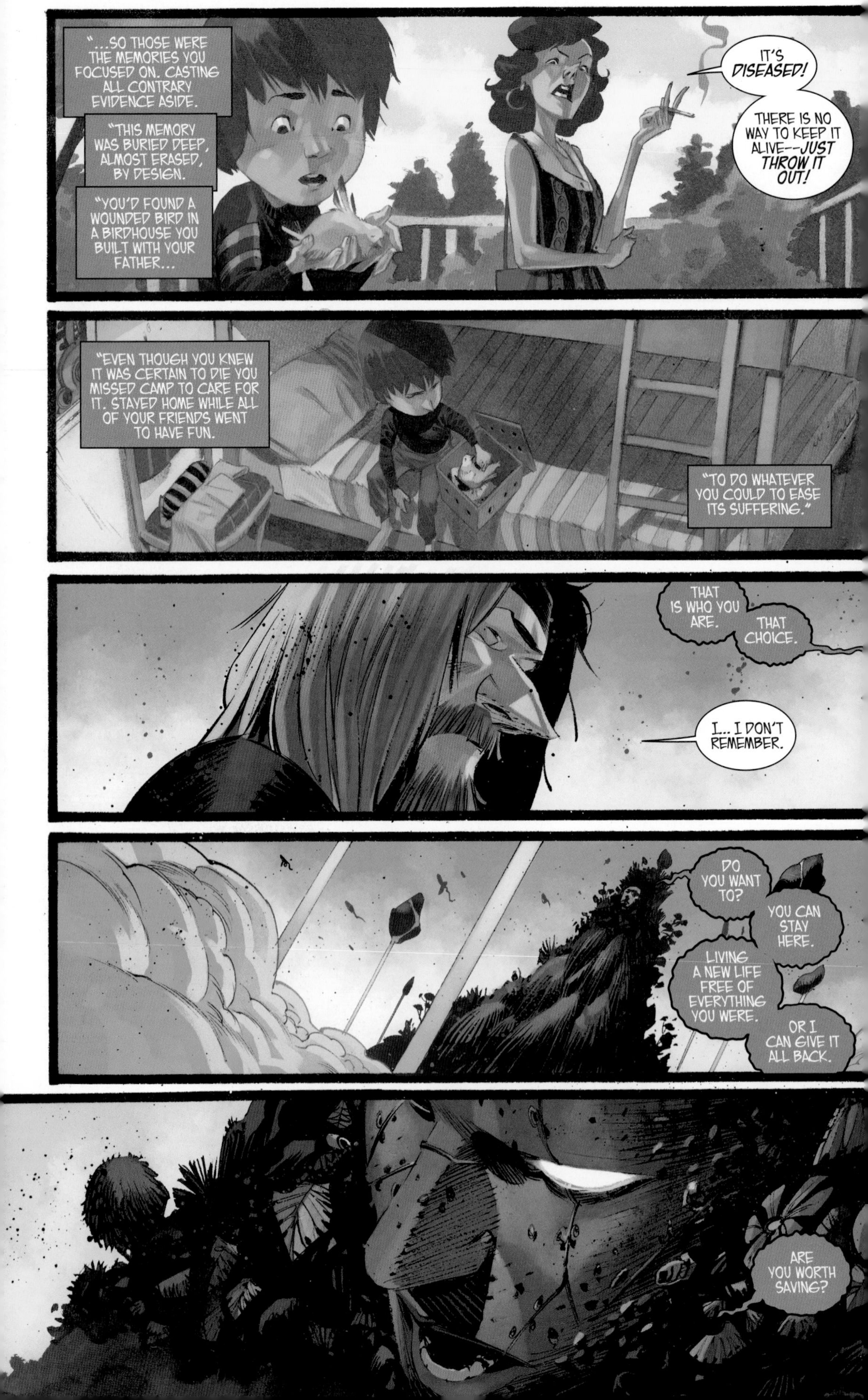
"...SO THOSE WERE THE MEMORIES YOU FOCUSED ON. CASTING ALL CONTRARY EVIDENCE ASIDE.
"THIS MEMORY WAS BURIED DEEP, ALMOST ERASED, BY DESIGN.
"YOU'D FOUND A WOUNDED BIRD IN A BIRDHOUSE YOU BUILT WITH YOUR FATHER...
IT'S *DISEASED!*
THERE IS NO WAY TO KEEP IT ALIVE--*JUST THROW IT OUT!*
"EVEN THOUGH YOU KNEW IT WAS CERTAIN TO DIE YOU MISSED CAMP TO CARE FOR IT. STAYED HOME WHILE ALL OF YOUR FRIENDS WENT TO HAVE FUN.
"TO DO WHATEVER YOU COULD TO EASE ITS SUFFERING."
THAT IS WHO YOU ARE.
THAT CHOICE.
I... I DON'T REMEMBER.
DO YOU WANT TO?
YOU CAN STAY HERE.
LIVING A NEW LIFE FREE OF EVERYTHING YOU WERE.
OR I CAN GIVE IT ALL BACK.
ARE YOU WORTH SAVING?

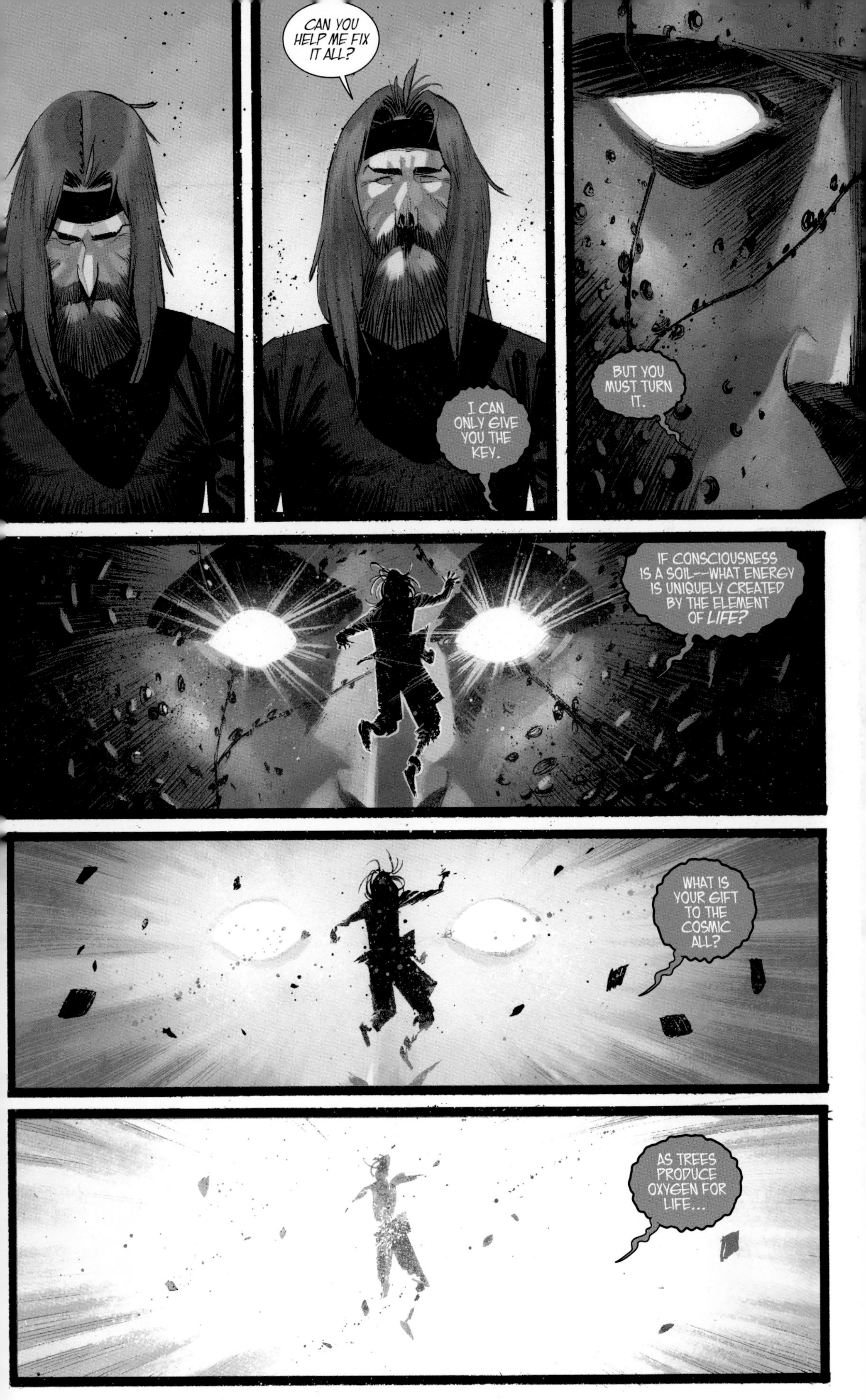
CAN YOU HELP ME FIX IT ALL?
I CAN ONLY GIVE YOU THE KEY.
BUT YOU MUST TURN IT.
IF CONSCIOUSNESS IS A SOIL--WHAT ENERGY IS UNIQUELY CREATED BY THE ELEMENT OF *LIFE?*
WHAT IS YOUR GIFT TO THE COSMIC ALL?
AS TREES PRODUCE OXYGEN FOR LIFE...

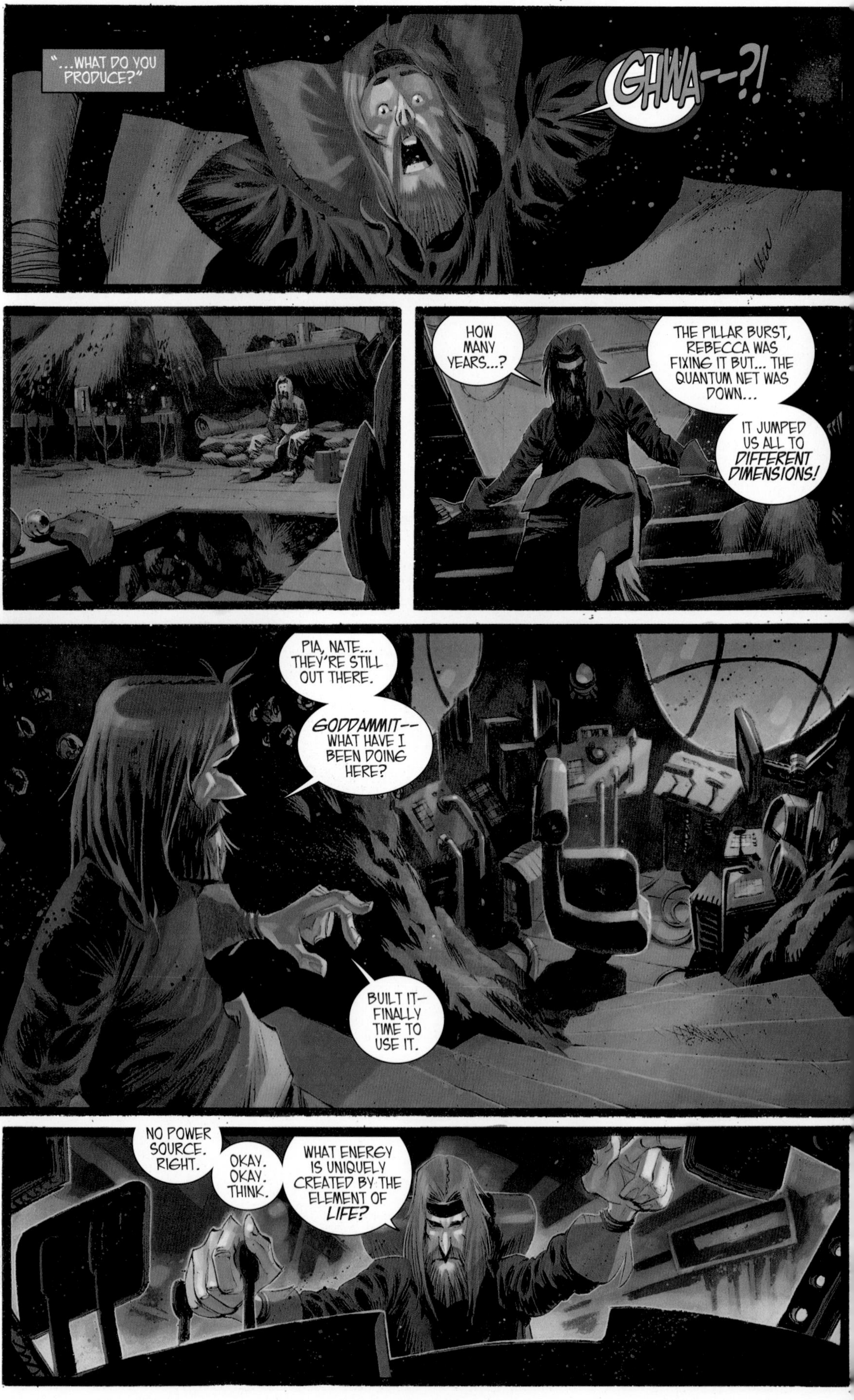
"...WHAT DO YOU PRODUCE?"
GHWA--?!
HOW MANY YEARS...?
THE PILLAR BURST, REBECCA WAS FIXING IT BUT... THE QUANTUM NET WAS DOWN...
IT JUMPED US ALL TO DIFFERENT DIMENSIONS!
PIA, NATE... THEY'RE STILL OUT THERE.
GODDAMMIT-- WHAT HAVE I BEEN DOING HERE?
BUILT IT-- FINALLY TIME TO USE IT.
NO POWER SOURCE. RIGHT.
OKAY. OKAY. THINK.
WHAT ENERGY IS UNIQUELY CREATED BY THE ELEMENT OF LIFE?

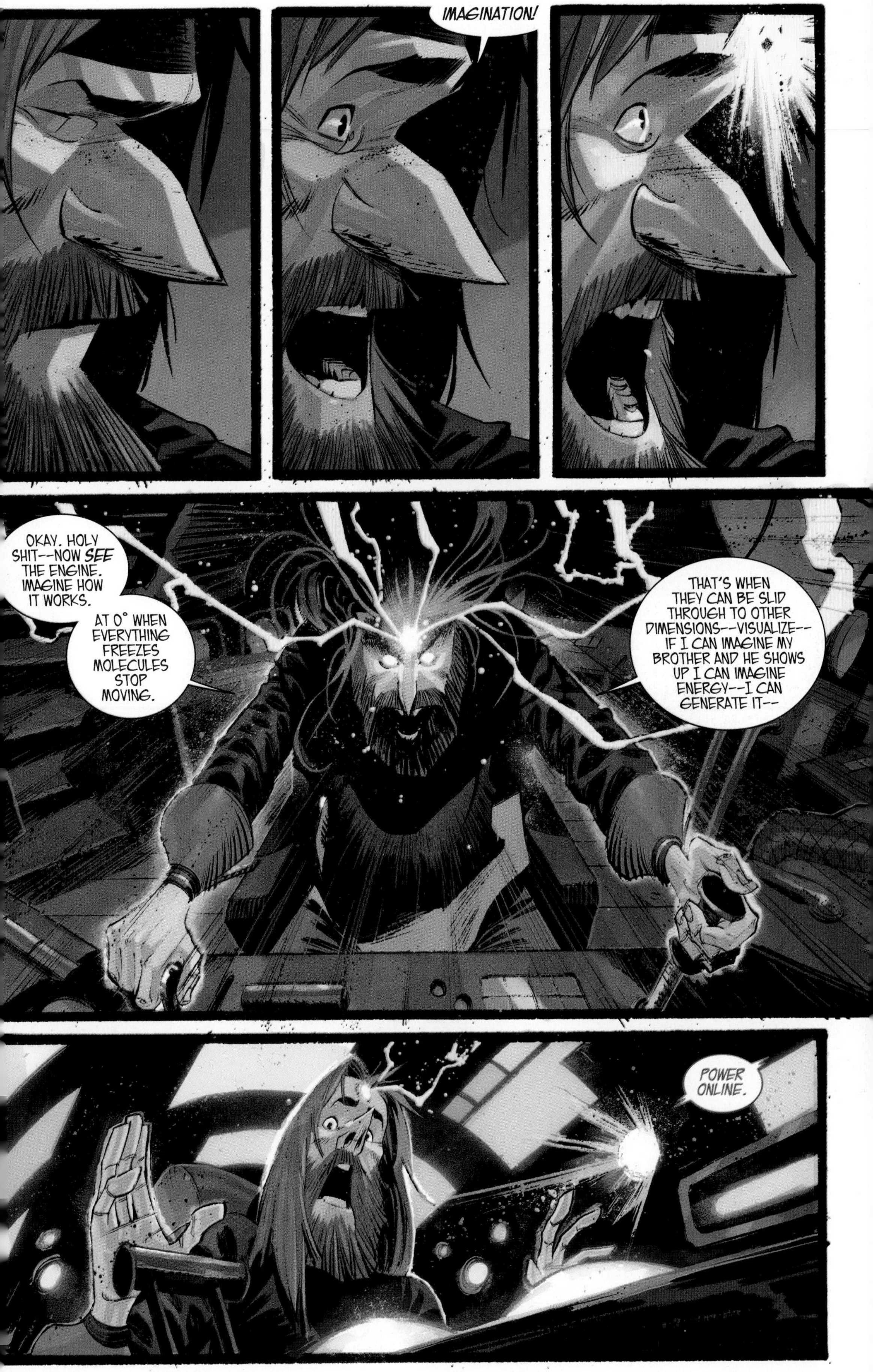

IMAGINATION!
OKAY. HOLY SHIT--NOW SEE THE ENGINE. IMAGINE HOW IT WORKS.
AT 0° WHEN EVERYTHING FREEZES MOLECULES STOP MOVING.
THAT'S WHEN THEY CAN BE SLID THROUGH TO OTHER DIMENSIONS--VISUALIZE--IF I CAN IMAGINE MY BROTHER AND HE SHOWS UP I CAN IMAGINE ENERGY--I CAN GENERATE IT--
POWER ONLINE.

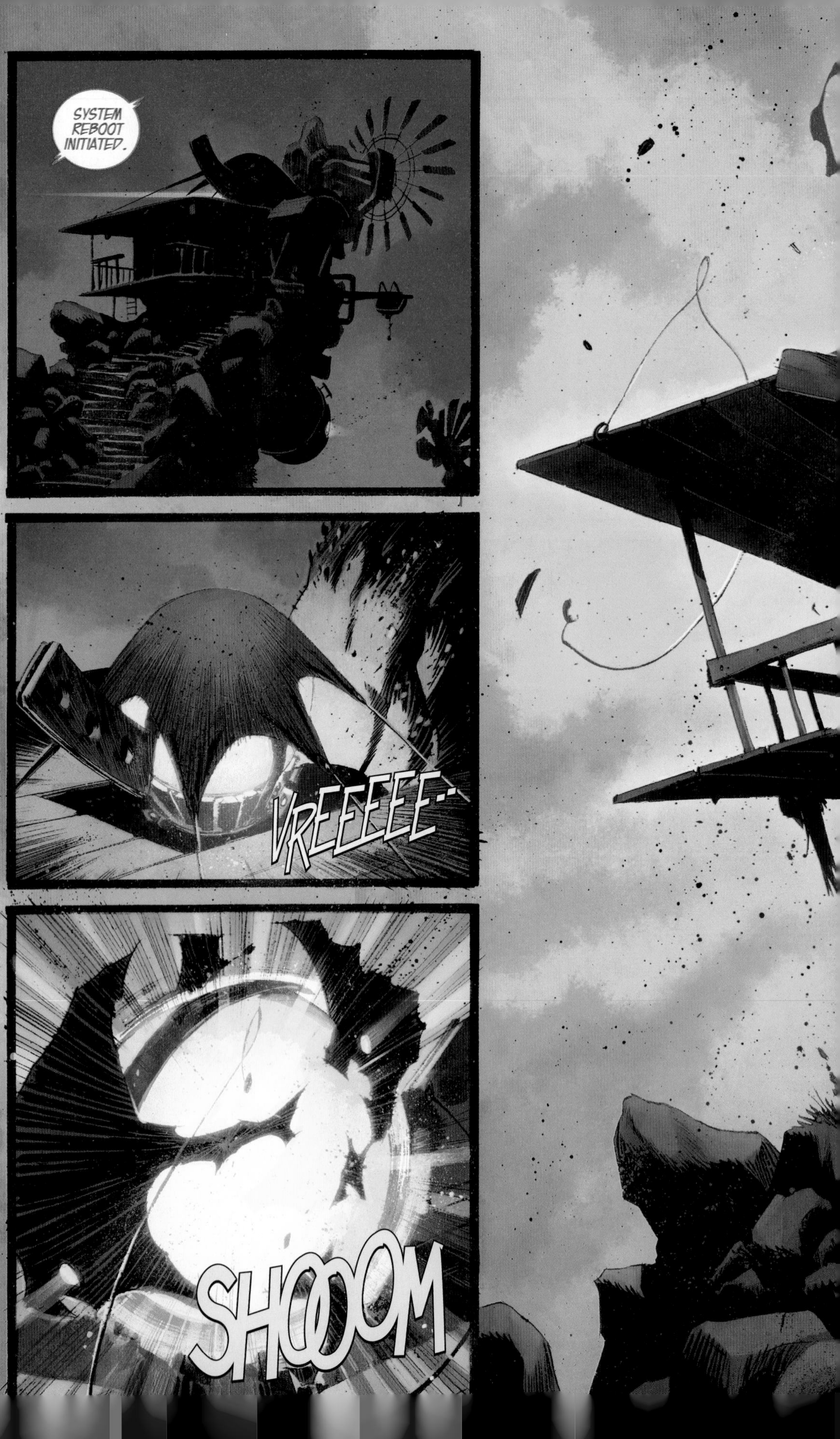
SYSTEM REBOOT INITIATED.
VREEEEE-
SHOOOM

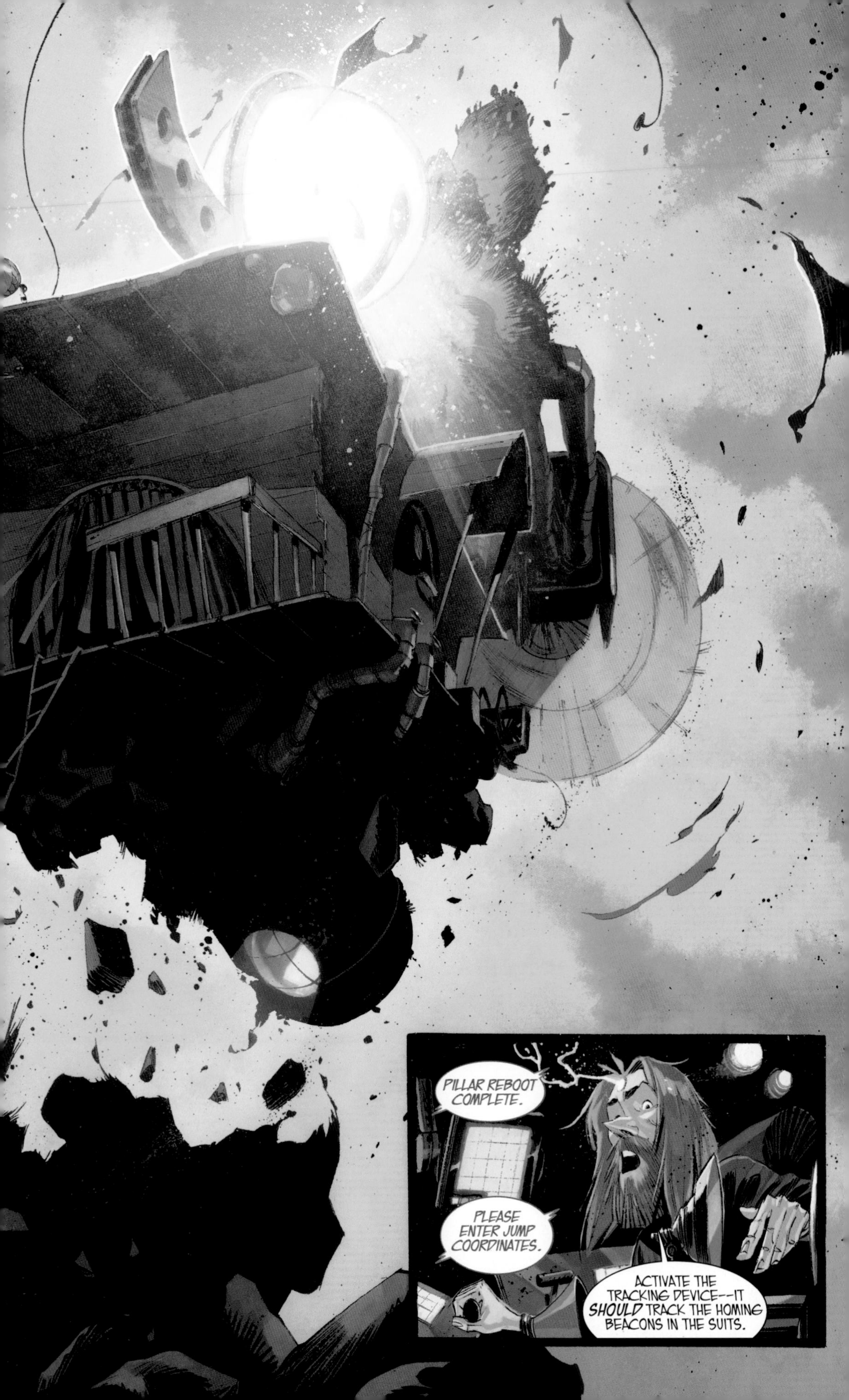
PILLAR REBOOT COMPLETE.
PLEASE ENTER JUMP COORDINATES.
ACTIVATE THE TRACKING DEVICE--IT SHOULD TRACK THE HOMING BEACONS IN THE SUITS.

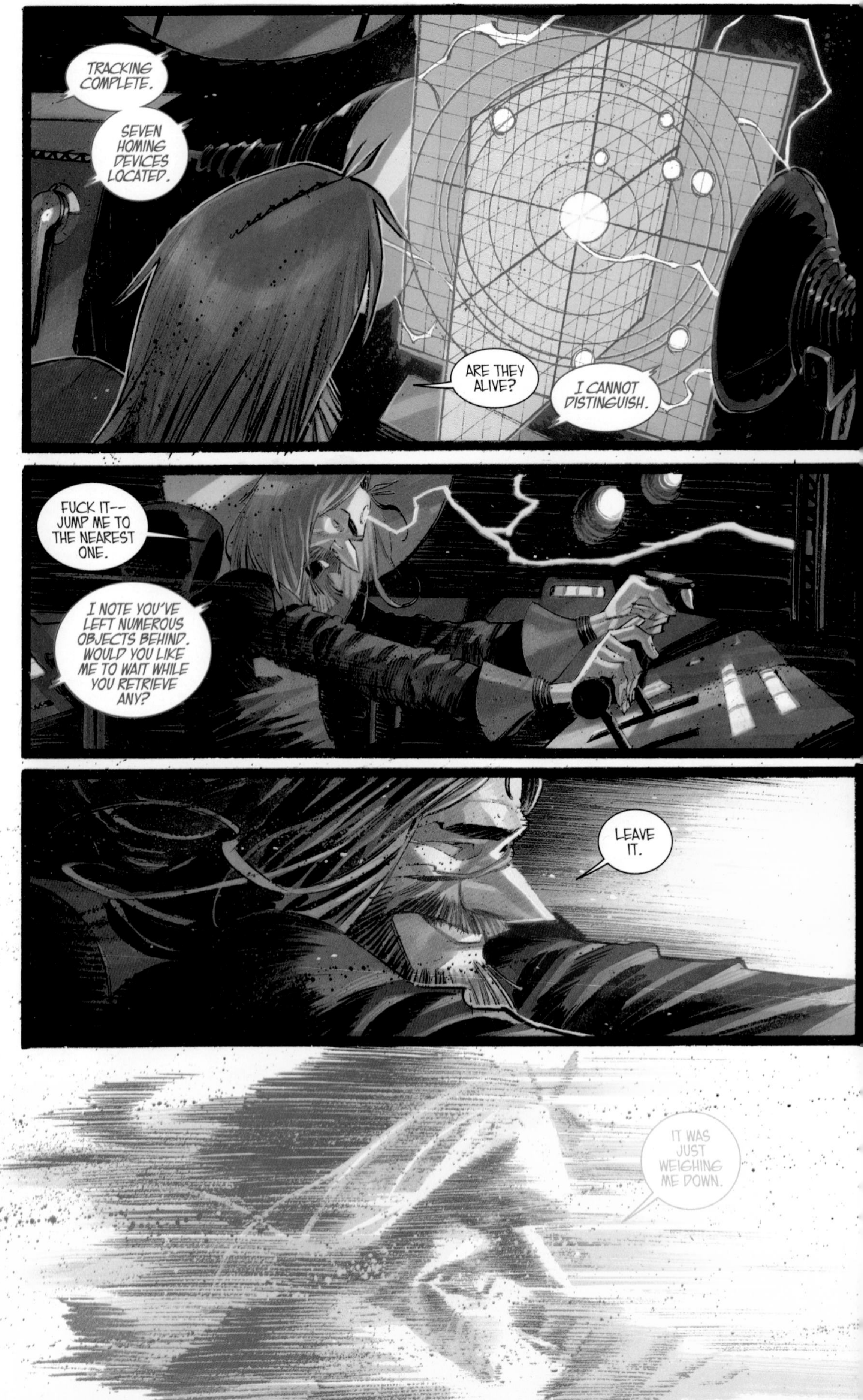
TRACKING COMPLETE.
SEVEN HOMING DEVICES LOCATED.
ARE THEY ALIVE?
I CANNOT DISTINGUISH.
FUCK IT-- JUMP ME TO THE NEAREST ONE.
I NOTE YOU'VE LEFT NUMEROUS OBJECTS BEHIND. WOULD YOU LIKE ME TO WAIT WHILE YOU RETRIEVE ANY?
LEAVE IT.
IT WAS JUST WEIGHING ME DOWN.

20

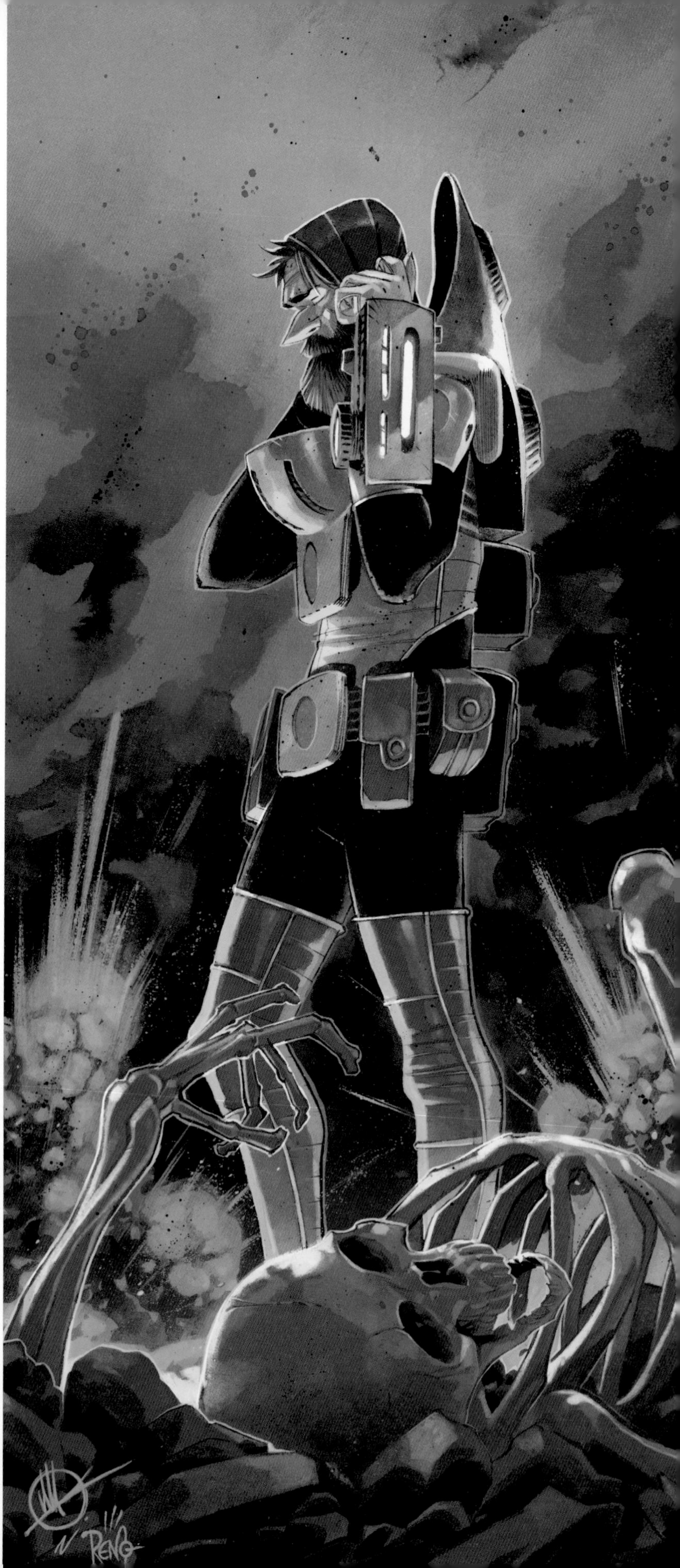

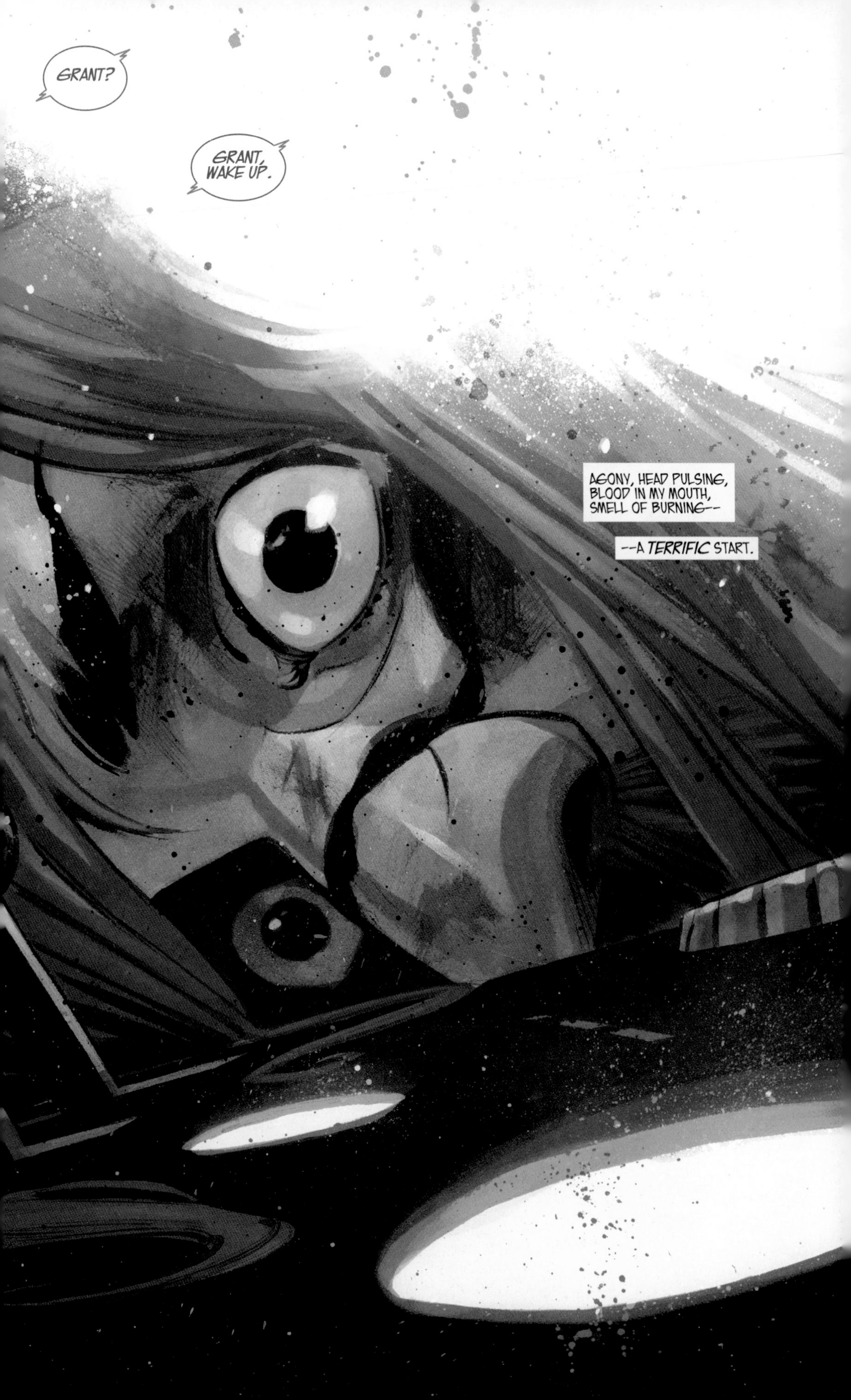
GRANT?
GRANT, WAKE UP.
AGONY, HEAD PULSING, BLOOD IN MY MOUTH, SMELL OF BURNING--
--A TERRIFIC START.

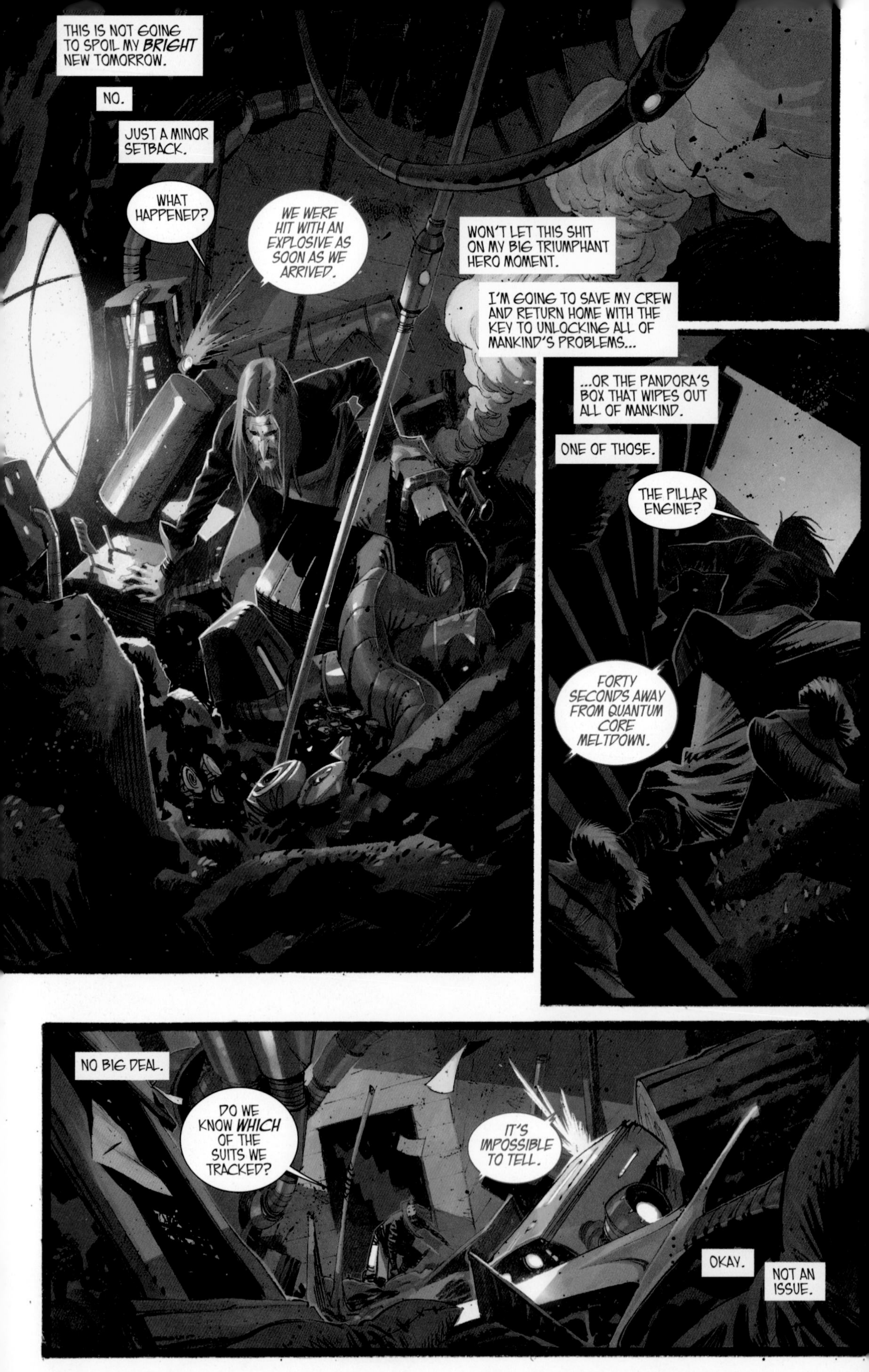
THIS IS NOT GOING TO SPOIL MY BRIGHT NEW TOMORROW.
NO.
JUST A MINOR SETBACK.
WHAT HAPPENED?
WE WERE HIT WITH AN EXPLOSIVE AS SOON AS WE ARRIVED.
WON'T LET THIS SHIT ON MY BIG TRIUMPHANT HERO MOMENT.
I'M GOING TO SAVE MY CREW AND RETURN HOME WITH THE KEY TO UNLOCKING ALL OF MANKIND'S PROBLEMS...
...OR THE PANDORA'S BOX THAT WIPES OUT ALL OF MANKIND.
ONE OF THOSE.
THE PILLAR ENGINE?
FORTY SECONDS AWAY FROM QUANTUM CORE MELTDOWN.
NO BIG DEAL.
DO WE KNOW WHICH OF THE SUITS WE TRACKED?
IT'S IMPOSSIBLE TO TELL.
OKAY.
NOT AN ISSUE.

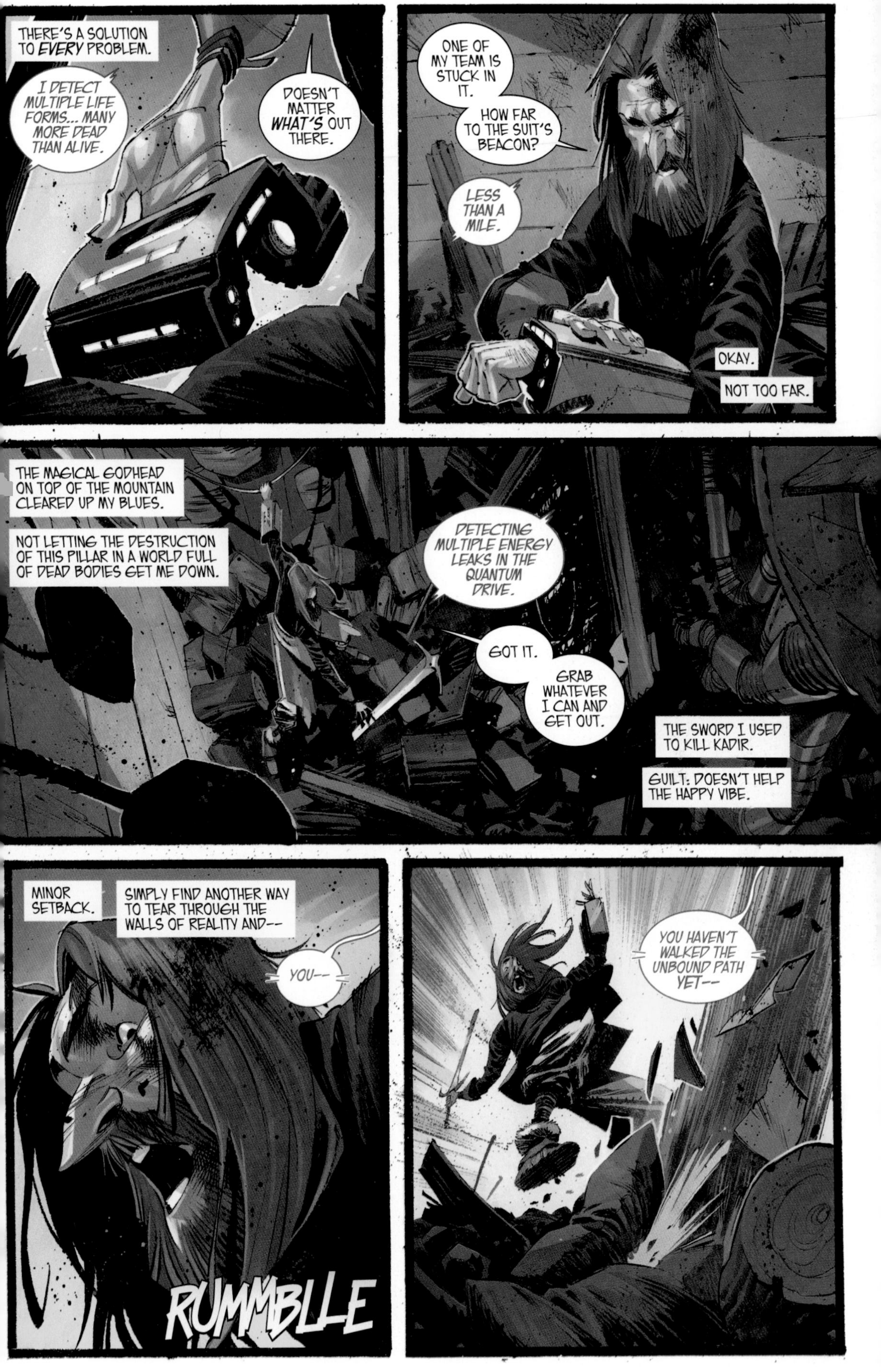
THERE'S A SOLUTION TO EVERY PROBLEM.
I DETECT MULTIPLE LIFE FORMS... MANY MORE DEAD THAN ALIVE.
DOESN'T MATTER WHAT'S OUT THERE.
ONE OF MY TEAM IS STUCK IN IT.
HOW FAR TO THE SUIT'S BEACON?
LESS THAN A MILE.
OKAY.
NOT TOO FAR.
THE MAGICAL GODHEAD ON TOP OF THE MOUNTAIN CLEARED UP MY BLUES.
NOT LETTING THE DESTRUCTION OF THIS PILLAR IN A WORLD FULL OF DEAD BODIES GET ME DOWN.
DETECTING MULTIPLE ENERGY LEAKS IN THE QUANTUM DRIVE.
GOT IT.
GRAB WHATEVER I CAN AND GET OUT.
THE SWORD I USED TO KILL KADIR.
GUILT: DOESN'T HELP THE HAPPY VIBE.
MINOR SETBACK.
SIMPLY FIND ANOTHER WAY TO TEAR THROUGH THE WALLS OF REALITY AND--
YOU--
RUMMBLLE
YOU HAVEN'T WALKED THE UNBOUND PATH YET--

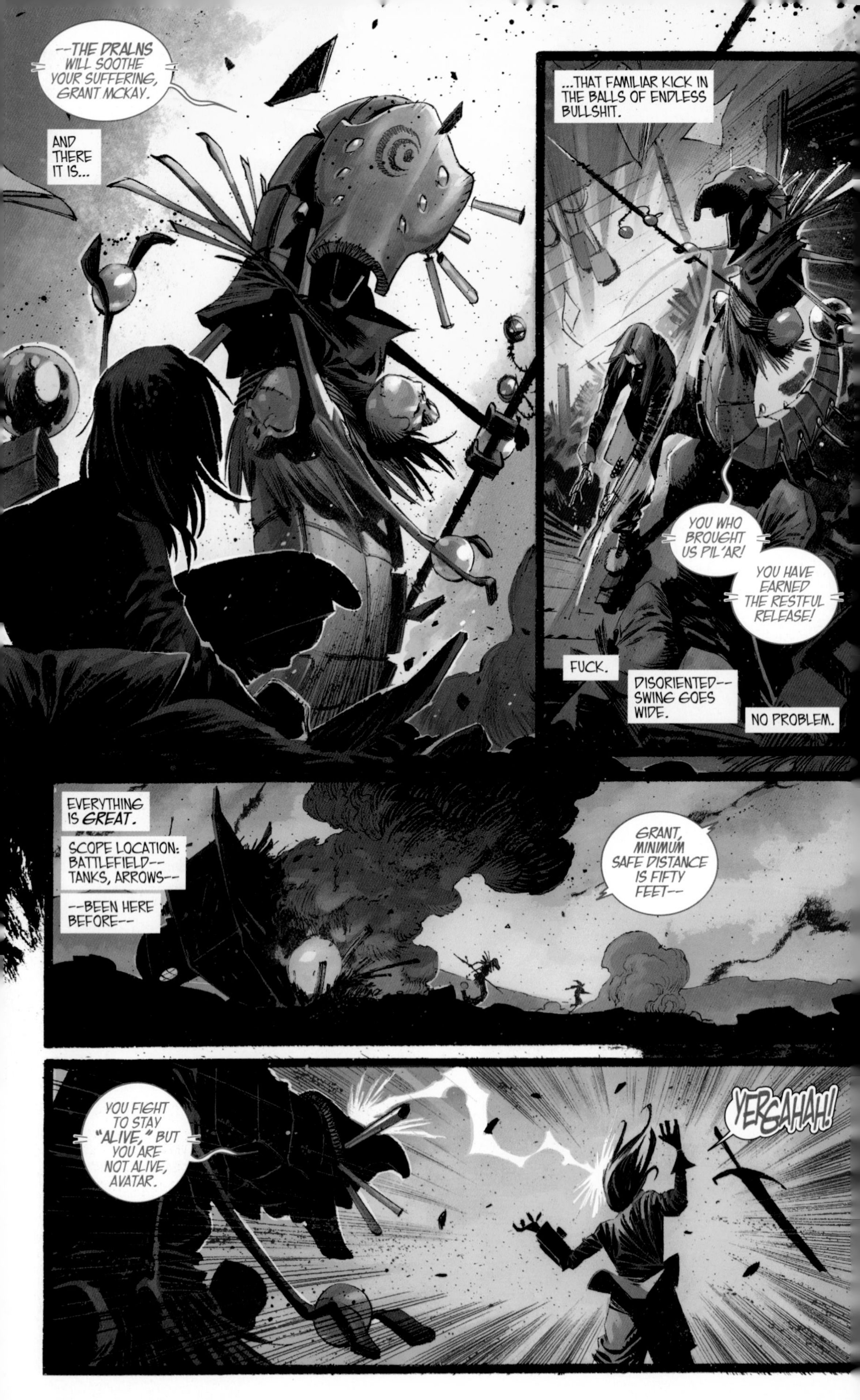
--THE DRALNS WILL SOOTHE YOUR SUFFERING, GRANT MCKAY.
AND THERE IT IS...
...THAT FAMILIAR KICK IN THE BALLS OF ENDLESS BULLSHIT.
YOU WHO BROUGHT US PIL'AR!
YOU HAVE EARNED THE RESTFUL RELEASE!
FUCK.
DISORIENTED--SWING GOES WIDE.
NO PROBLEM.
EVERYTHING IS GREAT.
SCOPE LOCATION: BATTLEFIELD--TANKS, ARROWS--
--BEEN HERE BEFORE--
GRANT, MINIMUM SAFE DISTANCE IS FIFTY FEET--
YOU FIGHT TO STAY "ALIVE," BUT YOU ARE NOT ALIVE, AVATAR.
YERGAHAH!

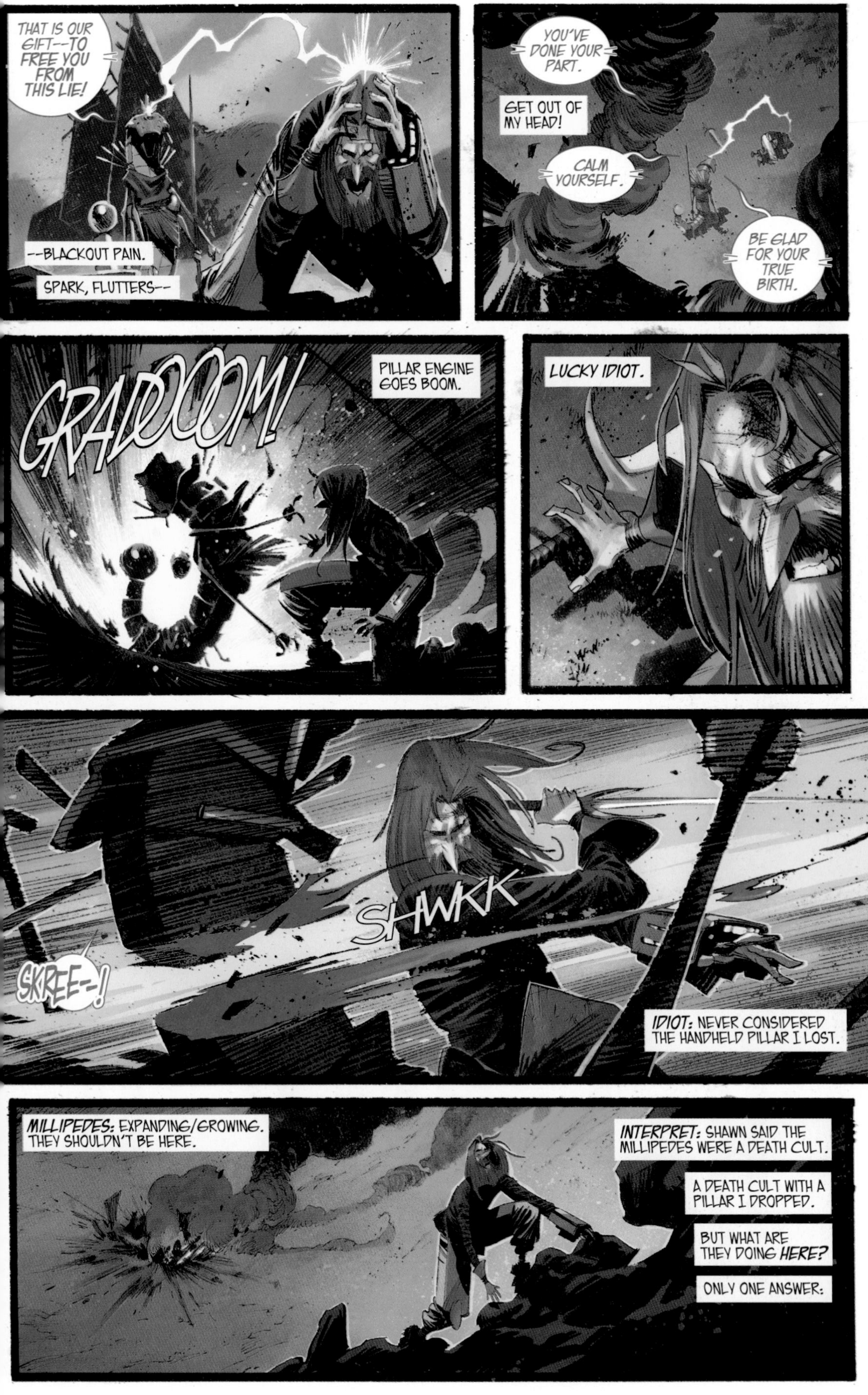

THAT IS OUR GIFT--TO FREE YOU FROM THIS LIE!
--BLACKOUT PAIN.
SPARK, FLUTTERS--
YOU'VE DONE YOUR PART.
GET OUT OF MY HEAD!
CALM YOURSELF.
BE GLAD FOR YOUR TRUE BIRTH.
GRADOOOM!
PILLAR ENGINE GOES BOOM.
LUCKY IDIOT.
SHWKK
SKREE--!
IDIOT: NEVER CONSIDERED THE HANDHELD PILLAR I LOST.
MILLIPEDES: EXPANDING/GROWING. THEY SHOULDN'T BE HERE.
INTERPRET: SHAWN SAID THE MILLIPEDES WERE A DEATH CULT.
A DEATH CULT WITH A PILLAR I DROPPED.
BUT WHAT ARE THEY DOING HERE?
ONLY ONE ANSWER:

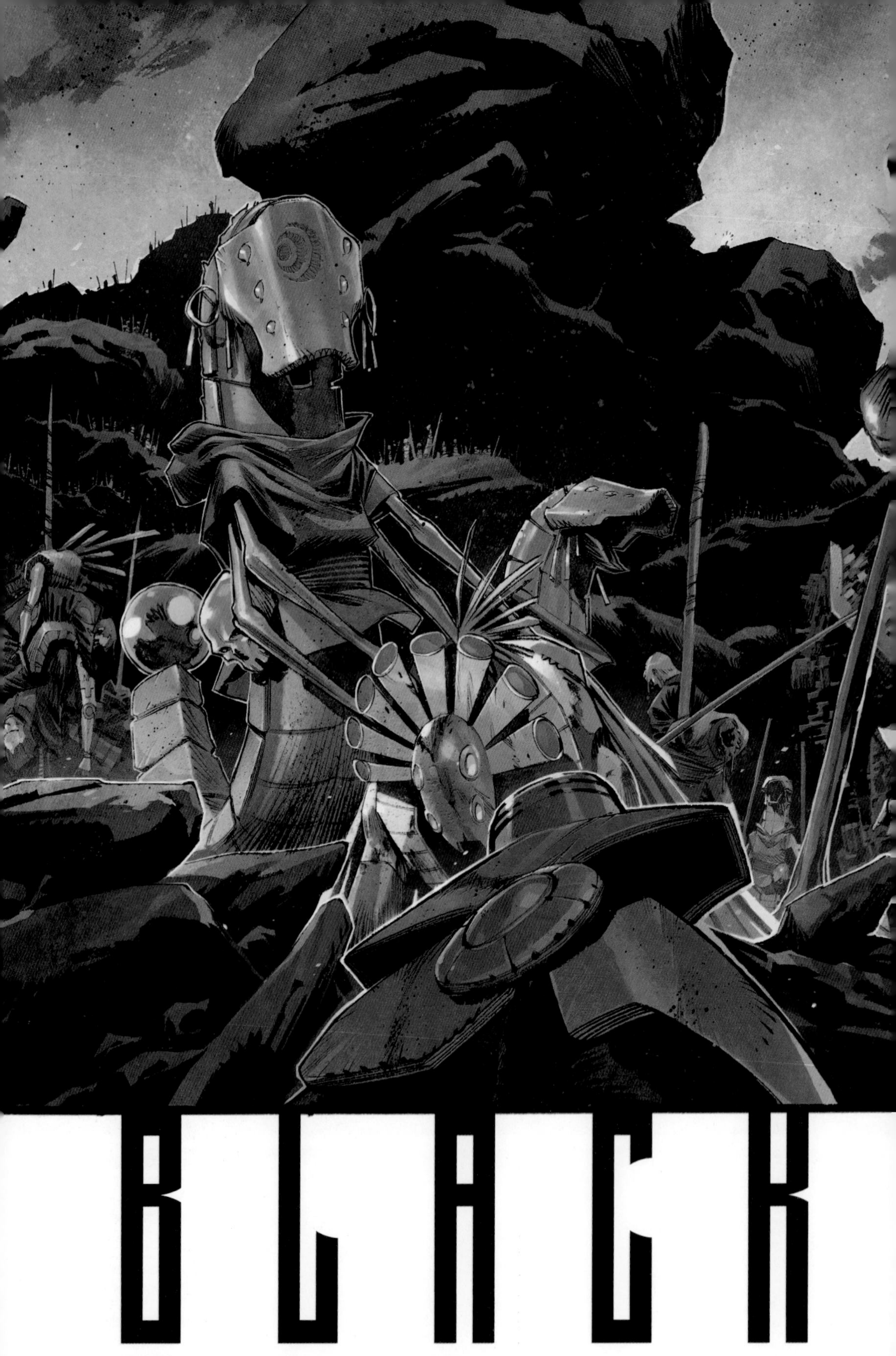

BLACK

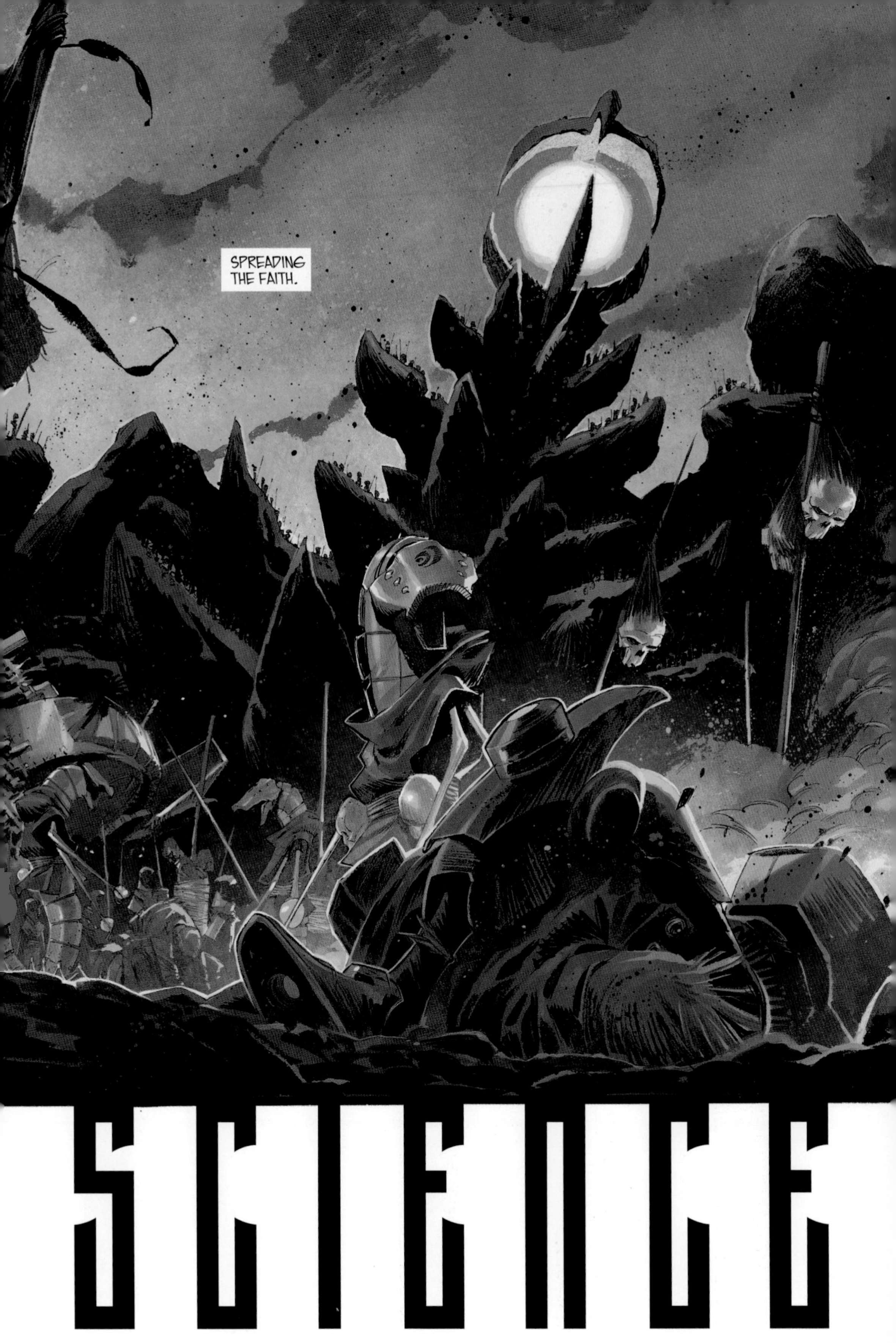
SPREADING THE FAITH.

SCIENCE

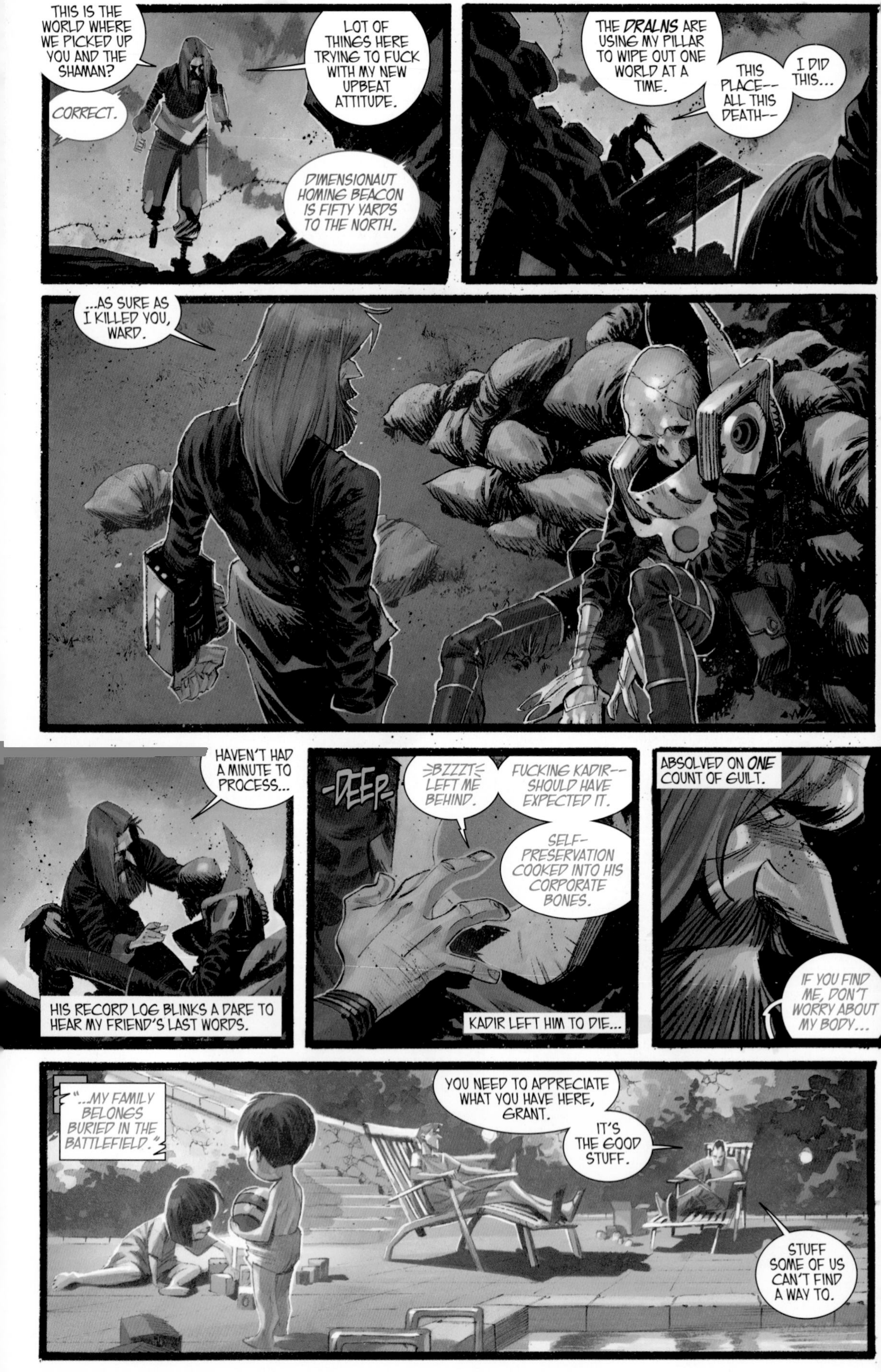
THIS IS THE WORLD WHERE WE PICKED UP YOU AND THE SHAMAN?
CORRECT.
LOT OF THINGS HERE TRYING TO FUCK WITH MY NEW UPBEAT ATTITUDE.
DIMENSIONAUT HOMING BEACON IS FIFTY YARDS TO THE NORTH.
THE DRALNS ARE USING MY PILLAR TO WIPE OUT ONE WORLD AT A TIME.
THIS PLACE-- ALL THIS DEATH--
I DID THIS...
...AS SURE AS I KILLED YOU, WARD.
HAVEN'T HAD A MINUTE TO PROCESS...
HIS RECORD LOG BLINKS A DARE TO HEAR MY FRIEND'S LAST WORDS.
-DEEP-
BZZZT LEFT ME BEHIND.
FUCKING KADIR-- SHOULD HAVE EXPECTED IT.
SELF-PRESERVATION COOKED INTO HIS CORPORATE BONES.
KADIR LEFT HIM TO DIE...
ABSOLVED ON ONE COUNT OF GUILT.
IF YOU FIND ME, DON'T WORRY ABOUT MY BODY...
"...MY FAMILY BELONGS BURIED IN THE BATTLEFIELD."
YOU NEED TO APPRECIATE WHAT YOU HAVE HERE, GRANT.
IT'S THE GOOD STUFF.
STUFF SOME OF US CAN'T FIND A WAY TO.

YOU'LL FIND THE RIGHT LADY.

I DUNNO.

I SPENT MOST OF MY LIFE UNDER THE ASSUMPTION THAT I MISSED AN IMPORTANT CHAPTER EARLY ON.

OUT SICK FOR THE LESSON ON LIVING A NORMAL, WELL-ADJUSTED LIFE.

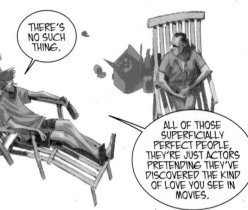

THERE'S NO SUCH THING.

ALL OF THOSE SUPERFICIALLY PERFECT PEOPLE, THEY'RE JUST ACTORS PRETENDING THEY'VE DISCOVERED THE KIND OF LOVE YOU SEE IN MOVIES.

DON'T JUDGE YOURSELF AGAINST THE NORMALS.

BEHIND CLOSED DOORS THEY *FIGHT*, DO *DRUGS*, *CHEAT*, AND *SCREAM*-- THEY JUST DO A BETTER JOB *PRETENDING* THEY DON'T.

FRAUDS MORE INTERESTED IN OTHER PEOPLE *THINKING* THEY'RE A THING THAN ACTUALLY *BEING* THAT THING.

AND THAT'S EVERYONE TO A DEGREE, AND WE DEMAND IT OF OTHERS.

WE GET TOGETHER, SMILE, PLAY PERFECT.

WE FUCKING LIE.

THIS SUNNY, POOLSIDE PERFECTION, THIS IS US HOLDING IT TOGETHER FOR COMPANY.

THIS ISN'T THE REALITY, WARD.

THE REALITY IS...

"...YOU'RE BETTER OFF ALONE."

JESUS.

ALL YOU WANTED WAS A FAMILY, A BACKYARD, AND ALL THE STUFF I SHAT ON--

I'M SORRY, WARD.

I'LL MAKE THIS MEAN SOMETHING.

NOW *THAT I* CAN HELP WITH.

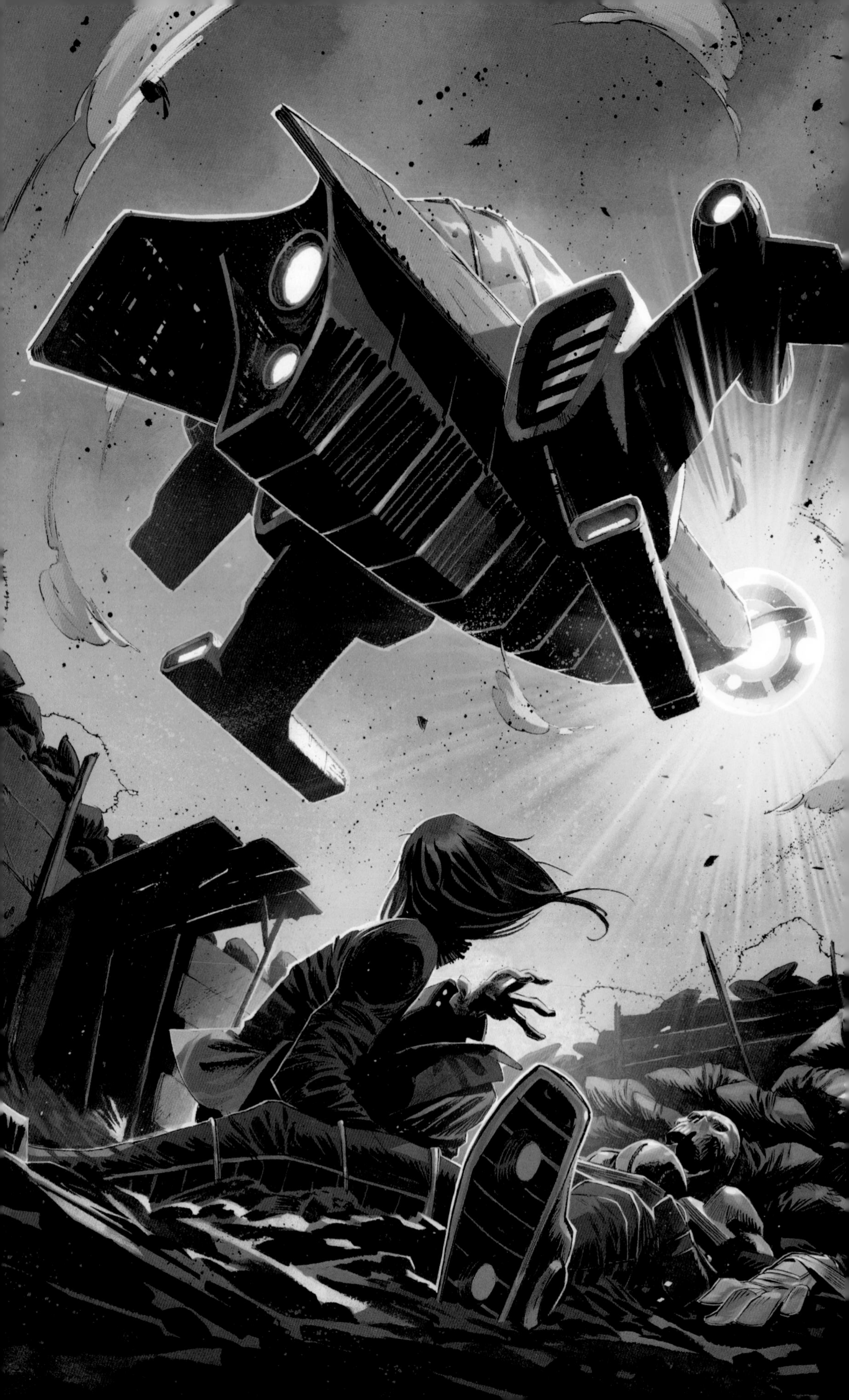

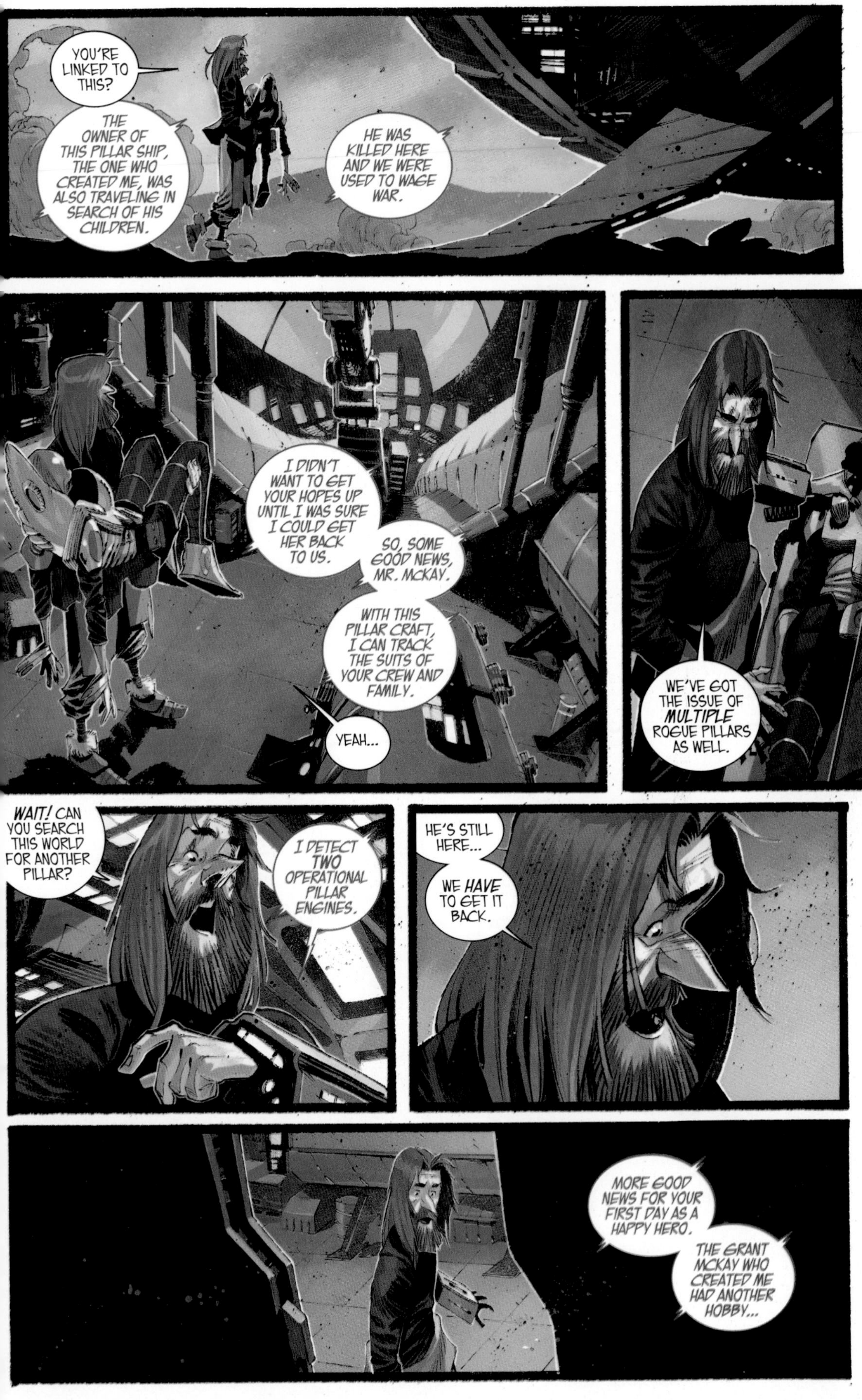
YOU'RE LINKED TO THIS?
THE OWNER OF THIS PILLAR SHIP, THE ONE WHO CREATED ME, WAS ALSO TRAVELING IN SEARCH OF HIS CHILDREN.
HE WAS KILLED HERE AND WE WERE USED TO WAGE WAR.
I DIDN'T WANT TO GET YOUR HOPES UP UNTIL I WAS SURE I COULD GET HER BACK TO US.
SO, SOME GOOD NEWS, MR. MCKAY.
WITH THIS PILLAR CRAFT, I CAN TRACK THE SUITS OF YOUR CREW AND FAMILY.
YEAH...
WE'VE GOT THE ISSUE OF MULTIPLE ROGUE PILLARS AS WELL.
WAIT! CAN YOU SEARCH THIS WORLD FOR ANOTHER PILLAR?
I DETECT TWO OPERATIONAL PILLAR ENGINES.
HE'S STILL HERE...
WE HAVE TO GET IT BACK.
MORE GOOD NEWS FOR YOUR FIRST DAY AS A HAPPY HERO.
THE GRANT MCKAY WHO CREATED ME HAD ANOTHER HOBBY...

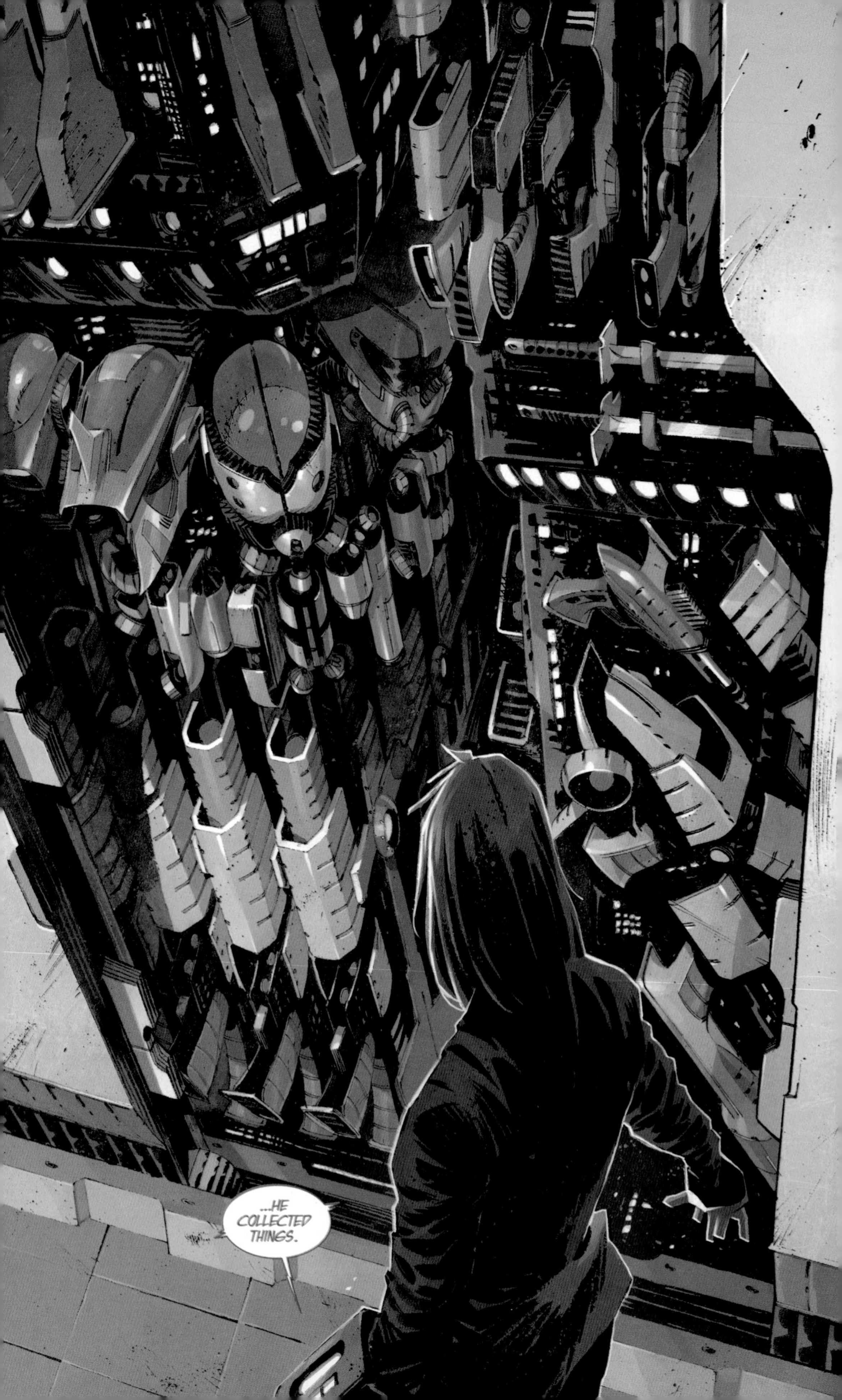
...HE COLLECTED THINGS.

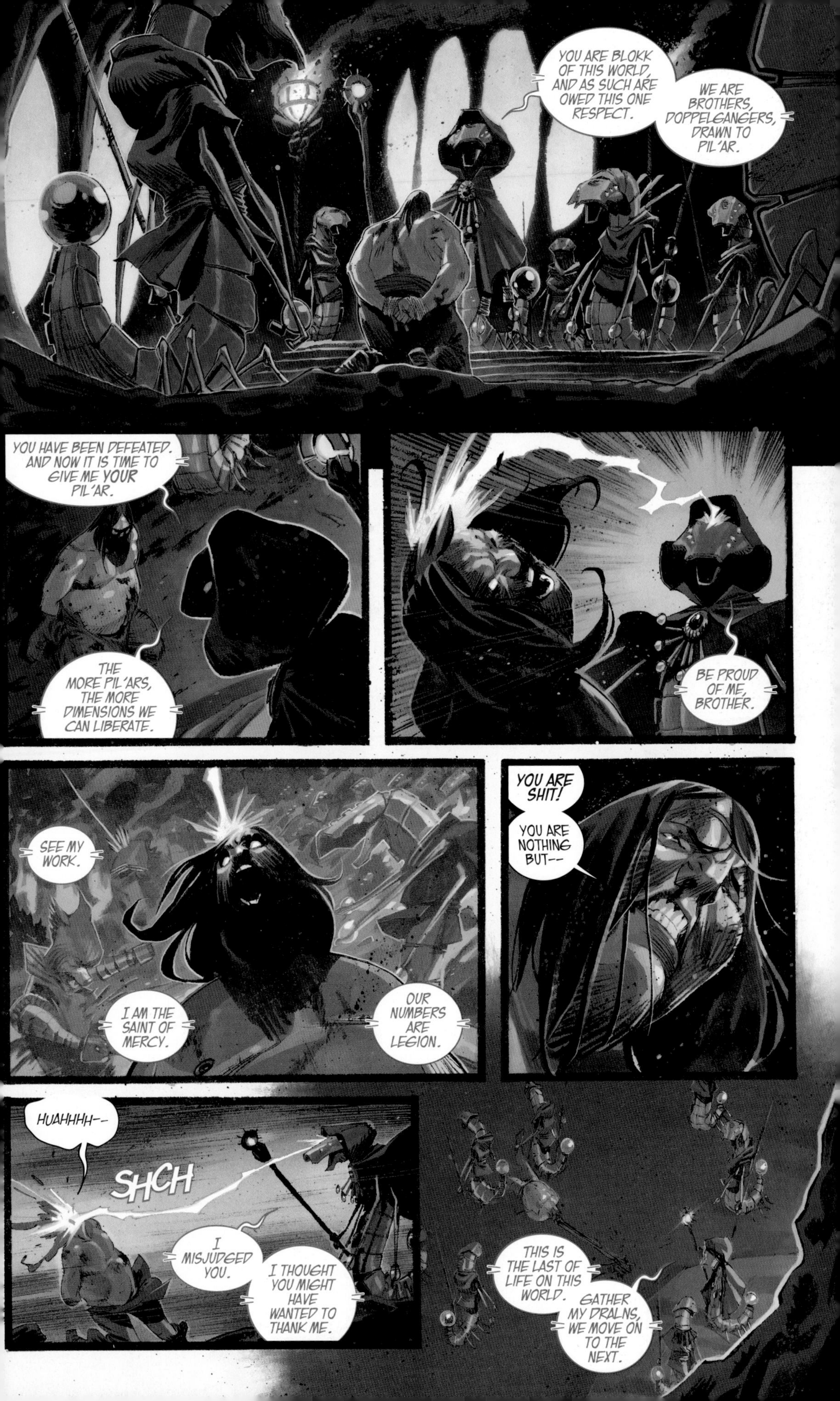

YOU ARE BLOKK OF THIS WORLD, AND AS SUCH ARE OWED THIS ONE RESPECT.
WE ARE BROTHERS, DOPPELGANGERS, DRAWN TO PIL'AR.
YOU HAVE BEEN DEFEATED. AND NOW IT IS TIME TO GIVE ME YOUR PIL'AR.
THE MORE PIL'ARS, THE MORE DIMENSIONS WE CAN LIBERATE.
BE PROUD OF ME, BROTHER.
SEE MY WORK.
I AM THE SAINT OF MERCY.
OUR NUMBERS ARE LEGION.
YOU ARE SHIT!
YOU ARE NOTHING BUT--
HUAHHHH--
SHCH
I MISJUDGED YOU.
I THOUGHT YOU MIGHT HAVE WANTED TO THANK ME.
THIS IS THE LAST OF LIFE ON THIS WORLD.
GATHER MY DRALNS, WE MOVE ON TO THE NEXT.

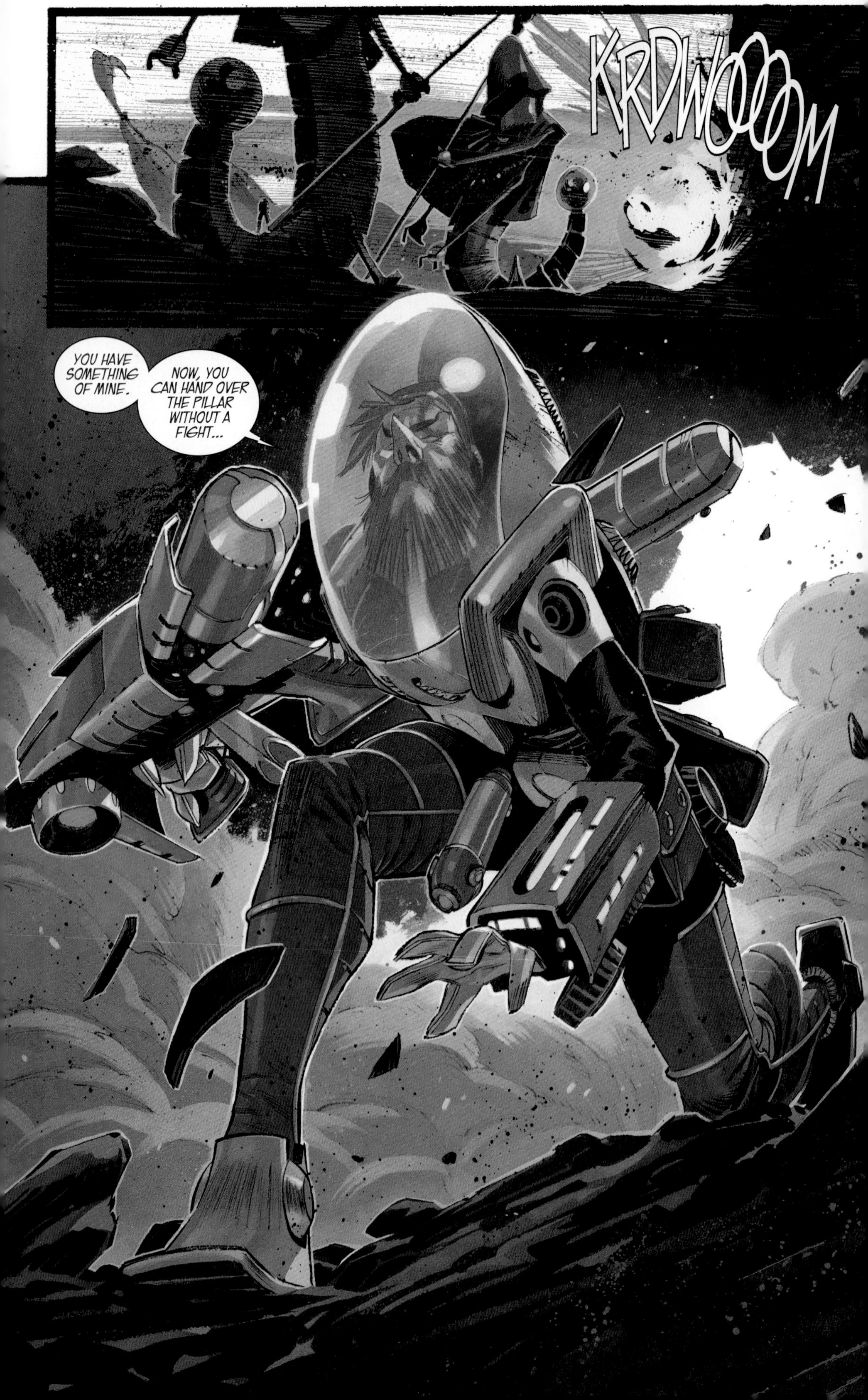
KRDWOOOOM
YOU HAVE SOMETHING OF MINE.
NOW, YOU CAN HAND OVER THE PILLAR WITHOUT A FIGHT...

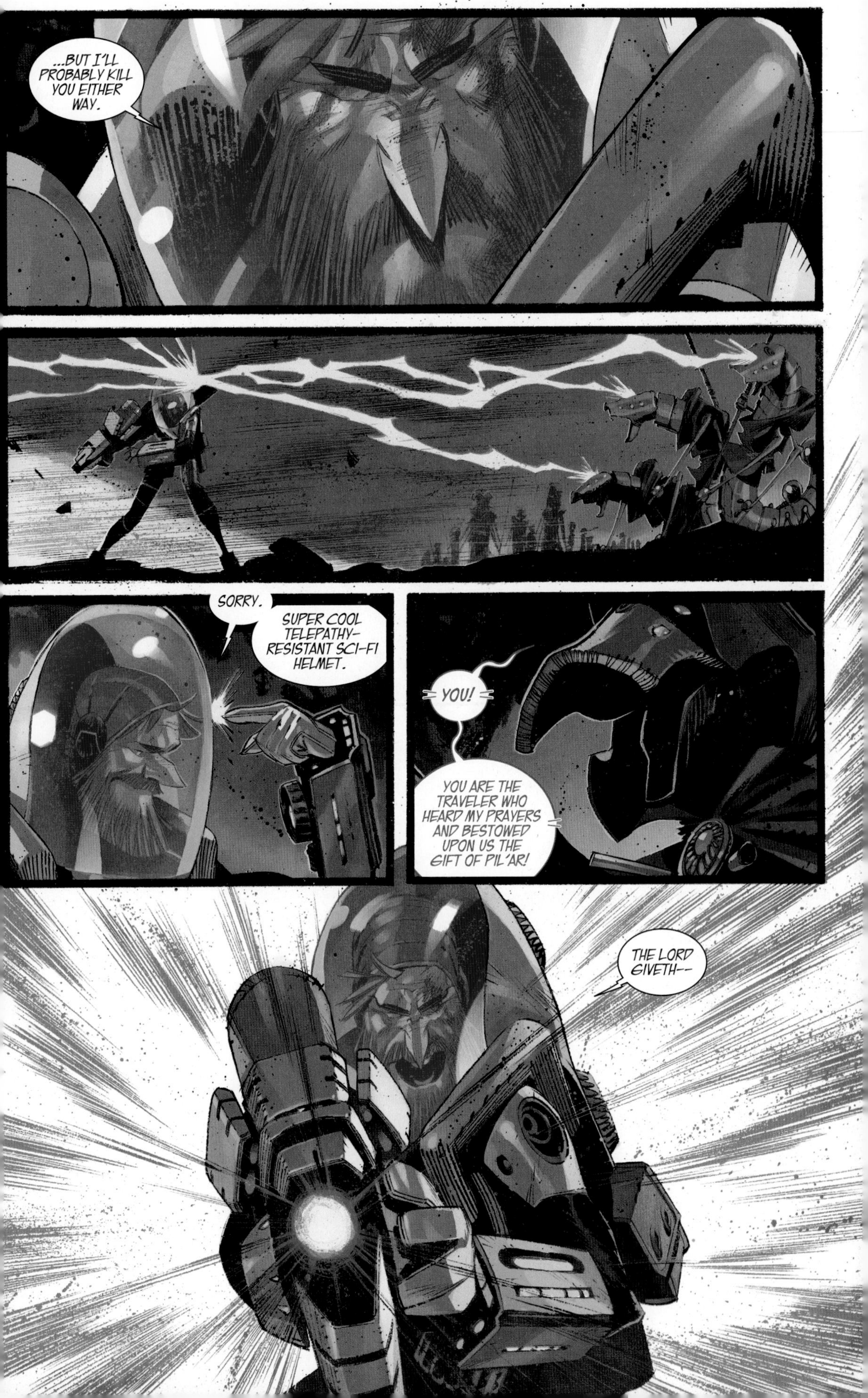
...BUT I'LL PROBABLY KILL YOU EITHER WAY.
SORRY.
SUPER COOL TELEPATHY-RESISTANT SCI-FI HELMET.
YOU!
YOU ARE THE TRAVELER WHO HEARD MY PRAYERS AND BESTOWED UPON US THE GIFT OF PIL'AR!
THE LORD GIVETH--

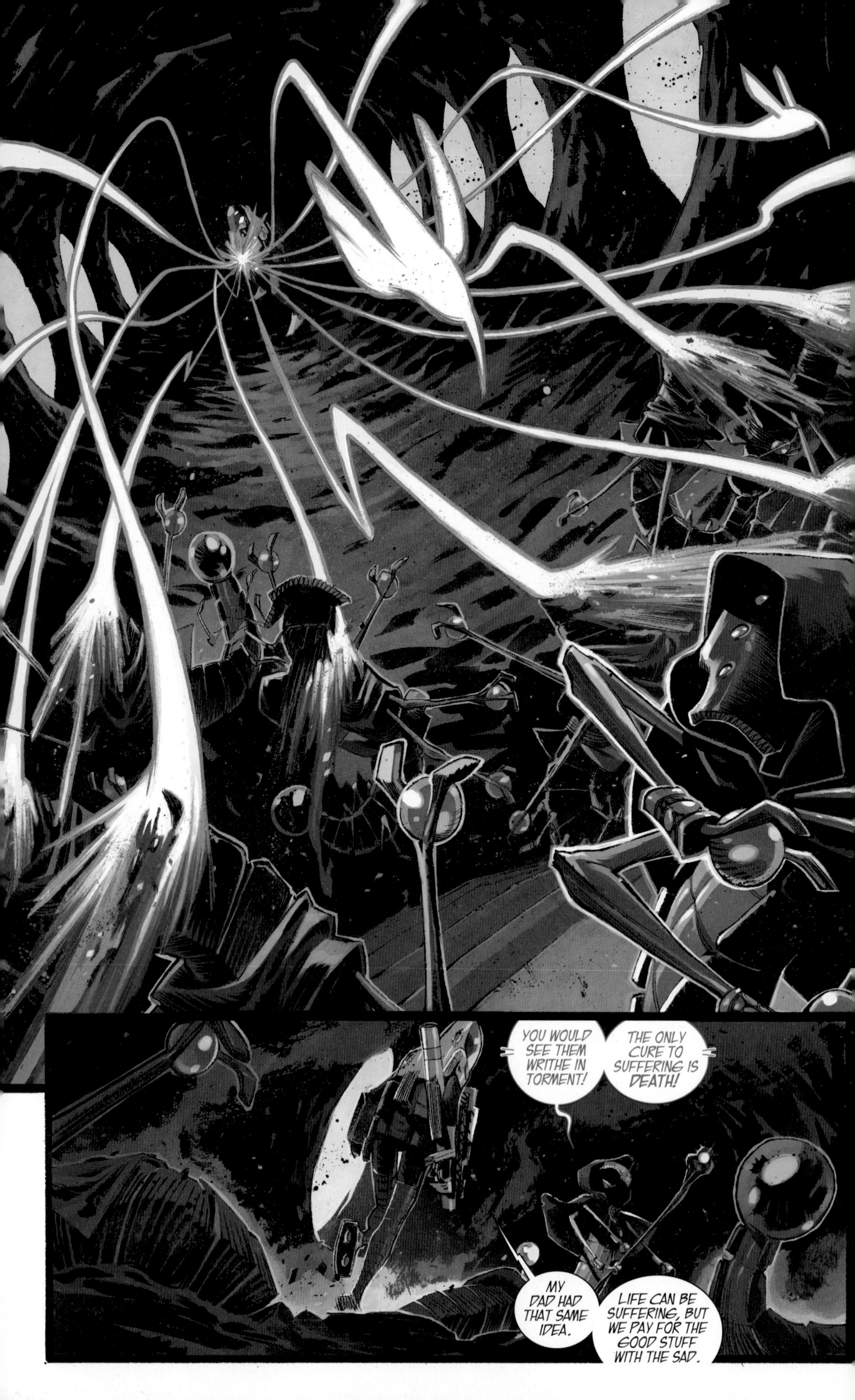

YOU WOULD SEE THEM WRITHE IN TORMENT!
THE ONLY CURE TO SUFFERING IS DEATH!
MY DAD HAD THAT SAME IDEA.
LIFE CAN BE SUFFERING, BUT WE PAY FOR THE GOOD STUFF WITH THE SAD.

YOU'RE NOT TAKING AWAY ANOTHER PERSON'S CHANCE AT *GOOD* DAYS BECAUSE YOU CAN'T DEAL WITH YOUR *BAD*--

--YOU SLIMY INSECT DICK!

KROKK

YOU LAY YOUR HANDS UPON BLOKK?!

LAY THEM ON YOU?

THEY'RE GOING TO TEAR YOU THE FUCK APART.

ANOTHER BLOCK--

PIECE IT TOGETHER.

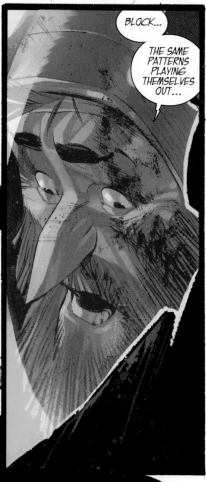

BLOCK...

THE SAME PATTERNS PLAYING THEMSELVES OUT...

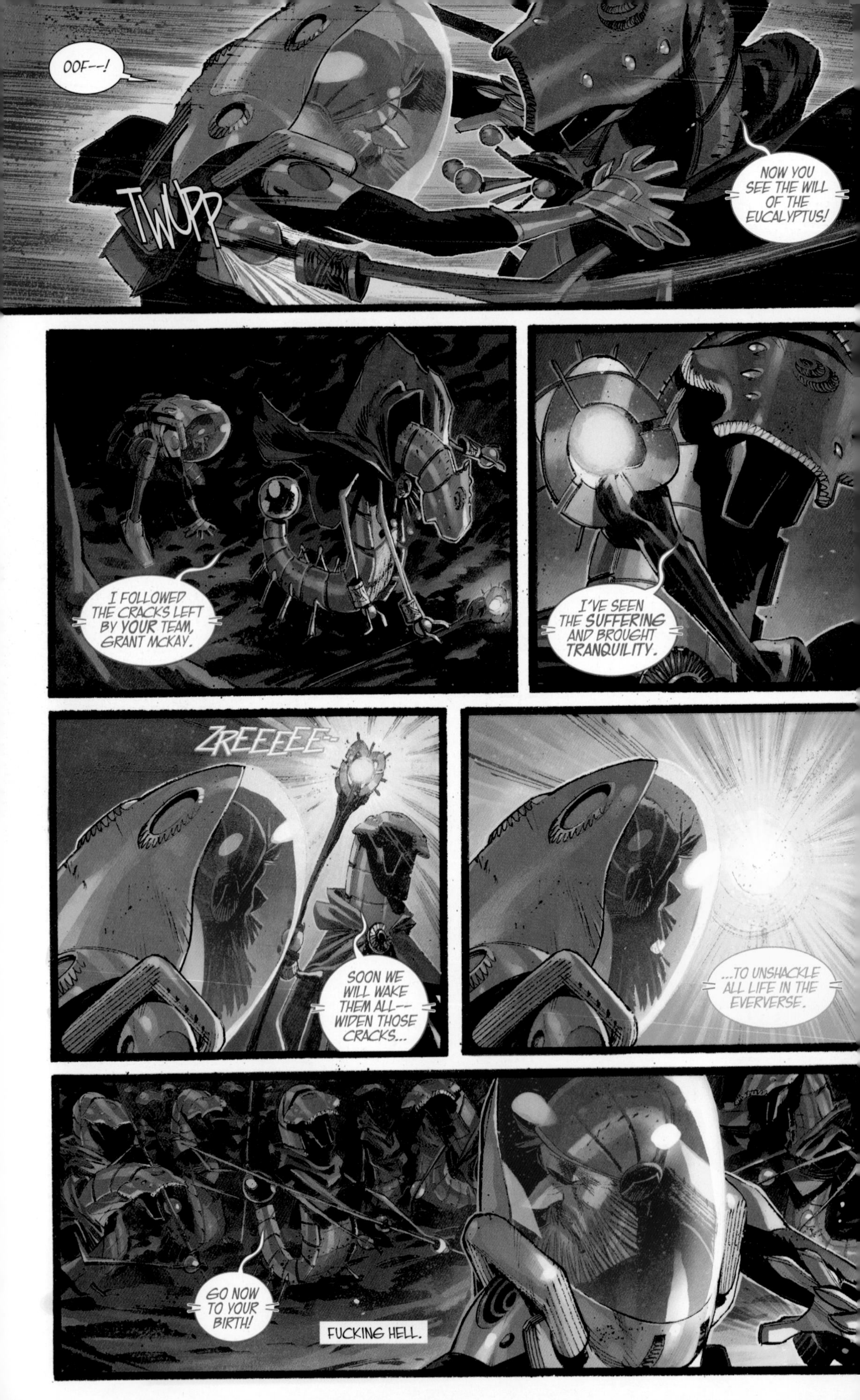
OOF--!
TWUPP
NOW YOU SEE THE WILL OF THE EUCALYPTUS!
I FOLLOWED THE CRACKS LEFT BY YOUR TEAM, GRANT MCKAY.
I'VE SEEN THE SUFFERING AND BROUGHT TRANQUILITY.
ZREEEEEE--
SOON WE WILL WAKE THEM ALL-- WIDEN THOSE CRACKS...
...TO UNSHACKLE ALL LIFE IN THE EVERVERSE.
GO NOW TO YOUR BIRTH!
FUCKING HELL.

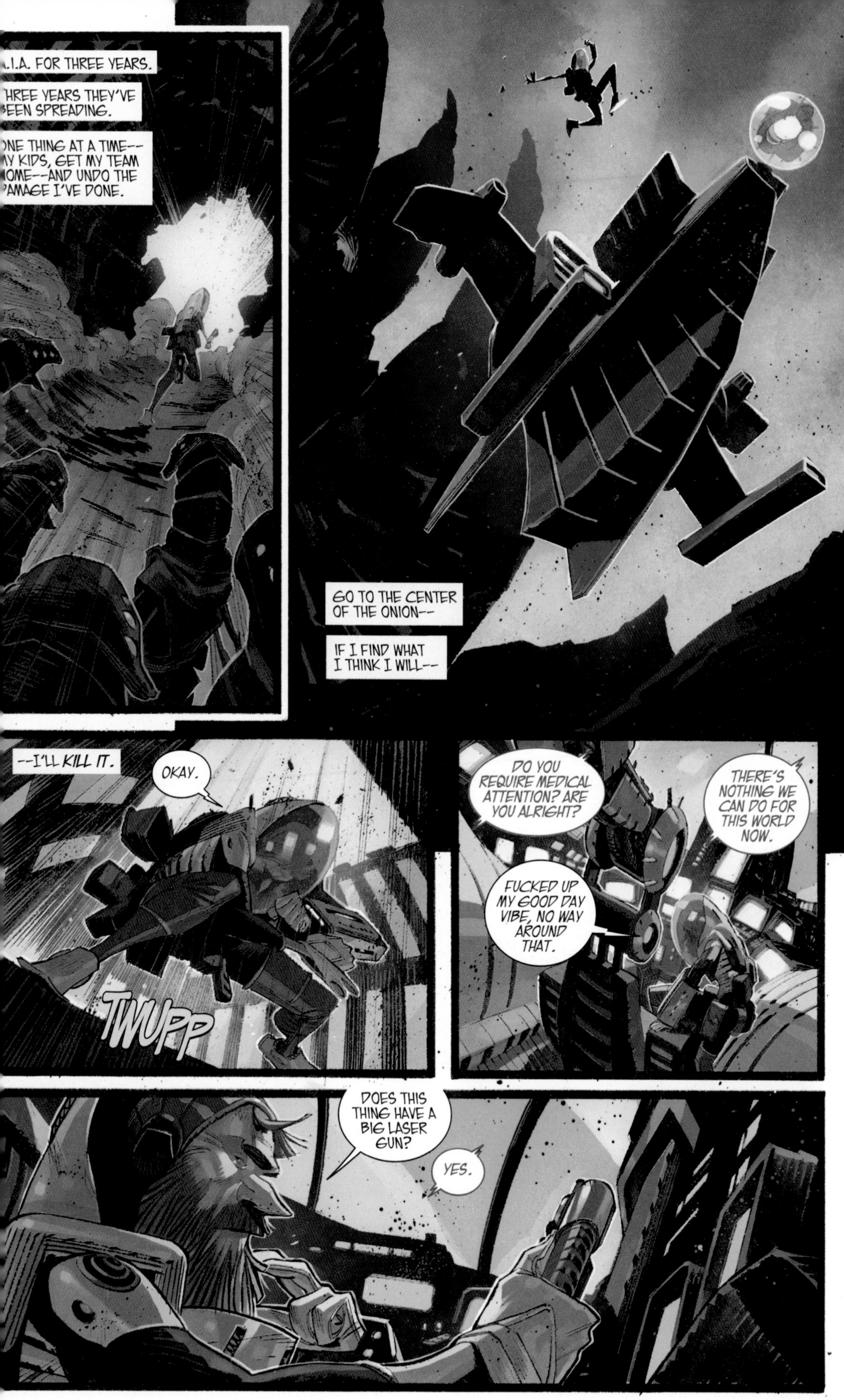

.I.A. FOR THREE YEARS.
THREE YEARS THEY'VE
BEEN SPREADING.
ONE THING AT A TIME--
MY KIDS, GET MY TEAM
HOME--AND UNDO THE
DAMAGE I'VE DONE.
GO TO THE CENTER OF THE ONION--
IF I FIND WHAT I THINK I WILL--
--I'LL KILL IT.
OKAY.
TWUPP
DO YOU REQUIRE MEDICAL ATTENTION? ARE YOU ALRIGHT?
THERE'S NOTHING WE CAN DO FOR THIS WORLD NOW.
FUCKED UP MY GOOD DAY VIBE, NO WAY AROUND THAT.
DOES THIS THING HAVE A BIG LASER GUN?
YES.

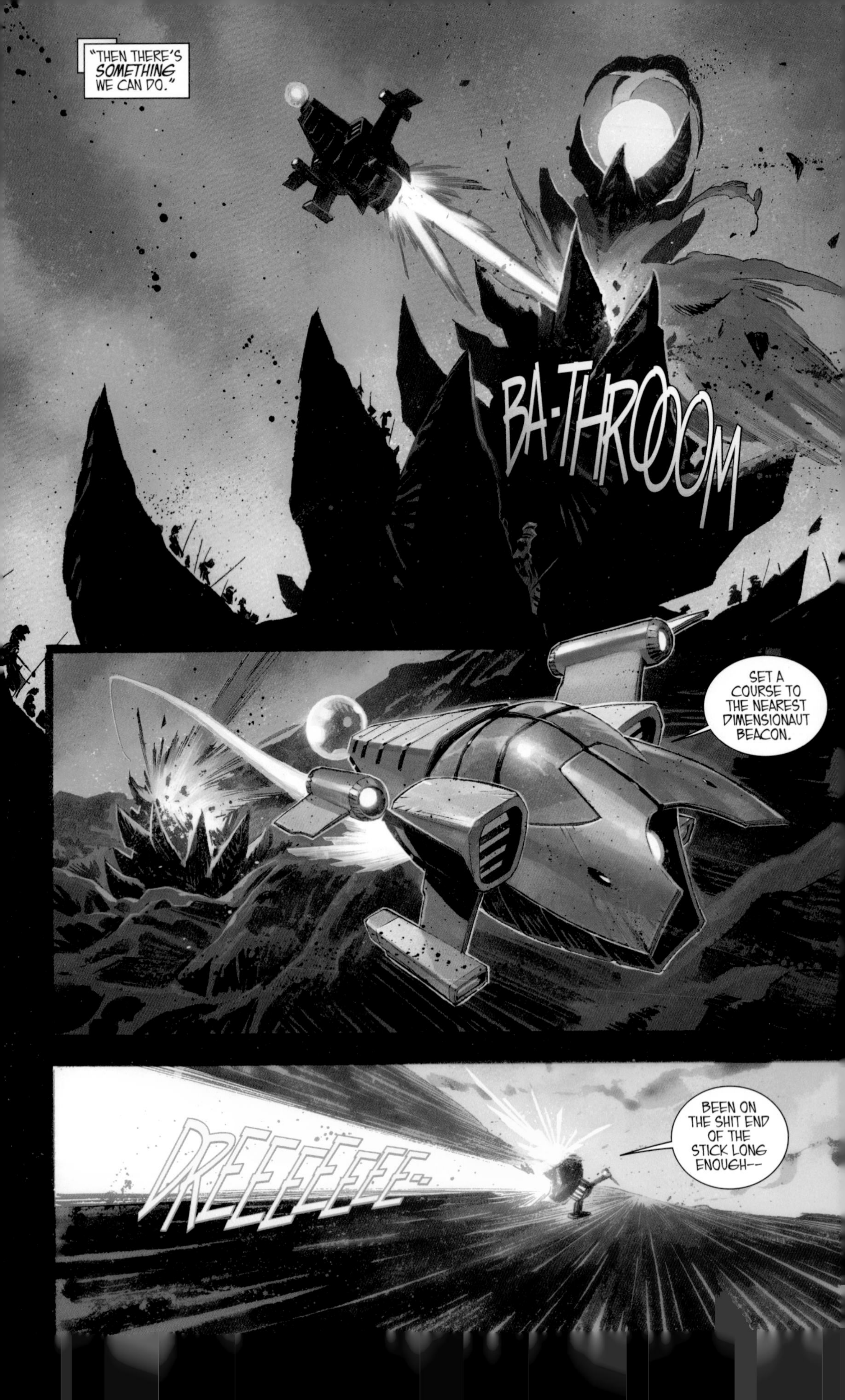
"THEN THERE'S SOMETHING WE CAN DO."
BA-THROOOM
SET A COURSE TO THE NEAREST DIMENSIONAUT BEACON.
DREEEEEEE--
BEEN ON THE SHIT END OF THE STICK LONG ENOUGH--

"--IT'S TIME TO GET
MY PEOPLE BACK."

21

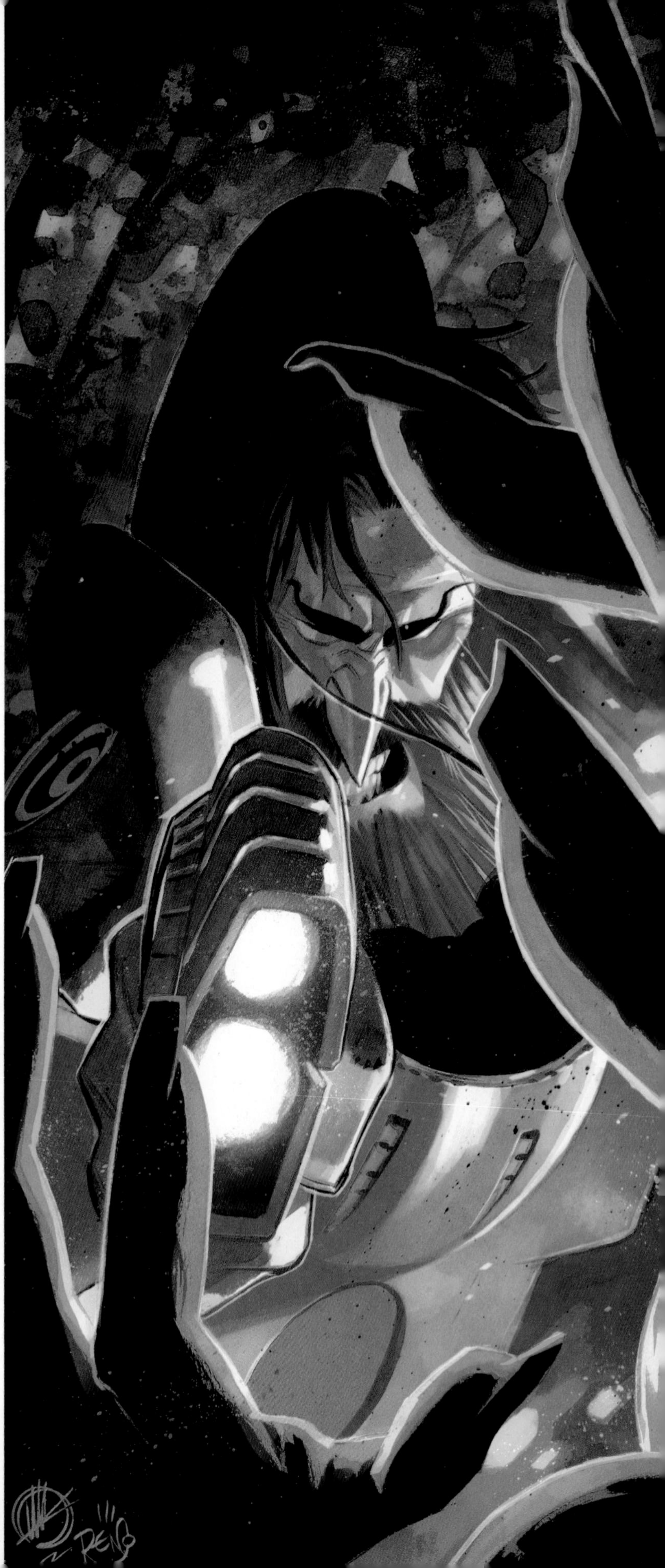

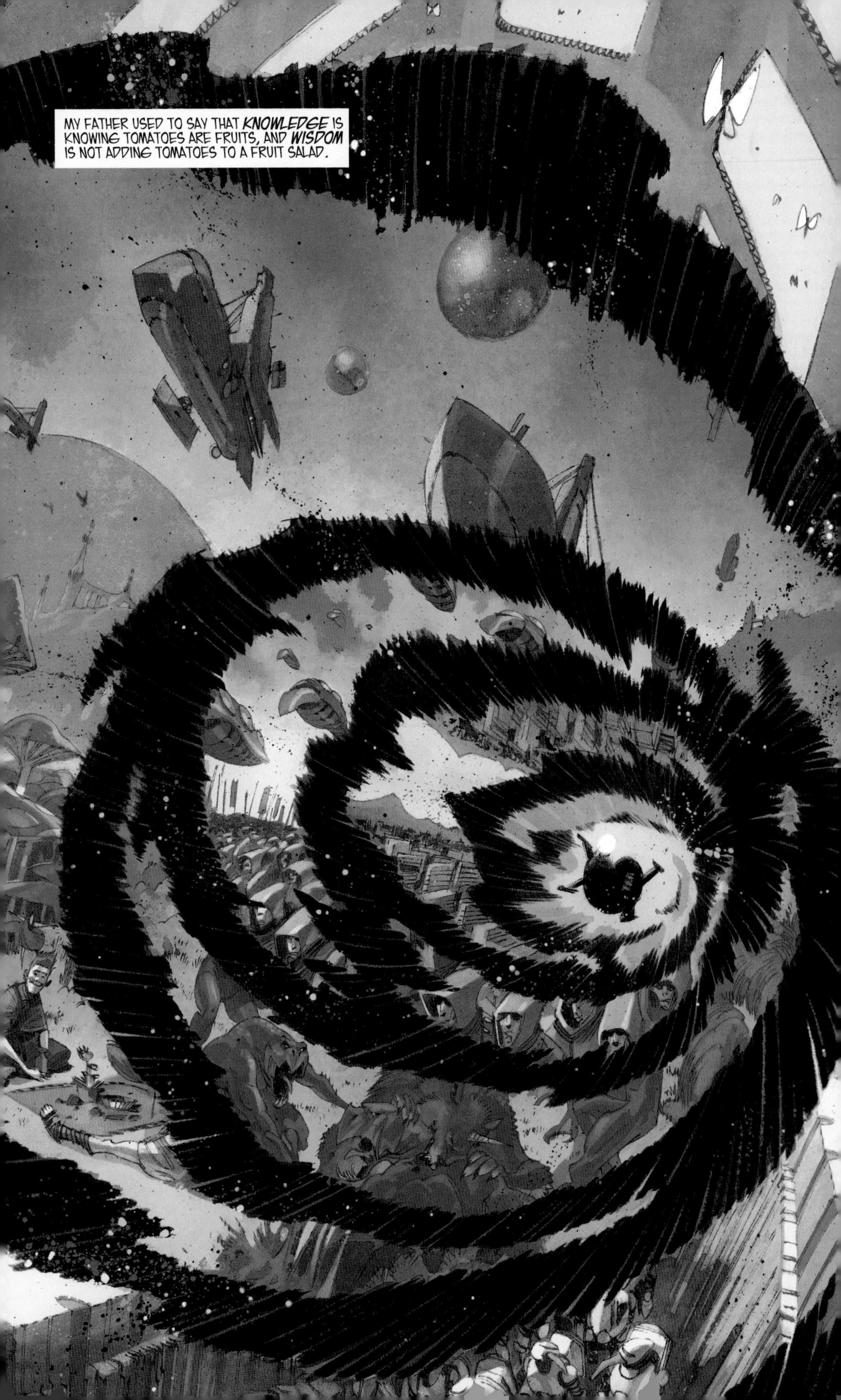
MY FATHER USED TO SAY THAT KNOWLEDGE IS KNOWING TOMATOES ARE FRUITS, AND WISDOM IS NOT ADDING TOMATOES TO A FRUIT SALAD.

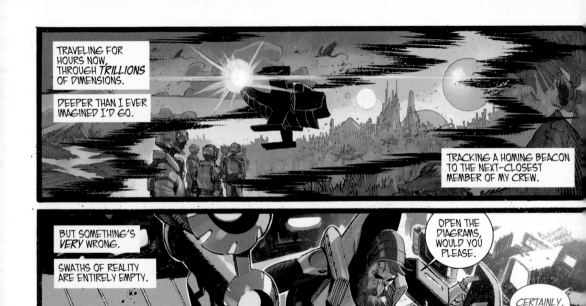

TRAVELING FOR HOURS NOW, THROUGH *TRILLIONS* OF DIMENSIONS.

DEEPER THAN I EVER IMAGINED I'D GO.

TRACKING A HOMING BEACON TO THE NEXT-CLOSEST MEMBER OF MY CREW.

BUT SOMETHING'S *VERY* WRONG.

SWATHS OF REALITY ARE ENTIRELY EMPTY.

OPEN THE DIAGRAMS, WOULD YOU PLEASE.

CERTAINLY.

I KNEW I'D MADE A MESS OF MY LIFE, BUT IF MY THEORY IS CORRECT...

...I'VE BEEN THROWING TOMATOES INTO *EVERYTHING*.

I'VE GOT SOME IDEAS ABOUT THE GIANT VOIDS WE'VE BEEN SEEING, HAL.

GRANT, I'M NOT SURE THIS NAME YOU'VE GIVEN ME IS APPROPRIATE--

THE NAME STAYS.

EVERY TIME THE PILLAR PUNCHES A HOLE TO ANOTHER DIMENSION, IT LEAVES A SMALL TEAR IN THE FIBER OF EACH REALITY.

A COSMIC UMBILICAL CORD, CONNECTING EVERY UNIVERSE WE'VE BEEN TO.

CORRECT.

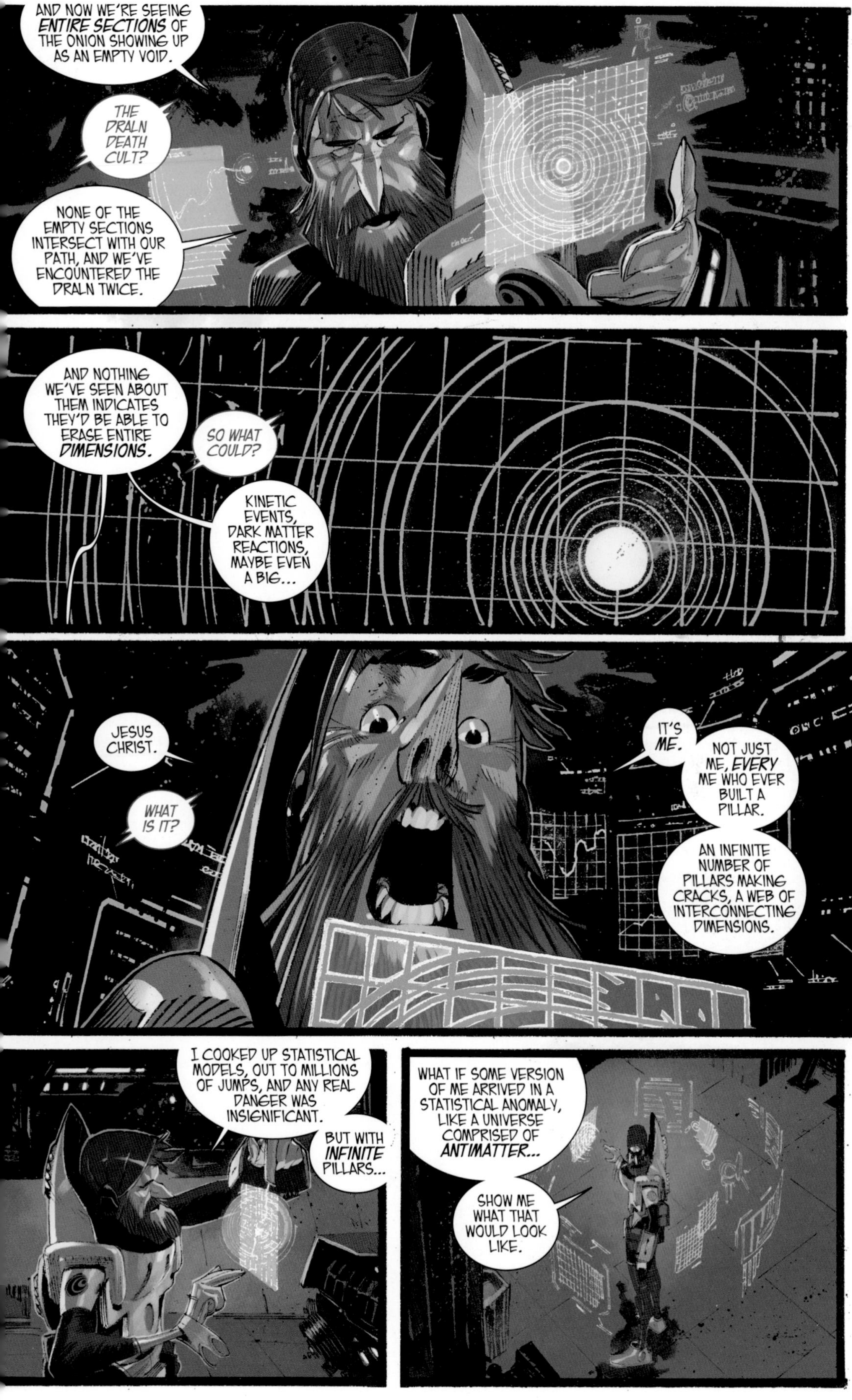

AND NOW WE'RE SEEING ENTIRE SECTIONS OF THE ONION SHOWING UP AS AN EMPTY VOID.
THE DRALN DEATH CULT?
NONE OF THE EMPTY SECTIONS INTERSECT WITH OUR PATH, AND WE'VE ENCOUNTERED THE DRALN TWICE.
AND NOTHING WE'VE SEEN ABOUT THEM INDICATES THEY'D BE ABLE TO ERASE ENTIRE DIMENSIONS.
SO WHAT COULD?
KINETIC EVENTS, DARK MATTER REACTIONS, MAYBE EVEN A BIG...
JESUS CHRIST.
WHAT IS IT?
IT'S ME.
NOT JUST ME, EVERY ME WHO EVER BUILT A PILLAR.
AN INFINITE NUMBER OF PILLARS MAKING CRACKS, A WEB OF INTERCONNECTING DIMENSIONS.
I COOKED UP STATISTICAL MODELS, OUT TO MILLIONS OF JUMPS, AND ANY REAL DANGER WAS INSIGNIFICANT.
BUT WITH INFINITE PILLARS...
WHAT IF SOME VERSION OF ME ARRIVED IN A STATISTICAL ANOMALY, LIKE A UNIVERSE COMPRISED OF ANTIMATTER...
SHOW ME WHAT THAT WOULD LOOK LIKE.

IN A MATTER-ANTIMATTER REACTION, ALL MATERIAL IS CONVERTED INTO ENERGY.

THE RESULTING ANNIHILATION WOULD WIDEN THE DIMENSIONAL TUNNEL AT THE POINT OF ENTRY.

THE BLAST WOULD TRAVEL THROUGH THE HOLES LEFT BEHIND BY THE PILLAR.

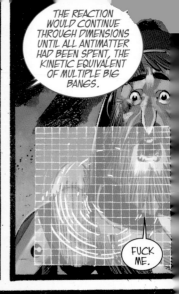

THE REACTION WOULD CONTINUE THROUGH DIMENSIONS UNTIL ALL ANTIMATTER HAD BEEN SPENT, THE KINETIC EQUIVALENT OF MULTIPLE BIG BANGS.

FUCK ME.

OKAY.

SO, EVERY JUMP WE ROLL THOSE DICE.

IS IT POSSIBLE TO DETECT IF WE ARE JUMPING INTO AN ANTIMATTER UNIVERSE BEFORE WE GET THERE?

THERE'S NO WAY TO DETECT ANYTHING OTHER THAN THE COORDINATES OF THE DIMENSION WE ARE TRAVELING TO.

I MEAN... THIS IS JUST TERRIBLY SHITTY NEWS. HOW DID I NOT CONSIDER THIS?

PERHAPS YOUR HEAVY USE OF MARIJUANA HAD AN ADVERSE IMPACT ON YOUR REASONING--

ALRIGHT. JUST PACK IT IN.

WELL, PEP UP, POT HEAD. I HAVE SOME GOOD NEWS.

WE'VE COMPLETED THE JUMP TO THE NEXT CREWMEMBER WITH NO CATASTROPHE...

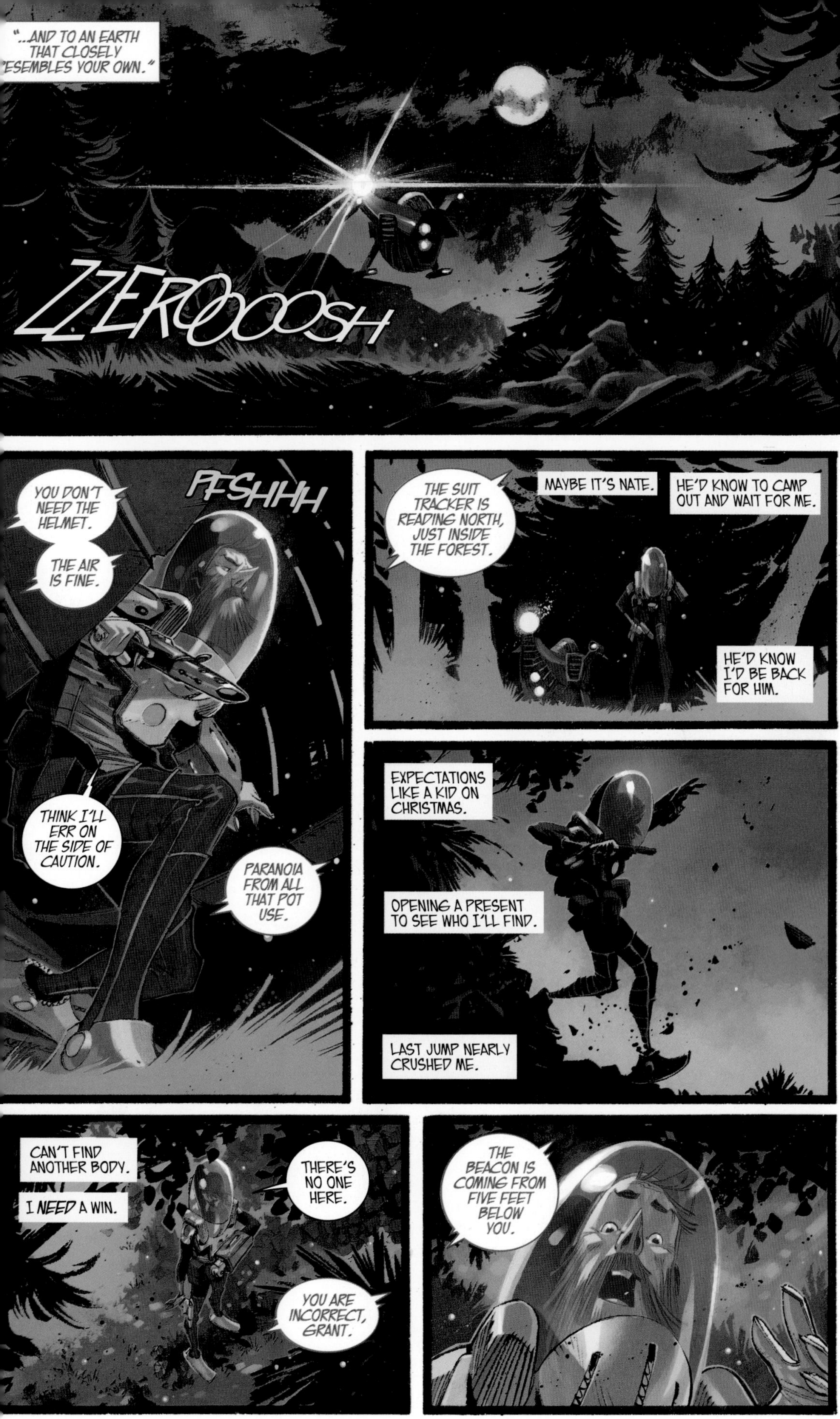
"...AND TO AN EARTH THAT CLOSELY RESEMBLES YOUR OWN."
ZZEROOOOOSH
PFSHHH
YOU DON'T NEED THE HELMET.
THE AIR IS FINE.
THINK I'LL ERR ON THE SIDE OF CAUTION.
PARANOIA FROM ALL THAT POT USE.
THE SUIT TRACKER IS READING NORTH, JUST INSIDE THE FOREST.
MAYBE IT'S NATE.
HE'D KNOW TO CAMP OUT AND WAIT FOR ME.
HE'D KNOW I'D BE BACK FOR HIM.
EXPECTATIONS LIKE A KID ON CHRISTMAS.
OPENING A PRESENT TO SEE WHO I'LL FIND.
LAST JUMP NEARLY CRUSHED ME.
CAN'T FIND ANOTHER BODY.
I NEED A WIN.
THERE'S NO ONE HERE.
YOU ARE INCORRECT, GRANT.
THE BEACON IS COMING FROM FIVE FEET BELOW YOU.

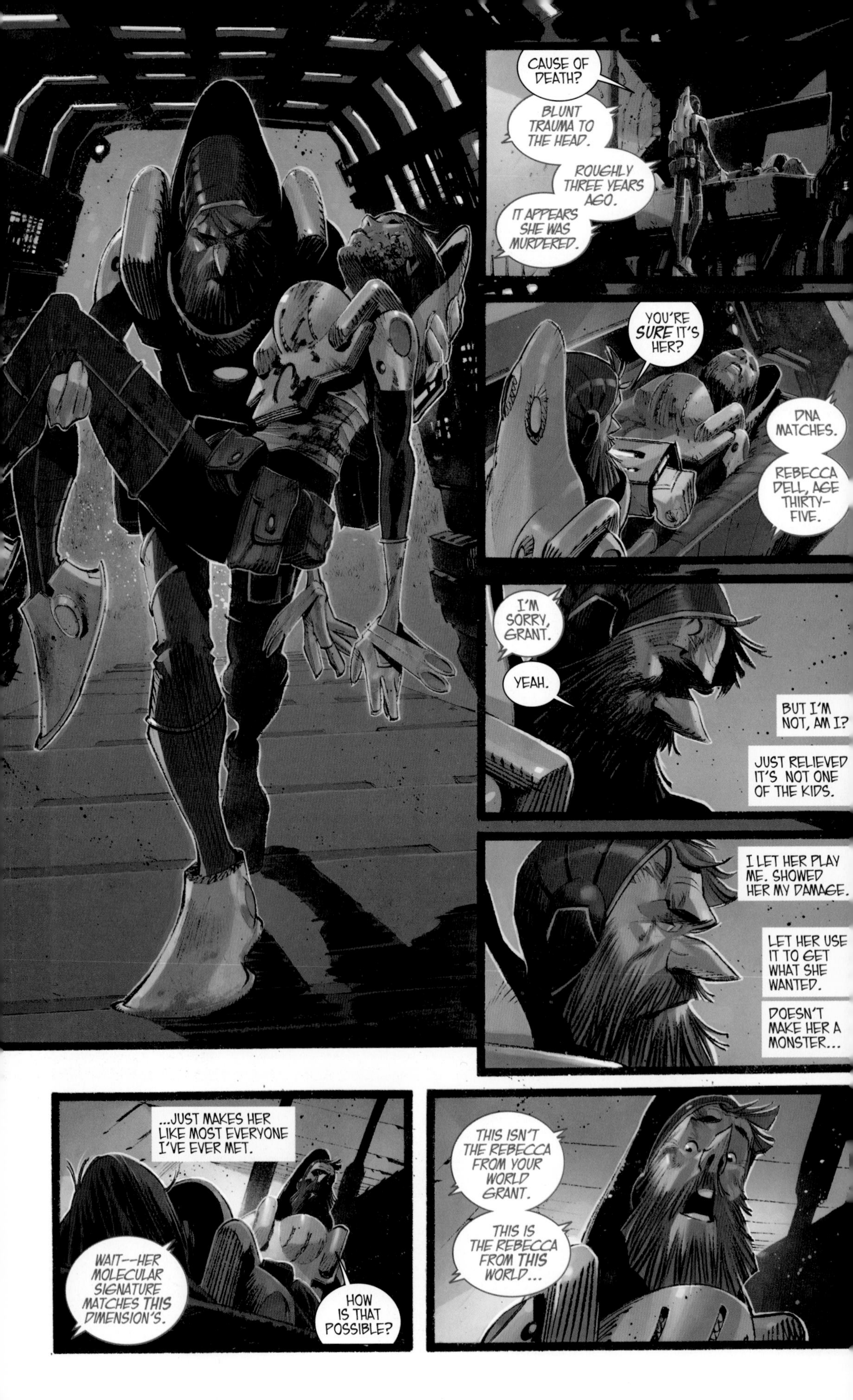
CAUSE OF DEATH?
BLUNT TRAUMA TO THE HEAD.
ROUGHLY THREE YEARS AGO.
IT APPEARS SHE WAS MURDERED.
YOU'RE SURE IT'S HER?
DNA MATCHES.
REBECCA DELL, AGE THIRTY-FIVE.
I'M SORRY, GRANT.
YEAH.
BUT I'M NOT, AM I?
JUST RELIEVED IT'S NOT ONE OF THE KIDS.
I LET HER PLAY ME. SHOWED HER MY DAMAGE.
LET HER USE IT TO GET WHAT SHE WANTED.
DOESN'T MAKE HER A MONSTER...
...JUST MAKES HER LIKE MOST EVERYONE I'VE EVER MET.
WAIT--HER MOLECULAR SIGNATURE MATCHES THIS DIMENSION'S.
HOW IS THAT POSSIBLE?
THIS ISN'T THE REBECCA FROM YOUR WORLD GRANT.
THIS IS THE REBECCA FROM THIS WORLD...

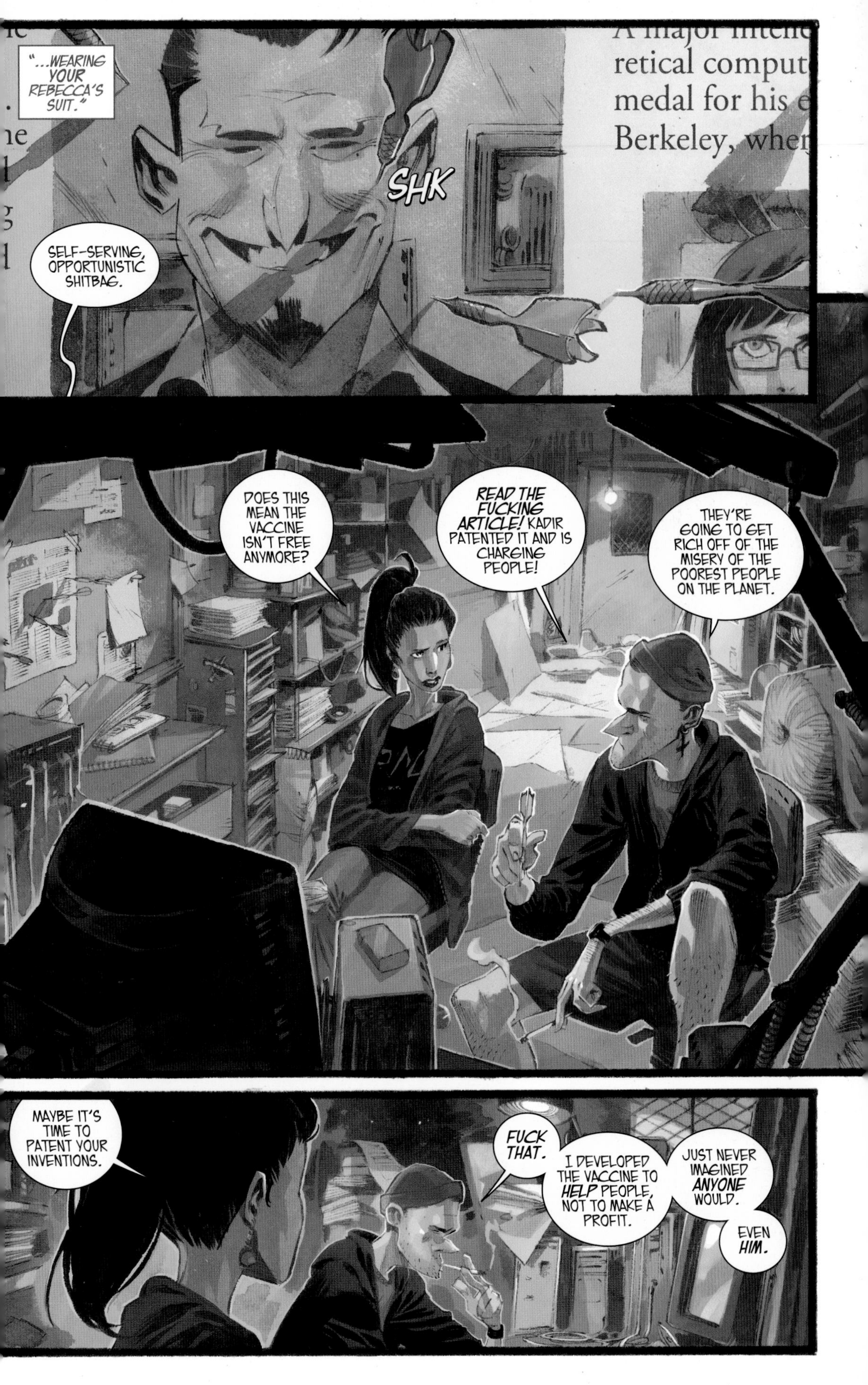
"...WEARING YOUR REBECCA'S SUIT."
SHK
SELF-SERVING, OPPORTUNISTIC SHITBAG.
DOES THIS MEAN THE VACCINE ISN'T FREE ANYMORE?
READ THE FUCKING ARTICLE! KADIR PATENTED IT AND IS CHARGING PEOPLE!
THEY'RE GOING TO GET RICH OFF OF THE MISERY OF THE POOREST PEOPLE ON THE PLANET.
MAYBE IT'S TIME TO PATENT YOUR INVENTIONS.
FUCK THAT.
I DEVELOPED THE VACCINE TO HELP PEOPLE, NOT TO MAKE A PROFIT.
JUST NEVER IMAGINED ANYONE WOULD.
EVEN HIM.

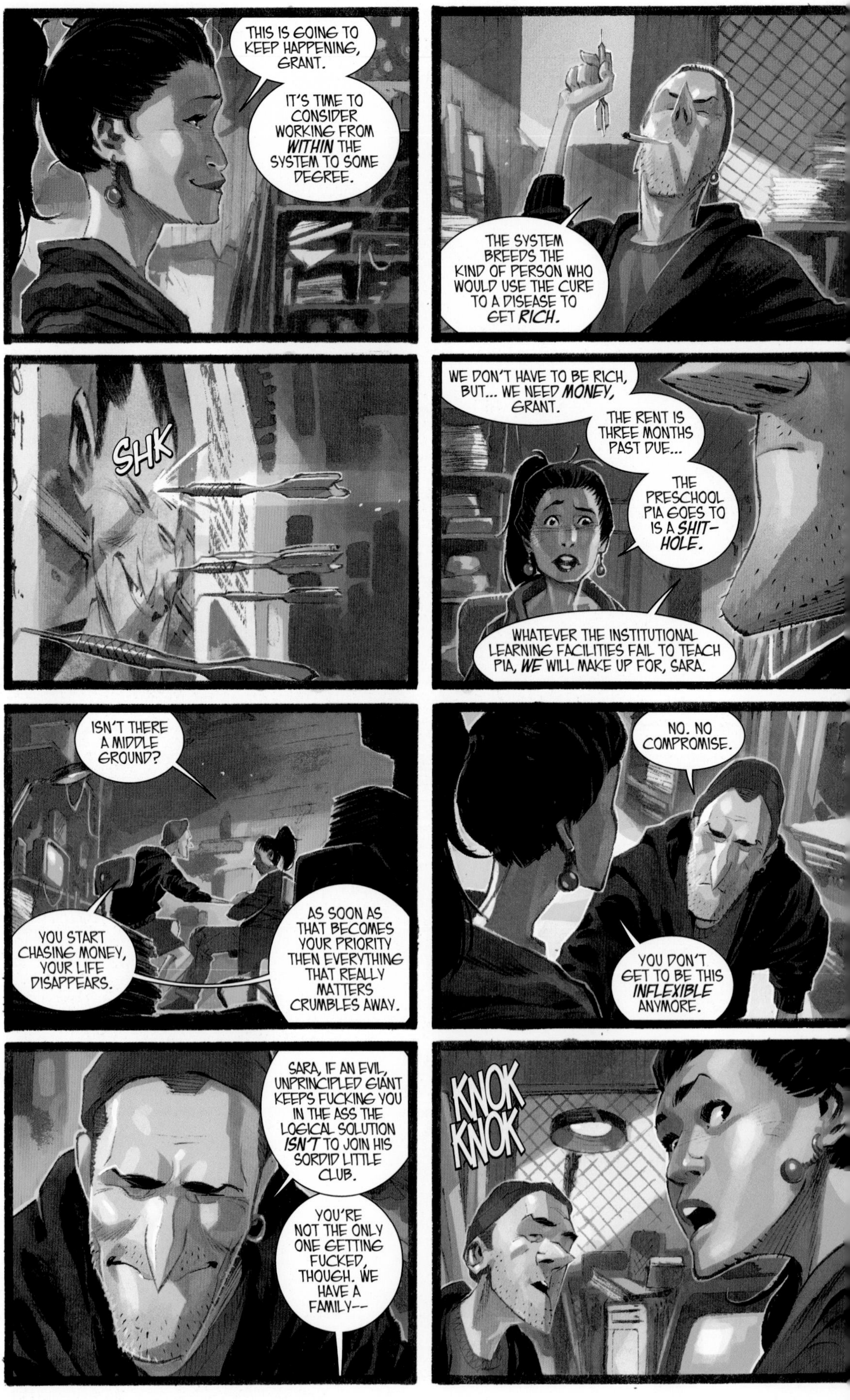
THIS IS GOING TO KEEP HAPPENING, GRANT.
IT'S TIME TO CONSIDER WORKING FROM WITHIN THE SYSTEM TO SOME DEGREE.
THE SYSTEM BREEDS THE KIND OF PERSON WHO WOULD USE THE CURE TO A DISEASE TO GET RICH.
SHK
WE DON'T HAVE TO BE RICH, BUT... WE NEED MONEY, GRANT.
THE RENT IS THREE MONTHS PAST DUE...
THE PRESCHOOL PIA GOES TO IS A SHIT-HOLE.
WHATEVER THE INSTITUTIONAL LEARNING FACILITIES FAIL TO TEACH PIA, WE WILL MAKE UP FOR, SARA.
ISN'T THERE A MIDDLE GROUND?
YOU START CHASING MONEY, YOUR LIFE DISAPPEARS.
AS SOON AS THAT BECOMES YOUR PRIORITY THEN EVERYTHING THAT REALLY MATTERS CRUMBLES AWAY.
NO. NO COMPROMISE.
YOU DON'T GET TO BE THIS INFLEXIBLE ANYMORE.
SARA, IF AN EVIL, UNPRINCIPLED GIANT KEEPS FUCKING YOU IN THE ASS THE LOGICAL SOLUTION ISN'T TO JOIN HIS SORDID LITTLE CLUB.
YOU'RE NOT THE ONLY ONE GETTING FUCKED, THOUGH. WE HAVE A FAMILY--
KNOK KNOK

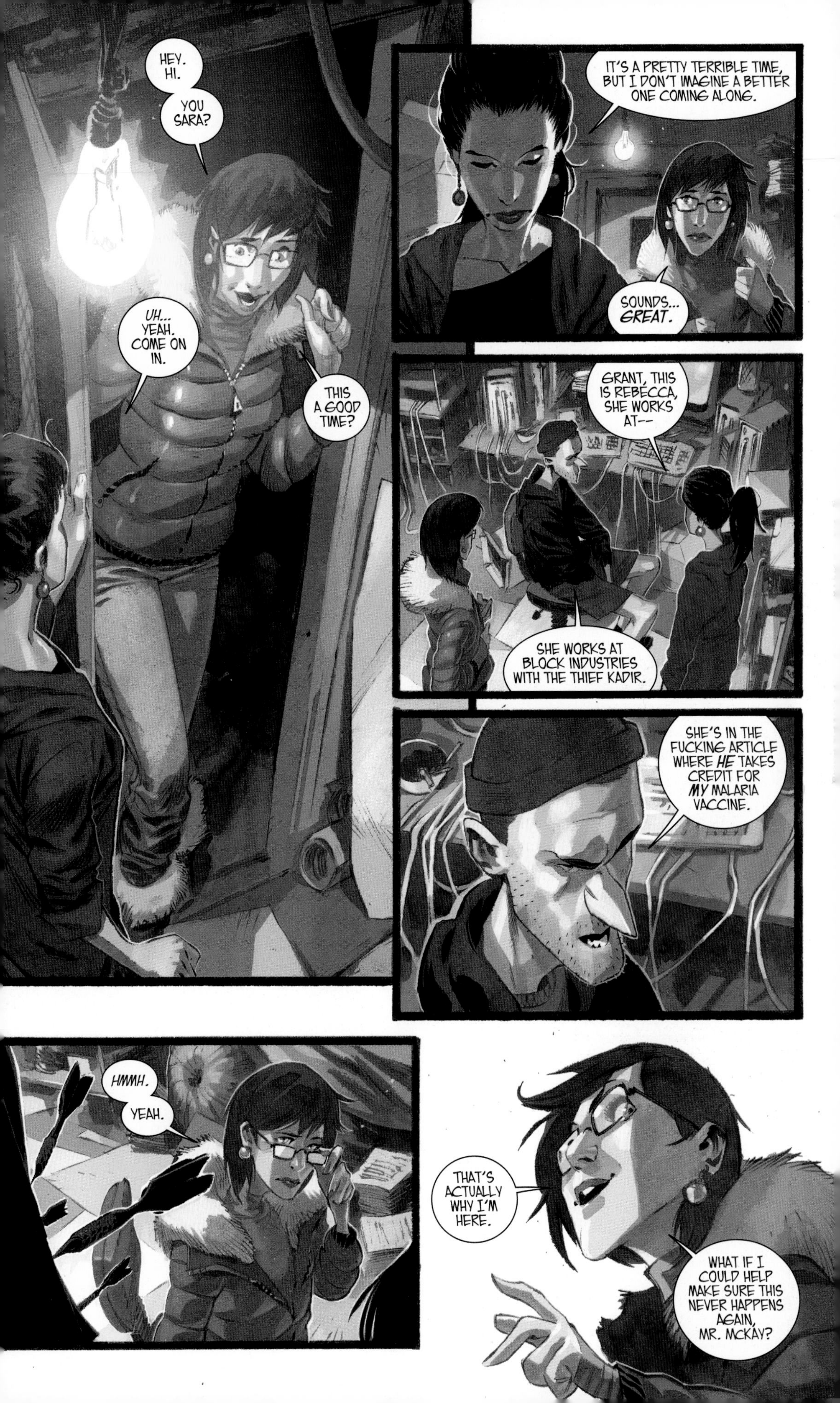

HEY. HI.
YOU SARA?
UH... YEAH. COME ON IN.
THIS A GOOD TIME?
IT'S A PRETTY TERRIBLE TIME, BUT I DON'T IMAGINE A BETTER ONE COMING ALONG.
SOUNDS... GREAT.
GRANT, THIS IS REBECCA, SHE WORKS AT--
SHE WORKS AT BLOCK INDUSTRIES WITH THE THIEF KADIR.
SHE'S IN THE FUCKING ARTICLE WHERE HE TAKES CREDIT FOR MY MALARIA VACCINE.
HMMH.
YEAH.
THAT'S ACTUALLY WHY I'M HERE.
WHAT IF I COULD HELP MAKE SURE THIS NEVER HAPPENS AGAIN, MR. MCKAY?

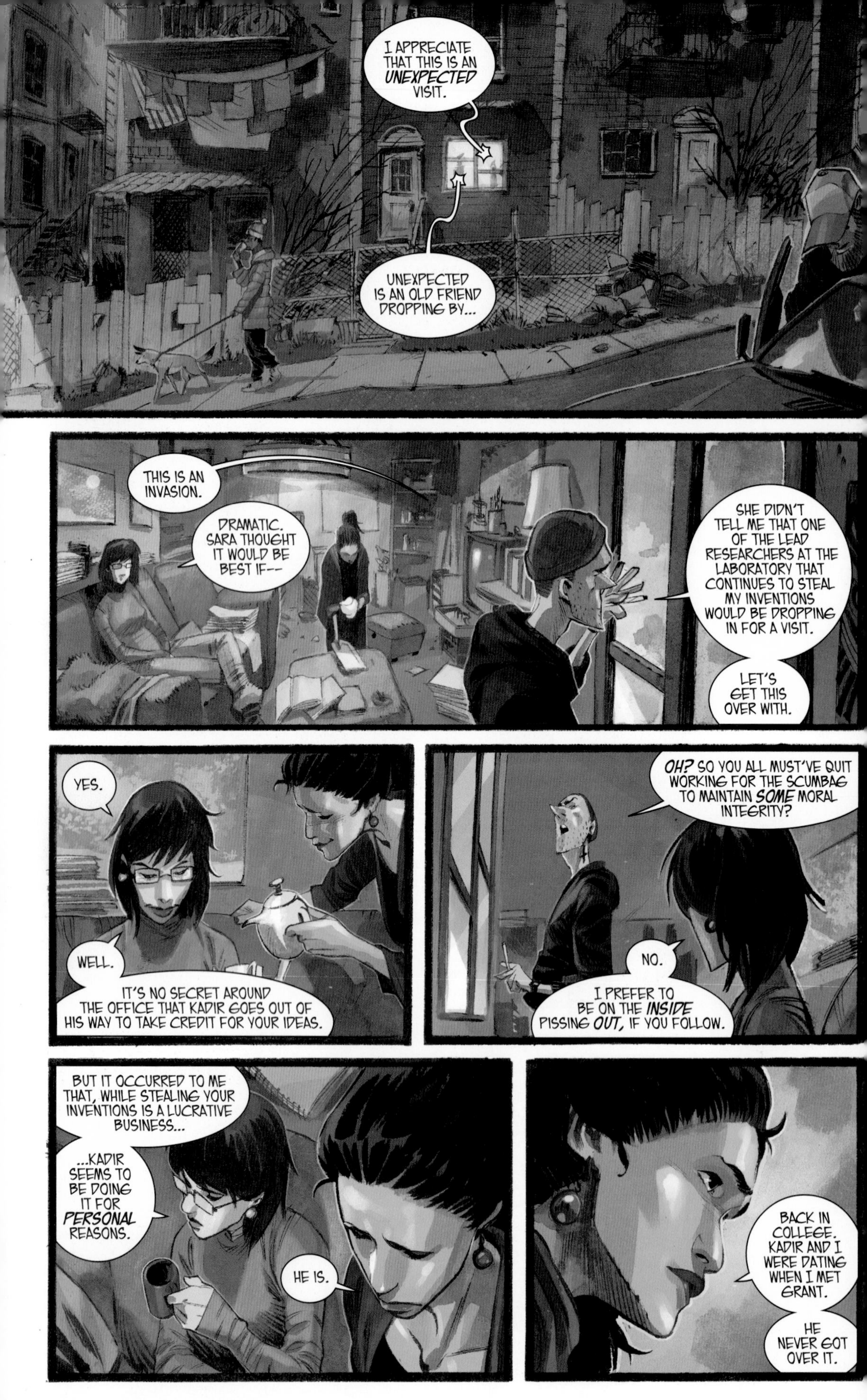
I APPRECIATE THAT THIS IS AN UNEXPECTED VISIT.
UNEXPECTED IS AN OLD FRIEND DROPPING BY...
THIS IS AN INVASION.
DRAMATIC. SARA THOUGHT IT WOULD BE BEST IF--
SHE DIDN'T TELL ME THAT ONE OF THE LEAD RESEARCHERS AT THE LABORATORY THAT CONTINUES TO STEAL MY INVENTIONS WOULD BE DROPPING IN FOR A VISIT.
LET'S GET THIS OVER WITH.
YES.
WELL.
IT'S NO SECRET AROUND THE OFFICE THAT KADIR GOES OUT OF HIS WAY TO TAKE CREDIT FOR YOUR IDEAS.
OH? SO YOU ALL MUST'VE QUIT WORKING FOR THE SCUMBAG TO MAINTAIN SOME MORAL INTEGRITY?
NO.
I PREFER TO BE ON THE INSIDE PISSING OUT, IF YOU FOLLOW.
BUT IT OCCURRED TO ME THAT, WHILE STEALING YOUR INVENTIONS IS A LUCRATIVE BUSINESS...
...KADIR SEEMS TO BE DOING IT FOR PERSONAL REASONS.
HE IS.
BACK IN COLLEGE. KADIR AND I WERE DATING WHEN I MET GRANT.
HE NEVER GOT OVER IT.

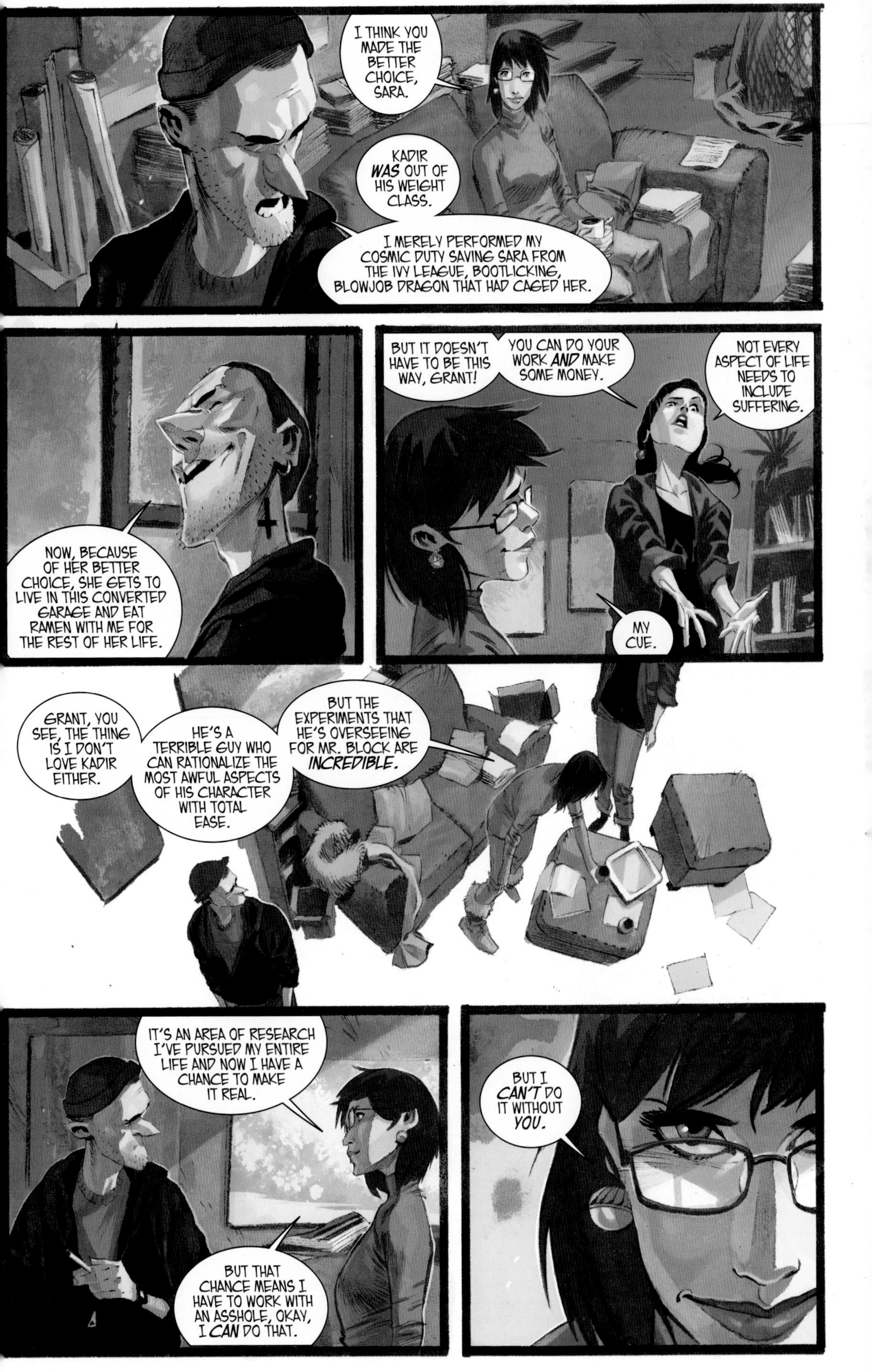

I THINK YOU MADE THE BETTER CHOICE, SARA.
KADIR WAS OUT OF HIS WEIGHT CLASS.
I MERELY PERFORMED MY COSMIC DUTY SAVING SARA FROM THE IVY LEAGUE, BOOTLICKING, BLOWJOB DRAGON THAT HAD CAGED HER.
NOW, BECAUSE OF HER BETTER CHOICE, SHE GETS TO LIVE IN THIS CONVERTED GARAGE AND EAT RAMEN WITH ME FOR THE REST OF HER LIFE.
MY CUE.
BUT IT DOESN'T HAVE TO BE THIS WAY, GRANT!
YOU CAN DO YOUR WORK AND MAKE SOME MONEY.
NOT EVERY ASPECT OF LIFE NEEDS TO INCLUDE SUFFERING.
GRANT, YOU SEE, THE THING IS I DON'T LOVE KADIR EITHER.
HE'S A TERRIBLE GUY WHO CAN RATIONALIZE THE MOST AWFUL ASPECTS OF HIS CHARACTER WITH TOTAL EASE.
BUT THE EXPERIMENTS THAT HE'S OVERSEEING FOR MR. BLOCK ARE INCREDIBLE.
IT'S AN AREA OF RESEARCH I'VE PURSUED MY ENTIRE LIFE AND NOW I HAVE A CHANCE TO MAKE IT REAL.
BUT THAT CHANCE MEANS I HAVE TO WORK WITH AN ASSHOLE, OKAY, I CAN DO THAT.
BUT I CAN'T DO IT WITHOUT YOU.

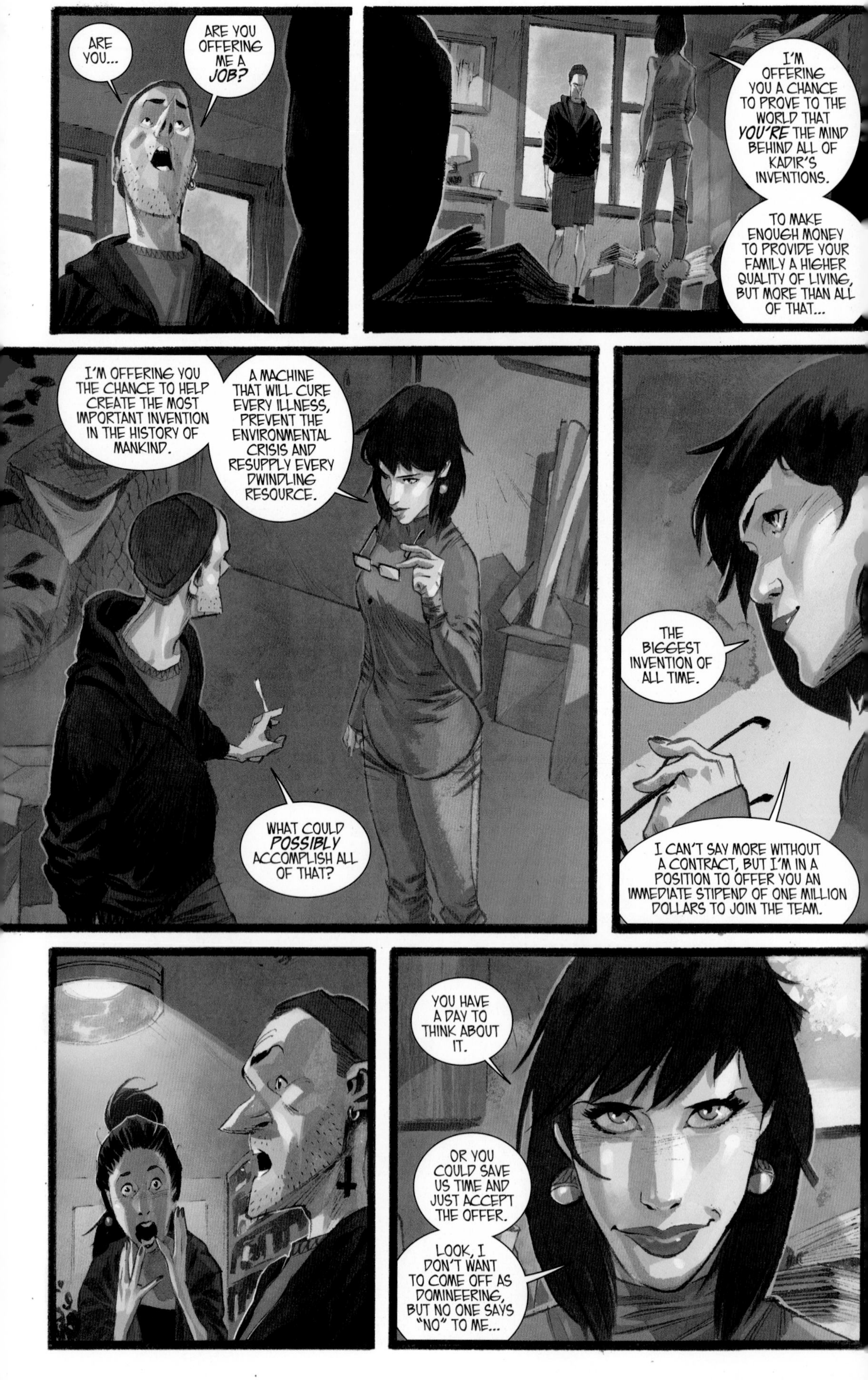
ARE YOU...
ARE YOU OFFERING ME A *JOB?*
I'M OFFERING YOU A CHANCE TO PROVE TO THE WORLD THAT *YOU'RE* THE MIND BEHIND ALL OF KADIR'S INVENTIONS.
TO MAKE ENOUGH MONEY TO PROVIDE YOUR FAMILY A HIGHER QUALITY OF LIVING, BUT MORE THAN ALL OF THAT...
I'M OFFERING YOU THE CHANCE TO HELP CREATE THE MOST IMPORTANT INVENTION IN THE HISTORY OF MANKIND.
A MACHINE THAT WILL CURE EVERY ILLNESS, PREVENT THE ENVIRONMENTAL CRISIS AND RESUPPLY EVERY DWINDLING RESOURCE.
WHAT COULD *POSSIBLY* ACCOMPLISH ALL OF THAT?
THE BIGGEST INVENTION OF ALL TIME.
I CAN'T SAY MORE WITHOUT A CONTRACT, BUT I'M IN A POSITION TO OFFER YOU AN IMMEDIATE STIPEND OF ONE MILLION DOLLARS TO JOIN THE TEAM.
YOU HAVE A DAY TO THINK ABOUT IT.
OR YOU COULD SAVE US TIME AND JUST ACCEPT THE OFFER.
LOOK, I DON'T WANT TO COME OFF AS DOMINEERING, BUT NO ONE SAYS "NO" TO ME...

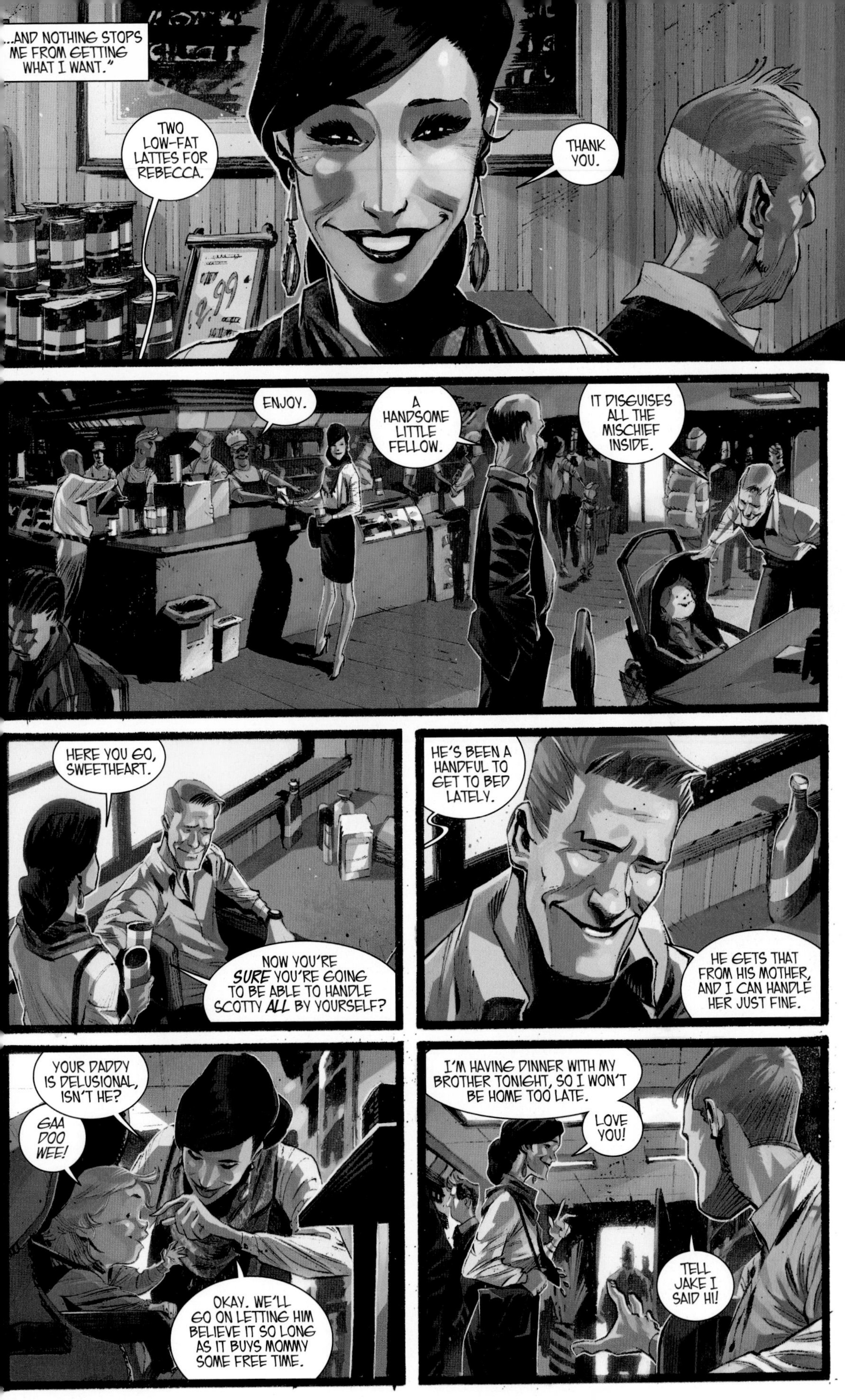
"...AND NOTHING STOPS ME FROM GETTING WHAT I WANT."
TWO LOW-FAT LATTES FOR REBECCA.
THANK YOU.
ENJOY.
A HANDSOME LITTLE FELLOW.
IT DISGUISES ALL THE MISCHIEF INSIDE.
HERE YOU GO, SWEETHEART.
NOW YOU'RE *SURE* YOU'RE GOING TO BE ABLE TO HANDLE SCOTTY *ALL* BY YOURSELF?
HE'S BEEN A HANDFUL TO GET TO BED LATELY.
HE GETS THAT FROM HIS MOTHER, AND I CAN HANDLE HER JUST FINE.
YOUR DADDY IS DELUSIONAL, ISN'T HE?
GAA DOO WEE!
OKAY. WE'LL GO ON LETTING HIM BELIEVE IT SO LONG AS IT BUYS MOMMY SOME FREE TIME.
I'M HAVING DINNER WITH MY BROTHER TONIGHT, SO I WON'T BE HOME TOO LATE.
LOVE YOU!
TELL JAKE I SAID HI!

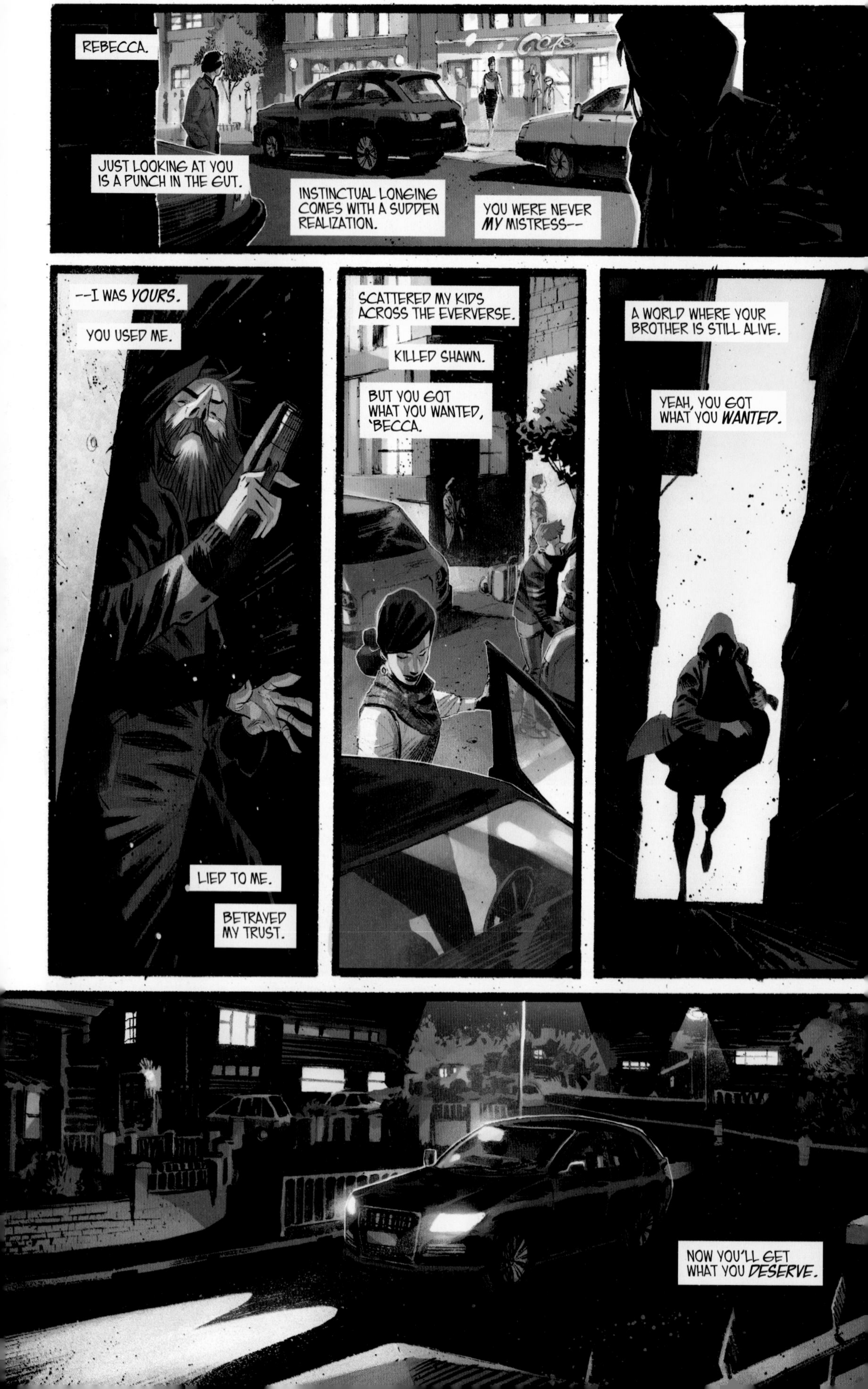
REBECCA.
JUST LOOKING AT YOU IS A PUNCH IN THE GUT.
INSTINCTUAL LONGING COMES WITH A SUDDEN REALIZATION.
YOU WERE NEVER MY MISTRESS--
--I WAS YOURS.
YOU USED ME.
LIED TO ME.
BETRAYED MY TRUST.
SCATTERED MY KIDS ACROSS THE EVERVERSE.
KILLED SHAWN.
BUT YOU GOT WHAT YOU WANTED, 'BECCA.
A WORLD WHERE YOUR BROTHER IS STILL ALIVE.
YEAH, YOU GOT WHAT YOU WANTED.
NOW YOU'LL GET WHAT YOU DESERVE.

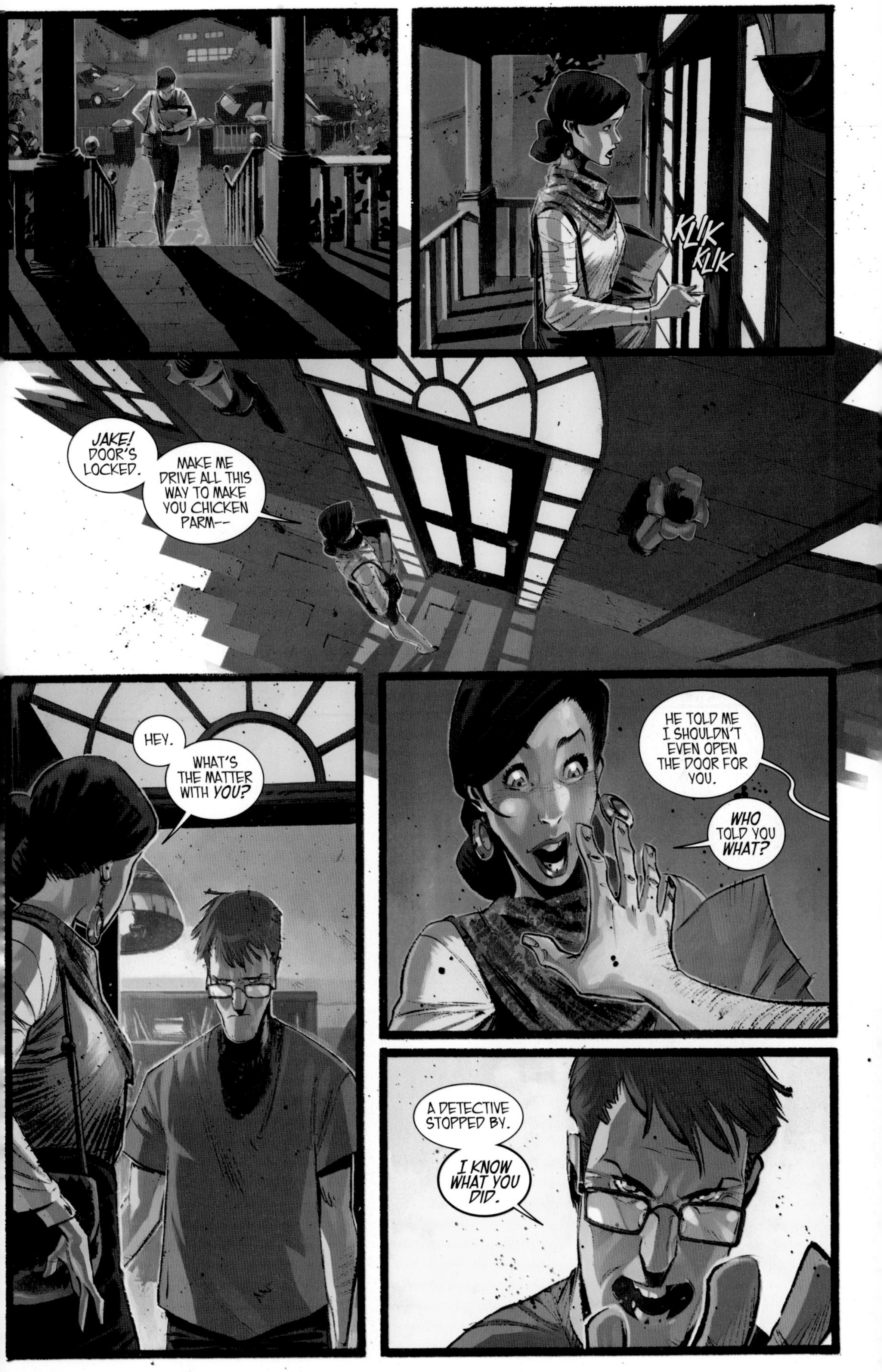
KLIK KLIK
JAKE! DOOR'S LOCKED.
MAKE ME DRIVE ALL THIS WAY TO MAKE YOU CHICKEN PARM--
HEY.
WHAT'S THE MATTER WITH YOU?
HE TOLD ME I SHOULDN'T EVEN OPEN THE DOOR FOR YOU.
WHO TOLD YOU WHAT?
A DETECTIVE STOPPED BY.
I KNOW WHAT YOU DID.

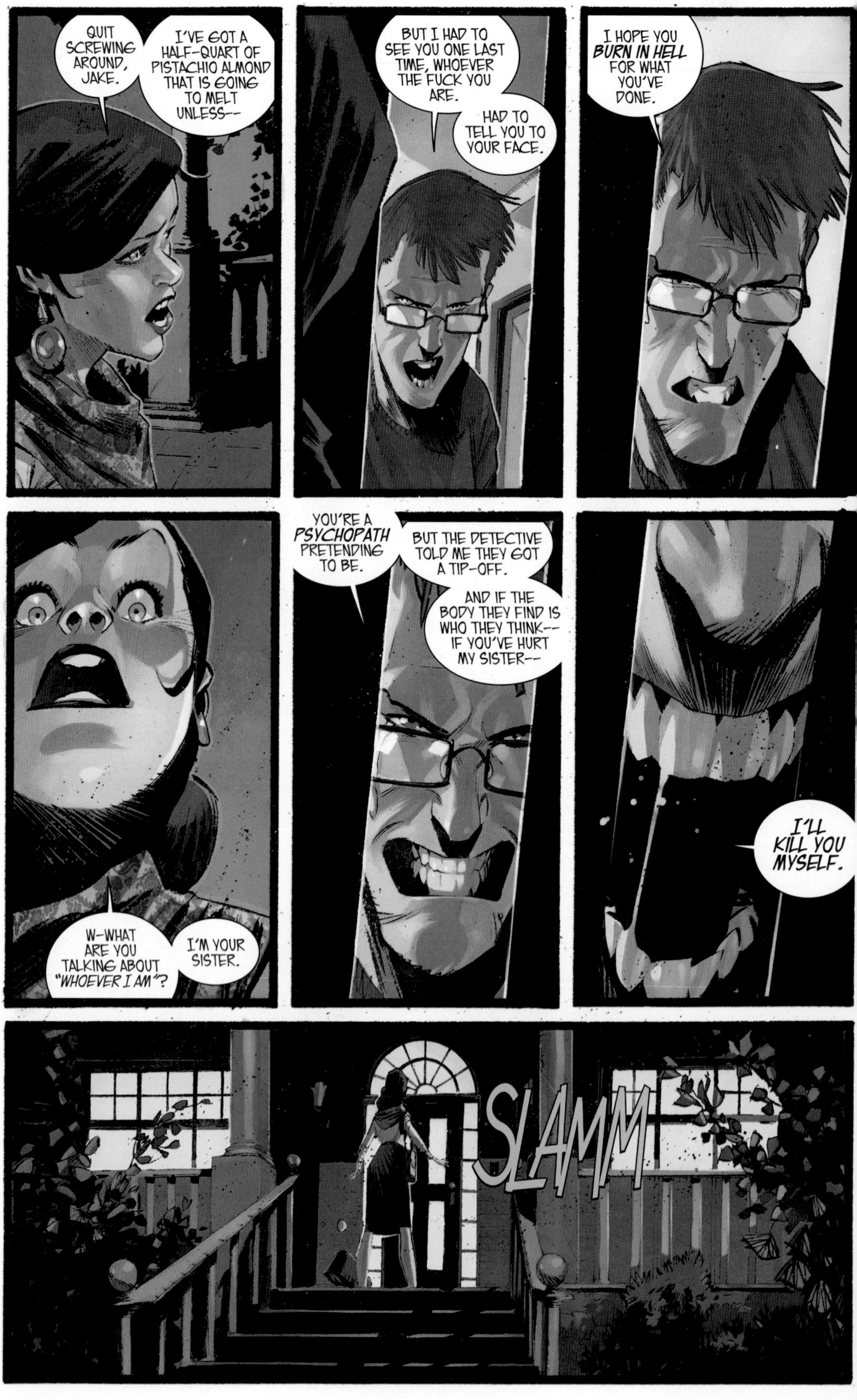
QUIT SCREWING AROUND, JAKE.
I'VE GOT A HALF-QUART OF PISTACHIO ALMOND THAT IS GOING TO MELT UNLESS--
BUT I HAD TO SEE YOU ONE LAST TIME, WHOEVER THE FUCK YOU ARE.
HAD TO TELL YOU TO YOUR FACE.
I HOPE YOU *BURN IN HELL* FOR WHAT YOU'VE DONE.
W-WHAT ARE YOU TALKING ABOUT "*WHOEVER I AM*"?
I'M YOUR SISTER.
YOU'RE A *PSYCHOPATH* PRETENDING TO BE.
BUT THE DETECTIVE TOLD ME THEY GOT A TIP-OFF.
AND IF THE BODY THEY FIND IS WHO THEY THINK-- IF YOU'VE HURT MY SISTER--
I'LL KILL YOU MYSELF.
SLAMM

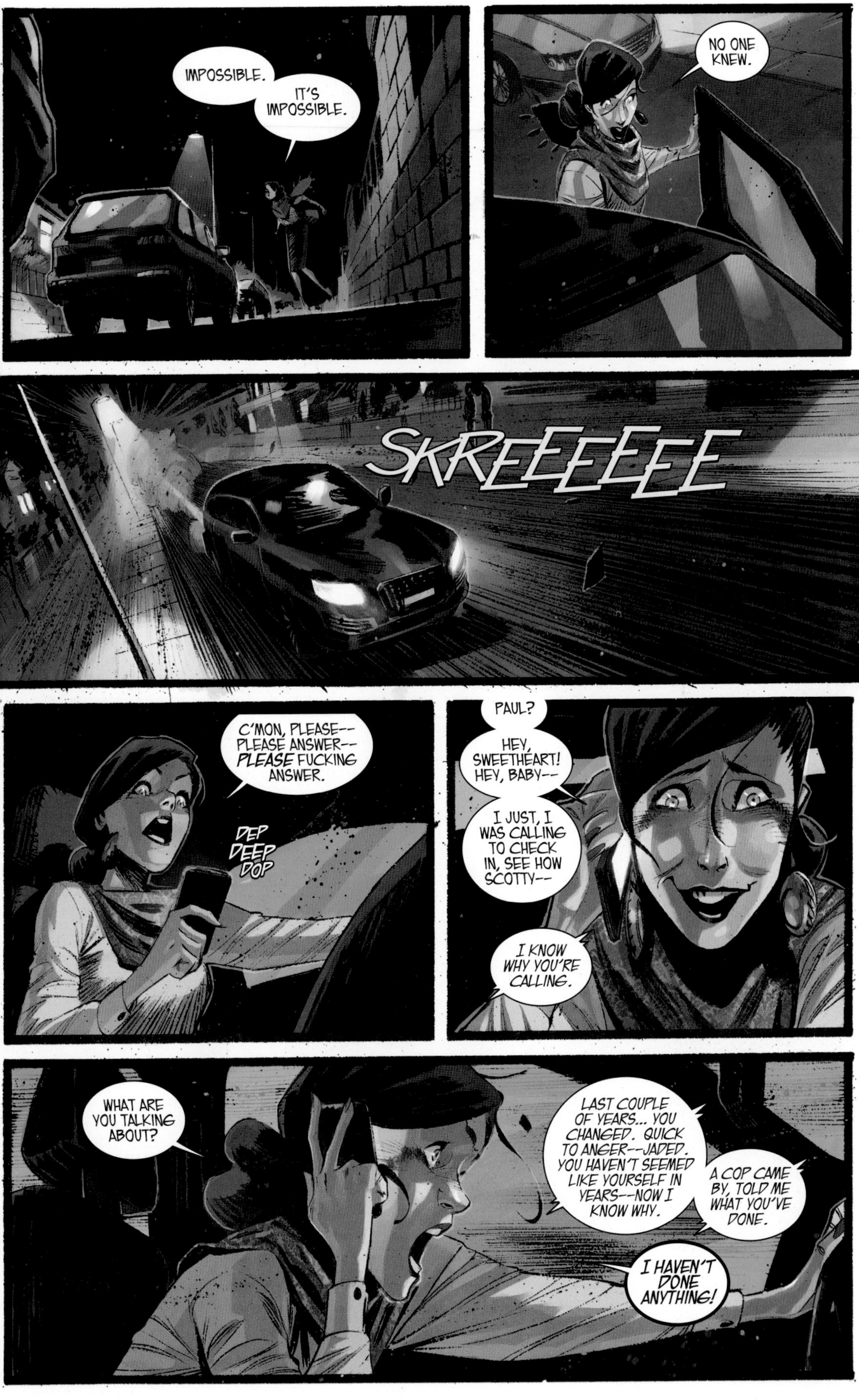
IMPOSSIBLE.
IT'S IMPOSSIBLE.
NO ONE KNEW.
SKREEEEEEE
C'MON, PLEASE-- PLEASE ANSWER-- PLEASE FUCKING ANSWER.
DEP DEEP DOP
PAUL?
HEY, SWEETHEART! HEY, BABY--
I JUST, I WAS CALLING TO CHECK IN, SEE HOW SCOTTY--
I KNOW WHY YOU'RE CALLING.
WHAT ARE YOU TALKING ABOUT?
LAST COUPLE OF YEARS... YOU CHANGED. QUICK TO ANGER--JADED. YOU HAVEN'T SEEMED LIKE YOURSELF IN YEARS--NOW I KNOW WHY.
A COP CAME BY, TOLD ME WHAT YOU'VE DONE.
I HAVEN'T DONE ANYTHING!

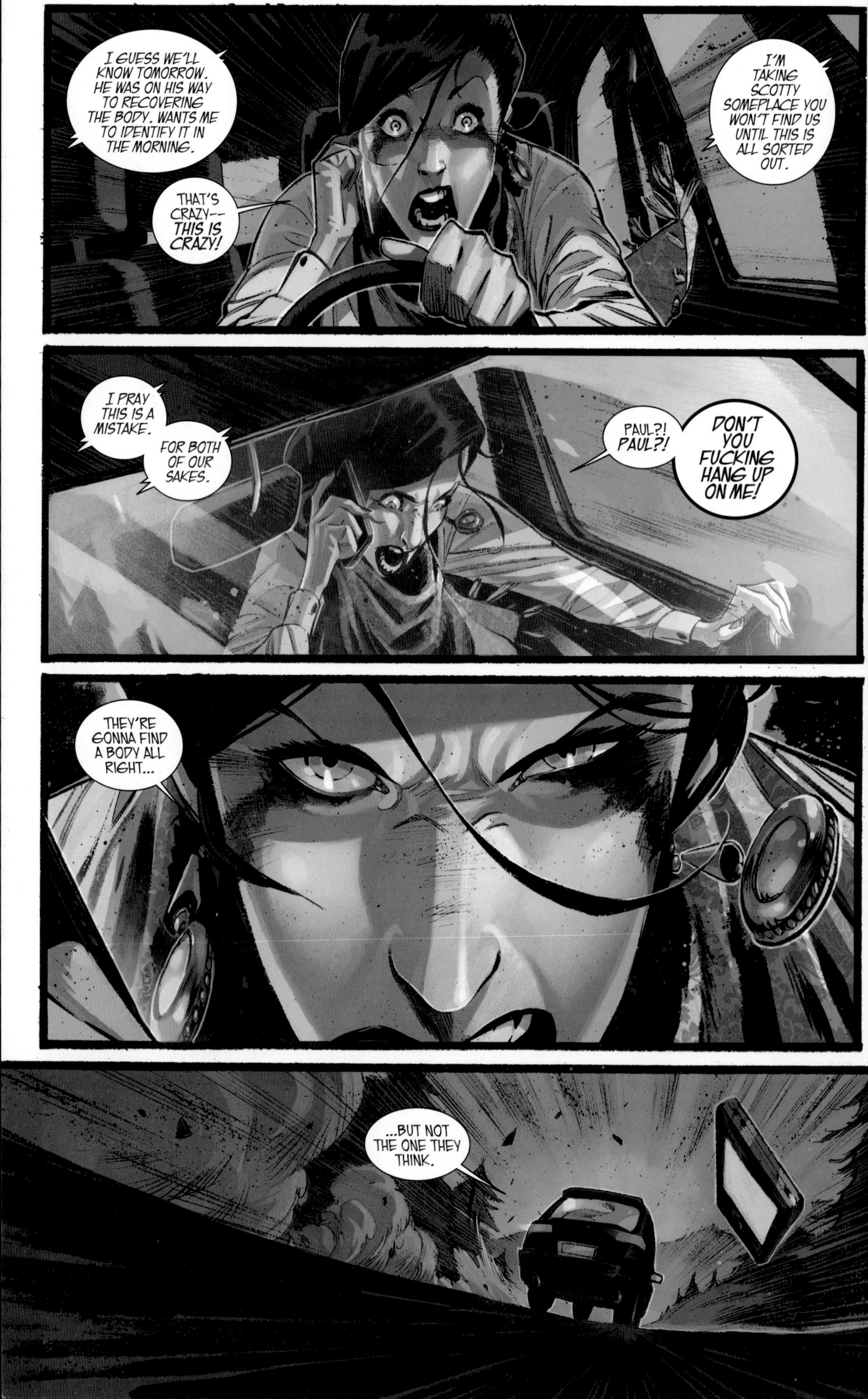
I GUESS WE'LL KNOW TOMORROW. HE WAS ON HIS WAY TO RECOVERING THE BODY. WANTS ME TO IDENTIFY IT IN THE MORNING.
THAT'S CRAZY-- THIS IS CRAZY!
I'M TAKING SCOTTY SOMEPLACE YOU WON'T FIND US UNTIL THIS IS ALL SORTED OUT.
I PRAY THIS IS A MISTAKE.
FOR BOTH OF OUR SAKES.
PAUL?! PAUL?!
DON'T YOU FUCKING HANG UP ON ME!
THEY'RE GONNA FIND A BODY ALL RIGHT...
...BUT NOT THE ONE THEY THINK.

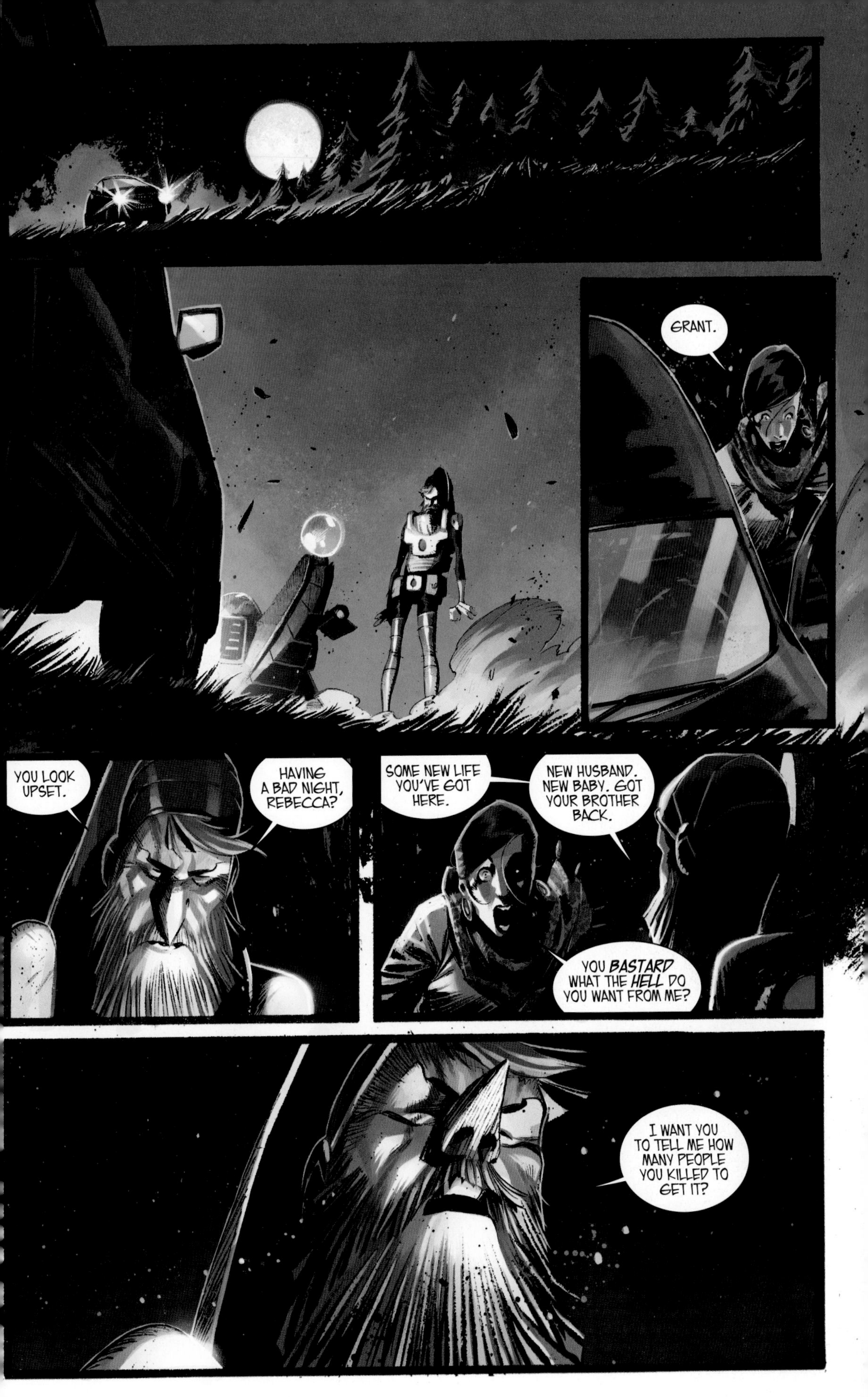
GRANT.
YOU LOOK UPSET.
HAVING A BAD NIGHT, REBECCA?
SOME NEW LIFE YOU'VE GOT HERE.
NEW HUSBAND. NEW BABY. GOT YOUR BROTHER BACK.
YOU BASTARD WHAT THE HELL DO YOU WANT FROM ME?
I WANT YOU TO TELL ME HOW MANY PEOPLE YOU KILLED TO GET IT?

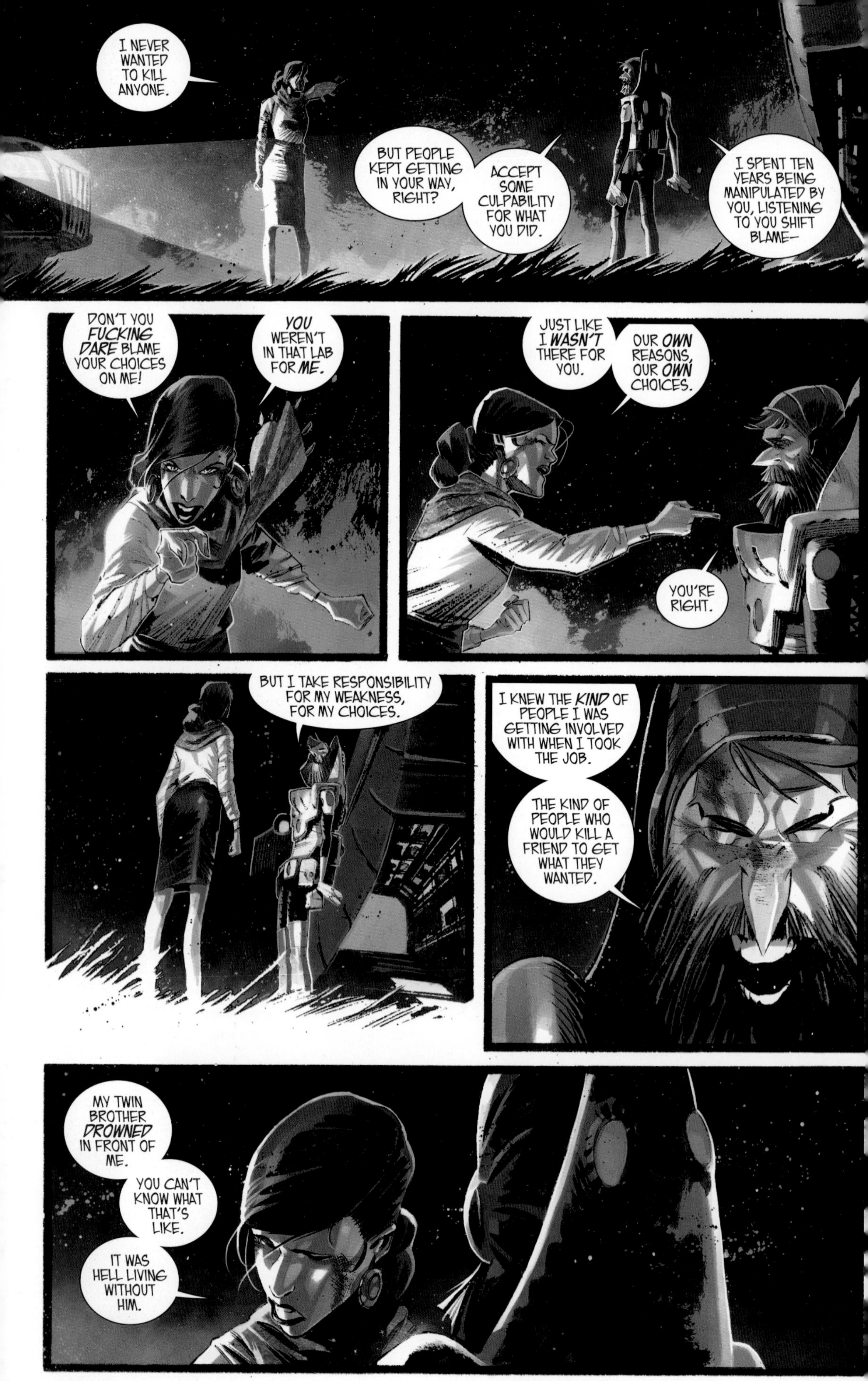
I NEVER WANTED TO KILL ANYONE.
BUT PEOPLE KEPT GETTING IN YOUR WAY, RIGHT?
ACCEPT SOME CULPABILITY FOR WHAT YOU DID.
I SPENT TEN YEARS BEING MANIPULATED BY YOU, LISTENING TO YOU SHIFT BLAME—
DON'T YOU FUCKING DARE BLAME YOUR CHOICES ON ME!
YOU WEREN'T IN THAT LAB FOR ME.
JUST LIKE I WASN'T THERE FOR YOU.
OUR OWN REASONS, OUR OWN CHOICES.
YOU'RE RIGHT.
BUT I TAKE RESPONSIBILITY FOR MY WEAKNESS, FOR MY CHOICES.
I KNEW THE KIND OF PEOPLE I WAS GETTING INVOLVED WITH WHEN I TOOK THE JOB.
THE KIND OF PEOPLE WHO WOULD KILL A FRIEND TO GET WHAT THEY WANTED.
MY TWIN BROTHER DROWNED IN FRONT OF ME.
YOU CAN'T KNOW WHAT THAT'S LIKE.
IT WAS HELL LIVING WITHOUT HIM.

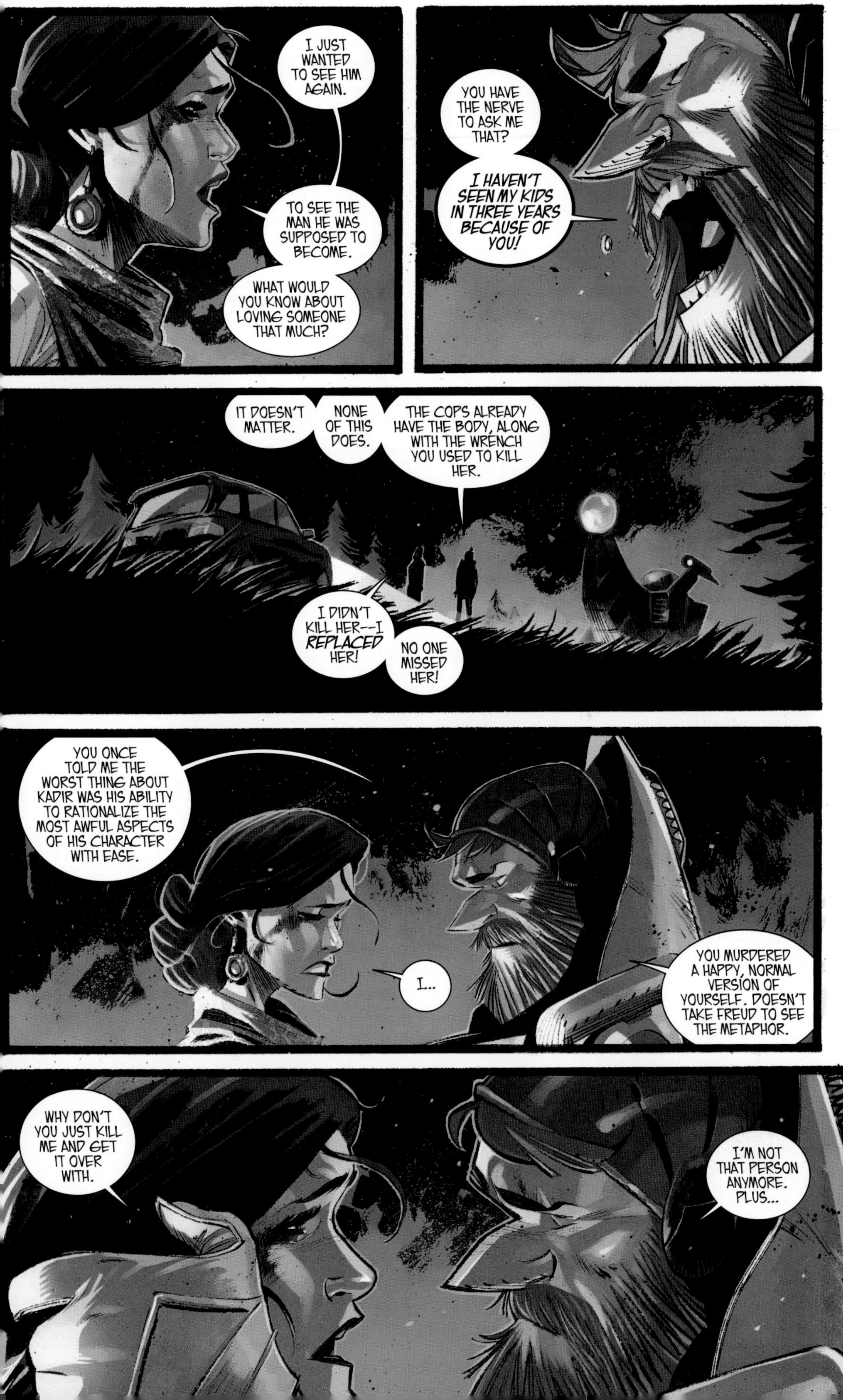
I JUST WANTED TO SEE HIM AGAIN.
TO SEE THE MAN HE WAS SUPPOSED TO BECOME.
WHAT WOULD YOU KNOW ABOUT LOVING SOMEONE THAT MUCH?
YOU HAVE THE NERVE TO ASK ME THAT?
I HAVEN'T SEEN MY KIDS IN THREE YEARS BECAUSE OF YOU!
IT DOESN'T MATTER.
NONE OF THIS DOES.
THE COPS ALREADY HAVE THE BODY, ALONG WITH THE WRENCH YOU USED TO KILL HER.
I DIDN'T KILL HER--I *REPLACED* HER!
NO ONE MISSED HER!
YOU ONCE TOLD ME THE WORST THING ABOUT KADIR WAS HIS ABILITY TO RATIONALIZE THE MOST AWFUL ASPECTS OF HIS CHARACTER WITH EASE.
I...
YOU MURDERED A HAPPY, NORMAL VERSION OF YOURSELF. DOESN'T TAKE FREUD TO SEE THE METAPHOR.
WHY DON'T YOU JUST KILL ME AND GET IT OVER WITH.
I'M NOT THAT PERSON ANYMORE. PLUS...

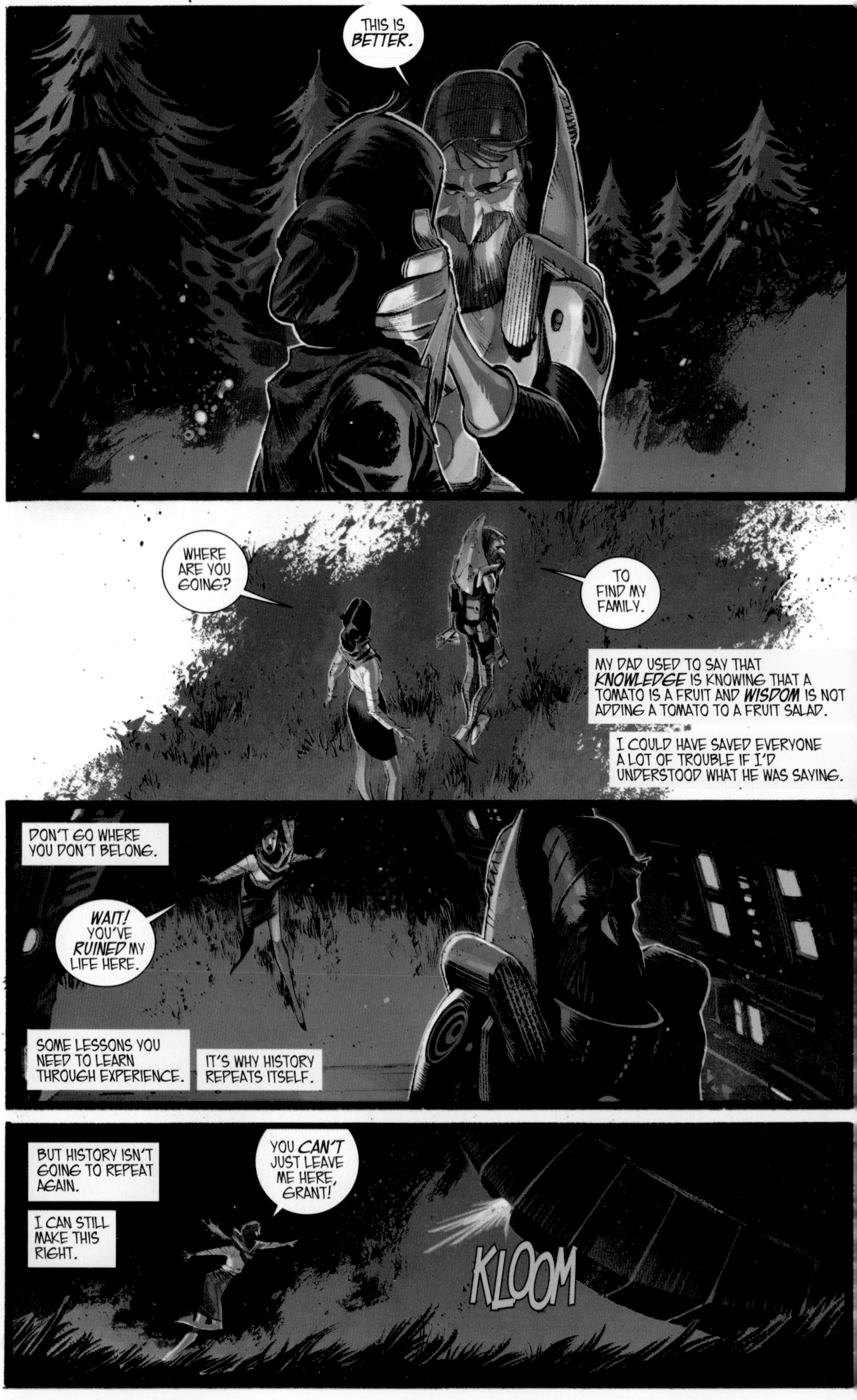
THIS IS BETTER.
WHERE ARE YOU GOING?
TO FIND MY FAMILY.
MY DAD USED TO SAY THAT KNOWLEDGE IS KNOWING THAT A TOMATO IS A FRUIT AND WISDOM IS NOT ADDING A TOMATO TO A FRUIT SALAD.
I COULD HAVE SAVED EVERYONE A LOT OF TROUBLE IF I'D UNDERSTOOD WHAT HE WAS SAYING.
DON'T GO WHERE YOU DON'T BELONG.
WAIT! YOU'VE RUINED MY LIFE HERE.
SOME LESSONS YOU NEED TO LEARN THROUGH EXPERIENCE.
IT'S WHY HISTORY REPEATS ITSELF.
BUT HISTORY ISN'T GOING TO REPEAT AGAIN.
I CAN STILL MAKE THIS RIGHT.
YOU CAN'T JUST LEAVE ME HERE, GRANT!
KLOOM

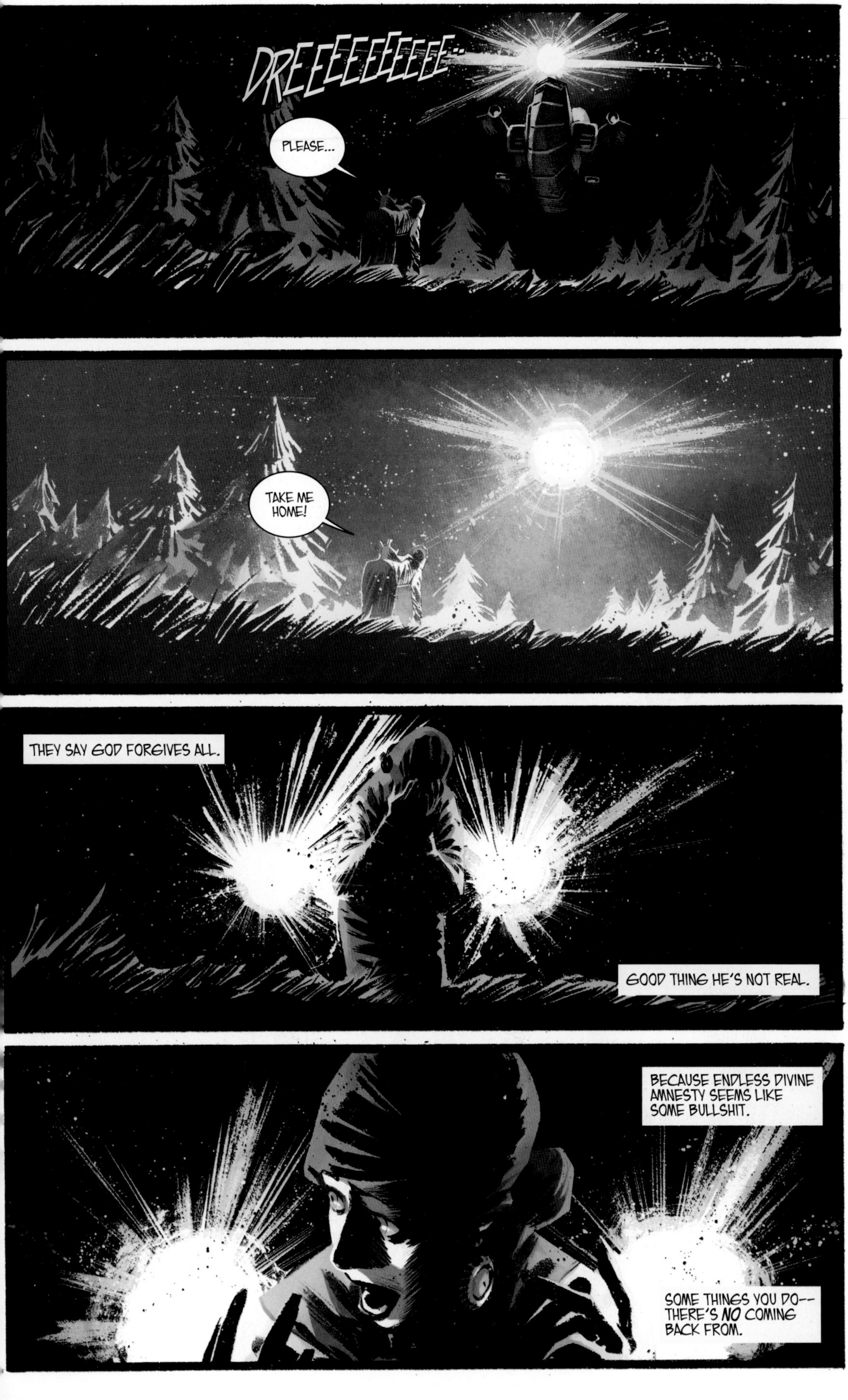
DREEEEEEEEEE...
PLEASE...
TAKE ME HOME!
THEY SAY GOD FORGIVES ALL.
GOOD THING HE'S NOT REAL.
BECAUSE ENDLESS DIVINE AMNESTY SEEMS LIKE SOME BULLSHIT.
SOME THINGS YOU DO-- THERE'S NO COMING BACK FROM.

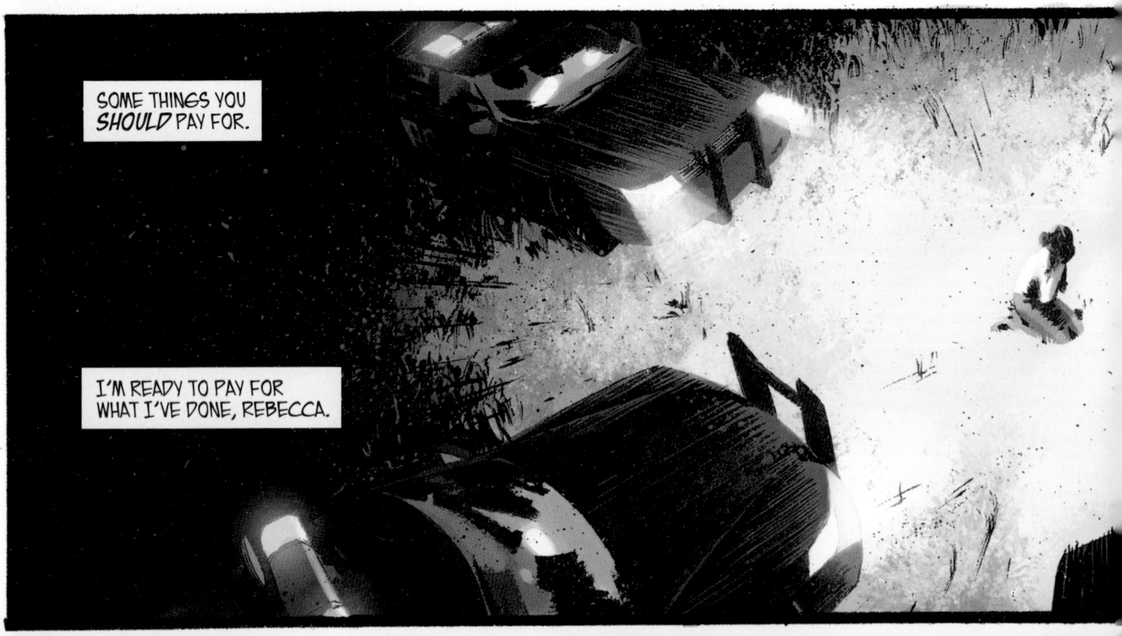
SOME THINGS YOU *SHOULD* PAY FOR.
I'M READY TO PAY FOR WHAT I'VE DONE, REBECCA.

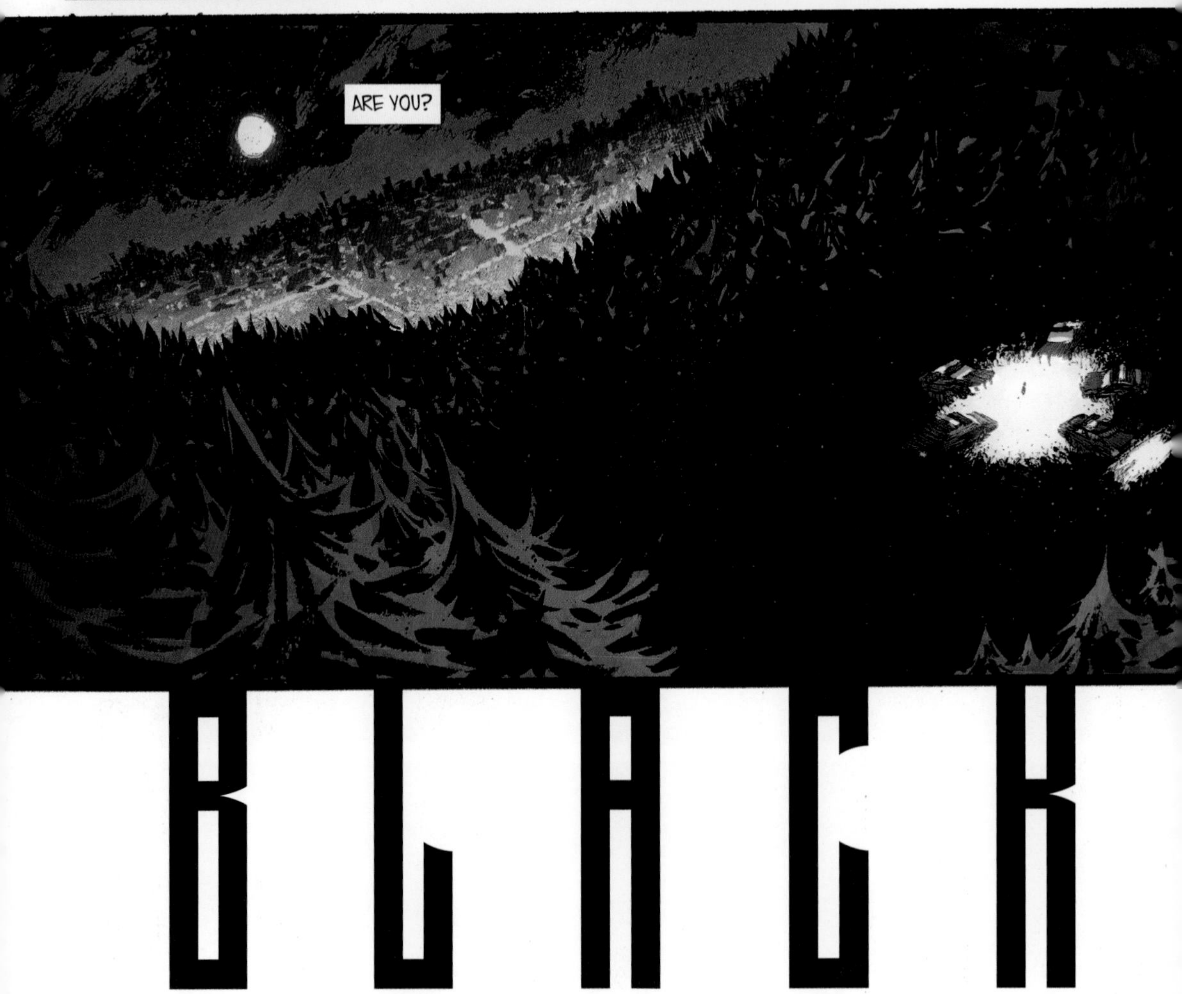
ARE YOU?

BLACK

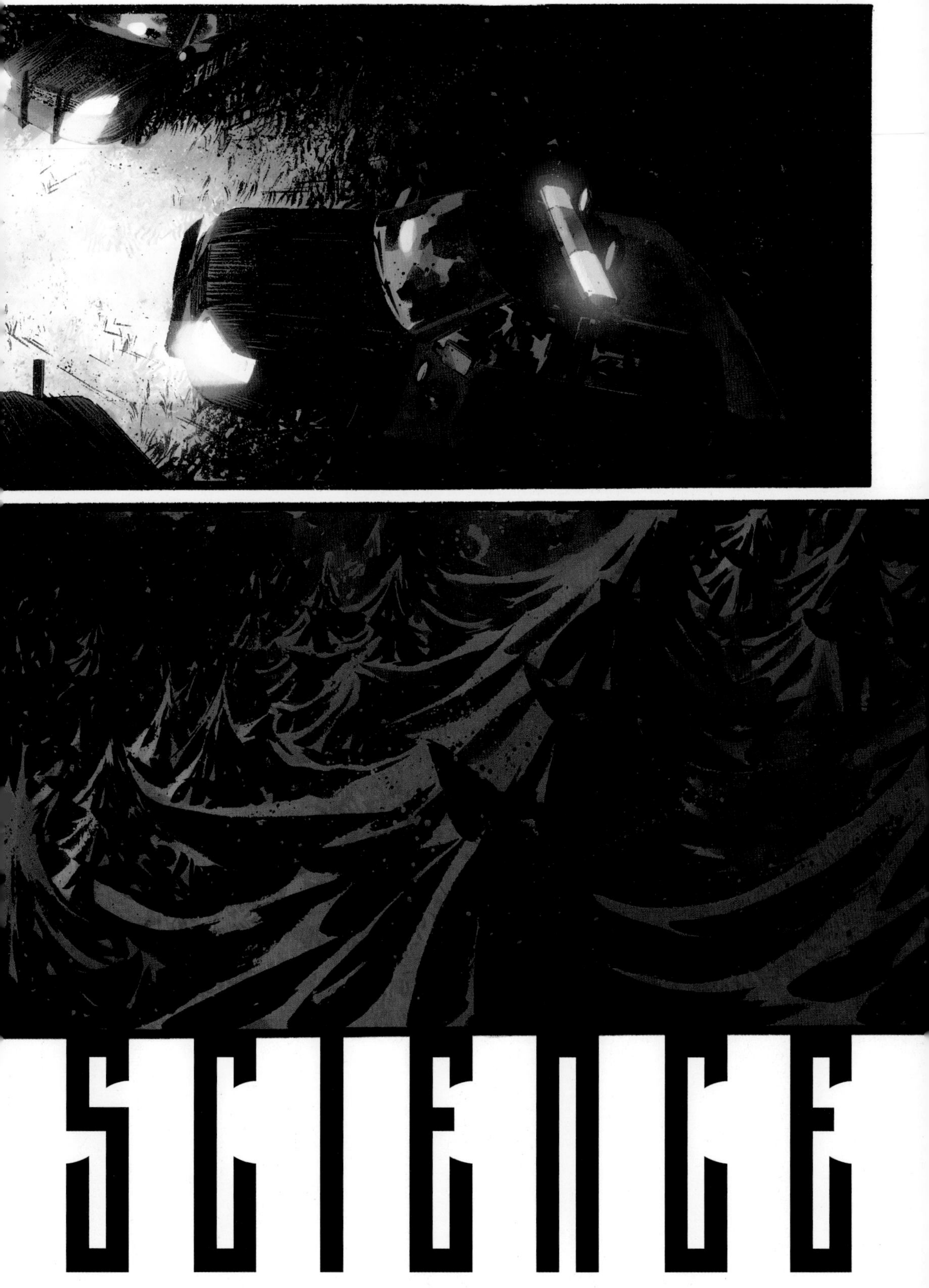

SCIENCE

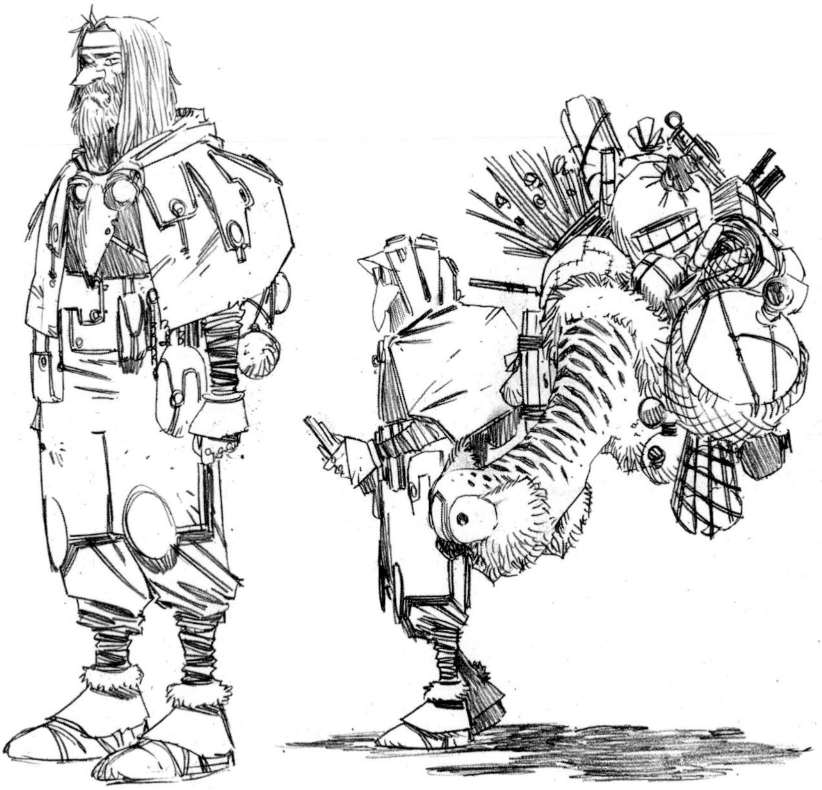

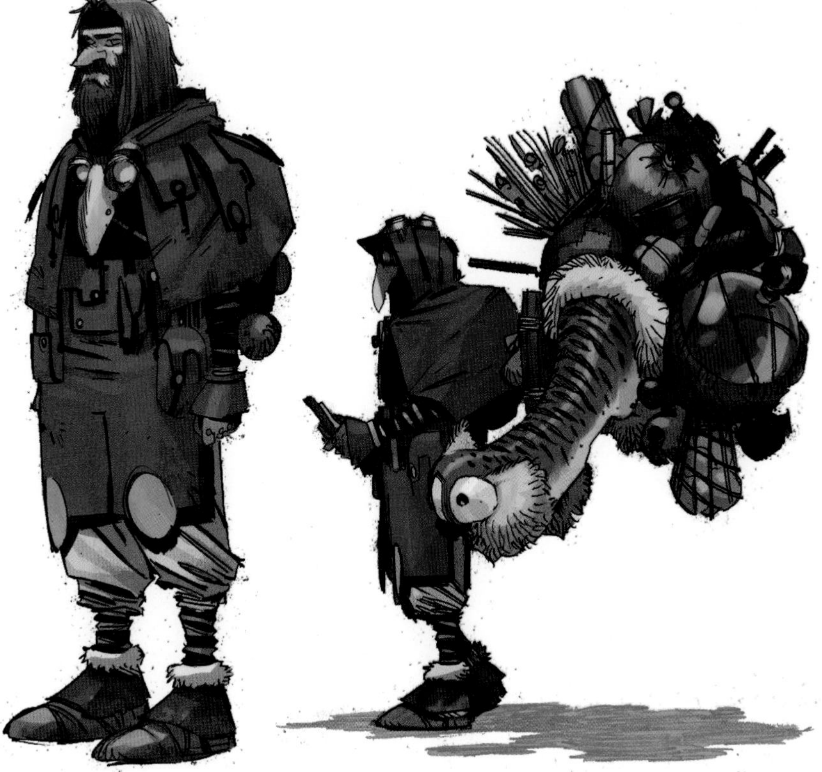

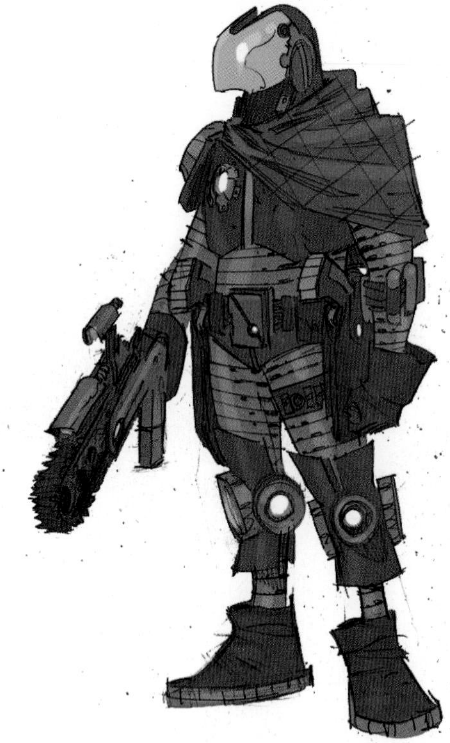

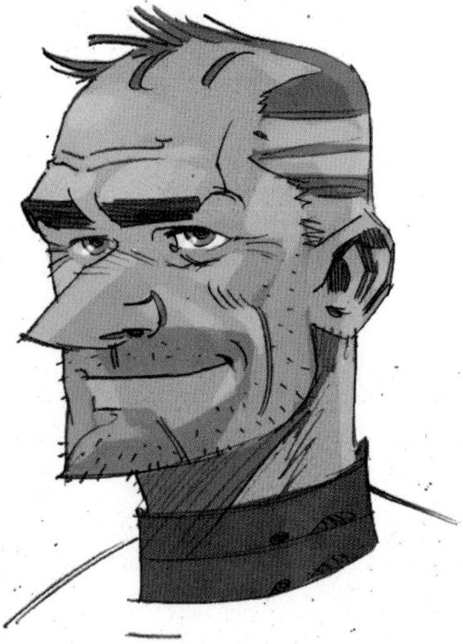

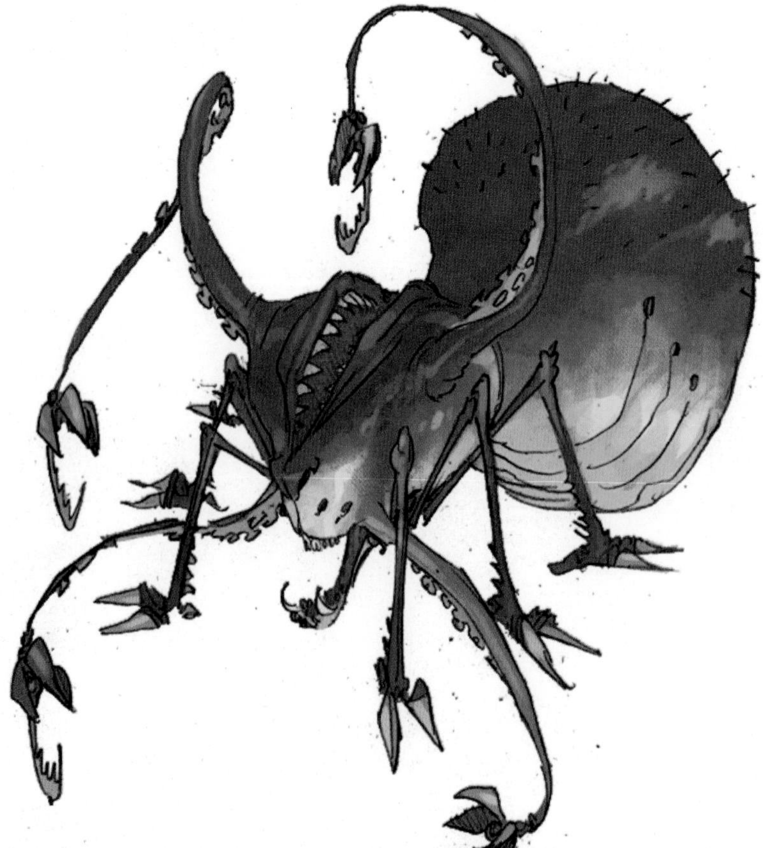

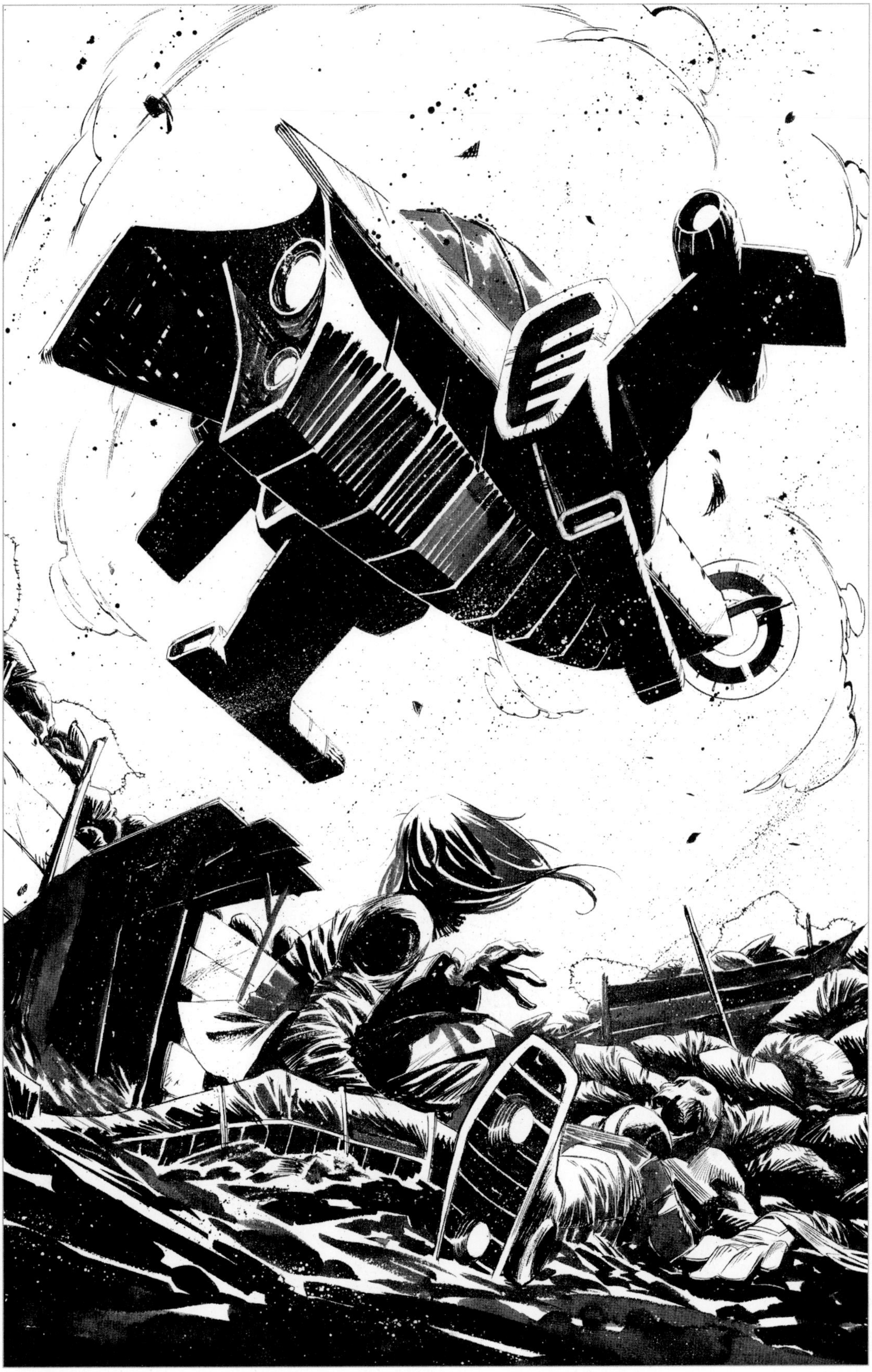

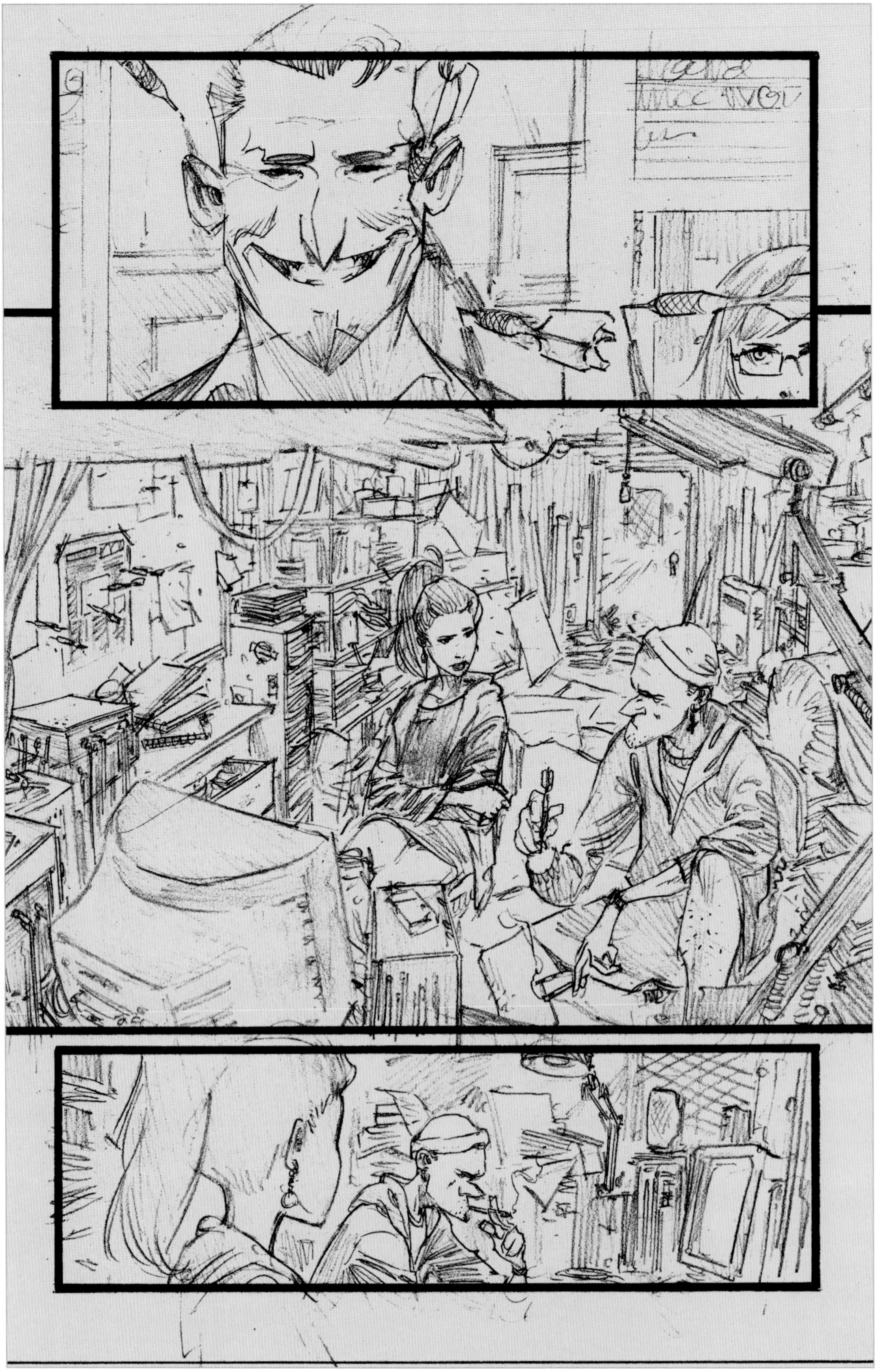

#21 PAGE 7 PENCILS

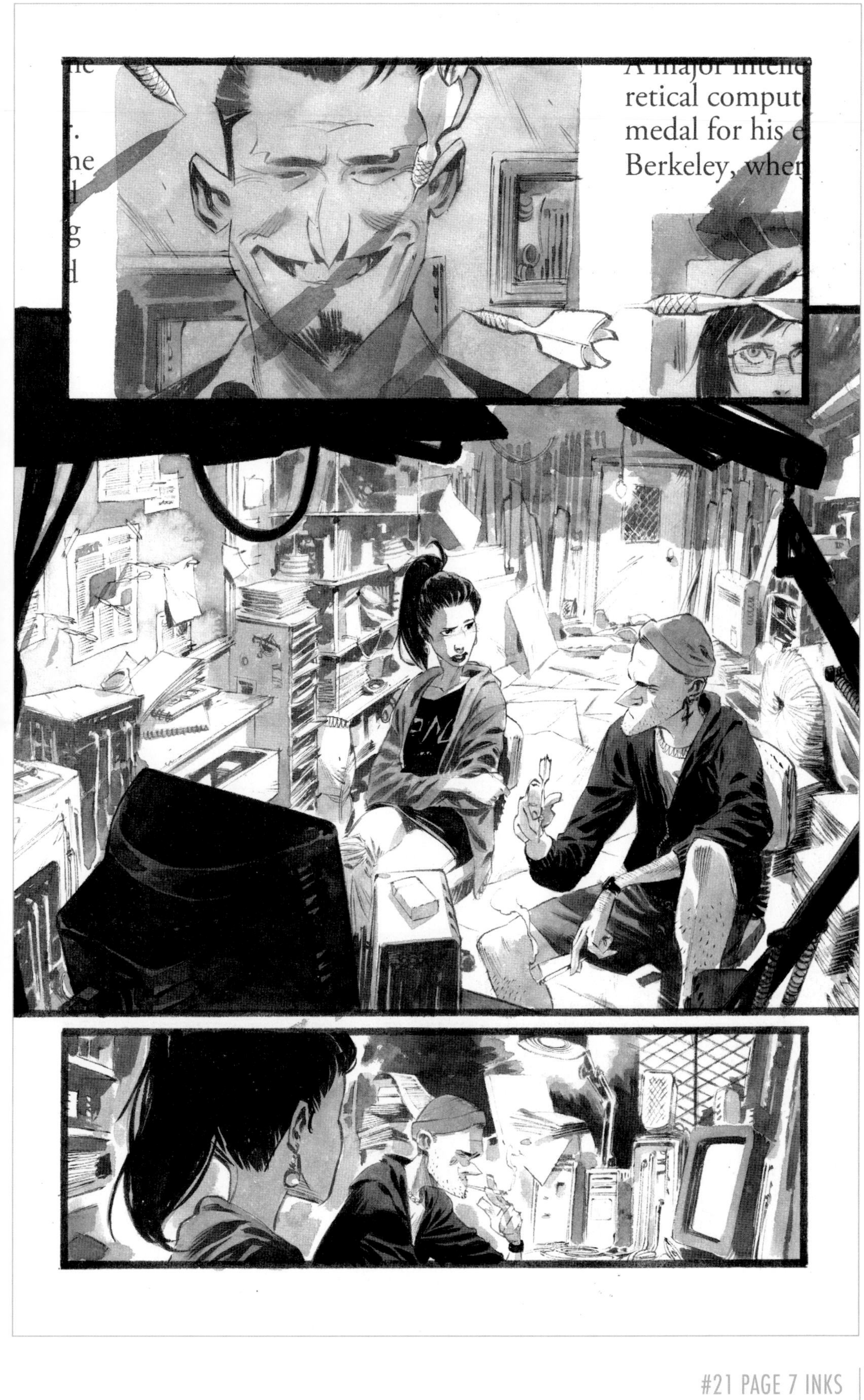
retical comput
medal for his e
Berkeley, wher

#21 PAGE 7 INKS

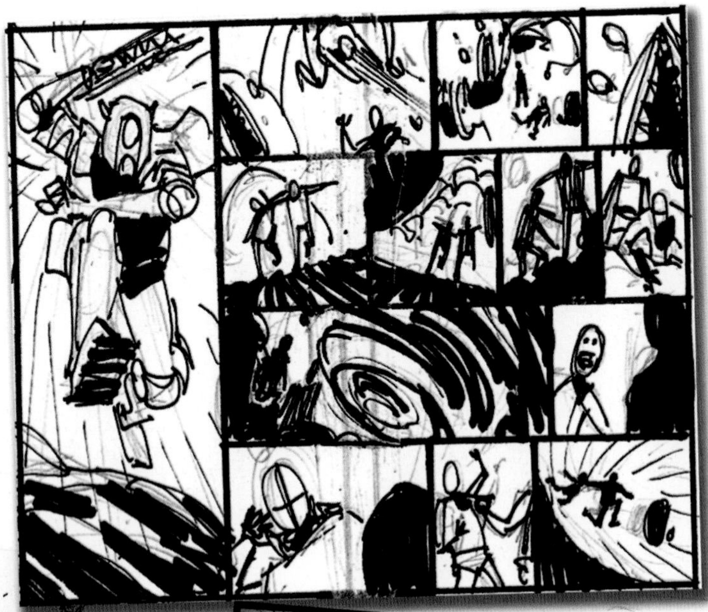

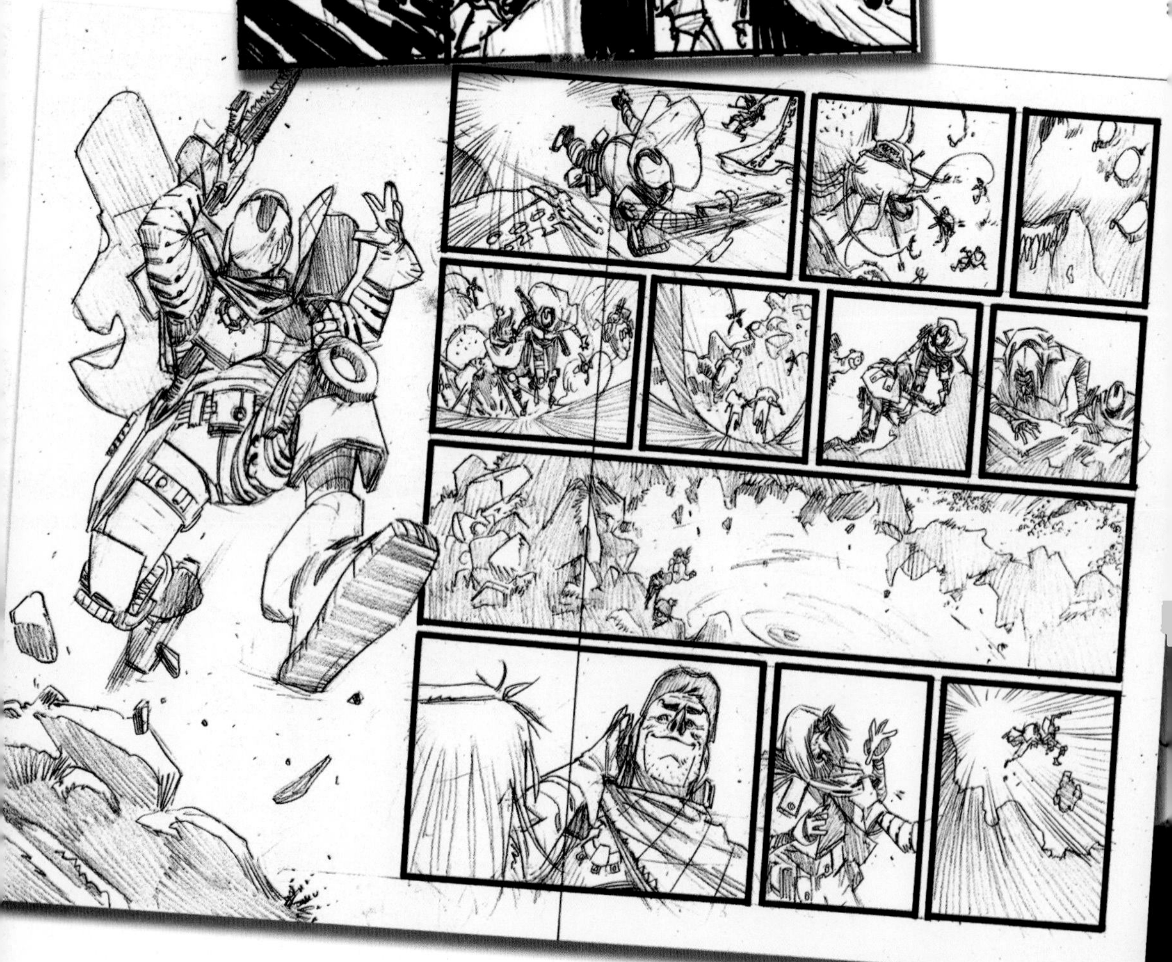

#17 PAGES 18-19

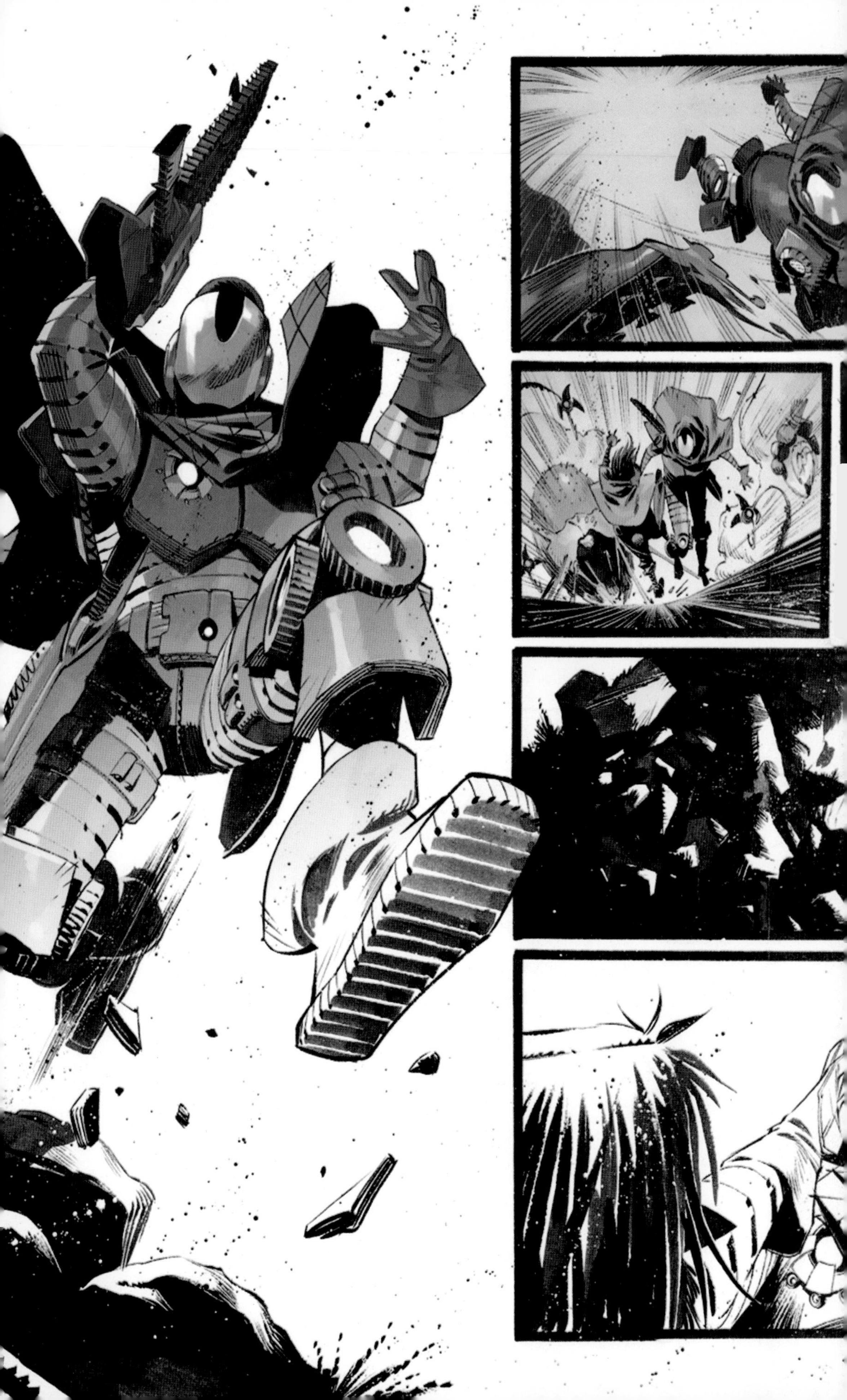

RICK REMENDER

Rick Remender is the writer/co-creator of comics such as *LOW*, *Fear Agent*, *Deadly Class*, *Tokyo Ghost*, and *Black Science*. For Marvel he has written titles such as *Uncanny Avengers*, *Captain America*, *Uncanny X-Force* and *Venom*. He's written video games such as *Bulletstorm* and *Dead Space*, worked on films such as *The Iron Giant*, *Anastasia*, and *Titan A.E.* He and his tea-sipping wife, Danni, currently reside in Los Angeles raising two beautiful mischief monkeys.

MATTEO SCALERA

Matteo Scalera was born in Parma, Italy, in 1982. His professional career started in 2007 with the publication of the miniseries *Hyperkinetic* for Image Comics. Over the next nine years he worked with all major U.S. publishers: Marvel (*Deadpool*, *Secret Avengers*, *Indestructible Hulk*), DC Comics (*Batman*), Boom! Studios (*Irredeemable*, *Valen the Outcast*, *Starborn*) and Skybound (*Dead Body Road*).

MORENO CARMINE DINISIO

Moreno Dinisio was born in 1987 in southern Italy. Holding a pencil since year one, thanks to the painter father, he grew up practicing with the aim of becoming a professional artist. After studying comic art in Milan, he went on to work as a comic and concept artist and character designer until 2013, when he made his debut in American comics, coloring *Clown Fatale* and *Resurrectionists* (*Dark Horse*). Dinisio first collaborated with Matteo Scalera on *Dead Body Road* (Skybound). Since December 2014, Moreno colors Matteo's art on *Black Science*.